THE
GAME
BIRD

✦ AIDAN R WALSH ✦

The Game Bird

First published 2018.

Copyright © Aidan R Walsh, 2018.

The right of Aidan R Walsh to be identified as author has been asserted.

ISBN 978-0-6482911-0-7 (paperback)

ISBN 978-0-6482911-1-4 (eBook)

For Libby.

Upon earth there is not his like, who is made without fear.
He beholdeth all high things: he is a king over all the children
of pride.

Job 41

Readers curious to learn more about the world of
The Game Bird, can do so at:

https://unpathedwaters.com/

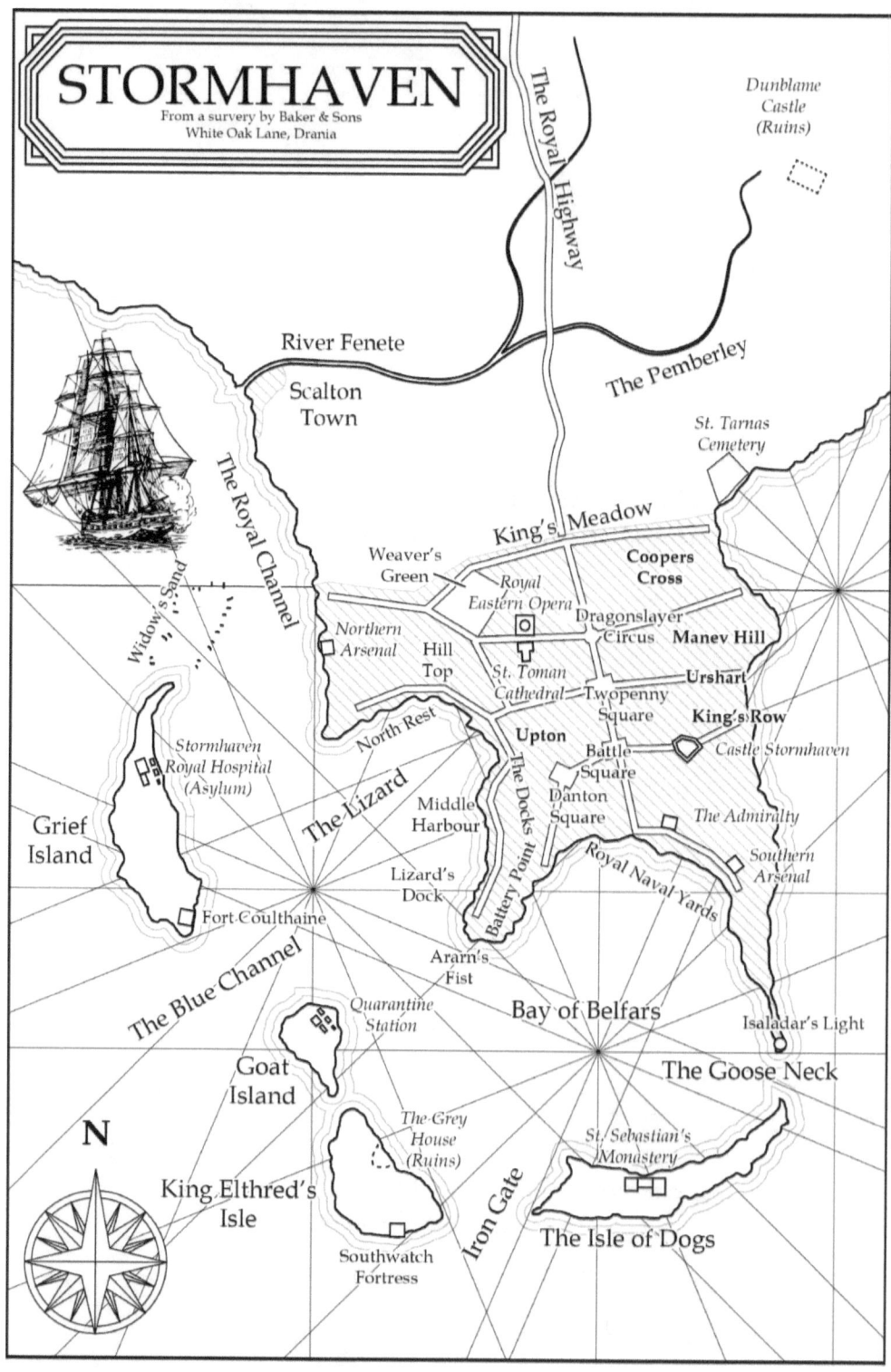

STORMHAVEN

From a survery by Baker & Sons
White Oak Lane, Drania

Dunblame
Castle
(Ruins)

The Royal Highway

River Fenete

Scalton
Town

The Pemberley

St. Tarnas
Cemetery

The Royal Channel

King's Meadow

Weaver's
Green

Coopers
Cross

Royal
Eastern Opera

Dragonslayer
Circus

Manev Hill

Widow's Sand

Northern
Arsenal

Hill
Top

St. Toman
Cathedral

Twopenny
Square

Urshart

King's Row

Upton

Battle
Square

Castle Stormhaven

Stormhaven
Royal Hospital
(Asylum)

North Rest

The Lizard

Danton
Square

The Admiralty

Grief
Island

Middle
Harbour

The Docks

Battery Point

Royal Naval Yards

Southern
Arsenal

Lizard's
Dock

Fort Coulthaine

The Blue Channel

Ararn's
Fist

Quarantine
Station

Bay of Belfars

Isaladar's Light

Goat
Island

N

The Goose Neck

The Grey
House
(Ruins)

St. Sebastian's
Monastery

King Elthred's
Isle

Iron Gate

The Isle of Dogs

Southwatch
Fortress

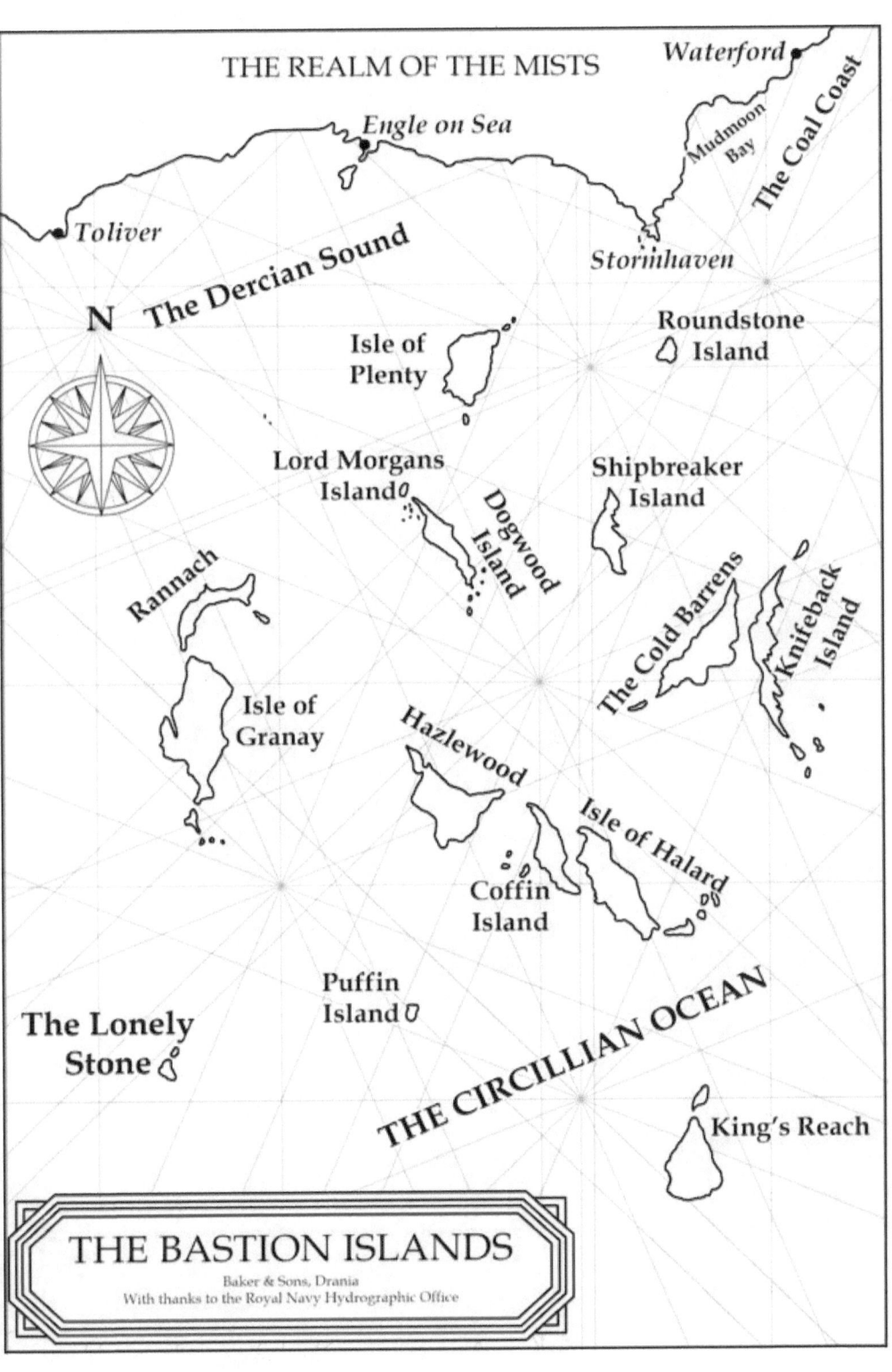

1.

JAMES FAULKNER'S HEART leapt and hammered. Sweat trickled down his back, the stitch in his side felt the size of an anchor and his boots could have been made from lead. He gulped down great gasps of air but he wasn't even close to catching his breath. Judging by the shrieks of their whistles, his pursuers were still close behind.

Faulkner was halfway up the hill and slowing when he spotted the entrance to a lane between two brick factories. Ducking past an ox-cart, he sprinted down the alley, his sword bouncing by his side. A hundred yards from the road, the lane turned sharply right and he hurled himself around the bend, desperate to get out of sight.

'Isaladar's blood,' Faulkner swore. Just around the corner the lane ended at two enormously broad, iron-studded doors. He skidded to a halt on the mossy stones. One look was enough to know he'd never be able to open the huge doors. He backtracked and peered around the corner. The men hunting him had paused at the mouth of the lane to draw their clubs and cudgels. The mills that loomed over him were three-stories tall and their few windows heavily barred. He cursed again. He had only succeeded in doing a better job of trapping himself.

In a few moments they would have him, and that would mean prison and the ruin of his career. He slid his sword a few inches out of its scabbard. Almost surprised, he looked down at the exposed steel for a moment and then slammed the blade back home. He would cheerfully crack the odd head when they found him, but he couldn't bring himself to use the blade. Not against poor men who were only trying to earn some honest coin. With a sigh, he spread his feet wide and balled his fists. At least he'd make them earn their bounty. As he rolled his head from side to side, loosening his neck in preparation for the inevitable brawl, his eyes fixed on a drainpipe next to the heavy doors.

He put a boot against the brick wall and gave the drainpipe a sharp yank. The metal groaned in protest and a shower of rust, damp stone and lichen rained down on him, but it held. Above him, the grey sky peeping between the dirty walls seemed miles away. But shinnying a few stories up a drainpipe couldn't be any harder than going aloft during a gale, could it?

Grasping the cold pipe, he began to climb. His expensive leather boots scrabbled on the wet bricks and the drainpipe cut his hands, but he quickly dragged himself up the side of the building. The bailiff's whistles echoed frighteningly close and loud in the confined space and he peered back over his shoulder. The lane was still empty. When he reached the eaves, he caught the edge of the overhanging tiles and looked down at the cobblestones below. A fall from his height would at least break his legs but he had to push on now so, with a grunt of effort, he heaved himself up. As he squirmed up and over the gutter, one of his coat's seams ripped with a sound like chain-shot hitting a full sail. If he'd breath to spare he would have sworn again; Donald would kill him. Safely up on the roof, he threw himself flat on his back on the cold slate tiles and put a hand over his mouth to quieten his gasping. He was not enjoying being hunted. Indeed, he was developing a marked sympathy for the foxes his countrymen so diligently pursued. Below him, the pack of bailiffs thundered around the corner. As his breathing slowed, he listened as they paused in front of the factory doors.

'You sure he came down 'ere?'

'Could 'ave sworn he did, Barlow.'

'Well, somehow he's just flown the coop then, hasn't he?' the man, Barlow, snarled.

The other men murmured in agreement.

'You don't have to look so fucking…' the first bailiff fumbled for a word, 'so cheerful about it.'

'I ain't cheerful, but it never seemed right running 'im down like a dog,' the man whined. 'Not after what he did in the war.'

Faulkner's mouth creased in the faintest of smiles.

'Shut it, Snapper. Hero or not, he's in a pile more debt than most we catch.'

'But Barlow...'

The sound of a muffled blow was followed by a cry. 'I told you to shut it.'

'What now, hey, Barlow?' a third man asked.

'Back to the *Pig and Whistle*. We'll get back after 'im Monday.'

Their footsteps retreated down the lane.

For a long time after they left, Faulkner lay on the roof, looking up at the clouds and breathing in the sooty and salty stench of the city. As the euphoria of his escape faded, a melancholy snuck in to take its place. His frantic climb, and the ancient law that prevented a debt being collected on a Saturday or Sunday, had bought him two and a half more days of freedom – but what did that matter? Come Monday his debts would still be gigantic.

He was an idiot. The red-tiled villa nestled amongst the vines, the priceless books, the expensive vintages, and the pretty little yacht. It had been so easy to justify his profligate spending when the war was raging, home was a thousand miles away, and death or fortune were his constant, competing companions. But then had come peace and both those imposters had departed, leaving him with half pay, no ship, and debts he couldn't even hope to service.

It began to drizzle and Faulkner scrambled to his feet and looked about to get his bearings. To the north the most obvious landmark was Fortress Stormhaven, her sloped walls and heavy gun batteries towering over the grimy tiled roofs of the city. The fortress couldn't hold his attention though. Not when just to the south, against the iron-grey waters of the Bay of Belfars, he could just make out the shapes of men of war through the rain. Their names came to him unbidden: dear old *Colossus*, where he had served as a mid; *Revenge*, the first to break the line at the Sunset Isles; the ancient *Furious*, whose timbers, the old sailors claimed, still bore the marks of dragon fire; and *Great Isaladar*, captured from the Caladians in the last days of the war.

Oblivious to the cold, he stared longingly at the warships for a long time. It was hard not to wonder if he would ever be lucky enough to walk their decks again. Finally he sighed, turned his back on the ships he had called his home for so long, and began to work out how to get off the roof without breaking his neck.

Faulkner rechecked the address, scanned the row of imposing terraces and then reread the rain- and sweat-dampened letter. He was fairly sure this was the right street, but it was so damn hard to tell, especially in the dark. As a boy he had spent days exploring Stormhaven's every nook and cranny but, while he had been away in the sun-drenched south, the city had rudely gone and changed.

'A pound o' crab, sir?' asked a voice behind him.

Faulkner turned and took an involuntary step back as the dirty-faced, longhaired costermonger brandished in front of his face a greasy morsel that, three or four days ago, might have indeed been crab. 'No, thank you, my man,' he replied, doing his best not to smell the thing.

The man dropped the crab back into his battered basket and brought out a fish. 'How 'bout a nice honest mackerel?'

'I don't want mackerel either, regardless of how honest it is.'

'Oh…' Downhearted but undefeated, the hawker threw the fish back into his basket and extracted a slimy, scaled thing that rolled lazily in his dirty hand. 'Perhaps wyvern's tail might do the trick then, Cap'n? Keeps a man's cannon primed, does wyvern's tail. That might tip the scales, mightn't it?' The man wheezed with laughter.

'I'll have neither crab, wyvern tail, mackerel, nor anything else you might have in there.'

The man lunged forward and caught Faulkner's hand. 'Please. My little ones are starvin'. Wife ran mad with the taint. It ain't easy raising the little ones on me own, Cap'n. Please just buy something.'

'Keep those dirty paws to yourself,' snapped Faulkner, shaking off the hawker's grip. He took a deep breath. 'But answer this honestly and you won't get a clip over the ear. Your wife, did she really suffer with the taint?'

'Oh, I swears it, sure as Isaladar killed the daemon, she did. One day she just upped and killed every dog on the street. Ripped 'em quite to shreds. Then she just jumped in the harbour and swam right out to sea. Breaks me heart, it does.'

All costermongers had a great talent for telling long and tragic lies, but the story did have a ring of sincerity. That, and only the most desperate liar would invent a link to the taint. 'I don't want any of your wares, but I'll pay you if you can tell me which house is Admiral Barry's.'

'You're a real gent, Cap'n, a real gent. Now that's it. Just there.' He pointed a crooked finger. 'That one there with the red door. He's just done it up he has, sir; finest house on this whole street it is now. Why, I was only sayin' the—'

'Thank you,' said Faulkner. He pushed two copper coins he couldn't spare into the fellow's filthy palm, then hurried across the street and knocked sharply on the freshly painted door. Footsteps echoed inside and a bolt was slid back. The door opened a crack and a uniformed servant peered out from beneath an old-fashioned wig. The leather-faced old man looked him up and down and wrinkled his nose. Faulkner couldn't blame him. With his wet, mud-coloured hair flattened against his skull and his coat scuffed, torn and rumpled about his tall frame, he must have looked the most down-at-heel post captain imaginable.

'Admiral Barry is not receiving,' the servant observed coolly, moving to shut the door.

Faulkner stopped him with a firm hand against the wood. 'Isaladar's blood, Atkins, is that you?'

'Captain Faulkner!' The old man's eyes widened with recognition and he grinned. 'It's good to see you, sir.'

'Still working for Barry, are you?'

'Aye, I was too old and broken down to do much good afloat, so Barry asked me to come ashore and work for him. Told him I'd take no charity, but he insisted.'

'Well, it's good to see you. But I'm not sure about you being broken down – you don't look a day older than when I first saw you when I was a mid.' Faulkner smiled a wide smile. 'That is to say, you still look ancient.'

'Well, I am afraid Captain Faulkner has changed – he is a little more rotund than when he went south,' Atkins replied loftily.

'It's all the dreary victory feasts and galas I've been getting dragged along to.' Faulkner patted his belly. 'Now, should I make an appointment?'

'No, no, of course not. The admiral will see you. He is just with his clerk at the moment and when you knocked he called down, "If that is another grasping bloody captain come looking for a blasted ship, you can tell him to…"' The old sailor petered out. 'Well, the rest should not be repeated. But come in, come in. He'd be furious if I left you out in this drizzle.'

Inside, Faulkner looked around the foyer and smiled. The house was splendidly appointed in marble and polished wood. His mentor had obviously done very well for himself with his share of the Northern Fleet's prize money. Atkins ushered him into a room off the antechamber and motioned for him to take a seat by the fire.

'Admiral Barry will be with you shortly.'

'Thank you, Atkins.'

The old sailor left, closing the door quietly behind him.

The room was obviously Barry's sanctuary. Above the fireplace was a very fine painting by Wilkinson that almost perfectly captured the pivotal moment at the Battle of the Iron Cape, when Barry, on his own initiative, had taken the *Colossus* out of the line to cut off the Auserwaldian escape. It was so flawlessly painted that Faulkner could almost hear the crash of the guns and feel the deck shudder under his feet again. Looking around, he saw that the study was filled with other icons and trophies of Barry's long and illustrious career that had taken him to all corners of the Circillian continent. Many of them Faulkner recognised. On the sideboard, the jewelled egg from the proud Countess Matejko and there, leaning against the writing desk like a common umbrella, the black iron mace given to Barry by the Great Elector of Garenburg for their help lifting the siege of his capital.

Turning eagerly to see what other curios the cluttered room held, he started in fright as he came face to face with a manticore. Set beside the door, so he had missed it when he entered, the thing's head was mounted on a wooden plinth like it was a common stag. The beast was no prettier in death than it had been in life. Even now its hideous combination of human and lion-like features, topped off with shark teeth, positively radiated hatred.

'I wonder…' Faulkner muttered to himself. Crossing the room he studied it closely. Sure enough, just beneath the thing's beady right eye and left unrepaired by the taxidermist was the mark his shot had made. He traced the groove with his finger and shuddered. In his desperate attempt to escape the lost battle at the Iron Cape, the enemy admiral had thrown all three of his irreplaceable manticores at the *Colossus*. Two of them had never reached the ship, the first had been shot through the brain by a marksman in the tops when it was still a hundred yards away and the second had one of its leathery wings torn clean away by a swivel gun. But the third and its rider had somehow come through the storm of shot unscathed and had smashed down on their quarterdeck, splintering timbers and pulping flesh. In seconds it had killed half the ship's officers and a blow from the beast's scorpion tail had hacked away Barry's leg just below the knee. In an effort to save his wounded captain, Faulkner had shot the beast at almost point-blank range.

The door banged open and Barry lurched into the room with the rolling gait his wooden leg had left him with. 'Looks rather less frightening mounted on the wall than rampaging across the quarterdeck, doesn't it?'

Faulkner turned and took Barry's offered hand. 'It does indeed, Knight Admiral.'

Barry motioned for him to take a seat and then stumped slowly across the room to sit down opposite him. 'Bravest thing I've ever seen, what you and Cumby did that day.'

'Major Cumby killed the beast. I only annoyed it.'

'Well, I've never forgotten what you did. Never shall.' The old admiral smiled. 'Now, how have you been, Faulkner?'

'Well, thank you, sir. Glad to be home. And you?'

'Me?' Barry's red face darkened redder. 'Horrible. My bloody clerk was just telling me he thinks the Century Council has only left me with money to keep a quarter of our ships at sea. A quarter! Can you believe that?'

'A quarter?' Faulkner's heart lurched. He knew it would be bad but he hadn't expected cuts that swift or that deep.

'Incredible, isn't it? The clerks and bankers well and truly have the reins at the Admiralty now. Leading a fleet into peace from behind a desk is going to be a damn sight more difficult than leading it into battle from the quarterdeck.' Barry paused and took a steadying breath. 'But now, enough of that grim talk. How have you been really been, Faulkner? And none of this "well, thank you, sir"!'

'I've been well.'

'Faulkner! Don't lie to me. You look positively harried.'

He sighed. 'It's been hard.'

'Well, there is no shame in that. The first time I was put ashore was back in '06 and I still remember it. One moment I was lord and commander of a warship, next I was wandering the streets as useless as any other feckless young man about town.'

'Being stuck ashore is a shock.'

'I detect a "but"?'

'But things are worse than that. I am in debt. Rather a lot of it. And I don't know how I am going to survive on half pay.' Faulkner spat the end of the sentence out, as if saying it quickly would diminish the shame.

'Oh.'

'You've been like a second father to me and I was hoping…'

'It is a little awkward you see, Faulkner.' Barry grimaced. 'I would dearly love to help you out, but the house's renovations have rather cleaned me out and I've no chance at all of getting you a ship and…'

Faulkner half rose from his chair. 'I had no intention of asking you for charity, Knight Admiral. Nor would I dream of accepting it if it was offered. I only came to ask your advice.'

'Oh.' Barry looked up, palpably relieved. 'Of course, of course, only too happy to give some advice. What did you want to know?'

'I suppose I'd take any suggestions as to how I might get by.'

Barry's brow furrowed. 'Well, first things first. How bad are your debts?'

'I can hardly pay my servant.'

'That bad? Would a merchant captain's wage cover it?'

'Not a chance.'

'What about entering foreign service? One of our Circillian allies on the continent? Taylach and Dasturia are both modernising their fleets and either of those navies would be hungry for an officer of your talents.'

'I shouldn't like to serve a foreign master.'

'No, nor should I. But if it is a choice between that and debtors' prison, perhaps you'd best consider it. There is no disgrace in serving with an ally and with your reputation…' Barry paused. 'Isaladar's blood, I haven't even congratulated you on your action at the Asare Roads. What a scrub I am. A third rate! A third rate, no less, captured by your little *Inflexible*! What a thing. I wouldn't have believed it possible.' He shook his head. 'What a thing!'

Faulkner smiled. 'Thank you, sir. But it wasn't as impressive as it sounds.'

'The Caladians didn't put up much of a fight?'

'No, her crew were most gallant. Captain Domitius still fought her until she was shot quite to pieces and even then didn't strike till we had boarded her. But their dockyards are so wretchedly corrupt the poor *Agrippa* was half a wreck before she even went to sea.' He crossed his arms. 'I felt very low when I got home and saw that the papers are all referring to the Caladians as blackguards and cowards.'

Barry snorted. 'What else would you expect from those scurrilous scribblers? The blighters are giving me a right hammering at this very moment over this bloody leviathan disaster. But what else am I meant to do? I've got half the fleet out hunting the blasted creature.'

'Leviathan disaster?'

'You haven't heard?'

'I caught some muttering on the docks when I came ashore but I didn't think much of it. You know merchantmen. They do go on like old women.'

'Unfortunately, with this leviathan thing marauding about they've got every right to mutter.' Barry hauled himself back upright. 'I'll tell you about it over dinner. You will stay, won't you? I've got a fine '28 Farron claret to open and I'd dearly like to hear a proper account of your pretty little action.'

Faulkner stood on Barry's top step and yawned. The dinner had been predictably excellent and he was pleasantly full, more than a little drunk, and in no mood to go back to his dismal boarding house. Instead, like he always did when he was low, he walked down towards the ocean. Not towards the Bay of Belfars and the men of war that his debts might have banished him from forever, but under the gnarled oak at the end of the road and down the worn stone steps towards the merchant harbour, the Lizard. As always, the waters of the Lizard were packed with the ships that made the Realm rich. Majestic southerners with holds full of peacocks, spices, apes and wonders; greasy whalers home from the wild northern seas; and dirty, tar-stained coasters all lying huddled together. Even at this late hour, dozens of lighters and barges scurried back and forth, unloading cargo by lantern light.

He wandered aimlessly along the waterfront, past the stinking, boisterous taverns and darkened warehouses. Halfway along the harbour, by the end of one of the ancient stone piers, a crowd of dockworkers had gathered together and were peering out over the dirty waters towards the ships. As he got closer he spied what had caught their attention. A longboat was making for the shore and in its bow, barely restrained by three big sailors, a man was thrashing around like he was possessed, the whites of his eyes flashing in the gloom. The man's frantic ravings carried faintly to the shore: 'Its... its... its... eyes, I saw hell in them eyes! I saw hell... its eyes... oh, its eyes.'

'What happened?' he asked a huge stevedore on the edge of the crowd.

'Leviathan attacked his ship,' the man rumbled. 'He was the only survivor.'

'Unlucky fellow.'

'Unlucky? It's a bloody miracle he's alive.' The stevedore looked Faulkner up and down and, noticing his uniform, the man's craggy face shifted into a frown. 'And what is the fuckin' navy doin' to help, Cap'n? You might have won this war, but you ain't helpin' them poor sailors now.'

'Watch your tongue. We're out hunting it.'

'Doing a useless job of it, if you ask me. It's no bloody wonder the insurance houses have put this bloody bounty on the monster's head.'

'Bounty?'

'You been livin' under a rock?' The stevedore shook his head. 'They've promised a hundred thousand bloody crowns to the bugger that kills it.'

'One hundred thousand?' Faulkner said.

'It's all every bloody sailor is talkin' about.'

One hundred thousand. The number rattled about inside his head. One hundred thousand would clear his debts. No, it would leave him comfortable for life. Lords of the North, it would set him up like a prince!

Without a word, he turned and ran back down the pier towards the lights of Stormhaven. Behind him the broken sailor's shrieking died away to a terrified whimper.

As soon as he was back in his crooked little room that smelled of polish, cabbage and pipe smoke, Faulkner sat at his cramped writing desk, turned up his battered oil lamp and took out his pen and ink. The effects of his exertions escaping the bailiffs, followed by the two good bottles of claret he had shared at Barry's, had left him exhausted and more than a little wine-fogged, but he was far too excited and far, far too desperate to let the letter wait until morning. Doing his best to ignore the noise of his servant Donald's thunderous snoring, which floated through the thin walls from the next room, he leant forward and wrote in a neat military hand: *Uriah Blake Esq., Prize Agent, Sapphire Row, Bromhead, Stormhaven*

2.

THEY CLIMBED THE moss-covered stairs together. The man walked with a hand held to the dull point of pain in the middle of his back and his daughter, her red hair whipping in the wind, held out her own hand to steady him.

'Are you all right, Father?' Sophia asked.

He nodded and flicked away a strand of horsehair that the wind had worked free from his wig. 'Too many hours spent hunched over my desk.'

They often came to this windswept cemetery perched on the cliffs above the restless ocean. As usual, they had taken the coach out from Stormhaven and, after paying for it to wait under the stunted poplars that clustered by the gates, they had entered the ancient graveyard on foot.

Reaching his wife's grave, Uriah stooped and carefully placed a sprig of rosemary on the cold stones, then sank to his knees and knelt in silence for a long moment, listening to the crashing of the distant waves.

'I miss you, Mother,' Sophia whispered at last.

Stiffly, Uriah climbed back to his feet and they stood side by side. Uriah sighed quietly to himself. He was a man of numbers and accounts and reason and logic, and unlike his daughter, he had never believed in an afterlife. He believed his wife's last shuddering breath had marked the point of her soul's absolute dissolution. Nevertheless, his love for her still brought him back here each month to lay a sprig of rosemary by her grave and miss her even more.

Uriah took off his spectacles, placed them in his top pocket and turned to his daughter. 'I am not a dramatic man,' he began slowly.

She smiled. 'You're the least theatrical man in the world.'

'Then you will appreciate that I am being serious now.' He coughed to hide his awkwardness. Mary had always been the disciplinarian. 'Is there anything you have been keeping from me?'

'Keeping from you?'

'Have you done anything you should tell me about?'

Before her mother died she would have happily lied that she had no idea how the window had been broken or how she had come to get home so late. She bit her lip. 'I rode the Burtons' new gelding yesterday, even though you asked me not to.'

'That is all?'

'Yes, Father, why? What's wrong?'

'You have just seemed distant lately,' he lied.

'You aren't angry about the gelding?'

'You are just like your mother. The Sophias and Marys of this world were born to ride horses they were told not to.'

'Well, he was fine anyway. Only a little skittish to start.'

'You have always been a much better rider than me.' He gestured back down the hill towards the gates of the cemetery. 'We have paid our respects and your mother would haunt me forever if I let you catch a cold so soon after you've been unwell. You take the coach. I have some business to attend to in town and my poor back could do with the walk.'

'Do you mind if I call on the Burtons?'

Uriah shook his head. 'Not at all. That sounds much more pleasant than going back to an empty house.'

'Are you even listening, Sophia?' asked Emma, the magistrate's prettier daughter.

Sophia had indeed not been listening. Instead she had been perched on the windowsill, watching the flow of people passing up and down the street. Unfortunately her vigil had gone largely unrewarded. Magistrate Burton's richly appointed townhouse sat just off Dragonslayer Circus and the majority of the passers-by were comfortable, well-dressed, upper class and, in Sophia's opinion, thoroughly boring.

She had seen a few naval officers though, and they always caught her attention. As a girl she had loved them. As a young woman she still liked them, but now it was a conflicted affection. She couldn't help but smile at the swaggering walk they now all affected following their successes during the war, and their blue coats still spoke of foreign shores, bloody battle and spirited adventure. But she couldn't bring herself to lionise them like she once had.

'I am sorry, I was miles away. What did you say?' she asked, blushing. Sophia disliked being poor company, especially as the magistrate's two daughters were always a bright and bubbly distraction.

Jane, the older of the sisters, looked up from her needlework. 'Emma asked who is going to be taking you to the Spring Ball.'

Sophia shrugged. 'I haven't the faintest idea.'

Emma stamped a slippered foot in gentle frustration. 'Oh come on, Sophia, don't be coy! The boys love your wild hair and that swishing walk you do. And the way you're so bold drives them absolutely wild. Surely you have someone in mind?'

'I promise I do not. Indeed, I don't even know if anyone will ask me at all.' In an effort to escape the familiar questions she fixed on the most obvious distraction. 'What about you though, Emma dear? I bet someone will ask you?'

Emma smiled the self-satisfied smile of a cat that had come across a fat, injured mouse in the dead centre of an empty room. 'I have it on the best authority that Reginald Anderson will ask me.'

'Lucky you,' she said. Anderson was a nice boy. Sedate, but nice.

'Have you considered Arthur Dennison?' asked Jane, fixing Sophia with a shrewd glance. 'My sources tell me that, even considering how bossy you are, he still thinks you most attractive.'

Sophia hoped her face didn't fall too obviously. Arthur was nice enough, but he was the respectable son of a respectable father. He worked in the respectable family concern and would no doubt one day marry a respectable wife and father respectable children 'I hadn't considered him,' she replied carefully.

'Sophia always gets so bored when we talk about eligible young men!' complained Emma.

'Well, enough of young men, then. What are your plans for this year, Sophia?'

'I would dearly like to go away. Just for the spring and summer. Just long enough for me to explore a bit, but not so long that Father gets too lonely.'

'Go away? Why?' the girls asked in unison.

A lone bird flew across the cloudy sky above the circus and Sophia watched it go wistfully. 'I love it here in Stormhaven, but don't you ever just want to go out into the world? Wouldn't you like to see the Ocean Gate at Scogolio or the Palace of the Great Republic in Dov or the spring flight of the wyverns at Jascarne? Even just once? We have to live a little before we are old and sedate matrons.'

Emma frowned. 'I like it here in Stormhaven. And I've never liked foreigners much.'

She gave up. It wasn't worth upsetting her friend. 'You're right. Ignore me. I'm just feeling restless because I was ill all winter. I'm sure I will be here to share the summer with you.' She turned to face the two sisters with a smile. 'Now, what dresses are you wearing to the dance? I saw a beautiful one in the window of de Launay's the other day.'

'De Launay's!' Emma almost squealed in delight. 'That's a little risqué, Sophia, even for you!'

An hour's brisk walk back from the cemetery later saw Uriah sitting at the bar of his local ale house, the *Stag and Hunter*, trying to enjoy the warmth of the cheery fire and the taste of good beer. He absently swirled the ale in its glass and admired the colour. He had always liked brown ale. He still didn't really approve of the modern trend of brewing with the cheaper, pale malt.

'What did he look like?' he asked finally.

Lambley, the Stag and Hunter's red-bearded publican shrugged and poured himself a beer. 'Like all tapmen, I fancy myself pretty good at reading men, but he was nondescript. If I had to guess I'd have figured he worked at a banking house or a merchants' firm.'

'And he definitely asked about Sophia?'

'Well, he didn't mention her by name, but yes, he described her quite clearly.'

'And he claimed he was an old friend of the family?'

'That was what made me suspicious. You've been in that same house on Sapphire Row for as long as I can remember. I figured if he was an old friend he shouldn't have had any trouble finding you.' Lambley nodded and took a long swig from his tankard. 'So I told him I had never seen a girl like the one he had described.'

'I should get home.' Nerves fluttered in Uriah's belly and he threw down the rest of the beer to drown them. 'Many thanks for letting me know.'

'I wouldn't like a strange gentleman sniffing around my daughters. That and I still owe you for all that legal work you did for me last summer.'

'Thanks again.' Uriah slid a few coins across the bar and stepped outside into the evening. The prosperous streets of King's Row were quiet and the only souls he passed on the short walk home were the Nightingales, who were dressed up for the theatre and waiting for their coachman.

At his front door, Uriah fumbled for his keys and then let himself inside. The house was dark and cold. Their servant had left for the night and Sophia still wasn't home from the Burtons'. For once he was glad for the solitude. He took an apple from the pantry and then walked upstairs to his study.

'How could I be so stupid?' Uriah muttered as he shut the door behind himself. With a groan, he sank into the hard-backed chair in front of his desk, then snatched off his wig and tossed it and the apple onto the mantle above the fire he never bothered to light any more. He turned in his chair to stare out over the moonlit garden. If Sophia had told the truth at the cemetery, and he was fairly certain that she had, then she had no idea that people were looking for her. That left one obvious and terrible explanation: someone else had discovered her secret and the men looking for her were almost certainly the secret police, the Camar Shiem.

The Camar Shiem!

He ran a hand over his unevenly shaven skull. The idea that the king's most implacable servants were probably searching for his daughter terrified him. He couldn't even plead ignorance. There wouldn't have been a soul in the entire country who didn't know that the tainted had to be registered at eighteen. But it had been so hard when her time had come; Mary had only just died and he hadn't been able to bear the prospect of losing his only child to an asylum as well.

He breathed out slowly and watched his breath fog the cold window-pane. Yes, his weakness had created terrible problems for his darling child, but he might still save her, if he acted wisely. Even though it scared him, he knew he had to arrange her registration. As one of the East's most respected prize agents, he had scores of contacts and, with any luck, his friends could use their political clout to arrange a pardon for Sophia and perhaps only a prison sentence for him.

He reached for his spectacles. It was just a question of getting Sophia out of the city for a month or so while he arranged it all. He knew very well from his own legal experience that a criminal who gave themselves up was always treated more kindly than one who was captured.

Yes. That was the best way forward. He just had to do it coolly – if the king's men caught Sophia fleeing Stormhaven it would only make things worse. It would have to look like a holiday, a country jaunt. He would write to some of his rustic friends and see where he could send Sophia. With any luck his friends would simply assume she'd fallen in with a bad crowd and was being punished with a summer in the counties. For a fraction of a moment he also considered telling her that he had known about her taint for almost a decade, but he still recoiled from the thought. He still wasn't ready for that dreaded conversation.

Satisfied that he had finally settled on a plan, he leant forward, turned up his lamp and then reached for his pile of daily correspondence. Correspondence that, before Mary died, would never have sat unopened till after dark.

Uriah smiled as he read the sender of the third letter.

Captain J. Faulkner. Lately of the Inflexible. *Breaker of Plates.*

He had met Faulkner when the lad was a shy midshipman freshly down from the North Country. He had taken a shine to the boy, and after that he and Mary often had the homesick lad to stay when he was in port. Since then, Uriah had followed the young man's career with an almost fatherly pride. He opened the letter.

Dearest Uriah,

I hope you are well. I was desperately sad to hear of Mary's death. I can hardly describe how terribly low I felt when I found out. I have often thought of her kindness to me when I was but a mere squeaker. My heart goes out to Sophia and yourself.

But I will not be mawkish. I have only a little time to write and I am sorry to be so brash, but I was wondering if you would like to meet me at my club the day after tomorrow. I will be there from one. Not only would I dearly like to see you, but I also have a proposition that may be of interest to you…

3.

'THAT IS ALL you have managed to find out?' the Tallowman snarled. Even muted by the thick, dirty bandages that covered its face, the thing's voice hummed with rage.

'Aye, Mr Savage. She 'as red hair. And she lives somewhere near the big Mournwood Estate,' replied Bulldog, the self-appointed leader of its new lackeys.

'So you have been watching this estate, then?'

'We go past once or twice a day, and we've been askin' around. Seein' if anyone's seen her and what not.'

'You go past once or twice a day. You've been asking around?' the Tallowman repeated slowly. 'Our last agent claimed you were dependable. Said you weren't complete fools.'

Bulldog gulped and took an involuntary step backwards into the forge that filled the centre of the abandoned workshop. 'It's a snobby bit of town, Mr Savage. They don't like our kind loitering about there.'

'He's right,' Franks, the better dressed and cleverer of the three, added. 'The watch are thick as fleas on a cur up King's Row.'

The Tallowman calmed itself with an effort. Killing the idiots would serve little purpose, and then it would simply have to hire replacements. 'Go to this King's Row immediately. Find a room with a view of this estate. Make some excuse and rent it. Then I want one of you watching out for this girl every single moment of every single day. Is that clear?'

'But... but... how will we pay the rent, Mr Savage, sir? Rooms by the row are worth a fortune,' Franks whinged.

Reaching under its tattered coat, the Tallowman drew out a heavy purse. It tossed it on the dusty floorboards in front of them. 'Questions?'

They shook their heads. Franks scrabbled up the purse and then the three of them scurried towards the doors.

'I will check on you,' it called after them. 'And if I catch you neglecting your watch or asleep at your posts, there will be a reckoning. Understood?'

'Yes, Mr Savage,' they chorused.

Bulldog threw open the workshop's double doors and the three men escaped into the evening gloom.

4.

FAULKNER YAWNED AND rubbed his bleary eyes. Although the rank of post captain called for a certain amount of unavoidable paperwork, he was still unused to spending most of his day at a desk.

He and Donald had come up to the office of the *Dercian Observer* straight after breakfast. Since it was Saturday, the building had been fairly empty, but the power of his fame had worked wonders on the few journalists at work. Not only had they let him in but they had also found him an empty office and brought him all the old editions of their paper that mentioned the leviathan. Now the day was almost gone and the desk in front of him was buried under a pile of crumpled newspapers, used pencil stubs and a notebook full of his neat writing.

Donald groaned, sat up in the chair where he had been sleeping, and scratched at his scraggly, soot-grey beard. 'You woke me up.'

'Sorry,' Faulkner replied absently, picking back up the paper he had been reading.

His servant turned to face the office's dirty window and his beady eyes narrowed. 'It must be the dog watch!'

'Mmm... I suppose so.'

'It ain't good for a man,' observed Donald accusingly. 'Ain't good at all. This workin' away cooped up all day.'

'A quarter of the city does this every day of their lives.'

Donald snorted. The sound spoke volumes for what he thought of that quarter. 'I'll go and get you a pie and a good black beer then. You're pale as a ghost, you are.'

'I haven't any money.'

'Luckily I saved some, got me month's pay and a bit more besides. I know what you and your generation are like with coin.'

Faulkner lowered the paper. 'I already have a mother, thank you, Donald.'

Donald swore under his breath and stalked out, slamming the door behind him. Faulkner stood up, folded the paper, tossed it on the pile and gathered up his notes. At least his day had been slightly productive. Even after his dinner with Barry he'd still been half convinced the leviathan was a sailor's fable. A myth, a daemon. But, judging by the accounts in the newspaper, the beast appeared real enough. From the no doubt exaggerated stories the paper had teased out of the few survivors of attacks, he had learned something of the leviathan's method of hunting and its raw, ship-breaking power. The paper's artists had also given him a rough idea of the thing's appearance. Although they were probably embellished for the paper's readers, the illustrations showed the beast as bigger than the biggest whale. It looked like a fish though, a hideous angler or groper perhaps, all snapping teeth and flat, evil eyes. It seemed leviathans would have to join rhinoceros, the tainted, basilisks and the odd honest dockyard overseer on his list of creatures that were mind-boggling but real. He had also charted, as well as he could from the journalist's utterly unnautical accounts anyway, the rough locations of each attack. Judging by this first rough attempts at a chart, the beast had made its home somewhere in the Bastion Islands, the wild, windlashed island chain just to the south of Stormhaven. Already, somewhere amongst the jumble of all this newly acquired information, he could feel the seed of an idea taking root.

Faulkner stretched and yawned again. Donald was right: a day at the desk was dreary work. At least with plenty of his brother officers cooling their heels in Stormhaven he should be able to find someone to buy him a drink or two.

While at sea Faulkner rose as if by clockwork, ashore he took great pleasure in lying about in bed, especially if he was hungover. So, it was with extreme reluctance that he threw off his covers and sat up. Donald hovered at the end of the bed, his long arms clutching the tray carrying his boiled egg and morning coffee.

'Morning, Donald,' he croaked. It appeared that something had died in his mouth during the night.

'It was morning when you came home. This is more like mid-morning.'

'I wasn't too loud, was I?'

Donald placed the egg and coffee on the sideboard. 'I believe your sword may have tripped you on the stairs.'

That would explain the ache in his lower back. He gulped down some coffee. 'Sorry.'

Donald muttered something surly and unintelligible under his breath.

Faulkner swung his legs to the floor and walked to the room's small window. The day was cloudy. In the distance he could see white sails upon the ocean. 'Did you deliver that letter to Mr Blake yesterday?'

'We don't all fritter away our time in drunken debauchery,' Donald muttered.

'I beg your pardon?'

'I did deliver it, sir,' Donald replied with a straight face. 'And what are your movements today, if I might ask?'

'Well, since you so kindly delivered my letter, I'll be going down to my club to meet Mr Blake.'

'You won't be wearing your good uniform though, will you?' Donald pointed to a crumpled heap of blue fabric in a corner of the room. 'I'd only just sewn that bloody coat back up.'

'Oh no, I suppose not. What about the brown one then?'

'The brown coat makes you look rather fat, sir. Wear the green one.'

'You do go on like an old woman, Donald.'

Donald sighed. 'Never a word of thanks.'

'I'll wear green if you're set on it.'

'Good.'

Breakfast and his walk across town improved his condition somewhat and he was feeling well enough to pause out the front of the Seahorse Club to watch a griffon-mounted messenger drift lazily down to land on the distant roof of what must have been the Stock Exchange.

'Impressive, isn't it, old boy?'

Faulkner turned, smiled and shook the fellow's outstretched hand.

'Hello, Algy, good to see you! It most certainly is, but what happened to the poor old pegasus that used to bring the news?'

Captain Sir Algernon James, Third Baron of Winthrope, grinned under his famously big nose. 'Oh, the merchants that run the Stock Exchange have been making a song and dance for years about how long it was taking the bulletins from the capital to get out here. Seems the king eventually got tired of their endless complaining and lent them a griffon.'

'And it's faster, is it? A griffon? We didn't have any flyers down south, not like you spoilt Northern Fleet types.'

'That bird does the trip in only three or four days. My butler was telling me the other day that it comes almost all the way from Barbonne in one hop.' The baron plucked an invisible speck off his jacket. 'Anyway, enough chatter about economics. How have you been, Faulkner?'

'Pretty well, thanks. Still finding my shore legs and acclimatising to our gloomy weather. What about you?'

'I've married, if you hadn't heard.'

'De Lacey told me. My heartiest congratulations.' They chatted for a while about marriage and other domestic subjects before Faulkner was able to navigate the conversation around to more interesting matters. 'Will you end up ashore?'

'I shan't have to worry about it. I mean to join the dark side and run for my father's old seat on the Century Council.'

'Politics? And I always liked you.'

'Ha, well be sure to vote for me then! What about you? Any luck getting a ship?'

Faulkner shook his head. 'I'm too junior on the lists by far. I've no hope. Believe it or not, I mean to have a crack at the reward for this leviathan. If I can manage to raise the capital.'

The baron's eyes widened. 'You don't do things by half, do you, Faulkner? It's no mere kraken – by all accounts the thing is smashing every ship it meets to splinters.'

'So the papers claim.'

'Brave of you.'

Faulkner shrugged. 'I haven't much choice. I'd go mad stuck ashore.' He didn't see any point in mentioning his penury.

'After the *Agrippa,* I suppose if anyone can dispatch it, you can.'

'Thank you.'

The baron skipped down the last few stairs and then stopped in the mud of the street. 'Now, when I saw you I had something I wanted to ask you.' He tapped his head as if to jog his memory. 'Ah, that's right. Will you be in Stormhaven this Sunday week?'

'I hope not.' Not when he saw bailiffs at every corner and imagined their whistles in every sound. 'Ideally I'd already be after this overgrown fish by then.'

'That's disappointing, old boy.' It started to rain and the baron clicked his fingers for his coach. 'Navy is playing army and we could desperately do with you opening. That cut shot of yours would put the cat amongst those grey-cloaked pigeons.'

The uniformed doorman bowed to Uriah and opened the door for him. Uriah's was a familiar face at the club. Naval officers were, with some justification, extremely nervous about the ancient and convoluted process that governed the awarding and payment of their prize money. Due to this understandable anxiety, Uriah had spent countless afternoons within the club's exclusive walls, providing reassurance or advice to his clients.

An attendant took his cloak and the club's butler glided up. 'Good afternoon, Mr Blake. Captain Faulkner will see you in the Iron Cape Room. Shall I have you shown through?'

Uriah shook his head. 'No, thank you, Sanders. I know the way well enough.'

The Seahorse Club had originally been built as a private residence, but the owner had been bankrupted in the Eastern Bubble not long after it was finished. The house had then sat empty and forlorn for some years before the club had acquired it. Now it was restored to its former glory, all gleaming wooden panels, sweeping stairs and shining glass. It was a friendly place Uriah liked visiting. The ceilings were high and the light always bright, even on gloomy days. The walls oozed a feeling of shop passionately talked, old friendships topped up and new ones forged.

Reaching the Iron Cape Room, Uriah knocked and entered. The room was richly appointed. Thick blue carpet covered the floor like a woollen lake, beautiful carved chairs and tables floating upon it like majestic ships. A fire crackled in the generous hearth.

Captain James Faulkner looked up from the paper he was reading. 'Hello, Uriah, nice to see you.'

They shook hands and Uriah studied James. The years had certainly changed him. The lanky, awkward lad had matured into a sturdy man. James' back was straight, his eyes bright and his grip strong. A slight redness to his cheeks hinted at maybe a little too much drink, but not so much as to be ruining him. Not yet anyway. But any change in his physical appearance paled in comparison to the change in his bearing. As a lad, James had been always ready for a game or lark, but there had also always been a shy and thoughtful side to him too. The man that stood before Uriah now had the hard look of someone used to giving orders. Orders promptly obeyed.

'You look well, my boy.'

James smiled and gestured to the rain-splotched window. 'It's my tan. Down in the south they have this wonderful thing they call summer. How are you?'

'Keeping well, thank you.'

'And Sophia?'

'You'll be shocked when you see her. She is quite grown up.'

James gave him a somewhat patronising smile that suggested he found that hard to believe. 'I'm looking forward to seeing her.'

'We will have you over for dinner. I'm sure she'd love to see you, too. It'll be just like the old days.'

The smile fled from James' face. 'I was so, so sorry to hear about Mary, Uriah. She was like a second mother to me.'

'Thank you. I am sure you know she was very fond of you.' He looked up and was surprised to see tears in James' eyes.

They stood in awkward silence for a moment before Uriah motioned for them to sit. 'Mary lived her own life with such energy, it does her memory no honour to let the day slip past lost in maudlin memories. Now, perhaps you might tell me about this venture?'

'The venture. Yes. Umm, well, Uriah, I mean to buy a ship and then hunt this leviathan…'

Once he had quickly sketched out his plan, James rocked back in his chair, anxiety etched in his face. 'So, how does that sound?'

Uriah looked down at the small diary that he had made notes in. 'I have some questions.'

'Of course.'

'What do you expect this venture to cost?'

'Between five and seven thousand crowns, I'd estimate.'

He noted that down. 'And, should you kill this leviathan, how would the prize be divided?'

'I figured we'd use the naval system and you would take the Admiral's and the Admiralty's share.'

Uriah made another mark on his page. That was a generous split. 'How hard would it be to find a crew?'

'Not too tricky. As a result of the peace, plenty of sailors, like their captains, will have found themselves marooned ashore and looking for a berth. I've already approached Lord de Lacey to be my first mate and Morgan to be my carpenter. Both were kind enough to accept.'

'I also can't imagine your reputation would hurt recruitment, my boy,' observed Uriah. 'Now, assuming you don't kill this beast, this leviathan, what happens to my investment then?'

'In the first instance, the ship gets sunk, either by the monster itself or storm or reef. In that case I'm afraid your investment would go to the bottom of the cold ocean along with our ship. But I assure you no one would be more disappointed with that result than me,' James said with a grin. 'In the second scenario we sail around for half a year without seeing anything and then come home empty-handed. In that case we pay the crew out and sell the ship. After all that, I suppose you'd get about a third of your coin back.'

'Hmm.'

They sat quietly for a while, with only the sound of the crackling of the fire and the patter of the rain at the window for accompaniment.

'Are you interested?' James asked at last.

'I am sorry to make you wait, but please, I need to think a little longer on this.'

'Of course.'

Uriah looked around the room, giving his analytical mind time to work. The idea was risky, more than a little mad and almost certain to fail. Uriah had always eschewed risk. He had been a builder and a grower. A sensible investment here, a shrewd buy there and a good deal of hard work everywhere else. He had become wealthy almost by accident. He had only wanted to provide a comfortable life for his family. But Mary's death had shaken him and he was gyrating off his familiar, sedate path like a child's top nearing the end of its spin. Maybe this once he could roll the dice? He had already made more than enough to ensure that Sophia would never want for anything – if the Camar Shiem spared her that was. The money certainly wouldn't be hard to arrange and it would hardly make a dent in his fortune. Even when he lost the lot.

He took a deep breath and looked at James. The man, the son he'd never had, was leaning forward like a boy waiting to open a birthday present. At twenty-four Captain James Faulkner had already given up ten years of his life and more than a few splashes of his own blood in the Realm's service and now, with the coming of the peace, she had cast him off. That counted for something.

'I'll provide the money.'

Faulkner's face lit up as brightly as the muzzle of a firing gun and he leapt to his feet in delight, scattering his papers. 'Isaladar bless you, Uriah!'

5.

'AFTERNOON, BART!' CALLED Sophia, as she strode into Lord Mournwood's spacious stone stables.

The grizzled stable master looked up from the bay mare he was busy shoeing. 'Oh hello, Sophia. We were just saying yesterday that you must have finally traded us in for poetry readings and embroidery.'

She ducked into the tack room. 'No! I've wanted to come, I just haven't been well,' she shouted. The Mournwood's town house was only few hundred yards from her home and, to the gentle consternation of that noble family, she had been helping in their stables since she was a little girl.

She quickly retrieved the trousers, plain shirt and work boots she kept hidden in a battered little chest. Her father put up with her working with the horses, but he would have had apoplexy if he knew about the boyish outfit she wore around the stables. 'Don't come in, Bart, I'm changing,' she called.

'I have my hands full enough here, thanks.'

'Where are Owen and Greg?' she asked, as she re-emerged dressed in her workingman's outfit.

'The yearling sale at Thornbrough. I sent them down to have a look.'

'Are you buying this year?'

'Just wanted to see how we measure against the competition.' He shut the door to the mare's stall. 'And what would you like to do today?'

'Do you mind if I see Warrior?'

Said to be descended from Prince Isaladar's horse Miazareth, Warrior was a giant old chestnut charger. During the Long War, Warrior had saved his master's life when the young lord had been grievously wounded by an Auserwaldian aerial dragoon. Now swaybacked and long past his prime,

Warrior was still kept on and pampered like a favourite child. Sophia had always liked that. Unlike most noble families, the Mournwoods didn't forget their debts.

The stable master nodded. 'The last time you were here was when he was so sick.'

She followed Bart out of the stable into the small, sandy courtyard at the back of the block. Warrior heard the door open and looked up. When he saw her, the old charger whickered softly and trotted up. She patted the old horse's nose gently. He was ancient enough now that in places he was even starting to lose his hair. She ran her other hand gently over the wicked old scars. The dragoon's wyvern had struck from above, and even after all this time the charger's neck and head were still crisscrossed with the marks left by the beast's vicious claws.

Bart shook his head. 'Every time I send the boys out to groom him one of them will come back in bitten or trodden on, but with you the old brute acts like a love-struck puppy.'

Warrior snorted and threw his head in the old man's direction.

To hide her nervousness, Sophia scratched Warrior's one remaining ear. She should have never asked after the old horse. 'He has good taste, that's all.'

'Well, he certainly likes you,' Bart agreed. 'I could almost swear it was the sight of you that healed him when he was so sick. I've never seen a horse recover from colic when they were as far gone as he was. Sure as Isaladar killed the daemon, I would have bet he'd be dead by nightfall. I even told Lord Mournwood he should come and say goodbye to his old friend. But within half an hour of you leaving he was prancing around like a six-month-old foal. Made a right fool out of me, he did.'

Sophia's heart raced. This conversation was getting riskier by the minute. 'You're far too sentimental about your horses, Bart. If anything healed him it was the vet's tonic.'

'True, true.' He patted the old charger's side. 'What about you? I hear you've been sick as well?'

'It was just a winter fever,' she lied. 'I've only been out of bed for a week or so.'

'It was a bad year for it. I'm glad you're feeling better.' He looked up and studied the clouds. 'We better get back to work, it'll rain soon. I'll have you groom Misty, if you don't mind.'

'Of course I don't.'

'And how is Mr Blake these days?' asked Bart as he swung the heavy door to the courtyard shut behind them. He hardly knew her father, but Bart had lost his wife as well and Sophia knew he understood the deep, lasting pain only too well.

'He is getting better. Very lonely though. It's hard.' She shook her head. 'Every day I still wish I hadn't been away at school when Mother got sick.' Particularly as then her mother wouldn't have died.

As they did every evening, Uriah and Sophia retired to their cosy sitting room after dinner. Uriah read the day's paper in his armchair and, it being an informal house, Sophia lay curled up like a cat in front of the fire reading her novel.

The door opened and their servant, Mrs Gilbert, poked her bonneted head into the room. 'Is there anything else you'd like before I go home?'

'No thanks, Gilly,' replied Sophia.

Uriah looked up from his paper. 'We're fine.'

'Night then.' She paused. 'I did mean to ask a favour of you, Mr Blake. I was hoping to take little Master Gilbert to see the Return. Do you think you could spare me the morning of the day after tomorrow?'

Duke Vomeryer held a colonelcy in the army and he had been away fighting on the continent for the better part of two years. Now he would be welcomed back with all the considerable pomp and ceremony Stormhaven could manage. 'As indispensable as you are to this house, Mrs Gilbert, I think we can spare you for the morning. Hopefully it is the last time in my life that we have to welcome home men who have been fighting abroad,' he said.

'Thank you, Mr Blake, Isaladar bless you both.' She left, gently shutting the door to the sitting room behind her.

'How was your day, Sophia?' Uriah asked as he carefully folded up his paper.

'Passable.' Sophia pushed her book away, yawned and rolled onto her back. 'I spent most of it helping with the Mournwood's horses.'

He frowned. 'I do worry you are imposing.'

'Relax, Father. Bart is glad for the extra pair of hands.'

'I hope so.'

'Stop fretting. How was your day?'

'I had the afternoon off and met a friend about a business venture.'

'Oh yes? Who?'

'James Faulkner, do you remember him?' He knew that she remembered him very, very well but it was a father's duty to tease sometimes.

'What?' She sat up, wide-eyed. 'James is home? When did he arrive?'

'A week or so ago.'

'The *Inflexible* isn't in the bay.'

'No. She is going into ordinary at Barbonne. He came down on the mail packet.'

Sophia looked crestfallen. 'You should have told me you were seeing him, I would have come along.'

'I would have, but we met at his club.'

'Oh.'

'He mentioned he might come for dinner.'

'Good. How was he? How did he look?'

'Very well.'

'Does he have an issue with his prize money?'

Uriah shook his head. 'No, he had a proposal for me.'

'A proposal?'

'Indeed.'

'Father! Don't make me suffer in suspense!'

Uriah relented and quickly outlined the nature of James' plan. Sophia listened intently, asking a question here and there.

'So?' he asked.

'According to the papers this leviathan is unstoppable.' Sophia pushed her hair back behind her ears. 'But if he did kill it, you two would be some of the richest men in the East.'

'We certainly would.' He paused. 'You keep abreast of naval matters. Do you think Faulkner is up to it?' He didn't mention that he had noticed that her naval scrapbook contained an exceedingly large number of newspaper clippings about Faulkner. He had already teased her enough for one afternoon.

'Probably. Frigate captains are handpicked from the most enterprising men in the fleet and James was generally considered the most enterprising of our frigate captains, so I've no doubt he could handle the nautical side of things.' She paused for a moment. 'But the financial side, why that is another matter entirely.'

'What do you mean?'

She laughed. 'Don't you remember what he was like when he lived with us? He was always down to his last few coppers. James couldn't hold onto money to save his life.'

'He might have changed.' Uriah pushed his spectacles back up onto the bridge of his crooked nose. She was right. James had always been terrible with money. 'Perhaps age and command has improved his grasp of finance. Anyhow, I've agreed to his plan already. I can hardly leave my business for three months just to oversee his spending.'

Sophia suddenly looked diffident. 'I might have an idea.'

'Go on.'

She took a deep breath. 'I could go. As your representative.'

'You can't be serious.'

'I am completely serious.'

'No.'

'Father! How many afternoons have I spent helping you with your books? You know that I know money. If you leave it up to James he'll be broke before he leaves port. I'll save you a fortune.'

'I've never heard such a fanciful notion in...' He trailed off as the first flicker of an idea bloomed. It was almost too perfect. He needed Sophia out of Stormhaven. What better and safer way to do it than in the company of a war hero?

'Father, are you all right?'

'What? Yes. Just thinking.' He found his hands were shaking and he gripped the folded paper tightly. 'Perhaps your scheme has merit.'

She opened her mouth and then closed it again. She blinked. 'Merit?'

'You can go. But there will be conditions. Many, many conditions.'

'Thank you!' She dashed across the room and threw her arms around him. 'Thank you! Thank you!'

Despite having packed and unpacked her trunks half a dozen times, Sophia was still too excited to sleep when the city's bells chimed three. Not that she minded – sleep was a waste anyway. This reality was far more exciting than any dream. She still couldn't quite believe it was happening. Her father was usually so protective of her. She'd really only suggested that she go along with James as a hopeful joke. If she'd been sitting on a chair when he said yes, she would have fallen off it.

Three months away would just be perfect too! Enough time for her to get out of the city and experience some of the world, but not so long that Father would be too lonely. It was also three months away from the fear of discovery and the terror of how her father and her friends would react when they found out. She pushed those depressing thoughts down. She had to concentrate on enjoying this one last breath of freedom. She could picture it already, ninety spring and summer days of strange villages, strange characters, desolate moors and the ocean shore! The possibilities made her heart lurch a little and she gave a tiny squeal of excitement.

Just resisting the temptation to do a silly little jig of happiness, she left her half-packed trunk and sat down at her dressing table to consider her outfit for the next day. A head scarf gave her a mysteriously gypsy-like air, but without it she could show off her golden eyes to the full effect. She tried both options a few times before giving up on the scarf. She couldn't imagine James liked fussy girls anyway. As a boy he had always been amused by her tomboyish antics.

The thought of the games he used to long-sufferingly play with her breathed sudden life into a long-dead memory and, dragging her dressing table's chair behind her, she went out into the shadowy hall. Setting the chair down in front of a large cupboard, she climbed up on its seat and began to ransack the cupboard's top shelves.

'Is that you, Sophia?' called out Uriah from his bedroom.

'Yes, Father, sorry to wake you.' Sophia smiled and rolled her eyes. Who else would be searching through their house in the dead of night?

'Do *try* to be quiet, dear, you sound like a herd of elephants,' muttered Uriah.

'Yes, Father.'

Finally she found the dusty old box she had been searching for. Leaving the chair and the mess behind, she lugged it into her bedroom and placed it gently near the glowing hearth, then opened the lid. The contents of the box were an archaeological dig through layers that marked out the stages of her life.

She ignored the first layer, carefully setting aside the beautiful dolls and painted horses she had treasured as a little girl. It was the next layer she wanted, the one that marked the best, the shiniest and the most sun-blessed part of her life. She smiled as she touched all these artefacts, turning them over in her hands, almost trying to awaken the contentment of that time.

The compass and knife her mother had given her for her eleventh birthday.

The lock from the mane of her first proper horse, Traveller.

The slingshot Faulkner had made her when the bullies had pulled her red hair. She had won a famous victory with it too and sent Fat Michael, the chief hair-puller, crying home to his nanny.

Her two favourite books from her first, long year at boarding school. *A Boy's Book of Ships* and *Jadwiga and the Thousand-Yard Boots*. She ran a finger over their familiar, battered covers.

Eventually she found what she was looking for: the boatswain's whistle James had given her when he left for the south. It shone in the firelight amongst the other jumble like gold on a stream bed. Its thin chain was curled around it. Even though years had passed, she could still picture the day he had given it to her, as clear as if it were a painting in front of her. It had been raining, of course, and James was trying to be brave, but she had realised even then that he was scared. It was no wonder, really: he was leaving his country and his family for what he must have known would be years. Despite the tears that shone in his eyes, he had smiled a courageous, boyish smile and pushed the whistle into her hand as they had hugged goodbye.

She grinned. After all these years she was finally going to get to go to sea as well. She picked the whistle up, slipped the chain over her head and carefully tucked it inside her nightgown. It just didn't seem right to put the little whistle back in that dusty box.

6.

IT WAS RAINING steadily, so Faulkner and Donald met under the lee of the building across the street from Uriah's office.

'What are you wearin' that for?' asked Donald. 'To hide from the bailiffs?'

Faulkner pulled down the scarf that covered most of his face and removed his battered tricorner hat. 'It'd be damned annoying to get caught now, just when I've got things sorted.' He looked his servant up and down. 'But you're hardly in a position to comment, not wearing that greasy sartorial mess.'

'This good, honest coat? Had this since I was on *Thunderer*. Seen many a scrape, it has.'

'Smells like it too.' Faulkner fished out his watch and checked the time. 'Fashion aside, are you clear on what you need to do?'

Donald nodded, instantly serious. 'Captain Murray will take me up to Mudmoon on the mail packet and Lord de Lacey and Morgan will meet me there. You'll join us as soon as you've sorted out our finances. The first crew will join us a few days after that.'

'Perfect. Now, you'd better hurry down to the docks, Murray has never liked waiting.'

'Very good, Captain. I'll see you up the coast.' Donald tapped a fist to his forehead and trotted off towards the naval yards.

Faulkner picked up his bag and splashed across the cobbled road. The bell above the door tinkled welcomingly as he stepped into the office and Uriah looked up from the pile of papers he had been working on.

'James! Come, my boy, sit by the fire and warm yourself. We can't have you catching your death. Can I get you a drink? Our leviathan is beginning to make coffee fiendishly expensive, but we've still some left.'

He nodded that he would take coffee and, despite being amused by the landsman's commonly held belief that a man who got wet promptly died, sat obediently near the fire. Uriah disappeared into a back room and soon the rich smell of roasting coffee filled the room.

Returning, Uriah handed a sheet of parchment to him. 'I had a pamphleteer mock this up. Do you like it?'

Faulkner took the parchment and quickly read over what Uriah had prepared.

VOLUNTEERS

*God save the **KING!***

*The heroic Captain James **FAULKNER**, victor of **ASARE ROADS**, lately of his Majesty's frigate **INFLEXIBLE**, seeks volunteers to aid in his hunt for the **LEVIATHAN**.*

*The **REWARD** of 100,000 crowns to be **DIVIDED** between all the crew as prize money.*

*Only **BRAVE** and **EXPERIENCED** tars need apply. If interested, **REPAIR***

to the offices of Uriah Blake Esq., worthy Prize Agent, Sapphire Row, Bromhead, STORMHAVEN

'It isn't a bit strong, is it?' Faulkner tried not to grimace. 'I don't want to sound the braggart.'

'Oh no, it's quite the done thing they tell me.'

'Thank you.' The pompous tone didn't sit well with him, but he had no desire to upset Uriah. 'They're very handsome. Can you arrange to post copies here and send others to Barbonne and Oldfort by the pegasus?'

'Are you sure the normal packet won't do? The Aerial Mail will be expensive.'

'I've no desire to waste your money, but the longer those flyers are up, if you pardon the pun, the more genuine sailors we'll catch ashore. And I need old tars. I have a feeling landsmen and leviathan hunting don't go well together.'

'Point taken. I'll have my clerk arrange it this afternoon.' Uriah took off his glasses. 'When these volunteers do begin to appear here, well, how am I to tell who is a competent sailor and who is not?'

'My old boatswain Jenkins lives up in Scalton. I've already sent word to him and he'll be down here tomorrow. You can send any volunteers to him at the Drum and Monkey on North Rest Road. He'll soon sort the wheat from the chaff.'

They were interrupted as a girl entered the room carrying the coffees on a silver tray. It took Faulkner a moment to realise it was Sophia and then a second moment to stop himself from staring too gormlessly. The skinny, carrot-haired tomboy he remembered was gone. She had been replaced by an elegant young woman. Putting down the tray, she turned to face him and red-golden hair fell over her shoulder to caress her neck. He swallowed and half rose from his chair, unsure if he should bow, shake hands or remain where he was.

She handed him his cup and saucer. 'Captain Faulkner. It's so nice to see you.' Brilliant golden eyes that carried more than a hint of laughter studied him impudently.

'Lovely to see you again, Sophia. You've changed.'

She laughed. 'I won't ask you to play with my dolls any more, if that's what you mean. You've changed as well, Captain. Last time I saw you, you were a boy pleased as punch with your new lieutenant's uniform. Now you're a naval hero.'

Annoyingly, Faulkner felt himself blush. 'Hero might be a bit much.'

'Oh?'

He shrugged his most nonchalant shrug. 'I knocked some holes in a few Caladian ships.'

Sophia stepped back out of Uriah's eyeshot and rolled her eyes. That was not at all the response Faulkner had expected and he fumbled for something, anything, intelligent to say.

'I'll be ready to leave within the hour, Father,' she said over her shoulder as she swished back out of the room without bothering to wait for his reply.

Faulkner turned to Uriah and narrowed his eyes. 'To leave?'

Uriah coughed nervously.

'Is there something you need to tell me?'

'Ah yes. There, ah, is.'

'And?'

'Sophia will be going with you.' Uriah coughed again. 'As my representative.'

'I beg your pardon?' Faulkner didn't remember Uriah as being particularly fond of pranks.

'Sophia will be my representative.'

A strange mixture of anger, embarrassment and shock bubbled up inside him. 'You can't be serious, sir?'

'I am.'

'You intend to send Sophia — as in your daughter, Sophia — along with me as your representative?'

'I do.'

'But—'

Uriah raised a hand to interrupt and drew himself up in his chair like a schoolmaster. 'I appreciate it is highly irregular, James, but my mind is utterly made up. Sophia will head north with you.'

'But—'

'My mind is quite made up, James. My investment is entirely dependent on it. There is no point in our discussing it further.'

Faulkner took a sip of his coffee and found it was scalding hot. For a long moment he was sorely tempted to call the entire venture off, but then he thought of the infernal bailiffs and their bloody whistles. Debtor's prison would probably be marginally less pleasant than this humiliation. 'Very good,' he said at last.

'I know Sophia is high-spirited, but she is a sensible girl and you two have always got on. You will be fine.' Uriah smiled at him. 'Now, the coach is collecting us from my house at three o'clock, so once you've finished your coffee we should walk up there to wait.'

The morning's rain had been blown away to the south by the cold blustery wind that now rattled at the windows, and the three of them sat together in Uriah's sitting room, waiting for the coach that would take James and Sophia north. In the long breaks in the fitful conversation, Uriah studied James and his daughter closely. Even as miserable as he was to be sending Sophia away, he couldn't help but be amused by the difference in their attitudes.

Sophia could not have looked happier as she leant against a window, keeping watch for the coach. He hadn't seen her this excited in years and he wished that it had not taken this nastiness of the strange men asking about her for him to finally let her go on a trip.

James, on the other hand, was slouched in his chair and looked as downcast as Uriah had ever seen him. The excitement he had shown for the venture back in the Seahorse Club had almost completely evaporated. Indeed, he had reacted so angrily to the idea of taking Sophia along with him that Uriah had thought for a moment the young captain might call the entire arrangement off.

'The coach is here!' Sophia announced.

Without a word, James stood and walked out into the hall to help the coachmen carry the bags out. Uriah and Sophia followed and watched from the top step. Once the baggage had all been loaded safely onto the coach, Uriah held out a hand to him. 'Good luck, my boy.'

James shook his hand firmly. 'I might need a dash of it.'

'Sophia has details of all the finances.'

'Very good.' James nodded, a slight hardness in the set of his mouth, the only sign of how much he disapproved of *that* arrangement. 'Hopefully when I next see you we can enjoy a very expensive meal of fish together to celebrate our success!'

'I can't imagine anything more pleasant, my boy. Now happy hunting!'

James waved farewell and climbed up into the coach.

Sophia turned to him and her voice wavered. 'I'll miss you, Father.'

'I'll miss you too, Sophia.' Uriah fought down the urge to cry. 'I want you to be sensible and listen to James' advice. He will keep you out of trouble.'

'Ha, I'll keep him out of trouble!'

He knew his daughter well enough to appreciate it was pointless to argue. 'Do you remember the financial arrangements?'

She rolled her eyes. 'You've only explained them to me a dozen times.'

'You have three promissory notes for two thousand five hundred crowns each. If, for whatever reason, you need more, you can draw from the Royal Eastern Bank.'

'I will be fine.' She kissed his cheek. 'I'll see you in no time at all.'

'You can only stay until James has whatever ship he finds outfitted and ready for sea. Under absolutely no circumstances are you to go out on the hunt itself.'

'Of course – you've told me that a hundred times already. I'm not stupid or deaf. I'd really better go, James is already shockingly grouchy. I love you. Don't get bored while I'm away! I love you. Don't look so sad, I'll only be gone for a month or two.'

Once the coach had clattered away down the street and out of sight, Uriah dabbed the tears away from his eyes, put his spectacles back on and checked his watch. He had no time to mope. Before he saw to Sophia's registration he had some investigating to do.

Leaving the stately homes of King's Row behind, he walked through the pleasant, orderly district of Urshart and then up the steep streets towards Manev Hill. The Hill was a strange suburb, its crooked buildings clustered so tightly together that, from a distance, they looked as if they were seeking shelter from the winds that howled in off the ocean. Over the years the place had developed a reputation as the home of Stormhaven's artists, poets and musicians. That was why, despite his significant holdings across the city, Uriah had never owned any property on the Hill. Long experience had taught him that the more creative his tenants were, the less likely they were to bother paying their rent. Twice he lost his way amongst the maze of twisting streets and turning lanes before he finally found the house he was looking for. Luckily the place was hard to miss, distinct as it was with its ironbound, yellow-painted door.

Taking a deep, steadying breath of cold, briny air, he lifted the heavy doorknocker and rapped three times. The door swung open a crack and a large, black-bearded head looked Uriah up and down coolly. 'Ja?'

'I've come to see Father Jan,' Uriah said.

'Why? Cannot heal now.' The man's accent was guttural and thick.

'I don't need him to heal.'

The big man scratched at his beard. 'Why see him then?'

'I want his advice.'

The man opened the door fully. He was built like a bear and his beard reached to his waist.

'All right. But he is weak. Make sick lady better only last month. Still tired. You try to make him heal for you, my brother and I throw you out on your head, ja?'

Uriah nodded and the bearded man motioned for him to enter. The house was heavy with the smell of peppery food, hard spirits and damp stone. He had been told that the man he sought, Father Jan, had emigrated from the Grand Duchy of Auserwald and the look of the room confirmed this. The open fire with the thick stew bubbling above it, the animal skins on the floor, the shiny bronze saucepans hanging from the roof and the household shrine to Isaladar all smacked of Northern Circillia.

'This Stefan. My brother.' The bearded fellow indicated another man who had been sitting silently in the shadows. The second man said nothing, but he watched Uriah keenly over a drooping moustache. A heavy blunderbuss lay cradled in his lap. 'Come. I take you to Father.'

Uriah followed him through the twisting corridors of the gloomy building. He had to duck to pass under the crooked doorways. In places the bearded man almost had to bend double.

Finally, the giant man pointed a thumb towards a nondescript doorway 'Father is outside. Remember, you ask him to heal, we throw you out. Gentleman or not.'

'I will remember.'

The big man opened the door and Uriah stepped through. On the other side he paused and blinked in surprise. Nestled in a space between the tenements was a tiny private courtyard and it was covered in a dazzling array of spring flowers. They climbed everywhere, vibrant and seemingly unrestrained by any rule of nature or season, obscuring the pitted stone walls to the height of a tall man. Uriah had always been a keen gardener and he was sure he recognised flowers that he had only ever seen before in books.

Indeed, he would have sworn that he even spotted some tropical species. It was as if a botanical garden's worth of flora had been lovingly gathered up and transplanted to fill this one ugly little courtyard.

'Are you a gardener?' asked a reed-thin voice from somewhere amongst the vibrant foliage.

'Yesterday I would have said yes, now I am not so sure.'

The speaker laughed softly and Uriah spotted a man nestled amongst a spray of purple fronds. Jan the Healer was even more ancient than Uriah had expected. Once he would have been a big man like his sons, but now he was just a jumble of bones poking at paper-thin skin. Despite his obvious frailty, clear grey eyes stared out from the old man's antique face.

Jan indicated a wooden stool next to the simple bench where he lay. 'You are too kind. Now come, sit.' Uriah sat, careful not to crush any of the plants that grew around the old man like courtiers striving for their monarch's attention.

'What is your name, my friend?'

'Uriah Blake.'

'Ah.' He nodded. 'Uriah Blake.'

'You know me, Father Jan?'

'Ja, lawyer. You come because of your daughter, Sophia.'

'How did you know that?' Uriah's heart suddenly felt like it was beating full of cold, rusty nails. 'You can recognise others with the taint?'

'I cannot, but another of my kind in the city can and we tainted are a tight clan. We gossip more than soldiers.' The man paused and studied Uriah. 'Now, this same friend says you do not fear your daughter. So why do you come for this old man's advice? Surely you must already know the taint has not made her a beast or a monster? You are not silly enough to believe the fairy-tale stories that we carry daemons inside us. You treat her with love.'

Uriah looked down into one of the brilliant purple flowers. The frost should have killed it long ago, he noted distractedly. 'No, I am not worried about her in that way. I would love her with or without the taint. I came because I have heard dark rumours about the Camar Shiem, the secret police... and... I... I have not had her registered yet.'

'Not registered?'

Uriah shook his head.

'That is very foolish, but not uncommon in these strange days. I still do not see how this old man can help?'

'I have heard you are a good and wise man, and I had hoped you could tell me what truly happens at registration and if Sophia is in any danger.'

Father Jan chuckled. 'Daughters make clever fathers silly men, Uriah Blake. Now come, put this blanket around me. Then I will tell you a story that will make things clearer.'

Uriah leant forward and tucked the blanket around Father Jan's frail chest.

The old man got comfortable and then began. 'On the Continent the tainted are hated. And I don't mean like here where they are disliked – overseas they are utterly reviled. In Auerswald, where I was born, a man could be executed for stealing a horse. But if the same man killed a so-called tainted he was unlikely even to be imprisoned. My dear mother and father were murdered, hung from the branches of a tree in our village, just because two seasons' crops had failed. Do you understand? The same villagers I had grown up with and played with all my life strung my parents up like deer after the hunt.' Father Jan paused and shook his head as if still shocked by the world's brutality. 'After my parents were murdered, I promised myself that I would raise my own family somewhere free from that kind of savagery. So I started walking south, but everywhere I stopped I found things were the same, even if the hate and prejudice was better hidden in some places. There would be an eclipse or a flood, or a deformed animal would be born and, driven by superstition and fear, ignorant peasants would kill my kind.'

'Was it always that bad?'

Jan shrugged. 'Some places were better. Further south they use my breed when they need them. A weather mage here, a diviner there. Over time the loathing would seem to disappear, but it always festered to the surface again when people were scared or threatened.'

'We have a proverb: the tailor did it, so they hung the tainted.'

Jan nodded. 'Exactly. I had almost given up hope of finding somewhere free of this hatred when I found myself in the Imperial Free City of Levestar and in the pay of a merchant from here in Stormhaven. He was a kindly man and took a liking to me. He even taught me to read and write and later, when he was almost blind, he had me read him the papers from his home each morning. One winter his normal paper did not arrive by ship because of a storm and I had to read to him from a newspaper he did not like. I couldn't believe what I saw in that newspaper. I'll show you.'

The old man took out a leather pouch from under the blanket and carefully unfolded an ancient scrap of yellowed paper. Uriah leant forward. It was an antique political drawing, in which a cruel caricature of King Alexander, grandfather of the current king, tipped a bag of gold coins into the ocean. A gaggle of naval officers stood off to one side, clapping. To their left a group of taxpayers wept and pulled at their hair in dismay. The caption read: *'Naval Taxes Well Spent.'*

'A satirical sketch? I don't understand.'

'I did not either. I asked my employer what had happened to the artist and the man said, "Nothing, Jan. He does it for a living, the republican rascal." I still remember his exact words. I was dumbfounded. I came from a land of proud soldier-princes who would strike down a man who looked at them without reverence, a land where rule and law lived only in cold steel or hot lead. I could not believe that my master came from a country where a man could make a living insulting his king. A king who could trace his line back to Prince Isaladar himself! At that very moment I decided to emigrate here. Six months later, when my employer came home to Stormhaven, I came with him.' The old man paused, carefully raised his head and took a swig from an earthenware jug by his side on the bench.

'I don't mean to be rude, Jan, but what does this have to do with the taint and Sophia's registration?' Uriah asked in the pause.

Jan wiped his mouth with his sleeve. 'My point is this, Uriah, I picked this nation because, out of all the places in the world, here law and liberty are king and queen. Even my kind are sheltered. Do not believe the rumours spreading in this city, Uriah. Yes, the Camar Shiem are a dark and terrible tool, but they serve this nation and its liberties just like the king, the army or the parliament do. All they ask of us tainted is that we all serve in our own way as well. They would only take Sophia away if the madness was about to consume her. Even then they would do so only reluctantly.'

'You are sure?'

'Of course I am sure. Nothing is worse than foolish advice freely given.'

'You mentioned that the tainted must serve? I mean no disrespect, but how do you serve, Jan?'

'They asked me to join the army as surgeon, but I refused. I had already seen enough blood to last a lifetime. They understood and said I could stay in Stormhaven, but I must promise to heal when they asked. Since then, they have only called on me a half dozen times. In two score years I have healed a prince, two dukes, a duchess, an astronomer, a philosopher and a general,' the old man said.

'And will Sophia be punished for not registering when she was eighteen?' Uriah asked, the lawyer in him stirring.

Jan waved a hand noncommittally. 'There is a fine. But if Captain-Constable Moreau's wife has not been pestering him about his drinking, he may choose to waive it.'

'So I should arrange her registration?'

'Have you been listening, Uriah Blake? You should have done so long before she was eighteen. The Camar Shiem does not only protect the common people from the tainted, they also protect the tainted from the things in the world that hate us far more than any superstitious peasant ever could. Sophia will be far safer on their books than off them.'

Uriah stood up. 'Your counsel has been invaluable. Can I pay you in any way?'

'No, I once asked exactly the same questions on my family's behalf as you now ask for Sophia. Now go, see to her registration.'

'Thank you very much, Jan.'

'Uriah Blake,' the old man called out to him as he reached the door. 'I have one last piece of advice for you.'

'Yes?'

'When people learn of your daughter's taint they will pour all manner of credulous nonsense in your ears. They will tell you we are moon-touched, or daemon-possessed or god-spoken. Ignore it all. Just remember that three centuries ago men thought the world was flat and they burned women who understood medicine. The taint is no different. It is simply a natural phenomenon we do not yet understand. So, when fools tell you your daughter consorts with daemons and fiends and other creatures of fairy tale, as I promise they will, remember this advice and just smile at their ignorant dread.'

7.

THE COACH RATTLED across an unusually rough part of the road and woke Faulkner from his fitful doze. He yawned and leant forward to peer out the coach's window. The sun had risen while he was asleep and for a time he studied the countryside. With its rolling green fields, stone walls and hilltop villages the view was pretty enough, but it soon bored him. He had grown up further to the north in the shadows of the borderlord's great fortresses and he was used to wilder lands. His was a country where the lonely cry of griffons still echoed at night and a man carried a musket for protection, not sport. Lying back in his hard seat he grimaced. He hated coaches. He hated the bone-jarring ride and the endless waiting for the next coach and the noise and the incessant changing of horses in dark, muddy and confused coach yards. He would take the leakiest old ship in the east over its finest coach.

Unfortunately, despite how much he hated the thing, the coach was the least of his current worries. He glanced across at Sophia and scowled. They had hardly spoken since they'd left. She'd spent the daylight hours reading over a pile of notes she had brought along and then had promptly fallen asleep as night fell. She was still asleep now, nodding to the sway of the coach and oblivious to his distemper. What had Uriah been thinking? Of course the man's investment gave him every right to send along a representative. But his twenty-year-old daughter? Had Mary's death driven him completely mad? What did Sophia know of the sea? Or even life outside the city? No doubt all she was going to do was complain and slow him down. Worse, unchaperoned as she was, the gossip back in Stormhaven would positively roast them. No doubt tongues would soon be wagging, if they weren't already.

'It's rude for a gentleman to stare, Captain Faulkner,' she said, without opening her eyes.

He jumped. 'It's just as impolite for a young lady to pretend to be asleep.'

She pursed her lips, but he was saved from any retort as the coach creaked and groaned to a stop. Glad to escape, he threw open the door and stepped down into the cool morning air.

'This is as far as we can go, Captain, it's too muddy from here on,' the coachman called down to him. 'You'll have to go on by foot for the last half mile. We'll carry the lady's bags down.'

'Thank you, my man.' Faulkner threw a purse up to the driver and turned to help Sophia out of the coach. She ignored his offered hand and jumped down.

With a sigh, he heaved his one bag up over his shoulder and turned towards the ocean. In the middle distance, nestled amongst the heather, sat the crooked old pub that was their destination. Beyond that was the muddy expanse of Mudmoon Bay and then, rippling like light on beaten tin, were the waters of the Circillian Ocean. In the far distance, a greyer smudge against the grey clouds, was the smog from the mills and factories of Stormhaven.

'Come on, Sophia. I've old friends to meet.'

He struck out towards the inn. The path by the side of the road was slippery and uneven but, even though he perhaps walked a trifle faster than he would have usually, Sophia kept up without complaint. As they rounded the last bend before the inn, the faint strains of fiddle music carried to them over the flowering heather and Faulkner rolled his eyes. Hopefully the inn didn't have too many other paying guests as he couldn't imagine they would have enjoyed being woken this early by the scratching of that bloody fiddle.

Sophia followed James down the muddy lane towards the picturesque little tavern. She almost had to skip to keep up with him and her dress caught on every infuriating thistle and weed they passed. Not for the first time since they'd left home she wished she had just worn her trousers and let manners and James' prudish sensibilities be damned. James ignored the inn's front door. Instead, apparently following the sound of the beautifully played fiddle, he led her around the back of the building and into a small and over-grown garden.

He pushed the rusty gate open and motioned for her to follow him. Two men were sitting at a rough wooden table. 'This is Lord de Lacey,' James said. 'He's the best lieutenant and by far the worst musician in the fleet. And this is Fredrick Morgan, who will be our carpenter. Gentlemen, let me introduce Sophia Blake.'

The two men could have hardly looked more different. The one who had been playing the fiddle, Lord de Lacey, was only a little older than she was. He had curly golden hair and plump, girlish lips that left him marooned somewhere between handsome and pretty. Morgan was grey-haired and might have been aged anywhere from forty to sixty. His hands were massive, his neck thick as a bull's and his nose was covered with thick red veins.

Holding out her hand, Sophia smiled her most devastating smile. 'Lord de Lacey. Mr Morgan.'

'Sophia,' said Lord de Lacey. He took her hand and kissed it.

'An honour,' Morgan muttered awkwardly.

'Isaladar's blood, Faulkner,' murmured the young lord in a stage whisper, 'for a plain-looking man, you've done well for yourself.'

'Miss Blake,' Faulkner replied quickly, 'is along as her father's representative.'

'Ah! Well then, Sophia, I hope I've not caused offence by suggesting you'd consort with the likes of our Captain Faulkner.'

'No,' she laughed. 'None taken. As long as you don't presume I would usually deign to keep such company.'

'I'd never dream of it! And how was your trip up, Sophia?' de Lacey asked.

'Oh, easy enough,' she replied in what she hoped was a bored-sounding fashion. 'James doesn't like coaches, though.'

'I've never found him much good on land. He's quite nautical, aquatic even.'

'We can chatter away about coaches and my dislike of them later,' snapped Faulkner. Was that a hint of a blush she saw at the base of his collar? 'Have you had any luck finding a ship?'

Lord de Lacey grinned. 'Oh, we've found one all right. She is just the thing. We can go straight out if you want.'

'Perhaps you two would like breakfast first? It must've been a long slog from Stormhaven for Miss Blake.' Morgan asked.

'Sophia?' James said.

'If you're fine, then I am fine.' She was hungry, but if James was going to skip breakfast then so would she.

James looked about. 'Where is Donald, by the by, de Lacey?'

'I couldn't stand his complaining any longer so I sent him up to Damstead to buy some supplies.'

'Then what are we waiting for?'

De Lacey nodded. 'I'll go and find the factor.'

The impeccably well-dressed factor, his expensive boots squelching in the mud, led them on a twisting route between the brackish pools. The factor was a senior agent for the Hortons, a famous shipping family. The man had been recommended to them by Uriah and had done well finding them a ship so quickly. Faulkner wasn't looking forward to arranging any potential purchase, however – the Hortons hadn't become astronomically wealthy by accident.

Although Faulkner had heard stories about Mudmoon Bay and peered at it once or twice through a glass as he had sailed his way up the coast, he was still awed by the sheer number of ships that littered the sludge. There were hundreds of them: barques, brigs, cutters, ketches, luggers, snows and types that even he couldn't name. They were in all states of repair too, from ships in such beautiful condition that they must have had caretakers living aboard, to others so decayed it was impossible to tell where ship ended and mire began. With the tide out, they all sat marooned on the mud like beached wooden whales.

Behind him, Sophia gave a little gasp as she slipped on the treacherous surface.

'Are you all right?' he asked, manners just fighting down his annoyance. He had hoped she wouldn't come with them.

'I'm fine, something just moved under my foot.'

'Crabs it'd be, Miss Blake,' Morgan said.

'Errgh. What a horrid place.'

'I did say you could stay back at the inn,' Faulkner said.

'And miss all the fun?'

'She is holding up rather better than I am,' de Lacey said.

He looked at his friend. 'You do look a little puce.'

'Too many boisterous nights, de Lacey?' Sophia asked.

'Me? Never. Though perhaps I did have a bottle or two too many last night.'

The factor waved them on. 'We are almost there, my lords, my lady.'

Faulkner liked the ship as soon as he saw her. A merchant collier by birth, she was ship-rigged and, even plastered with the mud of the bay, she still had a burly charm. Her hull was of good white oak, her keel and helm of fine Samaryani elm and her masts of pine and fir. She was not pretty by any measure, but only the foulest storms would bother her.

Unfortunately, she had not been looked after. Her topside was a mess of rotten lines, weatherworn timbers and faded paint. Below decks, dust rose in plumes where they walked, great ghostly curtains of spiderwebs hung from the bulkheads and the glinting eyes of rats stared out at them from the dark corners. But Morgan wasn't perturbed. 'No rot, no decay. I can make all this good again. A fine, well-built ship she still is.'

'How long has she been here?' Faulkner asked.

De Lacey pulled a notebook out of his pocket and flicked through it. 'Since '32.'

'What's she worth, Morgan?'

The carpenter shrugged. 'I would have said middle two thousands, but it's hard to know when you account for our merchant losses in the war and now the peace.'

Faulkner nodded. 'Let's have another look around.'

When their inspection was finished, the four of them gathered together in the mud on the lee side of the hull for one last conference. The factor stood some yards away by the bow, rubbing his pudgy hands together.

'So we are agreed?' Faulkner asked.

De Lacey nodded. 'She will do capitally.'

'You know my feelings, Captain,' added Morgan.

'So we are all settled then?'

The other two men nodded.

Sophia raised an eyebrow. 'All settled? It's all well and good you sailors want her, but what are they asking?'

Faulkner fought down a spurt of embarrassment and turned to the factor. 'What is your price?'

'Three thousand five hundred crowns,' the man shouted back.

Sophia blinked 'Three thousand five hundred? For that?' Her voice climbed effortlessly through the octaves.

'It's probably a good price for a ship like this, Sophia. With the war and all.' He clamped his mouth shut in an effort to avoid saying something rude that he'd later regret.

'A good price? A moment ago Morgan said it was worth about half that. And It looks like she will fall apart in the first strong breeze we encounter. I am going to talk to that factor.' She swept off across the mud.

He held a hand out uselessly after her. 'Sophia...'

'I'll buy it for two thousand crowns,' Sophia announced as she bore down on the Factor.

'Ahhhh...' began the Factor, looking towards Faulkner.

'Don't look at him,' Sophia snapped. 'I'm the buyer.'

The Factor shuffled his feet and looked away. 'My master will not sell for less than three thousand five hundred, princess.'

'I am no princess and your master said "sell it for three thousand five hundred if someone is stupid enough to pay that much".'

'No, miss, that is our best and final offer for the ship.'

'Nonsense it is. Your records show that she has sat here for almost four years. Do you want it to rot away completely? I will pay two thousand. Right now.'

The factor sighed deeply after a long pause. 'Three thousand two hundred.'

'For that rotting collection of timbers? Two thousand two hundred.'

'My master would have me flogged for selling this worthy vessel for less than three thousand.'

'Two thousand eight hundred. That is my last offer, Factor.'

'Master Horton won't be happy with that.'

'He'll be even less happy when we walk away and buy a different ship from one of the other agents.' Her voice was cool and steady.

'You drive a hard bargain.' The factor sighed an even more impressive sigh. 'But done.'

The factor and Sophia shook hands.

Realising that he had been holding his breath, Faulkner let it out slowly.

'If she ran your finances you might not be in this mess, Faulkner,' de Lacey whispered.

Faulkner raised an eyebrow. 'Says the man cut off by his father.'

After they'd signed the contract, which Sophia insisted was completed on the spot, Morgan produced a flask of rum and they stood under their ship's stern to have a celebratory drink. Sophia spluttered at her swig, but she still swallowed it down.

Faulkner stared up at the faded name painted beneath the stern windows. 'What is she called? *Earl Caskell*?'

Morgan shook his head. '*Earl Coxhell.*'

'We may need to change that,' de Lacey replied wryly.

Faulkner grimaced. 'Yes, he is in prison, isn't he?'

'That's right. Tainted Deviance.'

'Right, well, that probably does need to go then. *Warspite*? No, we shouldn't use a warship's name, that wouldn't quite do would it. Any ideas?'

It was Sophia who finally spoke up. 'What about the *Game Bird*? We are setting out to get ourselves hunted, and for your plan to work she will need to be a game little ship.'

'Aye.' Morgan grinned. 'That's a bonny name, Miss Blake.'

De Lacey nodded. '*Game Bird*.'

Faulkner met Sophia's eyes and found he was smiling too. '*Game Bird*.' He placed a hand on the ship's timbers. '*Game Bird*.'

8.

URIAH'S HAND SHOOK as he re-read the note.

Our friends are back. Know Sophia's name now – Lambley

He crumpled it up then threw it into the small coal fire by his desk and watched it burn. He had gone to the arsenal that morning but Moreau had been away and the men on duty had told him to come back the following day, so he had come in to work and found the note amongst his morning correspondence. The hardest thing was that Father Jan's assurances and the watchmen's apparent unconcern when he had told them he needed to register his tainted daughter had only seeded other doubts. If the Camar Shiem weren't looking for Sophia then who was?

Could she be in trouble of some kind that was unrelated to her taint? Had she led a boy on? Or borrowed money for a vice she had hidden from him? It seemed hard to believe, but the facts spoke for themselves. Ultimately, someone was going to a great deal of trouble to find her. By the time the note was ash, a string of fatherly nightmares had rattled through his troubled mind. He was also even gladder that he had sent her away.

Even with Sophia safe, when he turned back to his ledgers, he still couldn't concentrate. The sums that normally obligingly fell into place for him seemed almost unintelligible and after ten minutes of trying, he gave up on work for the day.

He stood and put on his cloak and hat.

'Thompson,' he said. 'I am coming down with a fever. I might go home. You can take the end of the day off.'

The ink-stained man blinked. 'Are you sure, sir?'

'Yes, my boy. Just remember to lock up when you leave. Take Jane to see the *Swaggering Sailor*, the papers say it is very funny,' he said.

With Sophia away, Uriah had let Mrs Gilbert go home early and then spent a miserable evening alone in the cold house. He retired early to bed but sleep eluded him and he tossed and turned, wracked with worry. Eventually, as the distant bells of St Danton the Seafarer rang four, he gave up on sleep, got dressed and padded down to his darkened kitchen to eat an apple.

At first he thought the noise was a stray cat. But then the sound came again, louder this time, a persistent scraping of metal on metal. He froze, fighting down the urge to run or scream, or do both at once. The lock clicked and he heard his back door swing open with its familiar creak. Half-eaten apple still in his hand, he froze, knees shaking.

He glanced frantically around his darkened kitchen. The loose board in the hallway groaned softly and whispered voices carried to him over the thunderous din of his hammering heart. He whirled about in panic, looking for an escape. A flash of inspiration cut through his terror and he opened the kitchen's potato bin, climbed down into it, and slowly closed the lid on top of him.

Jaw clenched in an effort to ignore the pain that radiated out from his back, he crouched in the musty, lumpy, earthy blackness for what seemed like an eternity. Each hand gripped a dirty potato and he squeezed them until his knuckles burned. Twice footsteps sounded impossibly close and he tensed, waiting for the lid to be flung open. But each time the footsteps moved away.

He almost convulsed in fear when a voice shattered the quiet.

'She's not fookin' here and nor is her old man. The fires ain't even lit.' The man's accent carried the thick lilt of the Lizard, the city docks. That was almost a relief. In the inky darkness it had been easy to imagine the intruders to be beasts or hunters of fable.

'Keep it down, Bulldog. Course she ain't, but do you wanna tell Mr Savage we didn't check proper?'

'Fook me, no.'

'You put everythin' back where you found it? Remember what he told us – any thieving and they'll find us face-down in ol' Brown Water.'

'I didn't touch nuffin'!' Bulldog whined.

'Right, then let's get out of here.'

'Mr Savage ain't gonna be happy.'

'Is he ever?'

The back door closed behind them and the latch clicked shut.

Uriah opened the lid to the potato bin and climbed stiffly out. Without quite thinking about it, he padded down the hall and quietly reopened the back door. His garden was already empty. He dashed across the dew-wet grass of his lawn, opened the gate in his garden's sandstone wall and peered carefully out onto the darkened street. The only people in sight, surely the two intruders, were already a few hundred yards away, walking quickly downhill towards the docks. He paused, frozen in the shadowy sanctuary of his garden. All he wanted to do was go back inside and hide, but Sophia's safety depended on finding out who they were.

So, without even closing his back door behind him, through the gloomy streets he followed them. Past the mostly darkened shops on High Street, through the crowds of perfumed young rakes just leaving the bawdy houses on Upton Way and under the stern, bronze gaze of the statue of Admiral de Minae who stood guard over Battle Square.

He knew nothing of spying, but Uriah wasn't a fool either and he stayed far behind them and moved swiftly between patches of deep shadow where he could. He wondered if he should be grateful or not for all the rugby he had played as a younger man. It had taught him to be swift and assertive on his feet, but it had also left him with his ruined back that ached with every step.

Downhill towards the harbour they went, till they reached the slums of Rumley. It was harder to follow them here, amongst the twisting lanes. But he stuck at it grimly and closed the distance between them until, at last, the two men stopped outside a sagging, rundown workshop. He watched as they knocked and then were quickly let in. A pale face – a third man, certainly not one of the intruders – peered furtively out into the dark and then the door was slammed shut.

Uriah paused, panting in the shadows cast by a sagging old boarding house. He was utterly sure now that these ruffians weren't King's men.

But then who were they?

Captain-Constable Moreau rearranged some papers on his messy desk and then looked around his cheery office as if searching for inspiration or insight in the pastoral landscapes that dotted his walls. The captain was not at all what Uriah had expected. Moreau was about forty, quite fat, and had seemed remarkably jovial. But that was before Uriah had recounted his story. Now the watchman looked pale and grim. 'So two unknown men broke into your house last night?' he asked at last.

'Correct,' said Uriah.

'And you believe they were looking for your daughter, Sophia. A girl who is both tainted and unregistered?'

'That's right.'

'For a start, I can assure you they were not my officers. We do not make a habit of breaking into citizens' houses in the dead of night and then sneaking away again.' He paused, pen raised. 'Just for my notes, you then followed the men down to a residence in Rumley.'

'Correct, an old workshop near the canal. I think I could find it again.'

'And then you came straight here?'

'As soon as the sun was up.'

The captain sighed and made a mark in his notes. 'I don't like the sound of this, Mr Blake. Not at all. It is possible your daughter has just fallen in with a bad set, but I've found in this game it generally pays to assume the worst.'

'What will you do?'

'My dealing with the tainted extends only to their registration and their breaking of common law. Other' – Moreau made a vague, twiddling gesture with his free hand – 'more serious matters I pass on to the relevant parties.'

'Relevant parties?' asked Uriah, his heart sinking.

'Well, in this case, Mr Otter. He is our Camar Shiem.'

'Mr Otter?'

'They give up their real names as part of their training.' Moreau leant forward and quickly wrote an address and a brief note on a scrap of paper. 'Go immediately to this address and tell Mr Otter exactly what you have just told me.'

'Thank you, Captain.'

'Think nothing of it, Mr Blake,' replied the watchman, opening a large ledger. 'But before you go, perhaps you should see to your daughter's registration.'

'I should.'

'Very wise, Mr Blake. You're safer on our books than off them, as they say.'

Once he had finished Sophia's surprisingly brief registration, Uriah paused in the warm morning sun outside the arsenal and checked the address that the captain had given him. It was for a street off Dragonslayer Circus. Uriah knew the area well, and although it was too leafy and exclusive an address for his tastes, his business took him there often. He set off through the crowded streets, keen to put a stop to the whole nasty business as soon as he could. Moreau's two watchmen, an escort the captain had politely but firmly insisted on, trotted along a few yards behind him like loyal hounds.

Reaching the circus, he paused briefly to get his breath in the shadow of the sixty-foot statue to Prince Isaladar the Dragon Slayer.

'You all right, Mr Blake?' asked one of his minders.

'Just my back. Hurt it in a scrum years ago.'

The man nodded and shouldered his halberd. 'Take your time, sir.'

But Uriah didn't want to wait. When the pain from his back had subsided a little he set off again, picking his way through the bustling crowd. Even the sight of the old griffon, long retired from the fleet, towing its brightly coloured hot air balloon full of laughing couples around the circus could not distract him. Walking under the spreading oaks that bordered the park, the three of them left the circus, picked their way between the press of pretty painted coaches, and crossed into Luthier Street.

The house when they found it was an unremarkable, well-presented terrace.

'Thank you for the escort, gentlemen.'

The older of the watchmen nodded. 'Our pleasure.'

He turned and knocked on the door.

'Come in,' a voice called almost immediately.

Uriah opened the door and stepped into a very simply appointed hallway. 'This way,' the voice called again. Uriah walked through an open door and into an almost empty study. A large desk and chair in one corner were the only large pieces of furniture.

'Can I help you, sir?' a swarthy young man asked from behind the desk.

'Ah yes, you can, I think. Captain-Constable Moreau sent me here to see a Mr Otter.'

The man nodded. 'Did he write you an introduction?'

Uriah waited patiently while the fellow read over Moreau's note. When he had finished, the man walked to a door leading further into the house. 'Excuse me for a moment.'

Uriah sighed and looked out the window at a wren hopping about on a flowering vine in the garden. Although he willed his nerves to settle, he still jumped when the man returned.

'Mr Otter will see you now.'

Every wall in the next room was covered by bookshelves that reached to the ceilings. A large and battered desk covered with neatly stacked papers filled the middle of the space. A man Uriah assumed to be Mr Otter stood behind the desk. He was older than Uriah had expected, his skin weathered and his hair white and his outfit austere. He had been working at his desk and was obviously distracted, but he stood and shook hands as soon as Uriah entered. Despite the man's age, his back was ramrod straight.

'Mr Blake,' the man spoke with a fighting soldier's crisp inflection. 'I am Mr Otter. Now that I am too old to fight, I serve as the Camar Shiem's eyes and ears in this city.'

'It's an honour to meet one of the Camar Shiem.'

The hint of a smile played across the old man's face. 'We don't often hear that. Now excuse my lack of small talk but I have an urgent matter to attend to this morning. So sit down and tell me why Captain-Constable Moreau has sent you to see me.'

Uriah quickly narrated his story again.

'You said you heard the intruders quite clearly. Are you positive none of them had a foreign accent?' asked Mr Otter when he had finished.

'I'd wager a fortune they were both Stormhaven born.'

'They referred to a third man not present by some kind of nickname. Are you positive you can't remember it?'

'Not Bulldog?'

'No, the other name.' The old warrior leant forward intently.

'I can't remember. Never been good with names.'

'Don't worry, Mr Blake, we'll soon find them anyway.' Mr Otter drummed his fingers on the table. 'Have you often spoken with your daughter about her taint?'

'We have never discussed it.'

'Never?'

Uriah shrugged wearily. 'My late wife and I realised she was tainted when she was only a little girl, but somehow we never had the courage to speak to her about it.'

Mr Otter nodded. 'Families are often reluctant to confront a child's taint.'

'Really?'

The Camar Shiem nodded. 'It is not an easy thing to discuss. Now, what aspect does your daughter's taint take?'

'Aspect?'

'Does she change the weather with her mood? Or perhaps she frightens every animal she meets? Curdles milk? Always wins at cards?'

'Oh…' Uriah faltered. It still seemed like a betrayal to reveal Sophia's secret that he and Mary had kept for so long. 'She seems to be able to heal wounds.'

Something close to fear flickered across the Camar Shiem's face. 'That's extraordinarily rare. You are sure?'

'F… fairly sure. Why?'

'We need to go to your daughter.' Mr Otter stood up and opened his desk's top drawer. 'Immediately.'

'What's happened? Why does the fact she can heal matter?'

'The only other tainted healer in Stormhaven died last night in a fire.'

'A healer? Dead?'

The old man nodded.

'It wasn't Father Jan from Manev Hill was it?'

'It was. You knew him, Mr Blake?'

'Not well. But I visited him on Monday to ask about Sophia's registration.' Uriah wanted to vomit. Had his visit somehow implicated or involved Jan? 'What happened?'

'I don't know. Jan and his family perished in the fire. I'd hoped the blaze was an accident, but I'm not stupid enough to believe your personal involvement with the man, followed by intruders at your house on the same night is an innocent coincidence. Now take me to your daughter.'

'We can't go to her. I sent her out of the city.' His voice quavering, Uriah quickly explained what he had done.

'Do you know where she is?'

'No. She was going to write but...' A sob swallowed the rest of his sentence.

'Her letters haven't reached you yet.'

Uriah nodded.

'Don't panic. This may still be something of a blessing. Her hunter still presumes she is in the city and that will buy us some time.' Mr Otter's gaze slid across his bookcases and settled on a thick volume by the door. 'But we do need to act quickly. For a start, I will arrange Moreau's men to watch this workshop in Rumley.'

'What about me? Can I help?'

The old warrior shook his head. 'You will only slow me down. I need you safe and out of the way. Do you have a weapon?'

Uriah gulped. 'No.'

The Camar Shiem reached into the open drawer and took out a pistol and some shot. 'Do you know how to use this?'

'I hunted as a boy.'

'Good. Leave here and go straight to the circus. Speak to no one. Not even your own mother. Are you familiar with Leopold's Coffee House?'

'I often meet people there.'

'Good. Go inside and take a seat where everyone can see you. I will send Captain-Constable Moreau to fetch you. He will approach you and say, "The roses will not bloom tonight, the frost will kill them." If anyone approaches and tries to insist that you leave the coffee house without utter-ing that phrase, shoot them and then run. Even Moreau. If he doesn't utter that phrase, warn him once and if he tries again to have you leave without speaking those words, you shoot him. Do you understand?'

Dazed, Uriah nodded again.

Mr Otter led him back through the first office and opened the front door. 'Remember, speak to no one, and if the person who meets you at the coffee house doesn't say the phrase, shoot them.'

Uriah stood on the doorstep, squinting into the bright sunshine. How could the city still look the same when his safe and calm world had just been ripped away like chaff on a breeze? 'But... but... how did my daughter end up being caught up in this?'

'I will not burden you with my speculation.' Mr Otter gave him a firm push in the direction of the circus. 'Go now, Mr Blake. Speak to no one and may Isaladar watch over you.'

9.

AT THE SIGHT of the Camar Shiem on the doorstep beside Uriah Blake, the Tallowman drew in a sharp hiss of breath and slunk back deeper into the shaded garden where it had been lurking. It had seen plenty of sketches of that hated face. Thirty-two years ago, Mr Otter had been part of the Camar Shiem band that had dispatched the Amynch Vampire. He had also been present when Rogathi the Unseen had been butchered.

Other than its master, the Tallowman feared few things. The Camar Shiem were one of them. They were loyal, driven, and as soon as the Camar Shiem had the scent of their prey they searched methodically till they had their quarry, like hounds at the hunt. It didn't matter how long it took them or what it cost, they came on and on relentlessly, armed with their bright blades and even brighter faith in their young god. They were the reason the Tallowman's kind so hated it when tasks took them into the Realm of the Mists.

Safely hidden behind a perfectly trimmed hedge, it fought down its initial spurt of panic and forced itself to think. Even though it had hidden last night's handiwork with the fire, its harvesting of the old healer, combined with whatever information Uriah Blake had just provided, would have been more than enough to alert this Camar Shiem to at least the possibility of its presence. That meant the old warrior would now alert his brothers and sisters at the Monastery of the Steadfast Knight in Barbonne and they would then send a band east. Then it would die. Or flee, in which case its master would destroy it anyway.

By the time the girl's father had disappeared down the street, its cold mind had reasoned out a solution. It obviously had to buy some time to flush out the girl for the harvest, and to do that it needed to swiftly deal with both the Camar Shiem and Uriah Blake.

Fortuitously, its masters had gifted it with a way to do just that.

Reluctantly, dreading the coming pain, it sank to its knees and leant forward into the hedge. Safely hidden in the dark, leafy recess it had made, it tore the bandages off its face and readied itself. The heat came first, spreading from the bridge of its nose, sliding, slashing and grinding down once-human nerves. As the agony reached its hands and feet it began to shake, mouth snapping open and closed in soundless torment. When the torture reached its searing climax, the skin of the Tallowman's face began to bubble and roll like boiling fat. Finally came the sharp cracks of breaking bone and flecks of blood splattered the damp earth in front of it.

Shuddering, it carefully wiped the gore off its new face with the discarded bandages and stood on slightly unsteady legs. At least the agony was spent on a worthwhile cause. When it stepped back out into the sunlit street, the face the Tallowman wore was Uriah Blake's.

It bluffed its way past the Camar Shiem secretary with a lie about forgetting its glasses. It found the old man in the next room, flicking urgently through a leather-bound book he had opened on the table. The monk looked up as the Tallowman entered and started in shock. The old warrior was not fooled by the false visage.

'I hadn't thought to see a Tallowman this far north again. Not in my lifetime,' he said.

The Tallowman smiled a savage grin that sat alien on Uriah's face. 'So it seems, or I assume you would have been better prepared.'

'Prepared or not, twenty years ago I would have killed you where you stood.'

'No, you wouldn't have. So, are you going to tell me where this girl, Sophia Blake, is before you die?'

'I have served my God and my king faithfully all my life. I shan't stop now.'

The Tallowman smirked as the old man's hand strayed towards something under his desk. 'Before I kill you, you should know that your sacrifice is worthless. I have never failed in a hunt. I was the one who killed Witch-Hunter General van Clausen and Monique de Salana. A vapid child cannot elude me for long. I will find her and then we will drink from her till we are satiated.'

The old fool lunged for the thing under his desk. He was pathetically slow.

The Tallowman drew its own pistol and fired in one smooth motion. The ball struck the Camar Shiem in the middle of his face and threw a flower of blood and brains on the bookcase behind him. The crack of the pistol echoed through the house. Dropping the empty pistol, the Tallowman drew two more from its belt and stepped back into the corner of the room to wait. Predictably, idiotically, the secretary burst in to help his dead master. The Tallowman shot him low in the stomach, taking care to make sure that the wound would not be immediately fatal.

Crossing the room, it kicked the secretary over. It needed him to see Uriah's face.

'My family,' the dying man whispered.

'Family!' it hissed. 'This is what you and your master get for trying to steal my Sophia.'

It walked quickly to the Camar Shiem's body and unclipped a heavy amulet from around the corpse's neck. A Camar Shiem's badge of office could be a useful thing to possess.

Stalking back through the house, it stepped out onto the street and was pleased to see that the shots had already attracted a crowd. It paused and, ignoring the shouted questions, made sure the dullards all had a good long look at Uriah's face.

Then it picked out a well-dressed woman at random and shot her through the heart.

The crowd screamed in panic and scattered.

10.

URIAH FOLLOWED MR Otter's instructions and walked straight down to Leopold's Coffee House. Unbelievably, the liveried doorman greeted him like it was just a normal day and his world hadn't just collapsed in on itself.

'Morning, Mr Blake. Your usual room?'

'No, thank you, Robson, I'm not on business today.'

'Just a public table then, sir?'

Uriah nodded.

'Please follow me.'

He took a seat in the manicured terraced garden outside and ordered a strong coffee. When it arrived, Uriah found he was too nervous to even drink it so, while it grew cold on the table in front of him, he tried to make sense of everything that had just occurred. All he knew for sure was that Mr Otter had been rattled and, if even a quarter of the tales about the Camar Shiem were true, the fact that the old man had been alarmed was very bad news.

Finally sick of just sitting worrying, he had one of the waiters bring him the day's *Financial Herald* and flicked through it listlessly. None of it could keep his attention, not even a strident editorial piece haranguing the navy for their lack of success hunting the leviathan. The dangers that James was going to face on the high seas suddenly seemed very remote and small compared to the nightmare he and Sophia had been swept up into.

Looking up from the paper, he spotted an old client of his, Dashiel Yates, enter the garden. Uriah usually would have waved hello, but remembering Mr Otter's instructions, he lifted the paper to hide his face. Oblivious to his presence, Yates crossed the lawn and sat at the table directly behind him.

'Are you all right, Yates? You look like you've had a turn,' asked a man who had already been sitting at the table.

'No, I'm not. I just saw a woman shot dead in cold blood. Right in the middle of the street, mind you.' Yates sounded like he might cry. 'Apparently the madman had shot another two people inside the house as well. Isaladar's blood, I can't remember ever being this shaken.'

'Are you serious?'

'Completely.'

'How terrible!'

'I don't think he even knew the woman he killed. He just smiled down at us all then shot her.' Yates drew in a long, shuddering breath. 'Worst part is that I know the fellow who did it, too. He acted as my lawyer when I bought Dawson's Hill. Uriah Blake is his name.'

At the mention of his name, Uriah started in shock and spilled some of his coffee. It took all his remaining reserves of courage not to just run headlong out of the coffee house. Instead, he forced himself to sit with his head down and watch the coffee stain expand across the pristine white tablecloth.

'Never heard of him. Did he seem queer when you knew him?'

'If anything he seemed quite staid and boring.'

'Perhaps he was tainted and ran mad?'

'Perhaps.'

'You're sure it was him?'

'Oh, it was definitely him. He didn't even try to hide. Another chap recognised him as well.'

What had happened? He and Dashiel Yates knew each other relatively well. They had worked on that contract for hours together. Surely Dashiel couldn't have confused him for another man? No, of course not, the timing was far too convenient for that. Had Mr Otter somehow framed him, then? Whatever had happened, he needed to get away. Leaving some money on the table, he stood and, trying to ignore the panic that had flooded his guts and threatened to turn his knees to water, walked slowly out onto the street. Back outside he set off aimlessly through the press of people going about their business on the circus. He was numb. Where could he go?

At the first corner he came to, he stopped near two gossiping bankers and pretended to straighten his wig in the reflection of a shop window while he listened to their excited chatter.

'Outrageous! And here in Dragonslayer, too! Down by the docks you almost expect it, but you don't imagine something this awful would happen *here!*'

'Think they'll catch him?'

'I should say so. I've just come up from Upton and I must've seen a hundred watchmen along the way. They even have soldiers from the garrison out helping.'

'Hope they hang the madman.'

A little way further down the street Uriah ducked into a lane and, once out of sight, he threw away his wig and fine jacket and then hurried on towards Twopenny Square. If he could get past the square he might just reach the Lizard. Even with its blood up, the watch had trouble finding men in that warren.

When he reached Twopenny he thought for a brief, glorious moment that he had escaped. The cobbled square was full of its normal crowd of hawkers, merchants, shoppers and rabble and the familiar, tattered banners of *Taxation without representation is tyranny* and *Universal suffrage* still fluttered over the stalls. His spurt of exultation only lasted a moment until a middled-aged woman in a broad, brightly coloured skirt, slunk up to him.

'Watch out, mate, the brown bullies are just on the uvver side of the square,' she whispered.

Following her sly nod he spotted the groups of brown-jacketed watchmen lurking by the exits on the far side of the square. Their traditional halberds were gone now and they all carried muskets.

He swore.

'They're always happy to crack the odd head for their lords, those dogs,' she murmured, turning him back towards Dragonslayer. 'If you're the one they're after, you'd better bolt. And try to look a bit less guilty, matey. You stick out like a sore thumb.'

He ran back towards Dragonslayer with only a rich, bubbling sickness in his guts for company. If the watchmen were already waiting this far away from the shootings, the net they must have cast was enormous. Isaladar!

Every constable in Stormhaven must be looking for him! Whoever had framed him had done an almost perfect job of it.

He slowed, mopped his brow with his handkerchief, and tried to force the panic from his face. He looked back over his shoulder. There was no sign the watchmen were following him.

The watchmen! He was fleeing the law and even the thought of that terrified him. All his life he had placed his trust in the watch and the magistrates, but now he knew his daughter's life depended on his staying out of their clutches, at least until he could work out how to clear his name.

He stepped back out onto the broad, spacious sweep of Dragonslayer Circus. The place was still packed with Stormhaven's worthies taking in the spring sun and he couldn't see any watchmen amongst the crowd yet. He dashed across the road and under the oaks. He was going to head west towards his home, but halfway across the grass in the middle of the circus he paused. There! By the great marble plinth a long line of people had queued up for a ride around the square with the griffon. The great beast itself was resting in the shade cast by the statue of Isaladar.

Uriah rudely pushed to the head of the line.

The attendant, a young girl with long black pigtails, looked at him with a raised eyebrow. 'Can I help you?'

He said a silent prayer that the sweat that by now completely soaked his shirt didn't arouse too much suspicion and nodded. 'Why yes, my girl, I completely forgot an important appointment I have to attend and my master will murder me if I don't make it. Is there any chance you can fly me out of the city so I don't miss it? I can pay well.'

'Mother!' the girl called over her shoulder to a wiry, grey haired woman feeding fish to the old griffon.

The woman patted the beast's beak and then walked over. 'Yes?'

'This man says he needs to get flown out of the city. Says he can pay.'

'How much can you pay and how far do you need to go?'

'If you could drop me near St Tarnas Cemetery that would be far enough.' He shook the remaining coins out of his purse. 'Please, my master has a terrible temper.'

'That's enough coin. But I'll still need to ask Moondancer. He has been working all morning.' She turned back to the griffon. 'Dancer, this man needs to be taken out of the city. Can you do it, or are you too tired?'

The griffon let out an eagle's piercing shriek and knocked over its bucket of fish.

'I was only trying to be well-mannered.'

The griffon shrieked again and rocked back on its lion's hindquarters, looking at its mistress with what appeared to be reproach.

The woman sighed. 'Well, I've upset the vain thing now. But he says yes, he can take you.'

With shaking hands, Uriah helped them unclip the griffon from the harness it used to tow the hot air balloon around the circus. At any moment he expected to hear a watchmen's whistle behind him. But the dreaded sound never came and with the beast unclipped from the balloon the woman climbed up into her saddle and then helped Uriah up behind her.

Once he was secure, she dug her heels into the griffon's flanks and the beast leapt up into the air. Uriah gasped and threw his arms around the woman's waist. With a few powerful beats of its wings, the griffon cleared the lofty oaks surrounding the park and they soared up above the circus. His stomach lurched and the wind tore at him. Opening his eyes, he looked down. In the gaps between the slate roofs he spotted the brown and grey uniforms of parties of watchmen and soldiers methodically searching the streets around the circus.

He had only just made it.

They landed near the cemetery and Uriah climbed gingerly down from the saddle. The woman waved to him as she took off again. 'I hope you make your appointment!'

He almost followed the familiar path to where Mary was buried. Alive, she would have been a pillar of strength, but the silent earth of her grave wouldn't help him now. So instead he clambered down the rocky slope beneath the cemetery to the beach. Reaching the sand, he turned north and walked along the windswept shoreline and away from Stormhaven.

He walked and he walked and he walked.

For the first few miles he passed fishermen and wreckers' little shacks with their boats and nets scattered about them, and the rush of his close escape and the remains of his terror carried him on. But soon the pain from his back overwhelmed even his anxiety. He limped on through the mid afternoon, his left leg dragging in the sand behind him. Despite the burning pain that gnawed at his back, the cold ocean breeze sliced through his sweat-soaked shirt and made him shiver.

Thirst rose in him like a terrible longing. Once or twice he looked longingly at the bubbling surf and was almost tempted to drink from the ocean. His tongue seemed to swell in his mouth until it was fat, prickly and heavy.

But he stumbled along with his head down, like he was battering his way through a violent storm. He was so tired he couldn't even spare the energy to look back to see if he was being pursued. Slowly midday gave away to afternoon and then afternoon to dusk. By the time the light faded his only company was the odd gull and the constant thunder of the surf. Still he went on, though his legs quivered with the effort and his spine burnt like molten iron.

The sun was setting when he spotted the mouth of the ocean cave and trudged tiredly inside. For a long time, he sat with his back to the cold stones and watched a lonely cloud drift across the otherwise empty sky. He was so exhausted, thirsty and tired that even his thoughts rolled thick and sluggish around inside his skull. Then he started to cry.

Someone had killed three people just to implicate him. Three people! He was a lawyer, a man of education and manners and weakness. The roughest parts of his life had been on the regulated grass of the rugby pitch. How then could he ever hope to protect his daughter from men who were so ruthless?

11.

ONCE THE FACTOR had left, Sophia returned to the little tavern with James, de Lacy and Morgan, where they collected their bags and then went back out to the *Game Bird*. Once aboard, they spent the remains of the afternoon making part of the ship vaguely habitable. James coolly insisted she take the captain's cabin and Morgan kindly helped her settle in by boarding up the broken windows and stopping the worst of the draughts.

As night fell they shared a simple meal of broth and hard bread under a canvas screen that Morgan rigged up on the deck. De Lacey produced a few bottles of wine from his enormous sea chest and the men chattered away into the evening. They didn't strictly ignore her, but all their talk of futtocks, keelson, yawls, skiffs, barks, aback and beams was alien enough that they might have well been speaking a foreign language. They laughed, joked and planned *Game Bird's* restoration while she sat there like an ignorant and ignored child. Finally, pleading a headache, she retired.

Afterwards she lay awake on her hard little cot and listened to their cheery babble. Eventually, de Lacey produced his fiddle and they began to sing. At some stage a bottle got smashed, accompanied by raucous laughter at some failed trick. She couldn't help feeling a little prudish. At home Uriah didn't drink more than a glass in an evening, but James and his friends sounded like they were trying to keep a vineyard in business.

Sometime around midnight, the tide must have finally floated the *Game Bird* free of the mud, as suddenly her swinging cot began to rock gently with the movements of the sea. The men must have noticed too, as the annoying fiddle finally stopped.

'She does swim after all. This calls for a drink!' called James, loudly.

The others answered with a slurred cheer.

She pulled the pillow out from under her head and put it over her face. Had she already wasted a small fortune of her father's money? James hardly seemed capable of managing a rowboat let alone hunting a sea monster. She had hoped for a moment's freedom before the truth of her taint swallowed her up, but instead she was just as trapped and useless as she had been in Stormhaven.

'Lords of the North take that workman,' Sophia groaned.

It was barely light and already the sound of incessant hammering reverberated through the ship. Curling her toes on the cold planks, she washed in the pitcher of fresh water Morgan had left her and then dressed quickly in the breeches, shirt, vest and riding boots that she usually wore in the Mournwood's stables. Fishing about in her bags, she found her little mirror and checked her hair. After running her comb through it a few times she deemed it a lost cause and tied the unruly mop back in a simple braid.

Up on deck, whatever mess the men had created the night before had been squared away. Unfortunately, the *Game Bird* herself appeared even more like a derelict hulk in the morning light. Pushing aside those concerns, Sophia leant over the rail and looked for the source of the hammering.

The tide had slunk back out during the night and James was standing ankle-deep in the mud belting a hammer against the hull. A collection of pots, buckets and coils of rope lay at his feet. She stood quietly and watched him work for a time. At home she had kept a scrapbook full of newspaper articles about the gallant Captain James Faulkner. She had read over them so many times she had come to picture him as the swaggering, serious, enormous and warlike man that the newspapers lionised. While he was certainly tall and had clean features and cheerful eyes, he was nothing like the beautiful hero of the public's imagination. He might have been older than her but he was still really only a boy. Ashore he would still have been a guildsman learning his trade or a subordinate clerk in some firm, carrying papers, writing minutes and scurrying about after his master. She just couldn't picture him taking a warship into action. The only hint that he was anything or anyone more than a clerk was the wicked scar across his left shoulder from when he had been so badly wounded back in '28.

'Morning, James.'

He stopped his hammering, looked up at her and then smiled. 'Morning. Nice of you to finally join us!'

With considerable effort she resisted the urge to drop something on his smug head. 'Where are the others?'

'Gone ashore to meet Donald. They'll be back soon.'

'What are you doing? Trying to knock our poor ship to pieces?'

'I thought I'd get started on caulking her.' Without waiting for a reply, he started to hammer away again.

Sophia wasn't used to being ignored. She clenched her fists and took a deep breath. Then she clambered over the side of the ship and jumped down into the mud next to him.

He paused and rudely looked her outfit up and down. 'Lost your horse, have you?' he asked with a grin.

She ignored that jibe. 'Would you like a hand?'

'What? With this?'

'Yes.'

'It's hard work. Perhaps you could...' He made a dismissive gesture in her general direction.

'Do *what* exactly, James? Something feminine?'

'Something' – he looked her up and down again – 'useful.'

'I can help here.'

'This is a tricky job.'

'Banging a ship with a hammer doesn't look that tricky.'

'It's a mallet and you'll just get in the way.'

'I want to help.'

'Then why don't you fix breakfast?'

'What did you say?'

'Breakfast. It's the first meal of the day.'

'It's the first meal of the day,' she mimicked. The flickering anger that had been simmering in her breast since the night before blossomed into an open flame. 'Go to hell, James. I realise you didn't want me to come, but that's no excuse for you to treat me like this. I mightn't know what "crossing the p" or "caulking" is, but I am happy enough to learn any job you give me. I'm not some fainting church mouse of a girl.'

'Sophia, be sensible…'

'*Sensible*? I am sensible! I've already saved you idiots from paying an extra seven hundred crowns for our ship. Seven hundred! You three nincompoops would have already thrown away a fortune of my father's money because you were too stubborn to haggle!'

'Nincompoops?' Faulkner's face went white then a deep, mottled shade of crimson. 'I'm not the spoilt brat who acts like a hunt for a bloody sea monster is going to be like some little jaunt to the zoo!'

'I am not acting like this is a jaunt!'

'Then why are you here? Have you ever even been in a bloody boat before?'

'Don't swear at me, Captain Faulkner. I'm not some press-ganged man you can whip into obedience. I'm so sick of all this… this…' She paused for inspiration. 'Nautical snobbery. You carry on like no one else in the universe could ever understand your stupid, closed little masculine world. We've been away, what, three days? And I am already sick of sailors and sick of you. You've grown up to be an utter boor!'

She turned, shinnied up the ladder, stormed back to her cabin and slammed the door behind her, which raised a great plume of dust. Once she had finished sneezing she kicked one of her bags across the cabin in frustration.

Why hadn't she just stayed in Stormhaven? To think she had hero-worshipped James and had longed to see him again. He was just as bad as the young men back home, so sure a girl was only a thing to marry, carry your brats, and then ignore for the rest of your life.

She would take the next coach back home. At least some people in Stormhaven took her seriously and treated her like an adult. She was already halfway through packing when there was a knock at the door.

'May I come in?' called James.

'No.'

James poked his head into the cabin anyway. He cleared his throat nervously. 'I'm sorry, Sophia. You're right. I have been a boor.'

'Why is it so terrible to have me here?' she asked.

'I've nothing against you…'

'Why are you being so dreadful to me then?'

'It's just this situation is most irregular. You know what gossip can be like. I felt some distance between us might, ah, take some of the, ah, the ah…' He petered out.

'Does it matter? That kind of babble is the last thing I could care about.'

'Well-bred ladies have long memories.'

'Well-bred ladies are fools.' Anyway, soon the well-bred ladies of Stormhaven would find out about her taint and then scandals like this would be the least of her old friend's concerns.

'I'm worried about your reputation, not mine.'

'And I'm not worried about it. So stop being a nervous ninny.'

'You might regret it later.'

'I won't.'

'Well, I've been a fool.' He held up his hands in mock surrender. 'Can we sign a peace treaty?'

She normally would have let him stew, but he looked so downhearted and genuinely sorry she gave in. 'On one condition.'

'Oh?'

'You teach me to caulk.'

He laughed. 'You'll come to regret asking. It's the dreariest work imaginable.'

'It's work better shared then.'

They climbed back down into the mud and James picked the mallet up again. 'All ships leak between their planks to some degree.'

Sophia nodded. 'That doesn't sound good.'

'It isn't. The idea with caulking is to stop that leaking as much as possible.'

'We aren't going to sea yet, so why are we doing this job first?'

He shrugged. 'It was just a job I could start on.'

'You don't like doing nothing, do you?' she asked.

He laughed. 'Only when a ship is involved. Ashore I do nothing but lie around eating, reading and drinking. I'd end up fat as an ox in no time! Now, no more interruptions. To stop the leaks we take this oakum' – he held up a bucket of what looked like hemp covered with tar – 'and using the mallet and this caulking iron we drive the oakum into the space between the planks.'

'Stopping the water getting in.'

'That's the idea,' he agreed. 'Would you like a turn?'

She reached for the mallet. 'I'm game.'

Within minutes her arms burned, both her hands were essentially one large, splinter-riddled blister, and the mallet felt like it was made from stone or solid lead. When she paused to catch her breath James looked up from where he had been mixing something in one of the pails. 'Take a break, it's nasty work.'

'It's just hard to get the oakum up under the plank.'

'It certainly is.' He held out a tin flask. 'Drink?'

She took the flask hesitantly. 'Grog?'

'Isaladar's blood no, not with this hangover. Strong coffee.'

'Thanks.'

'Don't think anything of it. I'll take the mallet and you can start puttying over what we have already done.'

'I can do more malleting. I'll be fine again in a second once I catch my breath.'

He smiled. 'Someone has to put this slop on and from the look of those blisters you could do with a rest. When I get tired of hammering, we can swap again. Deal?'

'Deal.'

12.

AS THE FIRST hints of dawn lit up the eastern horizon, Uriah clambered to his feet. He might have slept, but if he had it was only in jagged and fearful little slithers. The morning was chilly and as he shuffled around to loosen his aching back, he wished he hadn't thrown his coat away. By the mouth of the cave he found a pool of rainwater cupped in the black rock. He knelt, splashed his face and then drank his fill of the brackish water. The water did nothing for his hunger, but at least it killed the worst of his thirst.

By the time the first rays of sunrise spilled into the cave, he began to feel slightly more like himself again. Now the terror of his flight had faded, he desperately needed to work out what had happened and his logical mind required annotations and diagrams. Next to the pool he spied a long, thin piece of driftwood. He picked it up and then began to sketch notes and thoughts in the smooth sand of the cave floor. By the time the sun had driven some of the chill from his bones he had given up trying to fathom how they had managed to frame him. Yates, a man who knew him intimately well, had sworn it was him. Surely it couldn't have been a masked actor? Not even the finest theatre troupe from the capital could have managed that deception. Ignoring the rumbling from his empty belly he put aside that apparently unsolvable riddle and began to consider the murders themselves. Soon the floor of the cave was a mess of discarded ideas sketched and then scrubbed out in the sand, and all he had definitively concluded was that he could probably discount Mr Otter as having been involved. There was just no need for the Camar Shiem to bother. Mr Otter could have simply had him arrested, thrown in prison and then pursued Sophia at his leisure. But if the Camar Shiem weren't involved then that placed the suspicion squarely on the thugs who had broken into his house. But who were they? Who would dare dabble so aggressively in the Camar Shiem's business? He sat down in the sand to give his aching back a rest, looked at his useless scratching and sighed. He hadn't even told Moreau where Sophia was or when she was expected back. To make things worse, the description of the intruder's hideout in the docks he had given was vague enough that Moreau would probably never find it, even in the unlikely event the watchman decided to look.

He stopped.

The address in the docks!

That was it.

He drank down a few more gulps of water then stumbled back out onto the beach. Turning back towards Stormhaven he trudged down the beach until he came to the last shack that he had passed during his escape from the city. He hid in the dunes behind the hut and waited to make sure the place was empty. Once he was confident the fishermen were out at sea, he slunk down to the building, forced the door and stepped inside. The interior was dark and sooty. Hands shaking, he began his search. A battered trunk yielded a few coins. By the hearth he found half a loaf of hard black bread and some salted herring that he gulped down. In a weather-beaten old cupboard he found the disguise he had been looking for. Trying to ignore the pungent stench of fish and tobacco smoke, he pulled on the tattered old coat and jammed the fisherman's leather cap down low over his eyes. He dreaded to think how much his thieving would hurt the poor fishermen, but he had no choice. He promised himself he would repay the men if he ever got the chance, and then he shut the door and walked away.

Turning his back to the ocean he climbed the steep seashore and then walked west across the quiet fields at the northern end of the peninsular, avoiding the few farms he came across. After an hour or two, clouds rolled in off the sea and it started to drizzle. He walked up the slope for few more damp and unpleasant miles before he finally climbed a last ridge and looked down at the ocean on the western side of the peninsular.

Stolen oilskin flapping in the spring breeze, he walked down the rough path towards the village of Scalton. Scalton lay at the mouth of the River Fenete and the township's dilapidated houses clustered by the coast and riverbank, as if afraid to leave their source of income and sustenance. The beach by the village was a mess of discarded nets, lobster pots, boats and wheelbarrows. The muddy banks of the river were forested with the skeletons of half-built ships. The old men and women who sat on their porches smoking their pipes and mending their children's nets paid him no heed as he shuffled into the village. A flutter of relief ran through him. His disguise seemed to be working.

As it was almost dark and he felt weak enough to collapse, he decided to try to rent a place to sleep for the night. Right down by the waterfront Uriah found a dilapidated boarding house that suited his purposes. He rehearsed a number of stories and practised his best fisherman's accent, but the old woman who ran the place hardly looked up from her knitting when he paid her.

'Beds are upstairs. You need to be out by the eighth bell in the morning. Dinner is through there in the kitchen. Ends in half an hour.'

'Thank you.'

The woman didn't reply and went back to her knitting.

Dinner proved to be a lukewarm and bone-filled fish stew that was the worst thing Uriah had eaten since boarding school. Nevertheless, he was ravenous enough that he still forced down three bowls and would have had a fourth, except the bony cook looked at him sullenly.

The bedroom upstairs was a long cramped space, filled with ten thin beds. Three of them were already occupied by sleeping men, so Uriah picked an empty bed by the window. He took off his oilskin and boots, rolled down the stiff covers, carefully tucked away his glasses and crawled into bed. The mattress was full of old and lumpy straw, the pillow smelt of mildew and his feet hung over the end of the bed, but he fell asleep in moments.

Despite his exhaustion, Uriah slept badly. Throughout the evening more men came in to fill up the other beds, many of them drunk and apparently able to bump into every piece of furniture in the room. Also, at least four of Uriah's companions snored. He put his pillow over his face but that did nothing to kill the sounds of the other men and simply filled Uriah's nose with the stink of stale sweat and mould. He put the pillow back under his head and drifted back into a restless sleep.

It was still pitch dark when a piercing scream cut through his sleep.

Uriah opened his eyes and sat up. Had he imagined it?

The scream came again, high and animalistic.

A few of the soberer men in the room clambered out of their beds.

The screams cut through the thin walls a third, fourth and fifth time. They sounded close. The fishermen, traders and farmers Uriah shared the room with rubbed their eyes and looked around in confusion.

'Lords of the bloody North, what's that racket?'

'Some bugger has got himself in trouble.'

A braver fellow crept past him and up to the window. Against his better judgement, Uriah put on his spectacles and joined him. Uriah leant against the window and peered out through the salt-stained glass.

Directly below him, a dirty, naked man of about Uriah's age stood in the middle of the empty street. As Uriah watched the man raised his scarecrow-thin arms to the night sky and screamed again.

The man who Uriah had joined at the window, a fellow with a long farmer's beard, sucked in a surprised breath. 'Isaladar's blood, it's Old John!'

'You know him?' Uriah whispered.

The farmer nodded. 'He's our cow-charmer.'

The man screamed again, louder this time.

'He's tainted?'

'Yes, but he's a good, quiet fellow. Helps when the beasts gets sick and calms the cattle when we drive them down to the sea.' The farmer turned. 'I should try and do something.'

Uriah caught the man's arm. 'Just wait.'

The man shrieked again and suddenly the cobblestones around his feet seemed to writhe in the lantern light. Uriah was reaching up to take off his glasses and clean them when the farmer gasped. 'Rats.' He croaked in a broken voice. The man was right. A stream of rodents were pouring up from the nearby gutters and basements and converging on the man. When they reached him, the rats jumped up onto his legs and climbed their way up his body like a furry surge. The man's screaming intensified until it was almost unending. As Uriah watched on, frozen, more animals hurled themselves out of the dark and at the man. First came two street cats. They bounded over the tide of rats and leapt up onto the tainted man, hissing and scratching at his face and arms. More cats raced out of the night and threw themselves upon him. The man's screams became muffled as a big tomcat clawed its way up his chest and locked itself around his face. A pair of night owls and a crow circled Old John's head, snapping and scratching at his eyes and ears.

'No, no, no, no,' the farmer next to Uriah was muttering. None of the other men dared approach the window.

A big dog raced up the street, leapt up and caught the man's arm between its teeth. The man lurched forward, but did not fall. A second dog caught the man's left ankle and began to reef at it. The man stumbled to one knee. He was almost invisible now, buried under a writhing carpet of fur, fangs, feathers and claws. In their desperation to get at the man, the animals paid each other no heed. An even larger dog leapt up on the man's back and he toppled to the ground under the animal's weight and vanished under the great heaving pile. The big dog fought through the press and shook the man by the throat. After a moment Old John's screams petered out.

The animals tore at the tainted man for a few moments longer, until suddenly they stopped, almost as one. The creatures stood still for a fraction of a second and then scattered away into the shadows, the dogs barking as they ran and the birds wheeling away into the night. Soon all that was left of the animals was a scattering of dead rats and an injured cat mewing piteously.

What remained of the tainted man looked more like a butcher's leavings than a corpse.

A sob forced its way past the farmer's lips. 'Great Isaladar. Old John didn't deserve that.'

Uriah put a shaking hand against the window frame to steady himself. 'He must have run mad and broke himself.'

'Must have.' The farmer turned away. 'I... I should go and help.'

The other men in the room shouted questions, but Uriah couldn't find the words to answer them. He crawled back into his bed and pulled the covers up to his chin. He couldn't even think of sleep and simply lay in bed and listened to the fearful voices of the men working to clear up the mess in the street below.

How had he been coward enough to risk not registering his daughter?

When dawn finally broke, he rose, got dressed and walked down to the waterfront.

Uriah stood on the end of the pier and squinted down at the ferry. The dirty little pinnace was already half-full of passengers.

'Stormhaven?' he asked.

'Aye. We'll leave in a shake, too.'

The boatman helped Uriah down into the craft and found him a seat amongst the passengers and mounds of goods. Uriah muttered his thanks and paid his toll with the fisherman's stolen money.

'Hear about that ugly business last night?' the boatman asked.

'Bloody tainted. Should all be locked up,' Uriah growled in his best sailor's accent.

Thankfully, the ferryman cast off almost immediately and they were soon racing along on an impatient breeze towards the hazy spires of distant Stormhaven.

There were watchmen on the dock when they landed, but their muskets and keen eyes were gone and had been replaced by their usual halberds and unconcern. The men hardly gave him a second look as he hobbled past them. Perhaps he shouldn't have been surprised. They would be expecting him to be fleeing the city, not returning to it. Still, his heart lurched and thumped in his chest with relief as he disappeared into the Lizard. He was over the first hurdle.

He found a quiet, claustrophobic little lane and then glanced up and down the street. Once he was satisfied no one was watching him, he carefully checked the pistol Mr Otter had given him to make sure that no sand had fouled its mechanisms. Satisfied it appeared in working order, he tucked the gun back under his oilskin, put his spectacles back on and then stepped back out into the streets. Once he reached Blackroot Canal it took him less than half an hour to find his way back to the abandoned workshop. Strangely, his night-time pursuit of the two burglars felt like an eternity ago now.

He had to stop three doors away and fight down the urge to throw up. Once he had mastered himself, he knelt next to a pile of barrels and quickly ran through his plan one last time. Luckily it was simple in the extreme. Get into the building. Find out what they wanted with Sophia. Scare them off, or failing that… failing that… kill them.

Jangled as he was from his horrific last few days, he knew if he waited any longer he'd never do it.

He drew and cocked his pistol and then walked towards the old blacksmith's. He knocked hard on the heavy door. He was rewarded by the sound of confused mutterings from inside. He knocked again. Eventually, a sallow-faced man opened the door.

'Wrong address, old man,' the fellow hissed. He was smaller and better dressed than the men who had broken into his house.

'Step back inside.' Uriah raised his pistol and pointed it square between the man's eyes. 'Don't make a sound.'

The man's eyes widened and his mouth fell open, but he did as he was told. Uriah followed him and then nudged the door shut behind them. They were in what must once have been the building's main forge. A pair of anvils stood in the middle of the room and rusty tools still littered the dusty, cobwebbed workbenches.

'Call your friends,' Uriah whispered.

'Bulldog, Penn, get in here,' the man called in a wavering voice.

Two men ambled into the room. Uriah smiled grimly. At least he'd got the address right. He was certain they were the ones who had broken into his house.

'Who was that at the… well, fook me, that's 'im!' exclaimed the bigger of the two burglars.

Uriah kept his pistol on the pallid man. 'Are there only three of you?'

The man nodded and a bead of sweat trickled down out of his hair.

'Good. Now I'm going to ask you a question. Answer it truthfully and I won't kill you. Understand?'

The smaller man licked his lips. 'Y… yes.'

'What do you want with my daughter, Sophia Blake?'

'Sophia Blake?'

'Lie again and I will kill you. What do you want with Sophia Blake?'

'We were just hired, Mr Blake. We didn't mean her any harm ourselves. Honest.'

'Who hired you?'

'A strange man. Bandaged face. Calls himself Mr Savage.'

'What does he want with her?'

Uriah caught movement out of the corner of his eye and whirled about. One of the burglars had crept forward carrying a heavy length of wood.

'I will shoot you,' Uriah said.

They stared at each other for a long moment.

The thug's eyes widened. 'Go him, Bulldog! He won't fire that piece, he's got no fookin' ticker!'

Obedient to his mate's command, Bulldog bellowed, snatched up a rusty hammer and ran forward.

Uriah turned and fired.

The ball took Bulldog in the forearm, splintering bone. The man went down with an animal scream. Uriah turned back to face the first burglar, his empty pistol raised to ward off the blow he knew was coming.

But he was far too slow.

The big one smashed the heavy plank into his face and Uriah's world exploded into light and then tumbled away.

He swam in and out of consciousness, his thoughts fractured and unruly. He knew he was tied to a chair and that he had failed Sophia. Some of his teeth had been shattered and pieces of them floated free in his gagged and blood-filled mouth. He could feel a stream of blood and tears tracking down his smashed cheeks. Snippets of conversation still reached him, riding in on waves of agony.

'My arm is fookin' shattered! I'll fookin' smash the bastard!' The words came between agonised groans.

'Quiet, Bulldog. What do you reckon Mr Savage will do to you if you kill 'im?'

'I won't kill 'im, just want him to suffer.'

'Shut up, idiot. I need to think.'

The black, grasping well of unconsciousness swallowed him again.

'Did the watch send him?' the second burglar asked from a million miles away.

'Doubt it,' replied the pallid man. 'They really think he committed those murders. You saw the posters the watch's put up. Mr Savage set him up somehow.'

'That and if the watch knew we were here, they'd hardly send one fookin' old man, would they?'

'Right.'

'How'd he find us then?'

'No idea. But it's worked out well enough.'

'Reckon Mr Savage will be happy?'

'Doubt it.' Pallid man laughed nervously. 'He might be less furious though. You don't get this lucky often.'

Their voices grew jumbled and confused and the room fell away again.

A crash reverberated through the room and Uriah jerked back upright just as the skylight above them exploded inwards, showering broken glass and splintered wood down into the room. His captors shouted in alarm.

A pistol roared out from above them and something wet and hot splashed across Uriah's face. Pallid man crumpled and lay twitching on the floor. A dark figure dove through the broken skylight and landed on the table in front of Uriah. The unhurt burglar ran at the intruder with a screech of rage. The shadowy form danced forward. A blade flicked out and slid in and out of the burglar's chest with a squelch. The man dropped without a sound.

The remaining thug, Bulldog, backed away from the terrible shape, clutching his wounded arm and murmuring unintelligible apologies or pleas for mercy. The blood-splattered blade flashed again in the gloom. Bulldog screamed a choking, wet scream and died.

Uriah slipped back into the thick, clinging oil of oblivion.

The Tallowman stared down at its butchered henchmen.

It could work out some of what had happened easily enough. Its hire-lings had clearly captured someone, the blood-covered chair and ropes in the centre of the room were proof enough of that. But then someone (or more likely someones) had broken in, slaughtered its lackeys and rescued the captive. Behind its bandages the Tallowman scowled. While the dock-side thugs were no warriors, they were tough men well used to violence, and the three of them had been slaughtered with apparent ease. That did not bode well. However, the strangest part was that whoever had killed them had then just left. The alleys weren't thick with Camar Shiem and the roofs didn't crawl with soldiers from the garrison. The whole thing was strange. Very strange. And when the Tallowman was hunting it detested the strange. It turned to go.

It was halfway across the workshop floor when something caught its gaze. It drew in a hissing breath and leant forward. The glint of light it had spotted was from a broken and blood-flecked pair of spectacles. The same spectacles Uriah Blake had been wearing when he visited the Camar Shiem! A Tallowman did not mistake those kinds of details. With a shriek of rage it ground the glasses to splinters under its boot heel. Outside in the rain it screamed in fury and hammered its fists into the dirty brick wall so hard that the snap of breaking bones reverberated in the empty lane.

So close! The fool had been so close! Somehow those useless henchmen had managed to capture Uriah Blake and then… then… then… he must have somehow been stolen away. But by who? Not the watch; they thought him a murderer. So who then?

It raised its bloody fist again, ready to smash in the face of some harlot pictured on the bill poster.

But then it stopped and laughed aloud.

Under the bill for *The Swaggering Sailor*, dirty and wet with rain but still legible, was one of the posters Faulkner and Uriah had spread about Stormhaven.

Relief coursed through the Tallowman.

13.

THE BOAT BURST over the crest and then plunged down into the trough beyond. The vessel's bow slapped against the face of the next wave and a fine mist of cold ocean spray wet Sophia's face. They had left de Lacey and Morgan aboard the still mud-bound *Game Bird* that morning and set off up the coast towards the village of Waterford in a dinghy. Waterford was where James hoped to beg or buy an ancient gun from friends of de Lacey's family. Sophia wiped the sea spray from her eyes and looked up at the next bottle-green wave and then across to the distant white chalk cliffs. 'You're really sure we won't sink?' she asked.

'Sink? When *Furious* was wrecked back in '22, Crean sailed a boat not much bigger than this 800 leagues or so before our griffon scouts spotted him. If I sank us on this little cruise I'd never be able to show my face in the service again.'

'But the seas do seem a little heavy.'

'What, this little swell? Isaladar, no.'

Sophia wasn't convinced, but as she had no control over either boat or ocean, a change of subject was in order. 'How do you think your friends will go getting the *Game Bird* ready?'

'De Lacey and Morgan? Capitally, I expect.'

'They seem like very different men,' she said carefully. It was a wonder the tough old seadog and the raffish young lord got on at all.

'They work well together.'

'Really?'

'Morgan is one of the best carpenters in the fleet but he's the kind of man who, if left to his own devices, would spend an age getting one deck perfect while the rest of the ship fell apart about him. De Lacey isn't half the craftsman Morgan is, but he knows the running of a ship like the back of his hand. If it wasn't for this cursed peace, he'd have made the list months ago. Once my *Inflexibles* arrive they'll work up old *Game Bird* in no time.'

'Your *Inflexibles?*'

He nodded. 'My old crew.'

'Shouldn't they still be in the navy?'

'No,' he replied, a little evasively. 'It's an ancient tradition of the service that a captain can take a few men with him when he leaves a ship. And most of them would have ended up ashore anyway.'

'So they'll really get *Game Bird* up to Waterford in three or four days? She's almost a wreck.'

'It's only a day's sail. I imagine she'll still look a little irregular, but if the weather holds a jaunt up the coast won't trouble her.'

'And is de Lacey right about this gun?'

James did something to the sail and the boat swung her bow in towards the distant shore. 'Probably. He is pretty well acquainted with both guns and aristocratic women.'

She ignored that. 'Have you been to Waterford?'

'Once or twice, when I was a lad.'

'What's it like?'

'It's a crooked little town on a pretty, crooked little harbour. It's the kind of place that drives bad painters into paroxysms of delight.'

When Waterford finally hove into sight, it was just as picturesque as James had promised. The village nestled on the shore of a sheltered bay protected by a rocky promontory. Countless little boats dotted the deep harbour. An obscenely large manor house, a palace almost, lay fat and indolent on a hilltop behind the town. As they entered the bay and slid across the smooth waters of the harbour, it was obvious the town was busy and that the stone shops and warehouses that lined the quay were well maintained.

James ran the boat up on the pebble beach, helped Sophia out, and then threw their bags after her. Once he had hauled the dinghy up above the high-tide mark, he nodded towards a flight of stairs leading up off the beach. 'We'd better sort out rooms first.'

They found an inn easily enough. The one they picked was an attractive sandstone place called the Lark and Kestrel perched on the edge of the quay and offering a fine view out over the harbour. Inside it was clean and warm; the wooden floors were freshly polished and the walls were covered in paintings of vivid nautical scenes. The place smelled of brine and fresh paint. Their different last names and separate rooms sent a flash of surprise running across the innkeeper's kindly face, but he was too well-mannered to say anything. Once the inn's boy had taken their bags away, James turned to her. 'Ready?'

Their voyage had left her feeling hungry, wobbly and entirely salt-encrusted. Unfortunately it had only seemed to breathe a spark of energy into James and she still had no intention of letting him outpace her and confirm his opinion of women in general and her in particular. 'I'm ready.'

'Good.'

'But what's the plan?'

He held the door open for her. 'The plan?'

'Do we even have a plan?'

'De Lacey has already written ahead to introduce us, so there's no point mucking about. We'll just go straight up to the manor and ask if we might see the gun.'

'That sounds simple.'

'I'm a simple fellow. Now, I was just going to walk. Can you manage?' He shut the door and looked up and down the pier. 'Or should I hire you a cart or a pony or something?'

She raised an eyebrow. 'Do I look crippled?'

He sighed. 'Forget I asked.'

The road was well maintained and the manor only a little more than a mile from the village so the walk was easy enough. Entering the grounds through a pair of magnificent wrought-iron gates, they crunched up the gravel drive in silence. The facade was even more impressive up close than it had been from the sea. Indeed, the magnificently maintained sandstone edifice reared straight up out of the immaculately maintained gardens like some perfectly carved mountain and the better part of two hundred shining windows stared down on them. The place could have kept an entire village's population in complete luxury. As they approached the vaulted entrance-way, James' pace slowed. 'What do we do now?' he whispered.

She had no idea either. The money she knew was the comfortable wealth of lawyers and merchants, not this ridiculous aristocratic hauteur. 'Aren't we just going to ask about the gun?'

'We are.'

'Shouldn't we just knock then?'

'How should I know?' He laughed nervously. 'I've been at sea for ten years, how many manors do you think I've called on in the last decade?'

'We should just knock.'

He took his hat off, ran a hand through his hair and then nodded. 'Yes, I suppose we should.'

She followed him up the long flight of stairs and watched as he rapped sharply with the enormous lion-headed doorknocker. After a moment the door swung open silently and a balding middle-aged servant in a conservative coat stepped out. 'Yes?' the man asked. 'Can I help you?'

'I am Captain Faulkner and this is Miss Blake,' James stammered.

'And?'

'And?' James clenched his hand on the hilt of his sword. 'And we came to look over a cannon you have on your lands. A friend of mine, Lieutenant Lord de Lacey, wrote to introduce us.'

'Ah yes, Lady Whitelocke mentioned you might come calling.' He looked them both up and down and scrunched his nose up slightly, like he had caught the faintest whiff of an odour. 'It might be best if you met the baroness at the old tower. The gun is up there.' The servant waved towards a hilltop, just visible through a gap in the garden's spreading trees. 'I am sure Lady Whitelocke will join you there as soon as she is able.' Without another word the man stepped back inside and closed the door in their faces.

For a long moment James simply stared at the door, his face moving past bright red and into a kind of mottled maroon. Finally, worried he might do something he'd regret, Sophia took his hand and led him down the stairs and across the lawn towards the distant tower.

'I'd half a mind to box that rascal's ears,' he finally managed to spit out, once they'd already crossed about three hundred yards of verdant lawn.

She laughed and let go of his hand. 'Butlers are all tyrants. It never pays to argue with them. They run their houses with the same iron fist your admirals run their fleets.'

'Hmph.'

'James, if a butler likes you, you're not worth knowing.'

He smiled at that. 'Is that so? I am just too used to ordering people about.' He let out a deep breath and she heard his chagrin blow away on the breeze. 'Getting my own way.'

'I'll make sure I quake in reverential dread at your approach in future.'

'You? Dread? Reverence? The girl who bullied me into letting her caulk?'

'I didn't bully you, James. I just helped you see the error of your ways.'

He chuckled and they walked on in silence as the garden gave way to fields and then the fields to pretty seaside heather.

The afternoon sun was warm and the breeze off the ocean was cool. As they climbed the hill, the view back down to Waterford and its pretty little harbour was spectacular. Her hunger, their little voyage in the open boat, and now this idyllic stroll had all combined to have a euphoric effect on her. 'We were very close when we were young,' she said suddenly, without quite planning to.

'We were.'

'Well, I knew you as a boy and I think I'm starting to know you as Captain Faulkner, but what makes James the man he is when he stops being captain?'

He glanced at her with a look of surprise. 'I'm not all that exciting, I'm afraid.'

'I didn't ask to be entertained.'

'I suppose I'm like every other man of my generation.'

'What's that mean? What do you actually do?'

'At sea?'

'No, ashore.'

'Ashore? Ashore I suppose I like silly, normal things, like novels, plays, music, reading history and drinking too much. You'd find me dreadfully boring.'

Their talking had startled a large hare and it bounded into the open in front of them.

She pointed after it. 'And do you hunt?'

'No. I struggle to stay in a horse's saddle even when they're standing still. That and I've never thought killing defenceless creatures would bring me much joy.

'I like that very much James.' She looked at him. 'But you still want to kill this leviathan?'

'That hardly counts as hunting, not when the beast has the upper hand.'

'I suppose it doesn't.'

Behind them, two little grey ponies pulling a pretty gig trotted into view along the drive. 'This must be Baroness Whitelocke,' he said.

'Turning away the hero of Asare Roads, the current darling of the nation, for fear he might steal the silver,' laughed the elderly Baroness Whitelocke. 'Crawley will positively die of shame.'

'In his defence, this coat hardly has me looking my most dashing,' he replied.

'Nonsense. My brother said you were handsome and would drive the girls mad when you arrived home and he was quite right.'

Faulkner coughed nervously. 'Your brother, Baroness? You have me at a disadvantage.'

'The Duke of Yarmouth.'

'Ah, Admiral Rochfort. I served under him briefly in the Sunset Isles. A capital officer.' That was an exaggeration. But the duke was brave in battle and kept a good table, which more than made up for his occasionally exasperating level of disorganisation.

'And who is this beauty, Captain?'

Sophia curtseyed. 'Sophia Blake, Lady Whitelocke.'

'And are you a relation of the captain?'

'No, my father is the sponsor of our venture. I am his representative.'

'How progressive!' The baroness held out a plump and pink hand to Sophia. 'Now, come sit with me in my coach. I am far too fat to climb about on these ruins. We'll leave the men to their hobbies.' She raised her voice. 'Roland, come and show Captain Faulkner this cannon.'

'Yes, your ladyship.' A heavy-set man of about sixty clambered down from next to the driver and motioned for Faulkner to follow. 'This way please, sir.'

Faulkner followed the man inside the weathered fortification. The tower's interior was hollow and a spiral staircase that hugged the thick walls climbed away into the shadows above. The bottom of the tower was carpeted in moss and broken glass. The only illumination was a thick beam of sunlight cast by the single western window.

'The gun's up top,' the old man said as he led Faulkner up the stairs. When they reached a studded wooden door, black and red with age and rust, the man swung it open and stepped inside. Trotting across the circular room, the old man grabbed a large canvas tarpaulin and pulled it back to reveal one of the biggest artillery pieces Faulkner had ever seen.

'They don't make 'em like this any more, do they, sir?' asked Roland, rubbing a corner of the canvas across his sweaty brow.

'They certainly don't, Roland.' The gun was massive, bigger even than a first rate's thirty-two pounder. Big enough that when it was fired the cannon's mighty recoil would splinter the decking timbers of the *Game Bird* to matchwood. That hardly mattered though. They'd likely only get a couple of shots at the leviathan. Pure weight of shot was what they needed and there wouldn't have been more than a dozen heavier guns in the entire Realm. 'The thing is a monster.'

'It is. Her ladyship's grandfather was sold rather the pup if you ask me though, sir. I fancy he paid for someone's indulgent masterpiece. Why, the thing even has a poor view of the harbour,' the white-haired man said, pointing to the single small and badly sighted gunport.

The fellow knew his business. Even if it had been well positioned, the gun would have been foolishly heavy for most fortresses, let alone this fishing village's solitary stone tower. 'Were you a gunner, Roland?'

The old man nodded. 'Fought on the continent with General Alton. Hard man he was too, Captain. How we cursed his name, you'd blush to hear it. "Where a goat can go, a man can go, and where a man can go he can drag a gun," he used to say. We hated him then, but he taught me good habits. That's why I still come up here and clean the gun once a week. It's a foolish thing to do, but I can't leave it just rusting away.'

'Well, if it cheers you up, I think it suits my purpose perfectly.'

'Oh it does! Almost makes all those hours spent looking after the silly thing feel worthwhile. Do you need to see any more?'

Faulkner shook his head. 'No. It's perfect and you've kept it in beautiful condition.'

Roland beamed. 'Kind of you to say so, sir.'

Once the enormous gun was tucked safely away again beneath its tarpulin, they trooped back down the stairs and back out into the afternoon sun.

'How did it look, James?' Sophia called as they approached the coach.

'Perfect, Sophia, it's just what we need.'

The baroness heaved herself to her feet. 'Well then, Captain, we should have a talk. Sophia, Roland will fetch you something to drink.'

'But—'

'No, my dear, I have most enjoyed our little chat, but now I will speak to Captain Faulkner.' Sophia surprised him by quietly acquiescing and taking wheezing Roland over to stand in the shade by the tower door.

'Baroness Whitelocke, we are willing to offer a fair price for that gun,' Faulkner said, removing his tricorn hat.

'Shush, Captain,' the old noblewoman replied. 'I have more money than I could possibly spend in what's left of my life. However, as payment in lieu, I want two questions answered.'

'Go on.'

'Will this gun ever help defend my village?'

'No, Baroness.'

'Elaborate.'

'Not in this modern age. Any marauders that fought their way through the fleet and reached Waterford would pay no mind to one antique gun.'

'We will call that a pass. Now my second question is rather more personal.' She tapped a finger against one plump cheek. 'What are your intentions in regards to Sophia? I hope you are not playing on your fame.'

'Ah…' The directness of the question caught him completely by surprise and he fumbled for an answer. 'I, ah, I've known Sophia since she was only a girl. And, I, ah…'

'You didn't suggest she should come along with you?'

'It was her father's suggestion.' He blinked. 'Let me assure you I find the whole thing highly irregular. In fact, I argued strongly against it.'

'Very well. You pass. I will let you disarm my little village.'

They stayed on and had dinner with the baroness. The meal was a sumptuous affair, as extravagant as the room of gold thread, silver cutlery and shining mirrors they ate it in. The baroness was a consummate host as well, as free with her exquisite Farron reds as she was with her stories of a wild and tempestuous youth in the distant capital.

By the time dinner was over, Faulkner was more than a little drunk. Having said their goodbyes and refused for the fourth or fifth time to borrow the baroness' gig, they left the great house and walked back down the gently sloping road towards the lights of Waterford and their inn. The night smelled of dew, the sea and fresh cut grass. He could just hear the breaking of the surf in the distance.

'Despite a somewhat bumpy start, I think that went rather well,' he said.

'It certainly did.'

'The baroness is a fantastic woman, isn't she?'

Sophia nodded. 'She is. Did you like the house?'

'Oh yes, very elegant. Did you know Grainger designed it? It's his only house in the east.'

'It is very grand.'

He laughed. 'You manage to make that sound like a bad thing.'

'Doesn't her wealth strike you as a little unfair?

'Why would it?'

'Children are going hungry and cold in the poor houses tonight.'

'I suppose so'

'You suppose so?'

'I've never thought much on it.'

'Why not?'

'I just haven't.'

'Don't you ever feel like your poor sailors fight and die for those great families?'

'I'd argue that my poor sailors fight and die for all the country's families. Plus the baroness is hardly a monster. You've seen how well she keeps her people.'

'I like her personally; she is a charming old woman and open-handed too. I just hate to see so much money in one family's hands.'

He snorted. 'What do you suggest? The mob votes on these matters? Or maybe Mage Lords could divide it all evenly like they do out in Dasturia? You aren't a Ranter or an Evener are you?'

'Oh no, nothing like that. I just read Clancy's *Radical Democracy in the South* when I was sick last winter and it has stuck with me.'

'Hmph.'

'What?'

'When I sailed out of Republican Cartia, from what I saw of it, radical democracy is nothing but complaining at injustices, perceived or otherwise, and pulling down anyone seen to be too elegant or too wise. If that's your radical democracy, I want nothing of it.'

'You sound like a Royalist,' she said, crossing her arms.

'I suppose I am.'

'So you're happy with the state of the nation? With the slums? With child labour in the mills and in the pits?'

'Of course not. I want injustice overturned. I just believe that the rule of law is the least bloody way to do it.'

'It's a pity that all our laws are designed to keep baronesses as baronesses and the poor poor.'

He didn't have a reply to that and they walked on in awkward silence until they reached the inn and bid each other good night.

That night he dreamt of the leviathan.

Its teeth were taller and broader than coffins and between them were wedged anchors, timber, rope and sail. The detritus of its previous victims. Its eyes were milky grey discs, flat and deader than a week-old corpse. Its scales were the colour of bone, chipped and broken. As it swam through the gloomy depths they bulged and swayed as muscle and sinew, stronger and thicker than the stoutest ropes, slid up and down beneath them. The fins that thrashed at the cold waters were skeletal and tattered, like the wings of some arch-daemon. Although it was bigger than a whale, the beast threw itself through the water, hungrier and more urgent than a pike in a shallow pond.

He awoke terrified, his heart pounding. Throwing off the sweat-soaked bedclothes, he padded to the window and looked out over the safe little harbour.

He opened the shutters and breathed in the smell of the sea.

He didn't want to die.

James was quiet and withdrawn at breakfast and a nervous knot formed in Sophia's stomach. Just when she had almost won him over, had her politics driven a wedge between them? The navy was famously conservative after all, and it wouldn't have been the first time she had offended or intimidated a man by speaking her mind.

'We are still friends, aren't we?' she asked at last.

He almost looked surprised. 'What? Of course.'

'Why so grim then?'

'I had the strangest nightmare.'

'My politics weren't too strong for you then, Captain?'

'Your politics? Ha, no. The navy fights so you lot have the liberty to wreck the nation if you so choose.'

She stuck out her tongue at him. 'So, what did you dream about?'

'It was terrifying. I dreamt that a young woman I know and like is secretly an Evener.'

'I'm being serious!'

He speared the last of his egg and wolfed it down. 'I could hardly remember it when I awoke.'

'Liar.'

He shook his head. 'I truly can't remember it.'

She waited while the innkeeper leant over the table and took their plates. 'The *Game Bird* won't arrive today, will it?' she asked as the man left.

'No, we've the day to ourselves.'

'So what should we do?'

'I suppose we could walk up the beach a way? Unless that sounds boring?'

'It doesn't sound boring at all.'

They left the inn, walked through the little town and then up the folded, brush-covered dunes that sheltered Waterford from the worst of the south-easterly ocean storms. The sand shifted and slid underfoot and they walked mostly in silence. Cresting the last dune before the ocean, they paused and took in the great dark blue sweep of ocean in front of them. Sophia bored of the heaving of the empty sea long before James did, and she turned to study the beach. She spotted a man, accompanied by a small dog, pushing a cart slowly along the water's edge.

'What's that man doing?'

James looked along the beach to where she was pointing. 'He's a wrecker, I'd say.'

A wrecker! This was the kind of thing she'd been hoping for when she left Stormhaven. 'Does he use a lantern to lure ships onto the rocks on stormy nights?'

'Only in bad novels.'

'I've read plenty of stories where that happens.'

He shook his head. 'No.'

'I'm sure they do!'

'They don't. How would it work anyway? What idiot of a captain steers towards a strange light at night? The entire idea of lighthouses is that you're meant to avoid the things.'

She sighed. 'Fine then, spoilsport, if wreckers don't wreck ships, why are they called wreckers?'

'They loot the wrecks the sea gives up. Sometimes whole cargos or wrecks come ashore after a bad blow, other times it is only trunks and bags or just driftwood. Either way, the sea is fickle and her leavings are all worth something to a wrecker.'

She looked at him. He was staring out to sea with a thoughtful look on his face. 'For a sensible man, James, you get very poetic when you talk about the sea.'

'I suppose so.'

'Is that why you joined the navy?' she pressed.

'Because I loved the sea? No.' He paused. 'Well, yes, perhaps partly.'

'James!'

'What?'

'Why are you so reluctant to ever talk about yourself?'

'Reluctant?'

'Every other man your age won't shut up about how much money his father's company makes, or how quick his new horse is, or whom he last went hunting with – but finding out anything about you is harder than killing a daemon.' She set off down towards the beach, boots slipping and sliding in the dry sand of the dunes. She heard him trail after her.

'Sorry, Sophia. Since the Asare Roads I feel like I haven't been able to talk about anything other than myself. I'd be the first to admit I like attention, but I've always hated a braggart.'

'Well, I am far too unladylike to sit quietly feigning interest while someone bores me to death. If I ask you a question, I want an answer.'

'Point taken.'

'Good.' She turned back to him and raised an eyebrow. 'Well?'

'Well what?'

'Why did you join the navy?' She sat down in the sand and crossed her legs, waiting. 'I'm not giving up.'

'Tenacious, aren't you?'

'You've no idea.' She plunged a hand into the sand and then let the grains trickle away between her fingers. 'Last chance. Why did you join the navy?'

He unclipped his sword from his belt and sat down next to her. 'A big part was patriotism,' he said in a rush. 'Laugh all you want, but my boyhood heroes were men like Mayfield or de Minae.'

'And why would I laugh at that?'

'Last night you said—'

'Last night I said that the country could be more fairly run, not that I hated everyone in its service. It's the haughty aristocrats, grasping merchants and greedy bankers I don't like.'

'I thought I was lumped in with them.'

She rolled her eyes. 'No.'

'Good.'

'What were your other reasons?'

He groaned. 'I can't put it in your elegant words, but I didn't want to slave away all my life making a rich man richer. I saw what happened to the men who worked in the factories and mines and offices of Oldfort. The work crushed them down till little was left of them. The navy offered me an escape from all that and a chance for fortune and glory.'

'"Let other folk make money faster, in the air of darkroom'd towns?"'

'Something like that.'

Sophia considered him for a long moment. It was strange to hear him be so dismissive of shore life and home and she suddenly, uncharacteristically, felt tied to Stormhaven and its nice, quiet people. 'Life ashore isn't as grim as that,' she said at last.

'Of course it isn't. I was melodramatic as a boy.'

'Will you ever live on dry land again?'

'I've always fancied buying a farm and settling down in the high country north of Oldfort.' He grinned at her. 'But I want to have flown an admiral's broad and glorious pennant before then.'

She smiled back at him and began to unlace her boots. 'Ambitious, aren't you?'

'You've no idea.'

They spent the rest of the afternoon exploring further up the coast, peering into rock pools and wandering aimlessly along the sand, the only excitement coming when she embarrassingly mistook a gaggle of southbound colliers, their sails black with coal dust, for Druidic raiders.

They returned to their little inn in the particular glow that comes as a spring afternoon surrenders to twilight. Sophia excused herself to wash and Faulkner bought himself a pint and sat at a table outside to watch the return of the last few fishing boats to the safety of the harbour.

Finishing his beer he lay back against the still-warm stone of the inn. He hardly remembered having a nicer day. With a yawn he closed his eyes and almost dozed. As if on cue, wafting down from an open second-storey window floated the noise of someone splashing in a bath, followed by the sound of Sophia singing a folk song he didn't recognise. He stood up and looked around guiltily, almost expecting to get caught.

'I need a beer. No, two beers,' he muttered to himself.

When a freshly washed Sophia appeared downstairs again, they sat down to a simple dinner of mackerel together.

'So, Sophia, what do you want to do, then?' Faulkner asked once the serving girl had left them their meals.

'Sorry?'

He took a sip of his beer. 'Well you've grilled me all day about what I want out of life. But we haven't talked at all about what you want.'

'Well, thank you for asking, but...'

'But what?'

'What are my choices? Sedate wife with brats or mad old spinster with cats?'

'I am being serious, Sophia.' He swirled the beer in its tankard. 'You're far too spirited to live as either one of those. I assume you don't intend to spend the rest of your life helping work up ships for your father's friends.'

She tensed and met his gaze and for a moment he thought he saw something hard, almost impenetrable, in her eyes.

'Perhaps I could just flip a coin. Heads, wife; tails, spinster.'

Even as tipsy as he was, Faulkner realised that there was something lurking beneath the conversation. Not just a broad social pressure either, but an issue particular to just Sophia and, unwilling to ruin the mood, he shied away from it. Perhaps the pain left by the unexpected death of her mother? 'Well, let's play a different game then. What would you do if you could do whatever you wanted?'

'Secret agent,' she replied, the hint of a smile reappearing on her face.

'That would be right.'

'You don't think I could?'

He shook his head. 'You'd be perfect.'

'Really?'

'Well you're good at getting secrets out of other people.' He drained the last of his beer. 'While keeping your own safely locked away.'

She rolled her eyes. 'Maybe my secrets are just too terrible to reveal.'

Faulkner looked around the cheery little inn and then back to the beautiful girl he was sharing the table with. He doubted she had any secrets at all, let alone terrible ones. He sighed. 'I give up.'

'Good.' She smiled but there was no humour in it. 'What shall we talk about next?'

After dinner they parted at the top of the stairs and Sophia called out to him just as he reached the door to his room. 'I had a luminous day, James. You'll have sweet dreams tonight, won't you? No more nightmares.'

'You too, Sophia,' he replied, as he stepped into his room.

He shut the door. 'You too, Sophia? You too? Well done, you dullard.' He kicked off his boots, threw his sword in the corner and then hurled himself onto his bed.

14.

THEY HAD ONLY just sat down to breakfast the next morning when a dirty-faced boy came sidling up to their table. ''Scuse me, Captain, but your ship is comin' in,' he muttered.

'*Game Bird?*'

The boy nodded. 'My da reckons it is.'

'Thanks, lad.' James pushed a coin into the boy's hand and stood up. 'Come on, Sophia.'

Without the slightest regard for his heaped plate, James dashed from the inn. Sophia followed at a more serene pace. Outside she blinked against the bright sunlight and looked about. Sure enough, the *Game Bird* was tacking into the bay.

James turned back to her and grinned like a fool. 'Ha, see there, Sophia, what did I tell you? Easy as kiss my hand. To be sure, she is still a little dirty and somewhat unconventional in her tops, but by Isaladar's lance, we have a ship!'

His excitement was infectious. 'She is beautiful,' she said. Beautiful might have been an exaggeration, but at least at sea and with some canvas up she looked more like a ship and less like a decaying hulk.

'Let's get the boat and go straight out.'

'No,' she said and took his hand. 'Give them a minute to get ready. Walk with me a while and let them prepare.'

One turn along the pier was all they managed. By that point James was so impatient that she decided it'd be cruel to hold him back any longer and they pushed their dinghy out into the bay and climbed in. James slid the oars into the water and they glided out across the placid morning waters of the harbour. Although she was desperate not to show it, she was a little frightened. *Game Bird* had been an intimidating, alien place when she was still a dusty, empty shell. She could hardly imagine what it would be like now half the crew was aboard. The reputation of the men who lived below decks on the king's ships was daunting, to say the least. Afloat they were said to be vicious in action and cheerful in the face of storm. Ashore, if rumour and salacious playwrights were to be believed, their attentions were divided evenly between whoring, drinking and fighting. How would these hard men react to having her aboard their ship?

The boat bumped against the *Game Bird's* hull.

With a grunt of effort, James hurled his bag up onto the deck and then turned to her. 'Do you need the chair? We can't have you falling in!'

'The chair?'

'You sit in it and we lift you aboard.'

'I sit in it?' She sniffed. 'I told you, I'm not a cripple.' Before he could stop her, she stepped out of the dinghy and onto the ladder set in *Game Bird's* side. The little step was slippery with seawater and for a moment she thought she was going to fall.

'Are you alright?' James called.

'Of course.'

Once she had got her footing, she climbed carefully up the side. A man threw a rope down and James tied the boat to *Game Bird's* side and then clambered up after her.

On deck, de Lacey greeted them with a lazy salute. 'Welcome aboard.'

Sophia curtsied and looked around the deck. The timber was already cleaner, fresh lines lay neatly coiled by the masts, the brass shone, and most of the rubbish had been cleared away. 'I can't believe how much you've done, de Lacey!'

James nodded. 'Capital work by the look of it.'

'Thank you.' De Lacey smiled a wide, genuine smile, and for the first time Sophia saw just how much his captain's opinion mattered to the young lord. 'Now, shall we get Jenkins to take care of Sophia? I've got some figures I need you to look over.'

James nodded. 'Mr Jenkins!'

A monstrous red-haired man came lumbering up out of the open hatch. 'Good to see you, Cap'n,' he growled in a voice that rumbled like distant gunfire.

'How is the family?'

The boatswain grinned a wide, ugly grin. 'Good, sir, good. The wife is happy and the boys are already up to mischief.'

'I dread to think.' James turned to Sophia. 'Jenkins, this is Sophia Blake, our sponsor's daughter. Do you mind showing her about and introducing her to the *Inflexibles*?'

'Not at all. You ready, miss?'

She looked the huge man up and down and nerves fluttered in her belly. Jenkins was a terrifying fellow. His broad face was crisscrossed with a quilt of scars and his enormous, tattooed hands looked like they could bend a cannon out of shape. 'I'm ready.'

'What would you like to see first, miss? I can show you the cradle we're making to hold the gun? Damn interesting work that is.' If the boatswain was surprised to have her aboard he hid it well.

She took a deep breath and resisted the temptation to fiddle with her hair. 'If you don't mind, I think I'd like to meet the crew first.'

Jenkins laughed. 'Be warned, they're a sorry lot.'

Sophia soon found her nerves had been completely unwarranted. Indeed, everywhere she went about the ship her progress was marked by well-mannered salutes. They were so solicitous that she actually began to get a little cross. She wasn't the kind of girl to fall over the side or faint at the sight of blood. Not that the *Inflexibles* appreciated that; it seemed that every time she turned about Jenkins or another one of them was waiting half a pace behind her like a faithful hound.

They were a boastful, strangely childlike lot who were more than happy to share their stories. Within hours she already felt she knew a few of them well: Lewis, a fat ugly man who said he had come back to sea to escape his wife's nagging; Hook-Nose Simon who had already gambled and lost his prize money from the war; Black Patrick who sang with a high clear voice as he worked; Pincher who looked like a murderer but still carved her a rough little scrimshaw for luck; Giovanni and Giuseppe, two Cartian brothers who had enlisted in the south and stayed with the ship; and lastly, her initial favourite amongst the crew, Charley, the youngest of them, who played the hornpipe to amuse the rest when they stopped for their lunch, or whatever lunch was called aboard ship.

She hardly saw James, de Lacey or Morgan for the rest of that first day. The three of them spent almost the entire day in the main cabin, poring over an enormous list of supplies the *Game Bird* apparently needed. Not that she minded. By the time she had met the crew, had a look over the initial repairs, packed her things back at the inn, seen her bags ferried aboard and then made her cabin somewhat habitable, it was already dark. She ate a simple dinner, dashed off a rushed letter to her father by lantern light and then crawled into her little cot and fell almost instantly asleep.

She rose early the next morning but found that James had already disappeared into Waterford. After the way he had handled the purchase of *Game Bird*, the thought of him loose in the town with their money made her more than a little nervous so she bolted down a cold breakfast and then had Giovanni and Giuseppe row her ashore.

As she climbed the steps up to the old stone quay she bumped into Donald and a group of heavily laden *Inflexibles* staggering along under the mounds of rope, canvas and tools they carried.

'Morning, Donald! How did you get on?' she called.

'Terrible, miss, terrible. I swear, every man ashore is a robber.' Donald scowled. 'In my da's day a chandler would give a brave man like Captain Faulkner only the best of everything. Now it is all frayed rope and rotten bread. They're nothin' but thieves.'

Patrick nodded in agreement. 'Villains, the lot of them.'

'I hope your father is rich as a prince,' Simon muttered in her general direction.

'And where is Captain Faulkner?'

Donald nodded back up the steps. 'Sittin' down outside the Hammer and Tongs. No doubt wonderin' how we will ever afford to outfit the poor old *Game Bird* with only swindlers to buy from.'

As there were only five pubs in Waterford, it didn't take her long to spot him. She sat down next to him at a weather-beaten table outside. 'How did we get on?'

He glanced away from her. 'Oh, not too badly. Bear and Green weren't too bad.'

'James,' she said in her firmest tone, the one she usually reserved for an ill-behaved horse. 'Don't make me remind you I am here to oversee my father's investment. Tell me the truth: how did we really get on?'

He looked at her for a long moment.

'Now, James.'

He reluctantly slid the ledger across to her. 'Not so well, I'm afraid.' He sighed. 'I am no businessman, but I had still thought to do better than this.' He ran a hand through his hair. 'Prices and arrangements here are so different to what I'm used to in the service.'

'Let's see the damage then.' She opened the ledger and began to scan its pages. The sheer scale of supplies they needed was astonishing. Thousands of pounds of pork, beef, bread, flour and even raisins. Hundreds of bushels of wheat and pease. Thousands of gallons of beer and spirits. She shook her head. 'Isaladar wept! Do we really need all this?'

'If this hunt keeps us at sea for three or four months we will.'

She flipped through a few more pages of tidily written lists. The ledger even included live animals. A goat. Three pigs. A dozen chickens. 'Animals as well?'

'It's nice to have a fresh egg or some milk after a few weeks out at sea,' he said a little defensively.

'But the deck will be like a farmyard.' Her father hadn't even liked her cat coming inside.

'We're are used to having them aboard.'

'I'll have to take your word for it.' She tore her eyes away from the endless lists. James understood how much they needed, that clearly wasn't the issue. 'How much did you buy this morning and how badly did it work out?'

He leant forward and placed a finger on the page. 'These red marks here are what we bought. This first number is the quantity. The second is the price per unit. The third is the total.'

She had helped her father enough with his books that the total came to her easily enough. One hundred and eighty crowns. 'How far over your budget are you?' That was if James even had a budget.

'About a third.'

'A third over?'

He nodded.

'Ouch.' That would eat through her father's capital in no time. It would also leave very little over to cover them if something went unexpectedly wrong. 'Don't you usually have a purser to handle the financial side of things, James?'

He snorted. 'I've only known one honest purser and I buried poor Marlowe in the south.'

'So you don't usually see to these arrangements?'

'Not purchasing, no.'

'Will you let me see what I can do with these chandlers then?'

She could tell he thought about laughing at her, but he managed to fight it down. 'Sophia, do you have even the faintest idea what a yard of canvas or a pot of nails is worth?'

She tried to ignore the traitorous blush spreading across her cheeks. 'I had no real idea how much the *Game Bird* was worth either, but I saved you seven hundred crowns there.'

'Very true.'

'Let me try.'

He shut the ledger and picked it up. 'Fine. Let's give it a go then.'

'No.' She didn't want his help. The savings she had won them on the purchase of the ship could be disregarded as luck or bravado – this was her opportunity to prove herself a competent and confident business partner. 'I'll go on my own.'

'You'll go on your own?' He looked at her for a long moment, his eyes amused. Then he closed the ledger. 'I've got plenty to do on *Game Bird* anyway. See what you can do with these scoundrels. But don't agree to any arrangement until I have looked it over. Fair?'

She stood up. 'Fair.'

The first chandler's she came to was housed in a grand stone building that sat right on the waterfront. *Douglas and Sons, Est 581* the building's facade proudly proclaimed. Inside the shop everything gleamed and orderly piles of rope and canvas dotted the floors and hung from the walls. The clerk who stood behind the serving bench was perhaps one of the original 'sons'.

He was an elderly man now and was somewhat overdressed in a gentleman's cravat and high collar.

When she told him what she wanted, he actually smirked. 'Miss Blake, Douglas and Sons have served the sailors and tradesmen of Waterford well for more than fifty years. Our family has quite the reputation in these parts, you know.' He cleared his throat noisily. 'If your Captain Faulkner could come by tomorrow, then I am sure I would be able to take care of his little ship's needs.'

'Could you at least look over this now for me?' She put the ledger down on the gleaming wooden counter. 'Just to give me an idea of your prices.'

Mr Douglas looked down at the leather-bound book like it might bite him. 'Quite frankly, I don't see the point in wasting both our time, Miss Blake.'

'Captain Faulkner has asked me to arrange the rest of the victuals needed for our voyage.'

'Highly irregular.' He cleared his throat again and then dabbed at his lips with a spotless kerchief. 'Send your captain or your purser to see me.'

'But if you give me a rough quote, I could at least relay it to Captain Faulkner.' She grasped the side of the counter tightly and fought down the urge to punch the man's stuffy nose.

He sighed long-sufferingly. 'I will happily do a full and thorough quote for Captain Faulkner when I see him. I hope you do not find me rude, but I am a busy man and I do not have time to play at sailing with a mere slip of a girl.'

She recognised this type of man well. She could have had a fleet to refit and the treasure to pay for it and he still would have found a way to be difficult and patronising. 'I'll take my leave then, Mr Douglas.'

He bowed slightly like he had rendered her a great service. 'Before you go, my men tell me that your Captain Faulkner bought a load of supplies from Bear and Green this morning. I would not recommend dealing with them again. Their goods are almost unfailingly shoddy.'

She couldn't be bothered replying. She picked the ledger back up and walked for the door.

'And Miss Blake,' he called after her. 'Tell your Captain Faulkner that while our goods may not be the cheapest in Waterford, they are of the absolute finest quality.'

'Good day, Mr Douglas. And my commiserations to Mrs Douglas.' She slammed the door behind her. 'If there is one.'

She paused on the dock, took a deep breath and briefly considered throwing a cobblestone through Douglas and Sons' window. The ledger seemed to weigh a tonne and sweat prickled on her back. But she took another deep breath, quelled her anger and looked up and down the quay. Obviously going to the most snobbish shop might not have been the right idea. Luckily even a small town like Waterford boasted at least five or six chandlers. She started walking. What would have her father done? Firstly, he would have never gone to Douglas and Sons. It was too grand, too full of its own importance and always liable to be expensive and snobby. So where would her father have gone then? He would have picked somewhere in the middle. Not shabby, for that meant they got no business, but not somewhere too puffed up either. Mostly, he'd have picked somewhere the locals went.

Halfway down the quay she spotted a shop that looked perfect. A throng of fishermen were sitting on a pile of barrels outside smoking their long pipes. The fading blue and gold sign above the door read *Archers – Stevedores and Ship's Chandlers*.

She clutched the ledger tight against her chest and stepped inside, ignoring the glances from the men on the street. The building was much bigger than it had looked from the dockside and it took Sophia a moment to spot the shopkeeper as he was partially hidden by heaped mounds of gear and provisions.

'Joe Archer. How can I help you?' he called. He was tall, thin and so shy that he could hardly meet her eye.

She smiled brightly. 'My name is Sophia Blake. I'm from the—'

'*Game Bird*,' the man finished for her.

'Yes. Um, well, I was hoping to get a quote for the supplies we need.' She held up the ledger.

'All of the supplies?' Joe Archer turned, looked out the salt-grimed windows to where the admittedly rather derelict-looking *Game Bird* lay offshore. He gulped.

'I was hoping so.'

'I look after our usual customers.' The man looked around wildly like he might run away. 'We better go see Mrs Archer then. She handles our books,' he said finally.

He led Sophia up a rickety flight of stairs to a loft above the shop floor that stank of brine and tar. Although she would have thought it almost impossible, the room upstairs was even more cluttered than the store below. An anchor lay in one corner and a forest of fishing rods in another. A wide desk covered in papers sat before a window overlooking the harbour. A thick-armed, black-haired woman looked up from her paperwork as they entered. 'What's this, Joe?'

Joe Archer waved towards the *Game Bird*, which was just visible through the crooked little window. 'This is Miss Blake from that there collier. She was hoping to get a quote for outfitting her. The ship that is, Gerty.'

The woman motioned for Sophia to sit down. 'A pleasure, Miss Blake. I am Gertrude Archer. But call me Gerty.'

'Please to meet you, Gerty. I'm Sophia.'

Behind her, Joe slunk back down the stairs without another word.

Gerty crossed her big arms and looked her up and down. 'So, Sophia, looking for supplies are you?'

'For a quote, yes.'

Gerty nodded. 'I saw some lads from your wreck of a ship carting goods about this morning. Who'd you get that from?'

'Bear and Green.'

'I can do better than those robbers. Are we the first place you have come to this morning?' Gerty asked.

'No. I've just come from Douglas and Sons.'

'And how did they take a visit from a girl?'

'Not well,' Sophia replied with a wry smile.

'A woman with money and the freedom to spend it.' Gerty chortled at the thought. 'I'm surprised Douglas didn't up and have a stroke then and there.' She paused and leant forward, serious again. 'Now look, you seem a nice enough sort of lass so I'll be blunt with you. We are no shipyard, we normally serve fisher folk and the like. It's not every day someone just walks in here cold, looking to spend a small fortune. I'd also hazard by the look of you that you know little all about the sea or ships. So are you wasting my time? Is this some rich girl's prank or lark?'

'It's no prank.' Sincerity seemed like the best policy to Sophia. 'You're right though, I know almost nothing about the sea.'

'So what are you doing then?'

'The men on my ship know even less about money and the art of keeping it than I do about sailing.'

'That's men as a rule, Sophia. Bad with coin, one and all. Misers or wastrels the lot of 'em. Why do you think so many wives do the accounts for their husbands? We don't enjoy being harridans, we just understand numbers better.' The big woman cleared away some of the papers in front of her. 'So how will we do this then?'

Sophia put the ledger on the table. 'The prices Bear and Green charged us this morning are in here. I am sure it's bad form, but look them over. If you think you can do us a better deal then I'll have you do a full quote for the remainder of what we need. If Captain Faulkner thinks your prices are fair then we'll go with you.'

'And what's to stop you going to Parsons or back to Bear and Green and getting them to beat my quote?'

'My word.' Sophia met her gaze. 'You have my word. If your quote is competitive we'll purchase everything through you till we leave Waterford. As long as you keep to your terms, that is.'

'Gerty straightened some of the papers in front of her and shrugged. 'That will have to do then, won't it?'

Relief made Sophia's ears tingle. 'What now?'

'Now let's have a look at how our friends at Bear and Green robbed you this morning.'

After less than a minute's study, she spun the heavy book around so Sophia could see. 'It's an old trick this, but a good one and a favourite at Bear and Green. Now what they did was this.' She pointed at the page. 'Take powder and shot. They'd know your captain would have a rough idea of how much that should be worth, so they make it cheap, so cheap in fact that they probably make a loss on it. They do that on a few flagship items the captain would know, but on every single other bloody thing they make a very nice little profit indeed. The loss on the big stuff is soon clawed back, with interest.'

'So the poor simple sailor leaves thinking it's a good deal, but they really got robbed?' Sophia asked.

'Exactly.'

'So you can do better?'

Gerty snorted indignantly. 'I won't be cheaper on everything. But across the whole refit I'll save you an arm and a leg.'

'So what now?'

'Now we do you up a proper quote.'

'Can I help?' Sophia asked.

'You certainly can. Can you read and write?'

'Of course!'

'Good. You'll play scribe.' The big woman gestured to a cradle Sophia had missed nestled amongst a pile of cordage near the desk. 'And if the little Mister Archer wakes, you can rock him back to sleep once I've fed the little blighter.'

'Let's get to it then.'

It was well dark by the time they had finished the quote and fetched James from the *Game Bird*. Sophia stood at the window and watched the town's lights skip and jump across the black water towards where the *Game Bird* and a few other ships were just visible in the gloom. She was famished and tired and exhausted and excited. Baby Archer gooed quietly in her arms and as she soothed him back to sleep, she moved so she could watch James' reflection in the dirty glass of the window. He had been reading through the quote for the last half hour, only looking up to ask the odd question of her or Mrs Archer. At least he was interested.

He finally put the pile of parchment down. 'This is a very fair price, Mrs Archer.'

She nodded. 'I doubt you'll find cheaper between here and Barbonne.'

'I have one concern, however.'

Sophia's breath caught in her throat.

'Yes?' For the first time Sophia saw how much Gerty needed their business. It was written in the glitter in her eyes.

'You are only a small concern and time is of the essence. Are you going to be able to manage all this? I can't waste any time on a slow fitting out.'

'I have five brothers, Captain Faulkner, and Mr Archer, well, he has seven cousins. All of them are fishermen and I am damn sure they'll take a few days off the nets if I ask them for help. I figure they'll be glad to spend some time ashore, especially with that leviathan sniffing around.'

The baby stirred again in Sophia's arms and she gently hushed it.

'That's good enough for me, Mrs Archer.' James stood up and held out a hand to Gerty. 'You have my word as an officer, I'll go nowhere else.'

Sophia let out a quiet sigh of relief. She had done it! And in a single day too.

'Your word as an officer?' Gerty froze halfway out of her chair and the big woman's eyes widened. 'You aren't *the* Captain Faulkner are you?'

James then had to answer a string of questions about his war in the south, questions that Sophia couldn't help but notice that, despite his protestations, he was always quite flattered to be asked. By the time they had got down to signing the contract and determining what supplies James needed to be delivered first, she and baby Archer were cuddled together in a driftwood chair under the window. She only realised she had fallen asleep when James gently shook her awake. With a yawn she stood up, returned the sleeping child, said her farewells to Gerty, and then followed James downstairs and out into the cool evening air.

As the door to the shop was shut and bolted behind them she turned to James. 'So?'

'So what?'

'So? So, did I do a good job?'

'Oh that.'

'Oh that? That's all you have to say?'

'I was only teasing, Sophia.' His teeth flashed white in the dark as he smiled. 'How did you manage it? You must have saved us a thousand bloody crowns.'

A little spurt of joy flooded her heart, but she did her best to sound nonchalant. 'I was just honest. I told her what we needed and asked her if she could help us.'

'No manoeuvring then. Engage the enemy more closely.' He chuck-led. 'If only I knew it was that easy I might have saved us fifty crowns this morning!'

'So you're impressed?'

'Impressed? If I ever make lord admiral, I'll appoint you to run the dock-yards.' He laughed. 'You'd be the honest cat amongst the thieving pigeons.'

The next morning, with their line of supply secured, the transformation of the *Game Bird* began in earnest. Sophia had never seen a boiling cacoph-ony like it. It was utter, raving madness, but somehow James, de Lacey and Morgan seemed to be on top of it. Boats and barges rushed to and fro across the harbour bringing out what looked like enough supplies to build a town and then feed its population for a year. The great mounds of provisions were promptly winched aboard from the Archers' boats, only to disappear, almost as if by magic, down below decks. The air around the ship rang to the sounds of hammering and sawing and shouting and wherever she went or looked, sailors were hard at work. They swung in the rigging stringing ropes, hung over the side painting, crawled around the pitch-black hold like moles, and chopped and sawed their way through a forest's worth of timber – and above it all hung the stink of hot tar, warm paint and the sailor's inces-sant singing:

I'm sick in the head and I haven't been to bed

Since first I came ashore with me plunder,

For I spent all me tin on the lassies drinkin' gin

Far across the Western Ocean I must wander.

15.

FOR AN ETERNITY, time's passing was not marked in minutes, hours or even days but peaks and troughs of agony. He floated in this state, marooned. When he could, he thought of the happy days when Mary had been alive and Sophia had yet to leave for school. Other times nightmares, broken and distorted, swallowed him. Gradually he began to notice fragments of things again. The murmur of voices around him. The stink of blood and pus. A hint of light or warmth.

He was cleaned. The bandages on his face were changed. Sometimes a watery broth was forced gently between his smashed lips and other times a bitter paste. Eventually, slowly, time began to have meaning and he became Uriah Blake again.

He blinked owlishly. He was lying on a cramped cot in a small cabin. The red glow of sunset filtered through a grate above him. The earth felt like it was rocking under him.

'Can you hear me?' A man asked from close beside him.

The unseen man's voice was deep and heavily accented. Uriah turned his head and peered towards the speaker. Even that slight movement sent pain coursing through him. A silver-bearded, square-shouldered black man crouched next to his cot.

'Y… yes.' Uriah's voice was slurred and his tongue thick and sluggish. Language returned to him only with difficultly. 'Where am I?'

'On the *Palinurus*.'

'A ship?'

'Yes.'

'Who are you?'

'Marcellus.'

Uriah ran his tongue along the back of his teeth. His mouth was unfamiliar, jagged territory. A pounding headache leapt and kicked behind his eyes. 'Am I a prisoner?'

'No.' The black man shook his head. 'You are a guest of my mistress.'

'Your mistress?'

The man nodded.

'Who is she?'

'The Countessa Galliate.'

Uriah wanted to ask a thousand other questions, but a great, soft and prickly weight lay heavy on him. Although he fought against it, his eyes slowly closed and he fell back into a state somewhere between sleep and death.

The next time he awoke the tiny cabin was flooded with the grey light of dawn. He sat up slowly in the cot and touched a finger gently to his ruined face. His cheek were swollen and hot. He took the finger away and slowly turned his head to look around the cabin. It was empty. 'Hello?' he croaked. 'Hello?'

A moment later the door opened and the same man, Marcellus, stepped inside. 'You're awake again.' He took a leather water skin off his belt and held it out. 'Thirsty?'

Uriah suddenly realised he was parched. He took the skin with shaking hands and gulped down some water. Although his mouth stung and the water tasted of his own blood, it was worth it to kill some of his thirst.

'Can I get you anything else?'

Uriah ran a hand over his bristly, unshaven skull and tried to remember their earlier conversation. 'I need to speak to your mistress. The Countessa, ah, ah…'

'Galliate.'

'Yes, the Countessa Galliate. Can I see her?'

'I will find out.' The man stepped back out of the cabin. He returned a few minutes later with a much smaller, skeletally thin and bespectacled black man.

'I am Doctor Celsus.' The smaller man sat on the edge of the cot next to him and folded his brown hands in his lap in a peculiarly bird-like fashion. 'Now, do you remember what happened?'

Uriah nodded. 'I got hit in the head. With a plank.'

'And you should be dead.' The little man almost sounded aggrieved he had survived. 'You are just lucky I had some leeches to hand. Do you have a headache?'

Uriah nodded. 'Yes, a terrible one.'

'That is to be expected. Now, how many fingers am I holding up?'

'Three.'

'What was the name of the Caladian emperor who fought alongside your King Isaladar at Levestar?'

'Balbinus.'

The small man looked pleased. 'What is your name and profession?'

'Uriah Blake.' He didn't have the strength to lie. 'I am a lawyer by trade.'

'I was sure you would be much more addled when you awoke.' Celsus shook his head. 'The brain is a strange thing. You are lucky. Very, very lucky. But you will tell me if the headaches get worse, yes?'

'I will.' With a shudder of effort Uriah leant forward, threw back the covers and tried to kick his legs out of the cot. 'But now I really must see your mistress.'

The doctor nodded. 'I think you are strong enough. Marcellus, please take our guest up on deck.'

Despite Uriah's protestations that he was able to walk, Marcellus forced him to sit in a wicker chair and then bodily carried the chair, with him in it, up onto the deck. Once they were safely away from the hatch, Marcellus put the chair down, caught his breath and stretched with a grimace. Squinting against the morning sun, Uriah looked around. There was no land in sight and they were running before a slight breeze. The ship cut through the azure ocean with a lazy ease, her wake trailing razor-sharp behind her. Leaning back in the chair he studied the sail arrangement. The ship was propelled by three foreign-looking triangular sails. Around them the crew, all as black as Marcellus, were hard at work and Uriah was momentarily embarrassed that he was being carried about like a child.

'What strange type of ship is this, Marcellus?' he asked. Uriah had only seen a few such vessels in Stormhaven.

'The *Palinurus* is a xebec, sir.'

From what he remembered, xebecs were small, elegant ships native to the Tenebrarum Sea in the south. So what on earth was he doing on this strange ship, with its alien crew? He had been hurt in Stormhaven, hadn't he? Or had he dreamt the fight with the thugs? Or was he dreaming this? He'd heard of men being driven mad by a blow to the head.

Marcellus picked the chair back up and carried him astern. Mad or not, it wasn't hard to guess where he was being taken. The tall woman with her hands on the ship's helm must be the countessa. She was about forty and had the look of an eagle about her. Her skin was a dark olive and her mass of black hair was tied back to frame a proud, almost regal face. She wore working boots, breeches and a man's shirt, topped by a leather vest that looked thick enough that it might have been armour. As they approached she studied him, her amber eyes inquisitive.

'Is he well enough to be on deck, Marcellus?' she asked in faultless, slightly lyrically accented tone.

With a grunt Marcellus set Uriah and his chair down near the wheel. 'Doctor Celsus thinks so, Countessa.'

'Very well.' She turned to him. 'I am Fiora Varzi, Countessa Galliate, and I am glad to see you still with us.'

Like the ship her name was from southern Circillia, Caladian probably. But what were Caladians doing so far north? His thoughts were fuzzy and blunt. 'Uriah Blake. Pleased to meet you.' Not knowing what else to do, he held his hand out.

After a moment's pause, she shook his hand. Her grip was strong and her palms as rough as any of his naval clients. 'So, Mr Blake, to which Sacred Band do you belong?'

'Sacred Band?'

She nodded. 'What organisation?'

'I belong to the Club of Moderate Progressives…'

She blinked. 'I've never heard of them.'

'We are working to extend the voting franchise to all adult—'

'I am sworn to the Blessed Lance, you may speak freely to me.' She took a copper amulet out from under her shirt and held it out like it should mean something to him. 'I ask again, to what Sacred Band do you belong?'

'I am sorry, but I've no idea what you mean. Or what that amulet is.'

She made a sharp gesture with her free hand. 'Camar Shiem? Hammer of the Fiend? Blade of Morning? Do those names signify nothing to you?'

'The Camar Shiem are our secret police. But I've never heard of the hammer of the whatever and I've no idea what a Sacred Band is.'

'He says he is a lawyer, mistress,' Marcellus ventured.

'A lawyer?'

Uriah's neck was already aching from looking up from his chair.

'And you haven't even heard of the Sacred Bands?'

'No.'

She glanced up at the sails above them. 'You are out of your depth, then.'

'I have been for some time, Countessa. But please, what is a Sacred Band? And how did I come to be on this ship?'

'Sacred Bands are sworn to hunt the agents of the Great Enemy. We take an oath to remain aloof from the strife and bickering of the continent's kings and emperors and to work together to thwart our enemy.'

Uriah swallowed nervously. 'I'm definitely not in a Sacred Band then.'

She raised an eyebrow. 'Then how did you come to be a Tallowman's prisoner?'

'A what?'

'A Tallowman.'

'What in Isaladar's name is a Tallowman?'

'Great Samaryan! What have you stumbled into, Mr Blake?' She sighed. 'Perhaps you should tell me your story and then I will tell you mine. Yes?'

Uriah looked up at her for a long moment and weighed his options. No matter how he ran the sums, it felt like he had to risk telling her the truth. How long had he drifted in and out of consciousness for? Days? A week? A fortnight? If this countessa was allied to the men hunting Sophia then the game was almost certainly already lost and honesty would probably do no extra harm. On the other hand, if she was a genuine third party then he desperately needed her help.

He took a deep breath and told her his story.

Hands still firmly on the ship's wheel, the countessa listened attentively, only interrupting his story twice. When he described the rumours about the

Camar Shiem circulating in Stormhaven she shook her head angrily. 'Lies spread by the enemy to frighten people into inaction,' she hissed. Later, when he described how he was framed for the murders, she interrupted again. 'That is the Tallowman. They are a favoured agent of the enemy, able to take on another's face.'

'What do you mean, "take on another's face"?'

'They can mimic appearances almost perfectly.' An unreadable look flickered across her face. 'It is a scientific trick they've learned.'

'A scientific trick?'

'A mixture of alchemy and other arts. It's complex. Continue.'

When he was finally finished he leant back in his chair, exhausted by the effort.

The countessa nodded to Marcellus who stepped forward and gave him the water skin again. 'Drink,' she said.

'A few times now you've mentioned "the enemy".' He took a long sip. 'I don't understand. Do you mean us? The Realm?'

She laughed and shook her head. 'The Realm is not my enemy.'

'But we were at war only eight months ago!'

'The Emperor's War? Bah, that was a war between nations that should be brothers. An idiotic aberration that wasted countless lives and only further destabilised Caladia. The enemy I speak of is far worse than any nation.'

'Than any nation?'

She nodded. 'Nations mean nothing to our foes.'

'You aren't going to ask me to believe some fairy tale about an evil secret society or cult are you? I'm sorry, but you sound like a character from one of my daughter's dreadful novels.' He knew he was being rude, but his headache and his worry for Sophia had thoroughly dulled his manners. 'Don't tell me, they are trying to wake an ancient evil that lives on the sea floor or inside a volcano.'

'This is no fairy tale. The Great Enemy are real enough. Even now they plot to overthrow or subvert all Circillia.'

'Who are they then?'

'The Zakar Commune.'

'The Zakar,' he said. Lately rumours had reached Stormhaven of a savage war in the distant south, of armoured elephants and basilisks striding into battle, and of exotic nations slaughtered under a heavy, melting sun. But no matter how warlike the Commune was, the closest Zakar possession must have been the better part of 10,000 miles away. Uriah had never even heard of anyone who had even been south to Zakar. 'That's ridiculous!'

'It is the truth. Two centuries ago they were pushed almost to extinction and, at their nadir, the Zakar made a terrible pact from which they now find they cannot escape...' she noted his look of incredulity and stopped. 'Forget about the enemy for now. I will tell you my tale. You will not doubt the truth of it. Our stories are similar, my tragedy is simply more complete than yours.

'I will start by saying that I carry the taint.' She took a hand off the wheel and tapped her leather vest. 'Like your daughter, I carry the terrible, life-destroying taint. But I am fortunate in that my aspect is difficult for others to notice. All I was cursed with is the ability to detect when others use their taint. Even over great distances I can feel the use of someone else's aspect as a kind of distant echo.'

'That doesn't sound too bad. I mean...' Uriah trailed off. Did you treat the taint like a disease? Or was that patronising?

She appeared to take no offence. 'You are right. In many ways my taint is a very small thing, but it has still shaped my life. I was born to a family of noble Jaltanians loyal to Caladia. I will not bore you with the details of my childhood. Suffice to say when I came of age, like most Loyalists I was sent to be educated in Caladia and there I met my husband. I was mesmerised by his looks, his strength and the attention he paid me. My family approved of my choice. He could trace his ancestry back to emperors, so how could they do otherwise? We married.

'Our marriage was not a happy one. It quickly became apparent he did not desire a partner, only a string of eager girls to fan his vanity. Luckily our estates were vast and by the time I was twenty we only saw each other a couple of times a year. I could never hate him though, for by then he had given me a beautiful son, Lucullus.

'Looking back I can see in many ways it was an idyllic life. Materially, Lucullus and I had everything we wanted or needed. But, as they do, things changed. On a warm autumn afternoon a party from the Blessed Lance came to our estate.' She paused. 'Sorry, I forget this is all new to you. In my home country, the Blessed Lance fights the Great Enemy. They are Caladia's Sacred Band. Caladia's Camar Shiem. They told me they had scried out my taint and that they needed my aid.

'I should have said no. I should have sent them away. But by then I had lived in the country for almost ten years and, while I loved motherhood, I felt that life was passing me by. Initially, I was just flattered by their attention but what I saw when I accompanied them through that long winter changed my life. We faced down a true evil.' She shook her head. 'I had lived a pampered life and I could hardly believe that such cold savagery existed. But it did. Stopping these monsters became an obsession for me. When next they called there was no need for flattery or coercion on their part, and within months I had been sworn into the Blessed Lance proper. For years afterwards I served my band loyally and even directed much of my personal wealth to the cause. Over the years we uncovered and killed many of the Great Enemy's agents.

'However, like many who are taken up by a cause, I did not pay enough attention to my family. To my shame, Lucullus was fifteen before I even realised I had passed the taint onto him. He was much stronger in his taint than I am and, like your Sophia, his aspect was of healing. Worse, by then my constant absences had opened a gulf between us.

'I tried to speak to him, to warn him of the darkness that stalked the corners of the world and the danger to which his taint exposed him, but he wouldn't listen. I'm sure it all sounded like the efforts of an eccentric and absent mother to frighten and control a boy who was almost ready to go out into the world. I should have made more of an attempt to speak to him, but my attention was divided. There was a schism in my Blessed Lance and I foolishly gave this, rather than Lucullus, the majority of my attention. When the Emperor's War broke out, Lucullus waited for me to leave again and then snuck away. He travelled to Caladia and, with his father's help, enlisted in the emperor's Peacock Guard.'

'With his gold braided uniform and jewelled sword my son no doubt thought himself a proper soldier. But Tallowmen are not raised reading books of honour and glory, they are savage and efficient killers. From what I could gather later, the Tallowman murdered him in the privy house of a tavern where he was drinking with his new friends.' She paused for a long moment, her knuckles almost white against the dark wood of the ship's wheel. 'They found his body a week later. He had been left on a rubbish pile like common leavings. The Tallowman had torn out his heart, his genitals and eyes.'

Tears rolled freely down her cheeks and sparkled in the sunlight.

'I'm sorry, Countessa.'

'The fault is mine. You knew nothing of the evil that walks abroad in the world and you still did a better job of protecting your child than I did.' She raised a hand from the wheel and roughly scrubbed her tears away. 'We will speak more tonight. Marcellus can take you back to your cabin. You should rest.'

Marcellus carried him back below. The big man had hardly closed the door to his cabin before Uriah was asleep.

When he awoke the headache still thrummed against his skull and his face hurt like it had been branded.

'How is your headache, Uriah?'

He went to lift his head, but his pillow was stuck to the side of his face by suppurations from his wounds. He peeled himself free and rolled over. The little doctor, Celsus, was perched on a stool next to his bed, a leather purse in his lap. 'Terrible,' Uriah croaked.

The doctor bobbed his head. 'This is to be expected. Is the pain getting worse?'

'I don't think so.'

'Good.' The little man opened the purse and took out a small pair of scissors. 'Now, I think we should remove your bandages and let your wounds breathe in this nice sea air. Is there anything you need before we start?'

Uriah shook his head.

'Can you sit up, please?'

Uriah groaned and hauled himself up against the timbers of the cabin wall. 'I am very confused, Doctor.'

Celsus leant forward, pulled some bandages away from his face and then carefully snipped through them. 'I cannot speak of everything but I could answer any' – the doctor struggled for the word – 'general enquiries you might have.'

'Thank you, Doctor.' Uriah sat for a moment. A nagging thought prickled and writhed at the back of his skull, but his headache buried it and he couldn't quite catch it. He grimaced in frustration and settled for another question. 'So these Sacred Bands that the countessa mentioned, they are secret armies?'

'We are secretive. But Sacred Bands can be either private organisations or... ah, civic institutions. Is that the term?'

Uriah nodded.

'But we all swear the same oath and that is to cooperate in our resistance to the enemy, no matter what is happening between our home countries.'

'Even when our nations are at war?'

'Hold still.' Celsus gently tugged on a corner of the bandage and it came away from Uriah's face with a moist squelch. 'Especially then. This is the entire point of the Eternal Oath. The task of the Sacred Bands is to transcend these petty struggles and to present a unified front to our enemy, no matter what foolishness our nation's leaders are currently perpetrating. Why, the day before your army won their great victory against my emperor at Talamarno Field, the countessa was working alongside some of your Camar Shiem against the Great Enemy in the Sunset Isles.'

Uriah nodded again. The world needed more of that kind of philosophy. 'So are you like the Camar Shiem, does your...'

'Blessed Lance.'

'Are you funded by your emperor?'

'No. Our emperor is more cynical than your king.' Celsus carefully unwound a long snake of bandage from Uriah's head. Each layer of the fabric came away reluctantly, stiff and brown with dried blood.

'How so?'

'He does not believe in the threat posed by the Great Enemy and does not fund us.'

'What? You are vigilantes?'

'Yes, I suppose that is correct. We are.'

'What? Why?'

Celsus shrugged helplessly and then slid the scissors between Uriah's face and the bandages and snipped another break in their coils. 'It is not just my emperor. Many other rulers have convinced themselves this secret war is all superstitious panic.'

'But surely you must have proof to show them?'

Celsus shrugged again. 'The enemy's plots are so languid and careful, they can take decades to come to fruition and their agents are almost never taken alive. In the face of the few tenuous links that come to light, imagine how simple it is for a monarch to put their hands over their eyes and see no evil. Also, think what your Camar Shiem must cost to maintain – a fortune; even to us, their resources are legendary! Unfortunately, once a ruler has convinced himself that this threat is either a fabrication or a vast exaggeration that their army or militia can handle, they are free to waste money on things like…' The doctor smiled sadly. 'Bread and circuses.'

'So you get no help from your emperor at all?'

The little man gently peeled away another long thread of bandages. Pus had glued Uriah's eyebrows and the bandages together and Uriah flinched in pain as it came away. 'Sorry. Now we need to clean the wound. As for our emperor, no, we get no help from him.' The little man picked up a clean rag and a clay pot filled with salt water and began to dab at Uriah's wounds. 'We are in fact outlawed in Caladia and all her overseas provinces.'

'Outlawed?'

'Our emperor feels the church Templars are better equipped to handle these dark matters. Men and women have been executed just for belonging to our order.'

Uriah's shoulders slumped. He was a wanted criminal, and he had been rescued by members of an outlaw band of vigilantes. What possible hope did Sophia have of escaping this Tallowman assassin pursuing her?

Celsus put a hand on his shoulder. 'Take heart, Uriah. And remember we are in your country, not mine. Your king can trace his line back to Glorious Prince Isaladar himself and the Camar Shiem stand at his right hand!'

'I suppose so.'

'Don't look so glum – your daughter is not in the enemy's clutches yet.' The doctor put the little pot down and picked up two books from the floor. 'These may help keep your worries at bay. I am afraid my little library only has two manuscripts in your language.' He passed them to Uriah. '*The*

Bridge on the Moor and *Knight of Mourning*. Hopefully they are something of a distraction.'

'Thank you, Doctor.'

Celsus smiled and bowed. The little doctor then tucked the scissors and soiled bandages into his purse, gathered his other supplies and let himself out of the cabin. Once he was gone, Uriah lay back against the cabin wall and closed his eyes. The air was cold on the ruins of his face. He meant to read, but his eyes were so very heavy and the rocking of the ship was almost hypnotic. Again sleep crept up on him without warning.

It was after dark when the countessa sent Marcellus to fetch him again. This time the big man let him walk, supporting his arm against the roll of the ship. 'Where exactly are we, Marcellus? Geographically, I mean,' he asked as they shuffled through the cramped interior of the ship. Despite his abject weakness, he was glad to be back on his feet.

'About one hundred miles south-west of Stormhaven, I believe.'

'Why so far out to sea?'

Marcellus chuckled. 'There is nothing harder to find than a ship on the open ocean. And being hard to find is where you need to be when a Tallowman is hunting. I will leave you here.' Marcellus opened a door and motioned him through into what must have been the *Palinurus'* grand cabin. Through the stern windows the ship's milky wake trailed off into the moon-lit infinity. The countessa rose from behind a long table that almost ran the length of the cabin. She had changed into a simple robe that reminded him of the togas her ancestors would have worn.

She motioned for him to sit. 'You look much better, Mr Blake.'

'I still feel awful.' He noted in surprise that she had been working on a musket. Its complex mechanism was carefully spread out on the lacquered wood in front of her.

'Can I get you anything?'

He put a hand to his swollen jaw. 'You don't have a mirror do you?'

She walked to a small cupboard bolted to the bulkhead, took a small beaten metal mirror from one of the drawers and handed it to him. Even by lamplight the damage to his face was shocking. His features were so badly ruined he hardly recognised himself. Three teeth were missing and his left eye was almost swollen shut. Some of his bruises were the size of oranges and from forehead to collar his skin was mottled every colour between black and yellow.

'You are not a pretty sight, I'm afraid.'

Uriah placed the mirror on the table. 'Luckily I was never handsome enough to be awed by my own looks, Countessa.'

'We are both too old for such vanity anyway. Now, I must apologise for my behaviour earlier, the death of my son is still a very raw wound.' She waved away his conciliatory sounds. 'Did you understand my story, though?'

'I think so. You are hunting a man who killed your son. This same assassin, this Tallowman, is also hunting my daughter. But I still don't understand how your people came to find and rescue me?'

'Tallowmen are almost impossible to track. But they generally travel alone and often hire local help. It was by luck and the chatter of sailors I followed his trail to Stormhaven from Caladia. Once I was here it was the boasting of some thugs in a tavern about their strange, rich master that led me to their lair.'

'And which of your men do I have to thank for my rescue?'

'My men?' She smiled. 'I was the one who found you.'

'I… I didn't realise that a woman…' Uriah cleared his throat. 'I mean, thank you, Countessa.'

'I am not some soft northern girl.' She clicked two parts of the musket back together. 'And do not be too appreciative, Mr Blake, I had no idea you were there. I was hoping to catch the Tallowman.'

'And you would have killed him if he was?'

'Perhaps one time in three.' She tested the gun's mechanism. 'But the odds against a Tallowman are never much better than that. Even if you ambush them, they are still a terrible foe.'

'Why didn't you just wait for him to return?'

'Ha! Wait? The Tallowman is the snake and those fighting him the mongoose. You strike once and if you miss, you flee.'

'So you killed those ruffians and…'

'And as soon as I saw that the Tallowman was not amongst the dead I took you and escaped. I was hoping that you were Camar Shiem and could aid me.'

'I am not, Countessa, far from it.'

'So I see. But that still brings me to the proposal I have for you.'

'Proposal?'

'I am a stranger in this land. I can speak the language and I have plenty of gold, but I know nothing of your nation's customs or laws. I need you to help me hunt this beast. I need you to be my local guide, at least until more of your Camar Shiem arrive out here in the east.'

'I'm no soldier.'

'You have already proven yourself to be brave.'

'And incompetent. You had to rescue me.'

She shrugged. 'I already have plenty of warriors aboard. I need your knowledge, Uriah Blake.'

It sounded preposterous. A strange foreign warrior woman wanted his help catching some assassin of fable. He wasn't sure if he should laugh or cry. 'But...'

'As a wanted murderer there is nothing you can do by yourself to help your daughter. But you can help me find and kill the Tallowman. If we do that your Sophia will be safe, for a time anyway.'

'Can't we rescue Sophia first?'

'Tallowmen are consummate killers. Once assigned to his prey he will hunt and hunt and hunt until either he succeeds or is killed. I swear on my son's grave that your daughter will not be safe until this Tallowman is dead. The only way you can truly help your daughter now is by helping me hunt him.'

He looked out the stern windows at the darkening ocean. Could he trust this driven, vengeful woman? Did he even have a choice? 'Can't we, I mean you, just talk to the Stormhaven Watch? Get them to help?'

'Not against a Tallowman. They'd only blunder about like blind men and alert our foe.'

'I see.' He took a long breath. 'I will help you. But I have one stipulation.'

She crossed her arms. 'Go on.'

'At least let me write to Captain-Constable Moreau detailing roughly when I expect Sophia might return to the city and asking him to take her into protective custody when she does. Wanted murderer or not, I think he'd follow that advice. I swear I will say nothing of this Tallowman fellow.'

She thought for a long moment. 'I suppose it will do little harm.'

16.

THE BARONESS SHIFTED on the soft green leather of the gig's seat and glanced up towards the old watchtower. 'I've never seen a man crushed to death,' remarked the old woman conversationally.

Sophia tilted the parasol the baroness had made her carry and followed the older woman's gaze. Getting the enormous cannon down from the top of its thirty-foot tower did look dangerous. The *Game Birds* had spent the last two days carefully removing the roof of the tower to expose the gun. Once the roof was off they had built intricate wooden scaffolding up and over the tower. Now, under James and de Lacey's direction, they were stringing up a mad spiderweb worth of block, tackle and rope. 'I'm sure they know what they're doing,' Sophia said.

'I hope so.'

'Of course they do. At Garenburg James hoisted two eighteen pounders from a barge's deck and up onto the old city walls, all without crushing anyone. Plus he was only a midshipman then.'

'Did he indeed? At the great siege of Garenburg?' The faintest hint of a smile danced around the edges of the baroness' mouth. 'A clever man, that captain of yours.'

'He's not my captain,' Sophia said absently. James was in the thick of it as usual, barking orders and pulling on a rope like a common sailor; his height made him easy to spot. She had always expected a naval captain to do little more than stand on his quarterdeck with his hands behind his back looking stern and patrician, but James wasn't anything like that. Indeed, he had been working so hard she'd hardly spoken to him since she'd organised their supplies.

The sudden, piercing shriek of the boatswain's whistle reached them.

'Well, here we go,' said the baroness.

With a collective grunt of effort the *Game Birds* hauled away on their lines. The remaining slack in the ropes leapt taut and the makeshift scaffolding groaned in protest. 'Heave away, lads!' James yelled. Sophia watched him strain as he hauled on his own lead. It was hard not to notice that all the work he had been doing had left him hard and brown, and the little paunch he'd carried in Stormhaven was long gone.

The scaffolding flexed and groaned again. For a moment she was sure it'd collapse, but then the massive ugly black shape of the gun, suspended beneath its webbing of rope, wobbled free of the tower. A group of men under Morgan pulled on another line and the cannon swung away from the stone. The gun began to rock wildly back and forth like a clock's pendulum. 'Steady, you lubbers! Steady!' Jenkins roared. Ropes shifted, the swing promptly died away and soon the gun was only twisting gently in the breeze. Inch by painful inch, they lowered the cannon down until it settled with a dull thump on the bed of shorn tree trunks they meant to roll it down to the harbour on.

Once James had checked on the gun, he wandered down the hill towards Sophia and the baroness. His face was red, his hair damp and his plain white shirt was plastered to his chest with sweat.

'What did you think?' he called as he got close.

The baroness clapped. 'Very impressive, Captain. I was sure someone would end up crushed.'

'Crushed? No, that was a piece of cake.' His somewhat relieved and utterly smug smile suggested it was anything but.

'Nothing compared to Garenburg?' the baroness asked.

'You're familiar with the siege, Baroness?'

'No, Sophia was just telling me all about it.'

He glanced at her with a strange look on his face. 'Sophia was?'

'Not *all* about it, just what I read in the papers.' She could have kicked the old woman. 'Father likes to keep abreast of naval goings on.'

'Uriah? Yes, I suppose he would.' He smiled up at them, but this time the smile didn't quite reach his eyes. 'I should get back to work. Baroness. Sophia.' He bowed and then turned and jogged back up the hill.

'Good-looking devil,' the baroness remarked once he was out of earshot.
'What? James?'

The baroness smiled at her. 'You don't think so?'

'Oh, I've known him since we were little. And he's not my type.'

'Little?'

'His parents live in Oldfort and when James had his first shore leave in Stormhaven he didn't know anyone, so Mother and Father invited him to stay with us. After that it became a bit of a ritual, until he went south, anyway.'

'Well, childhood friend or not, I think you're very wise to pay him no heed. I'm sure handsome war heroes are thoroughly overrated.' The baroness shifted in her seat. 'I think all the excitement is over, Claude. Can you please take us home?' she called back over her shoulder.

'Ma'am.' The driver flicked his reins and the carriage lurched forward.

They passed the trip back down the hill in silence. When the carriage had rolled to a stop on the sweeping gravel driveway, the baroness motioned for Sophia to follow her. 'We'll sit on the new terrace. That way we'll be able to watch your sailors manhandle your gun down the hill.' The old woman led Sophia through the enormous manor and out onto a broad, sunlit terrace Sophia hadn't even seen before.

'We'll take champagne, thank you, Martin,' the baroness told one of the ever-present liveried servants. When the baroness had discovered Sophia's cabin was being rearranged to house the great gun, she had bullied and nagged Sophia into staying with her at the manor. Despite her initial reservations, Sophia had come to enjoy their fortnight of long evenings together chatting and playing cards. The old lady may have been revoltingly wealthy, but she was also kind, intelligent and a born raconteur. The manor house was also distinctly more comfortable and quiet than the *Game Bird*.

The drinks soon appeared, condensation glistening on the crystal glasses. Ice houses were becoming increasingly common in Stormhaven, but Sophia still hadn't got completely used to the baroness' ability to have her servants produce chilled drinks at all hours of the day and night.

They passed the middle of the day very pleasantly. The sun was warm and Sophia's glass was refilled more often than she strictly needed. The baroness was amusing as always and in the distance they had the spectacle of the men labouring to manoeuvre the gun safely down the hill to entertain them.

By the time the *Game Birds* and their gun had disappeared from view behind the houses of Waterford it was almost dusk and Sophia was feeling quite tipsy. She should have been more careful; the baroness was a dangerous woman to share a drink with. Standing up, she walked back and forth beside the lichen-covered stone parapet in an effort to sober herself up a little. On her third or fifth turn, something about the design of the windows above her caught her eye and she turned to the baroness. 'This looks a bit different.' She gestured at the manor with her glass. 'This part of the house.'

'Yes, this wing isn't original.'

'Not Grainger?'

'No.'

'But Grainger's famous, why alter his work?'

'We had no choice, unfortunately. My great uncle was tainted. He was a vile man, able to compel people to do as he wished.'

'Against their will?'

'Yes. He liked to spend his time dominat—' Even the baroness blushed at that. 'Let us just say he liked pretty chambermaids, especially *compliant* chambermaids. Eventually he started liking them a little too often and his taint drove him insane. He destroyed a good chunk of the house in his madness. Thankfully the gamekeeper at the time shot him before he could reduce the entire edifice to pebbles and twist all the servants into mindless thralls.'

The mixture of champagne and the sheer unexpected horror of the story almost caught Sophia with her guard down. But she forced herself to smile, sit down and make a few efforts at insipid conversation. Once she thought she wouldn't cause any offence she made her excuse and stood up.

'My admission of a tainted blood hasn't frightened you off, has it, Sophia?'

'Not at all. My mother and father raised me to treat the tainted as normal men and women.' She forced herself to smile. 'But I do need to check on how things are going with the *Game Bird*.'

'Well, make sure you have a sailor walk you back up the hill tonight. I won't have you sleeping on that cramped little ship.'

'I will.' Sophia waved goodbye and then walked down the steps, across the manicured gardens and through the gate in the high wall around the manor. The fields beyond the wall were quiet. The tenants and copyholders had returned to their cottages for the evening and only the twittering of the small birds in the ancient hedges and the smoke curling from the chimneys of Waterford showed that the world was still inhabited.

'Thankfully the gamekeeper shot him...' The baroness' words continued to rattle through Sophia's head. The old lady had spoken about her relative's death in the same kind of way a yeoman might describe having to shoot a neighbour's rabid dog. The old woman was cosmopolitan and open-minded, indeed she'd spent her youth in the capital fraternising with actors, sodomites, writers and whores, and still counted many of that rakish set her friends but, even to her, tainted were still the other. The beast.

The worst thing was that Sophia couldn't really be angry at the baroness. The tainted were dangerous. She was dangerous. Genuinely, horrifically dangerous.

She was so lost in her gloomy reverie she hardly noticed when the fields and lanes gave way to the streets and houses of Waterford.

'Make a lane there, Miss Blake!'

A group of half a dozen *Game Birds,* led by Jenkins, were rolling a load of laden kegs and barrels down the hill. She stepped out of their way. 'I thought all the supplies were already aboard, Jenkins?' she asked as they passed.

'They are, miss.' Unlike the other sailors, the boatswain was carrying two barrels, one over each huge shoulder. 'These are for the party.'

'Party?'

Giuseppe put his barrel down carefully and grinned up at her like a madman. 'You know, the big revel. We are so grateful. So excited!'

Jenkins nodded. 'Tomorrow's dance or what have you, after the match.'

She frowned. 'Dance, match? I've still no idea what you're talking about.'

'Oh.' Jenkins cleared his throat nervously. 'Perhaps you should go and see the captain. He's just up at the brewery sorting the rest of the order.'

'There's more?'

Jenkins gulped. 'Quite a bit more.'

'Bloody mounds of the stuff,' Simon said morosely. 'I didn't join the navy to stuff about hauling bloody food and grog up hill and down dale all day. You'd think we were servants.'

'Thank you, gentlemen.' Sophia took a very deep breath and then stalked off in the direction Jenkins had indicated and soon found James. He was standing outside the brewery, deep in conversation with a short, bald and red-faced man she assumed must be the brewer.

James grinned when he saw her. 'What a day! Morgan's done a really capital job and the gun's snug aboard in her carriage. With a bit of luck we'll be at sea within the week.'

'Good.' She nodded a curt greeting to the brewer. 'And when were you going to tell me about all this?'

'All this?'

'This dance.'

He blinked. 'I asked the baroness' permission to use the village green. I just assumed she would have…'

A powerful mixture of champagne-fuelled anger coursed through her. 'You just assumed.'

'I did.'

The brewer coughed nervously. 'It's past my dinner time, Captain, I should be getting home to the wife. You have any more questions, just send a man up to my house.' Without waiting for a reply, the man fled inside and slammed the heavy door of the brewery behind him.

'So how much is this all going to cost?' she asked once they were alone in the street.

'Just the beer and cider?'

'What? There's more?'

'Well, of course. There's food too.' James shifted from foot to foot. 'And some musicians. Oh, and some wine.'

She almost choked. 'Just how much is this little party going to set my father back?'

'I doubt it will come to more than sixty crowns.'

'Sixty crowns!'

He spread his hands innocently. 'It's to thank the villagers and the crew for all their hard work. And to cheer the lads up before we go to sea. After all, *Game Bird's* not a man of war and the fitting out has been damned hard work for the hands not used to our navy ways.'

'This is my father's money!'

'And I'm the captain.'

'James!'

'You saved us so much money I thought…'

You didn't think at all, James.' A vein pulsed on the side of her head. 'I'm meant to be your partner in this. You can't just use me for the jobs you hate and then run off and do all the fun things.'

'It's not like that.'

'It's exactly bloody like that.'

'Calm down, Sophia.'

'Calm down? Calm down while you waste a fortune on some dance? I want you to cancel it. Right now.'

He blinked. 'What? I've already told the crew.'

'Cancel it.'

'I'll be humiliated.'

'You should have thought of that before.'

'I won't.' He set his jaw. 'You can cancel it if you feel that strongly.'

'Coward.'

'Coward?' His eyes widened. 'How dare you.'

'How dare I? I'm not the one throwing away someone else's hard-earned money on frivolities!'

'Sophia, I…' She didn't wait to hear what he had to say. She knew her temper well enough to realise she was very close to making some choice remarks she'd never be able to take back, so she turned her back on him and walked briskly back up the hill and into the darkened fields. He called out after her, but she pretended she hadn't heard him.

Back at the manor Sophia found the baroness reading in her study. She let herself in and threw herself down on an overstuffed chaise longue with enough force to make the hunting scenes and landscapes that festooned the green painted walls rattle.

The baroness shut her book. 'Something's wrong with the ship?'

'No. The stupid ship's fine.'

'What then?'

'Nothing.'

The baroness sighed. 'Sophia.'

'Did you know about this dance tomorrow?'

'Of course. Captain Faulkner asked my permission to use the green.' Baroness Whitelocke put her book down on her writing table. 'I take it he neglected to mention it to you.'

Sophia blinked back her traitorous tears and nodded. She suddenly felt almost exhausted. It must have been the champagne and the day's sun.

'Ah.'

'He said he assumed you would have told me.'

'I suppose I should have. But as you are down at the ship every day, I figured he would have spoken to you already.'

'He should have.'

'Agreed. I take it you had a disagreement?'

'I told him to cancel the stupid thing.'

'Ah.'

'Ah?'

'He can't do that.'

'Why not? He organised it.'

'Captains must maintain a certain aura of dignity and authority. I don't feel cancelling this, ah, treat he has organised for his crew would be wise.'

'You sound like you think it is a good idea!'

The baroness nodded. 'I do.'

'What? Sixty crowns wasted on a party is a good idea?'

'Sophia dear, your annoyance at Captain Faulkner's rather high-handed conduct is completely understandable, but don't let it cloud your judgement. Ultimately, he has to take an untried crew to sea in a little ship to hunt a sea monster that quite literally eats ships for its breakfast. If he feels he needs to raise their spirits, he's probably right.'

'But sixty crowns for a feast!'

'Sixty crowns is nothing if it will help him knit his crew together.'

Sophia lay back on the longue and flicked an errant strand of hair out of her face. Unfortunately the baroness was right. 'So what should I do then?'

'Three things.' The baroness raised a plump finger. 'Firstly, let this party go ahead. You're far too pretty to cut off your nose to spite your face.' She raised a second finger. 'Secondly, be sure to make him very aware that he has done the wrong thing.'

Sophia snorted. 'I think I've already managed that. What was the third thing?'

'Don't be too hard on yourself. Sea captains are all far too used to playing god, so the fact you've forced any concessions out of him is a miracle.'

They crested the rise above Waterford and looked down on the village green.

'If I'd known there was going to be cricket involved I really would have made him cancel his silly party,' Sophia said.

The day had dawned clear, blue and breezy, although a towering mass of white clouds marched along the eastern horizon. The village green was nestled in a sheltered dell on the landward side of Waterford. A crowd of villagers were already gathered around the tables and sailcloth tents that the *Game Birds* had set up under the tall elms that lined the edge of the open space. The cricketers were clustered together in the middle of the green and still seemed to be in the process of setting up their game.

'You don't like cricket, Sophia?' the baroness asked.

'You do?'

'Of course. My brother and I were raised on it.'

Even the thought of cricket had intensified the slight headache yesterday's champagne had gifted her. 'I've no idea what you see in it.'

'It's sacrifice and duty.'

Sophia laughed despite herself. 'That's why I avoid it!'

'It is an acquired taste.' The old woman smiled. 'Now help me down the path. We can't lurk up here all day.'

Sophia had to grudgingly admit James appeared to have done a good job of arranging things. Tables were already laden with pastries, cakes, apples and drink, and a hay cart had been dragooned into service to bring lunch down from the village when it was ready. The crowd was in a jovial mood (the ladies in their finest dresses and the men in their church-going best) and the baroness received an almost rapturous welcome. She waved her reception away with a grin and found them the two wicker chairs her servants had set up in the shade with a good view of the field.

They had only just sat down when de Lacey came wandering in out of the sun. 'Sophia,' he called with a smile and a wave. He then bowed and kissed the baroness' cheek. 'Auntie.'

'What are the teams?' the baroness asked as soon as she had worked her way through the minimum of pleasantries.

'*Game Birds* against the Waterford Eleven.'

'And you're batting first?' she asked.

He nodded.

'Who's opening?'

'Captain Faulkner and Jenkins, our boatswain.'

'He's good, is he?' Sophia asked, curiosity getting the better of her.

'Faulkner?' de Lacey asked. 'Oh yes, he's devastating at his best. Though he's in a high dudgeon today for some reason, so we shall see.'

The match got under way only minutes later. James blocked the first three balls he faced. It was obvious he was unhappy with this inactivity and as the bowler walked back to his mark each time, James paced back and forth in front of his wicket like a particularly belligerent bull. The fourth ball was a rising bouncer that reared up at James off the pitch and he hacked at it with an ugly flourish. The ball only caught the edge of his bat and it lobbed high up into the air and then down to one of the Waterford fielders for an easy catch. The villagers cheered.

'One for none.' De Lacey sighed and picked up his bat. 'See you soon.'

James stalked off the pitch, looking about as pleased as a king who had just been told his barons were in open rebellion. His course took him past where they were sitting.

'A rather unorthodox hook, Captain Faulkner,' the baroness called out to him when he was close.

He turned towards them, blinking as his eyes adjusted to the shade under the trees. 'Unorthodox? It was bloody stu—' He collected himself. 'It was an ill-advised shot, Baroness.'

'I'm sure you have much on your mind,' the baroness said, perhaps a little archly. 'Now, will you stay and keep us company for a while?'

James' gaze flicked from the baroness to Sophia and his eyes narrowed for a fraction of a second. 'No, I'd better not. I should go and check on our lunch arrangements. If the rest of my team is as pitiful as I was, we'll be out in the field shortly.'

The rest of the *Game Birds* were far from pitiful. Jenkins took to the bowling with the same kind of gusto some of the more rotund villagers had taken to the treats on offer, and on more than one occasion the crowd had to scatter as the huge boatswain sent a ball careening through the branches above their heads. De Lacey wasn't as brutal as Jenkins, but his more elegant flicks and jabs still sent ball after ball bouncing away between the fielders and across the freshly cut grass. Sophia soon lost interest. Thankfully the warm spring day and the dappled sun sneaking its way down through the foliage was soothing and she leant back in her chair and closed her eyes. For a long time she drifted along half asleep and half-heartedly listening to the crack of leather on willow, the cheers of the players and the steady stream of locals who approached the baroness with problems, requests, favours and gossip. After the unpleasantness of the night before, it was so peaceful she was a little disappointed when a bell rang for lunch.

The meal James had arranged was a simple country affair of cold roast beef, pickles, cheese and a selection of vegetables. Walking away from the table after she had been served by an even sourer than usual Donald, she spotted de Lacey picking at a rather small plate of food and walked over to stand with him. 'What happened?' she asked.

'Weren't you watching?'

'I may have closed my eyes for a moment.'

The young lord shook his head and grinned at her. 'And you call your-self a Realmswoman. We made a hundred and sixty-one. A decent score on that somewhat agricultural pitch.'

'How did you do?'

'Me? Oh, not too bad. Made forty-three.'

'Did you win?'

'What? Win? We haven't even fielded yet.'

She was aghast. 'There's more?'

'De Lacey!' James suddenly roared in a sea-going voice from somewhere close by. 'De Lacey!'

'Here!'

James picked his way through the press to reach them. 'Come on, we're back on. You can finish gossiping once the match is over.' Without waiting for a reply he marched off.

De Lacey handed her his plate and rolled his eyes. 'The captain is obviously enjoying his party.'

The afternoon sun rolled sluggishly through the high blue sky. The men ran to and fro across the green, balls were hit here and there and batsmen came and went. From what Sophia saw, James seemed to enjoy this spell in the middle. When he was fielding he lurked close to the bat, eager and hungry and he bowled spitefully fast when it was his turn with the ball. The end of the game came quite suddenly when he knocked the last two batsmen's stumps over with consecutive balls.

The baroness took Sophia's hand firmly and led her out to meet the two teams. 'Your batting might have left something to be desired, Captain Faulkner, but your bowling was superb!' the old woman called out to him.

'Hardly superb.' His mood must have improved because he grinned. 'I had a bumping pitch and a good team on my side.'

'I am not convinced. But enough about cricket, I'm sure Sophia is heartily sick of it by now. Is everything in hand with dinner?'

'Yes, Donald will have things under control.'

'Would he like help? I could lend you some of my people.'

James shifted awkwardly. 'No, no, I think he will manage. He has some *Game Birds* helping him.'

'Are you sure? He is feeding quite a horde.'

'No, I imagine he'll be fine.'

Sophia rolled her eyes. 'Baroness, what Captain Faulkner is trying to avoid saying is that his servant Donald is the bossiest and most cross-grained man ever born and is exceedingly unlikely to desire or even accept any help.'

'Thank you, Sophia, I always appreciate your honesty.' He smiled an exceedingly thin smile in her direction. 'Now, if you would excuse me, I must go and get changed before dinner.'

As night fell and the smell of cooking began to waft through the air, two huge bonfires were lit and dozens of lanterns were hung from the lower branches of the trees. The lights also seemed to attract Waterford's wealthier residents who came up from the village in a procession of carriages and carts. The arrival of these worthies demanded the baroness' attention and Sophia suddenly found herself quite abandoned. Once or twice she drifted slowly past a group of village girls or boys but they made no effort to welcome her.

Perhaps put off by her city clothes or maybe, she thought as her melancholy deepened, they felt some faint and unidentifiable revulsion at the presence of her taint. For what seemed like an hour she drifted around the party, doing her best to look anything other than forlorn and aimless. She had always thought being alone at a party was the loneliest thing.

Finally she came upon Donald, Patrick and Simon sitting down with their backs against a hay bale, tankards of ale in hand.

'You did a good job with the food, Donald,' she said as she got close.

He shook his head. 'Bah, it was nothin'. A fine lady like you should have better than those poor country scraps.'

'No, it was lovely.'

'Lovely? I told Faulkner we needed some pheasant or a nice swan to lift the occasion. But would he listen? Of course not. Never does.'

'Stop your whingeing.' Simon took a long swig from his tankard. 'The young miss is right, it was a good cook up.' He must have already had a few tankards, Sophia thought. It was the first nice thing she'd heard out of Simon's lips.

'Delicious!' Patrick agreed with a wide grin.

Donald finished his beer. 'You, miss, are just bein' nice. And as for these two poor sailors, why Simon couldn't tell boot leather from venison and Isaladar knows what spices and such Black Patrick was raised on.'

'Reckon I've had more venison than a soft Stormhaven man like you,' Simon scoffed.

Patrick rolled his eyes. 'More drinking, less arguing.' He reached behind the hay bale for a small keg and topped up their tankards. Once he had finished he looked up at her. 'And how have you found putting up with us sailors, miss? Not too rough?'

She grinned. 'Rough? It's been fun.'

They chatted on for a time about the party and the ship until Donald dragged Patrick and an irate Simon off to help with the clean up and Sophia drifted through the party alone again.

When the musicians started up by the flickering light of one of the fires, she was thankful for the distraction and wandered over to watch the few revellers who had already begun to dance. She had hardly arrived when she caught sight of James among the dancers. He had changed into his full uniform of white breeches, black boots and a fine blue coat with gold embroidery. The heavy epaulettes of a post captain adorned each of his shoulders and his medals and sword glinted red in the firelight. Annoyingly, he looked extremely impressive. Even worse, the traitor was dancing with some busty village wench. She watched as he laughed and leant forward to whisper something in the slattern's ear. He looked like he didn't have a single care in the world. He could, of course, dance with whomever he pleased, but the way he was obviously completely unmoved by their argument and the dismissive way he had treated her all day was more than she could stand. The temerity of the man! His manners would suit some simple country girl perfectly.

Gritting her teeth she turned and walked away. It was a boring party anyway. She'd plead a headache and get a servant to walk her back up to the manor. She soon found the baroness sitting down at a table under one of the great trees. Unfortunately, the old woman was still mobbed by a grasping gaggle of locals and, try as she might, Sophia couldn't catch the old lady's eye. Giving up, she leant back against the rough bark of a gnarled tree trunk and waited. After a while a group of finely dressed men and women came and stood near her. It took her a moment to realise that they hadn't seen her shrouded in the shadows.

'It's all most irregular,' a middle-aged man complained.

'Most irregular.' The speaker shook his head and Sophia saw with a spark of annoyance it was Mr Douglas, the chandler who had refused to serve her. 'A captain playing games with his men. No wonder they say the modern navy is going to the dogs.'

'And his men are still here.' The plump woman cast a horrified look back towards the bonfires. 'And they're drinking.'

'Common tars marauding about our pretty little town.' The first speaker straightened his red cravat and then patted at a crease in his vest. 'This is not Stormhaven! Has the man no decency?'

Douglas snorted. 'From what I have seen, Captain Faulkner has neither decency nor sense. Did you know he sent a woman, a girl, to my shop to organise his victuals?'

'No!'

Sophia dug her fingernails into the bark behind her and willed herself to behave. She was Baroness Whitelocke's guest after all.

'Oh yes. A mere slip of a girl and she had a positively scandalous amount of flesh showing. I tried my best to help her, but she was quite impossible to deal with. Very rude and quite high-strung.'

'Like all her generation, husband,' one of the women ventured.

Mr Douglas ignored her. 'Once it was clear she wasn't willing to pay for our quality, I recommend she go back to you at Bear and Green, but I understand she eventually settled on Archers.' He snorted at the very thought. *'Archers.'*

'I've never heard anything so preposterous.' The first merchant, Bear or Green, shook his head. 'From what I've read of Faulkner's wartime service, you'd have thought he'd have the sense to put the girl in her place.'

'She is a belligerent young thing,' Douglas replied. 'Perhaps it's courage not sense he lacks.'

That was too much for Sophia. She pushed off the tree trunk and barged into their circle. 'What would you lot know of courage?'

They turned to stare at her, their faces a perfect mixture of surprise and irritation.

'Oh, I'd hazard they know plenty of courage, Sophia.' She wasn't really sure where he had come from or how long he had been listening but James was suddenly beside her. His face, its features cut harshly by the torchlight, was like a thundercloud and his hand was resting on the pommel of his sword. 'Take Mr Green here – he has courage to try to sell frayed rope and rotten biscuits to his customers.'

The man spluttered. 'How dare you?'

James smiled down at him. 'As a mere customer commenting on goods purchased, I dare very easily. And look, here is Mr Douglas. He too is a courageous man.' James turned to face Mrs Douglas. 'Your husband had the courage to follow his strong moral compass. He was so sure, so utterly confident, that it was wrong to do business with a woman that he passed up a five thousand crown contract.' He held out a hand in gesture of placation. 'Yes, five thousand crowns were forgone, but he stayed true to his belief that a woman's place is in the home! It was five thousand crowns wasn't it, Sophia?'

'It was 4,889 crowns, four plums and three nails.'

James shook his head ruefully. 'True courage.'

Mrs Douglas made a retching sound and clutched at her throat.

James bowed to the circle. 'I would stay and discuss courage at greater length, but I am a vain man and I thoroughly detest being surrounded by my betters.' He took Sophia's hand and the hardness of his grip surprised her. 'Would you dance with me, Sophia?' he asked.

'Of course.'

He led her back through the throng towards the fires.

'I don't need protecting, James,' she said.

'No, having been on the receiving end of some of your reprimands, I don't think you do.' He squeezed her hand. 'But after my little oversight I thought it was the least I could do.'

'Your little oversight?'

'With the party.'

'Your *little* oversight?'

'All right, my large mistake.' He stopped, turned to face her, and took her other hand. 'I seem to say this to you a lot, but I was an idiot and I'm deeply sorry. I've always been a fool with money. Forgive me?'

'I do. As long as you don't do it again.'

'I won't. You've done a brilliant job organising everything so far and I had no right to rush off without consulting you.'

'No you did not, but you're still forgiven. We'll talk of it no more.' Behind him the musicians struck up the lively traveller's tune, 'Bride of Ravenmark'. 'Do you know this piece, James?'

'I do, but be warned I am an awful dancer. I wallow about like a becalmed first rate in a decent swell.'

He placed a hand on her hip and they whirled out to join the other dancers. James certainly wasn't a natural, but at least he was happy to lead.

'Who was the pretty girl you were dancing with earlier?' she asked.

'The girl?'

'Yes, James, the girl you were dancing with. About ten minutes ago.'

'Oh, that girl! That was Sarah Henslowe. She was just telling me that her uncle was the master on *Indomitable*. Knew him quite well. Why do you ask?'

They swayed around a slower-moving couple. 'Just curious.'

'Hmm.' He held her gaze and a strange thrill ran through her. She glanced away. His coat smelled of the sea and of him. 'Other than the few times I've been worried you might murder me, I've really enjoyed having you along, Sophia. It almost feels like old times again,' he said softly.

'It has been fun, hasn't it?'

'It has. You know...' He paused for a long, long moment and they danced on in silence. 'I don't think I realised how much I missed you while I was away.'

Against her better judgement she looked back up and her heart leapt in her chest. Surely he wasn't..? He leant forward a little. She closed her eyes and pursed her lips. A tingle of excitement flowed through her.

'Gaaargh!' someone shrieked, and James almost lurched out of her arms.

Behind them a portly matron was rubbing her shin while her partner supported her. 'That sword of yours just gouged me most cruelly,' the woman wailed.

'I am so terribly sorry. I crash the stupid bloody thing into people whenever I wear it. Oh, Isaladar wept, you're bleeding.' James fumbled in one of his pockets. 'Take my handkerchief. I am mortified. Here, if you'll just let me...'

Directly above them a dazzling flash of lightning suddenly split the night, followed quickly by a great crack of thunder and the first heavy drops of rain.

As the dancers scurried for the cover of the elms, Sophia glared skyward accusingly.

17.

A WEEK LATER and with *Game Bird* almost ready for sea, Faulkner, Sophia, de Lacey, Morgan and Jenkins gathered in the *Game Bird's* freshly painted wardroom for dinner. Donald had prepared a fine suckling pig and to wash it down de Lacey had, from his seemingly bottomless supply, produced a few bottles of fine Mandor claret. The dinner whirled past in the usual procession of progressively more and more unlikely stories and anecdotes. However, as the plates were cleared, they got down to business. Moving aside the wine glasses, Faulkner rolled out a large chart he had prepared and then held it in place with empty bottles and his heavy notebook.

'The Bastion Islands?' Sophia asked.

Faulkner nodded.

'Your chart looks like it has caught a bad case of the pox, Faulkner,' de Lacey observed.

'Each of those red marks, as well as I could position them from newspaper articles and such, indicates where the leviathan is known to have sunk a ship. The notes next to each mark are the ship's name, type and the approximate date when she was sunk,' he replied.

While the others all leant forward to study the map, Faulkner read back over the few notes closest to where he stood.

Cormorant – whaler – 13/3

Lady Eliza – mail packet – 27/2

Amalfi – southerner – 7/3

City of Farron – brig – ??

Möwe – ship rigged bark – 29/1

Dolphin – brig – 23/1

As he read each simple little note it was hard not to picture the last moments of each ship's crew as the beast tore their vessel apart. When he had first heard about the reward for the leviathan, he had struggled to imagine how the merchants and brokers could afford to offer the princely sum of 100,000 crowns for its death. But now, as he stared down at his chart, it was obvious. The beast had already killed hundreds of sailors and sent millions of crowns worth of shipping to the bottom. Even without taking the wider disruption to trade into account, the grasping insurance houses would consider 100,000 crowns very well spent if it did away with this terror.

He refilled his glass and gave the others time to study the chart. 'At my last count I had listed almost two score ships sunk by the leviathan. Based on the rate of attacks to date, I assume it has attacked again since we left Stormhaven and also that other ships went down with all hands so we have no records of their loss.'

Morgan scratched at his grey beard. 'Does it sink every bloody ship it attacks?'

'Just about. One or two have managed to either limp into port or beach themselves.'

De Lacey moved his glass to get a better view of the map. 'And none of our ships have even seen it?'

Faulkner nodded. By 'our ships' de Lacey was, of course, referring to the navy. 'Correct. Since the peace we've had half the warships of the Eastern Fleet combing the islands and they haven't seen so much as a scale on the thing's back.' He paused and weighed up whether he should proceed. 'I've been wondering if it can recognise a warship enough to avoid it.'

'What? Surely not?' said Morgan.

'I think the numbers speak for themselves. More than three vessels are being sunk each week and yet we've had twenty men of war scouring the islands for sixty days and they haven't seen a sausage.'

De Lacey shrugged. 'Crows learn to pick out the man with a musket. I suppose a leviathan could learn to spot a man of war.'

Sophia clicked her fingers. 'So that's why we've bought such a small ship and enormous gun!'

'Exactly. We can play the innocent lamb, lure it to the surface and then hopefully show the beast that our bite is worse than our bark.'

Morgan frowned. 'Does it always attack on the surface, though?'

'It does.' Faulkner picked up his notebook and flicked through it. 'Or at least, all the survivors' accounts are the same – the leviathan attacks along the surface from astern, sinking each ship with one or two blows that cave in the stern.'

'Well, I suppose when we sail south we better keep that big gun loaded then,' observed Jenkins.

Once Donald had cleared the dinner away and a sailor had been sent to walk Sophia back up the hill, Faulkner and de Lacey stood together at the taffrail, looking out over the dark water. De Lacey took a deep pull from his cigar and its spark illuminated his face. 'Morgan was a little twitchy, but Jenkins was unworried,' he said.

'I could tell Jenkins I planned to sail the ship directly to hell and he'd only ask if he was likely to meet any doxys down there. Morgan we'll just have to be careful with. He's no coward, but he detests the unusual.'

'What about the crew? Do you think they'll bear up?'

Faulkner shrugged. 'The men we poached from the fleet should be right enough. The merchantmen we will have to look after; it's one thing to sign on to hunt a sea monster in the warmth of a tavern with a belly full of beer, it's quite another when the beast is lurking somewhere under the futtocks planning your murder.'

De Lacey nodded. 'On the subject of our oversized bloody fish, I finally got our reply from Baron Elphinstone. Came by pegasus in today's mail.'

'What did that most eminent man say?'

'Nothing particularly useful, unfortunately, but fetch that lantern and I'll give you the summary.' De Lacey took the letter out of his coat and unfolded it. He cleared his throat and then began.

'"*Dear Lord de Lacey,*

'"*Let me say I was most flattered to receive your letter. I believe that the Royal Zoological Society has a very great debt to the men of the Royal Navy. I, for one, will never forget the help your service provided me during my great voyages to the south to observe the blue-toothed basilisk...*" He rambles on a bit here, James. Although he also writes some very pretty words about our little action with the *Agrippa* that you might like to read at your leisure. Ah! Here is the more pertinent part.

"'Although I am no expert on matters marine, I have consulted my more learned colleagues and attempted to answer your questions as best I can. You asked if a leviathan has ever before been recorded attacking shipping before. The consensus among my colleagues is 'no'. Our records hold scores of accounts of ships attacked by kraken or sea serpents and even occasionally by whales, but none describing leviathan attacks."

'Our professor has kindly added *"Or perhaps no previous survivors?"* in red ink in the margin there,' added de Lacey with a thin smile.

"'Our library has only has a few records of the leviathan's appearance. The best comes from Eumenes of Datria. During his travels to Imperial Iperus in the year 274 he was taken to see the corpse of a leviathan that had washed up on a beach. He writes, and I quote here: 'the great beast looks much like a deep sea fish, but was perhaps half again as big as the largest whale I have observed. It is protected by thick mottled scales and its mouth is lined with banks of shark-like fangs. My guide tells me even sea dragons do not hunt these beasts. Looking at its savage appearance I had no reason to doubt him. My man Lysander also demonstrated the toughness of its hide. His spear, thrown from only a few paces, left no mark on the leviathan's scales. When I asked him how the local men had the courage to go to sea knowing this beast was beneath them, he only laughed. 'The leviathan does not bother men,' he said, 'it lurks in the silent depths hunting other monsters.'"

'And that's about it, at least in terms of anything that may be of use to us.' De Lacey handed the letter to him.

'That doesn't help much.'

'It doesn't, no.'

Faulkner folded the letter and slid it into his coat pocket. 'Something just doesn't feel right about this leviathan, does it? How has one never, ever preyed on ships before? Men have sailed these waters in one form or another for at least three thousand years.'

De Lacey shrugged, stubbed out his cigar on the rail and lit another. 'Perhaps it is lame or hurt? When I was a lad I read the biography of an army officer who served in the colonies and he claimed many of the tigers or manticores that become man-eaters are lame and they only attack villagers because they can't catch their usual prey.'

'I hope you're right.'

They stood in silence for a long moment.

'Do you really think we can we kill this thing?' de Lacey asked at last.

Faulkner shrugged. 'It'll be touch and go. That's if we even manage to find it.'

'High stakes for touch and go.'

'I'd understand if you didn't come with us.'

'Didn't come?' De Lacey let out a snort that ended in a series of hacking coughs. 'What else would I do? Go slowly insane with boredom at staid dinner parties until someone starts another little war for us to amuse ourselves with?'

Faulkner knelt down on the deck and forced his hand as far into the pile of neatly folded canvas as he could. He had known more than one captain who had pulled out his spare sail canvas only to find it completely rotten away with mildew. Thankfully his set was dry, all the way to his fingertips.

'All shipshape, sir?' Jenkins asked.

'Bone-dry, thank you, Boatswain.' Faulkner stood and then rattled the heavy locks on the nearby storeroom doors. They were locked nice and fast to stop any pilfering. Walking back across the deck he ran a hand down the whitewashing on the hull. The mixture of ground chalk and glue was smooth and firm to the touch and he nodded in satisfaction. 'Mess deck now.'

Their first stop on the mess deck was the fire hearth, which Donald had predictably polished until it shone. The stores that would be consumed first were also stowed away neatly. The only disappointment on the entire deck was a mess of personal possessions scattered about one sailor's sea chest. 'See that stowed.'

Anger flashed in Jenkins' eyes and he turned to a group of sailors carrying some last supplies below. 'Whose bloody mess is this?' he roared at them.

'Nagel's,' said one of them.

'Find him. And get him to clean his scraps up. I'm not his fucking nursemaid.' The men dashed off to find the offending Nagel and Jenkins turned back to Faulkner. 'Sorry, Captain.'

'It's always tricky with a new crew. Just make sure you keep at them.' He nodded towards the ladder leading up to the weather deck. 'Now let's have a last look around above.'

Back out in the bright sunlight, Faulkner walked the freshly scrubbed deck and smiled. The *Game Bird* didn't yet boast the gleaming sparkle he had expected on the *Inflexible*, but she was already far more shipshape than most merchantmen. He paced the weather deck one last time, checking the little things that were often easy for a crew to miss.

They were ready. He took a deep breath. He was normally in a mad rush to get to sea, but now he was strangely reluctant to leave. It had been such a nice couple of weeks in Waterford. But it was hardly as if he would never see Sophia again – of course he would write during the voyage and could call on her as soon as they got back from the hunt. With a quiet snort at his own foolishness, he turned back to Jenkins who had been following a half-pace behind him. 'You and Morgan have done a really superb job with the repair, Boatswain. We'll sail this next tide. Send a man ashore to fetch Sophia. I imagine she would like to see us bless the ship and say her goodbyes.'

Jenkins disappeared to see to his request and a rather tired and red-faced de Lacey took the boatswain's place at his side. The young lord saluted. 'A fellow has arrived from Stormhaven. Walked all the way to join us.'

'One of our old crew?'

'Never seen him before.'

'Strange.' Could the fellow be a particularly enterprising bailiff? He doubted it; even with his mountainous debts he doubted any bailiff would be brave enough to come aboard, not with his entire crew only a shout away. 'I'd be a poor scrub not to give him the time of day if he really has walked all that way. I'll see him in what passes for the great cabin. And go and have a drink, de Lacey, you look like you're about to expire.'

The great cabin had never been very large, but now that the huge gun had been rigged to fire out the stern, thus dividing the cabin in half, it was tiny. The other side had been given over to Sophia as a kind of sitting room, although that would be reclaimed once they'd put to sea.

His visitor was a severe-looking fellow of about fifty. His clothes were dour and, if his thick, wiry beard was anything to go by, Faulkner figured he belonged to the Orthodox Church. Not that he minded: despite their difficult reputation, he had always thought they made for good crew, particularly as they often didn't drink.

'The name's Boscawen, Captain Faulkner. I need to join you,' the man said as soon as he had entered the cabin.

Faulkner raised an eyebrow. 'You *need* to?'

'I've a score to settle with that leviathan and I hear you mean to hunt the beast down.'

'I do.'

'Will you take me then?'

'I might. But I've already got a full crew and before I make any decision I'll hear your story, Boscawen.'

'My story?'

Faulkner nodded and sat down at his tiny desk. 'You said you had a score to settle?'

'Aye.'

'Well then, let's hear it.'

'My last berth was the whaler *Clermont,* out of Mandor. She was a good ship, with plenty of my cousins aboard.' Boscawen was clearly not a talkative man and the story came slowly out as if dragged painfully from him. 'We had been down south and it had been a lucky trip, our holds were full and we were thinking of the warmth of hearth and home. But the leviathan hit us off Dogwood Island, shook us like a dog shakes off water and brought down all the masts at once. Poor *Clermont* sank before we could even swing the boats out...' The man gulped as he recalled the terrible scene. 'In all my years I've never seen a boat founder so fast. But the beast wasn't content with that. It came back and swallowed the men swimming in the water one by one. I hung to a spar, said my prayers and waited for my end. But... but... for some reason it left me on my own amongst the wreckage.'

'You were the only survivor?'

'I was.'

'Well, I can see why you want to level your score with the leviathan then.' Faulkner considered the hard old sailor. The whaler would be useful hand, particularly as he had actually seen the leviathan. 'I can't turn you away then, can I, Boscawen? But you be careful telling that story to your mess mates. I don't want you putting the wind up the other men.'

They left Giovanni standing awkwardly in the splendour of Waterford

Manor's hallway and Sophia and the baroness retreated into the drawing room to say their farewells.

'Thank you, Lady Whitelocke, you have looked after me very kindly.' Sophia did her best to look happy, but the thought of the *Game Bird* sailing off into the great ocean without her lay on her chest like a great weight, heavy and cold.

'Don't be silly. It's been a pleasure. You've been good company, Sophia, and I don't get nearly enough good company out here in the counties.'

'Well, I'm still very grateful for your hospitality.'

'Pish posh. I'd never let you leave if I had my way.' The baroness smiled and picked up an ivory-handled letter opener. 'As you've been such a delightful guest, I will give you some advice before you go, however.'

'I… ah…'

'Shush, my dear. I may be old now, but I still remember what it was to be young.' She pointed the little blade at Sophia's heart. 'And your feelings are written plainly on your face.'

'My feelings?'

Baroness Whitelocke rolled her eyes theatrically. 'You're not stupid, Sophia, so don't pretend to be. Never let a chance like this slip away. I know Faulkner's type – they're far too gallant and not nearly interested enough in their own pleasures.'

'James? We're just frie—'

'Oh, do be quiet. You're no more friends than my husband and I were. Friends enjoy each other's company. You two young idiots swing between wanting to kill each other and never wanting to be apart. If you have half a heart and a bit of stomach you'll go away to sea with your ship.'

'What? Go with *Game Bird?*'

'Exactly.'

'I can't!'

The baroness sighed and rolled her eyes again. 'Why? I would have when I was your age. The Faulkners of the world are worth chasing.'

'My father said I wasn't to go to sea.'

'We all upset our parents, dear, that is half of growing up. You need to decide if Faulkner and a trip to sea are worth the fight with your father.'

Sophia turned and looked out the wide windows. In the distance the waters of the harbour flashed and glinted in the sun. Through the glare she could just make out the *Game Bird* lying at anchor among the local ships. All she had wanted was one adventure before she surrendered to the truth of her taint and a life cloistered away in some damp asylum. But they had got the ship ready so quickly. It felt as if only a few moments had passed since she left Stormhaven, not weeks. She wasn't ready to go home and face her taint and the revulsion that came with it. She deserved a little bit more joy before her life was ruined. Didn't she? She hadn't done anything to deserve the taint. 'But I can't go, I shouldn't!' Sophia said.

'Then you must admit that Captain Faulkner has escaped you. He will either disappear at sea or he will come back having killed this monster. And, if he does come back rolling in gold to go with the wartime fame, how long will it be before some precocious young noblewoman snaps him up?'

Tears pricked at Sophia's eyes and she blinked them away. 'It doesn't matter if I go to sea or not. James and I can't ever be together.'

'Nonsense, girl! Don't be such a wet blanket. Faulkner might be famous, but you come from a far better family. His father is only a teacher after all.'

She started to protest again but the baroness shushed her again. 'Don't make excuses, Sophia. Go to sea with him. Show him he would be lucky to have you! My family were once poor knights; I am just lucky that one of them had the stomach to go after what he wanted. You should do the same.'

The baroness' enthusiasm was infectious. That the old woman was unaware of her taint hardly mattered. It would still be amazing to go with the *Game Bird*. What a way to enjoy her last few weeks of freedom. It would be a true adventure. 'Maybe I could go with them...'

'Of course you can. Who is going to stop you?'

'James won't be happy.'

The baroness waved that away with an imperious gesture. 'In time, Sophia, you'll come to find that the men and women of this world that are worth having are not interested in those who make them happy. They're interested in those who keep them interested.'

Sophia took a deep breath. Her father would be shockingly worried when he found out she had gone to sea. But he'd be no happier to find out about her taint if she went home. Delaying the revelation of her taint could almost be seen as a kindness, couldn't it?

'You need to make your mind up, Sophia. We can't leave that poor sailor standing in the hall all day.'

The faintest sound of lark song drifted through the open window and Sophia turned back to the baroness. 'Can I borrow a pen and paper then? I suppose I should write to my father. He will be furious when he finds out, the poor man.'

By the time she had written her letter, walked down the hill, kissed the baroness goodbye half a dozen times, been rowed out to the *Game Bird* and then climbed aboard, all seventy of the crew were gathered together on the deck, murmuring to each other in excited whispers. James waved to her over the press of sailors and she walked astern to join him.

'Sophia,' he said, doffing his hat formally. 'I thought you might like to see the blessing.'

Feeling the eyes of the crew upon her, Sophia decided it wasn't the best time to announce her intention to go to sea with them.

'I would be delighted, Captain Faulkner.'

'Good, it would have been a pity just to throw you ashore without a proper farewell.' He turned to de Lacey. 'Are we ready?'

'We are.'

James stepped forward and raised his voice. 'Lads, I'll have your attention, please.'

The men fell silent.

'First I have to commend the effort you have all made this past fortnight. You have done very well fitting out *Game Bird*.' The men grinned and she saw the odd wink or grin exchanged between old friends. 'But our work has hardly begun. We still have this terrible fish to find and kill. Many of you have sailed with me before, or at least know my reputation. For those that don't, I flatter myself a hard but fair captain.' Faulkner stood in silence for a moment. 'I hope each of you has thought long and hard on the dangers this voyage will involve. You must make no mistake, this leviathan is a dangerous foe and I don't want any man with us whose heart is not in the venture. I won't ask you to embarrass yourself here before your mates, but if you have thought it over and decided you want out, see Mr Jenkins before we sail. They will give you coin and supplies enough to tide you over until you can find a safer berth.'

'We ain't scared, Captain. We'll smoke that beast good an' proper!' a sailor yelled.

Faulkner grinned. 'We will. Now, on the subject of coin, is every man clear on how the reward, should we win it, will be divided?'

The press of sailors muttered their understanding.

'Good.' James turned back to de Lacey. 'Perhaps Sophia would like to do the honours?'

De Lacey handed her a simple tin cup full of wine. 'Don't worry, I'll tell you what to do.'

James bowed his head and, seeing the sailors follow his lead, Sophia quickly did the same.

He cleared his throat and began.

'Isaladar, guard this ship.
You walked and died as a man,
You know our terror of the shade of death.
Isaladar, defend this ship,
Hold back the tireless anger of the great ocean,
Send us not down into the sea's cold embrace.
Isaladar, guide this ship,
Keep us in your hands when the wrathful deep grasps for us,
And shelter us until we are safe again ashore.'

Finished, he motioned to Sophia. 'Throw the wine over the lee side, Sophia.'

'Lee side?' she hissed.

'Left with this wind,' whispered de Lacey.

She threw the wine over the side and as it splashed into the water below, the crew let out a loud cheer.

James raised his hat. 'The voyage is blessed. Now Mr Morgan and Mr Jenkins, have the men stand to, we shall leave as soon as Miss Blake is safely put ashore.'

She took a deep breath. 'James, perhaps we should, ah, have a word in private.'

Their inventible fight wasn't pretty. They had discussed things for a little while and then argued reasonably for a time and then James had yelled that she couldn't come and she had yelled that she could. That had gone on for a time until Sophia had pointed out that, in the absence of her father, she owned the ship and would be taking it back if she couldn't come. That had rather taken the wind out of his sails and he had stormed out off in a huff.

Although Donald quickly arranged a cabin for her somehow, Sophia still wasn't able to sleep that first night at sea. In the still of the night, the tolling of the bell, the creaking of the timbers, the thump of bare feet on the deck and even the bleating of the goat all sounded deafeningly loud and funerary in tone. It was almost dawn when she fell asleep.

By the time she came up on deck, the sun was high in the sapphire sky and land had long ago melted away below the western horizon. With no one to speak to and nothing to do, she leant against the main mast and watched as *Game Bird* wove a bewildering course across the surface of the sea. Sometimes she pointed almost directly into the wind, only a few small scraps of canvas aloft, strung from the masts like washing on the line. Then the men would swing about in the rigging, the sails would come to bloom and she would run due south with the breeze, under a forest of cloud-white sail. Not wanting to get in the way and further annoy James, she moved to sit on the chicken coop and continued to watch the mayhem.

And up and down, James and de Lacey paced, staring intently at a pocket watch Faulkner carried. At the end of each drill de Lacey made notes in a small book. James didn't even bother to acknowledge her. De Lacey at least grinned at her the first time they passed.

James had just ordered another change of course when a sailor in the tops suddenly screamed out in agony and blood rained down on the deck near her in fat, wet drops. For a sickening moment Sophia thought the injured sailor would fall, but the men near him caught him and held him fast. As they brought him down she saw it was the boy, Charley. He held the bloody wreck of a hand to his chest and his face was white with agony.

'Got his hand caught,' one of the old hands said.

'I swear I'll lose the hand. I swear I will. Isaladar's blood, I felt the bones snap,' Charley moaned.

Heart hammering in her chest, Sophia pushed through the gaggle of sailors around the boy.

'Give me your hand, Charley, I know a little medicine.'

With a wince he held it out to her. Before any of the other sailors had a chance to see the damage, she quickly covered the boy's hand with hers. The lad's diagnosis had been right, his hand was shattered and two fingers were almost severed.

Her heart sank. She knew what she had to do, her conscience demanded it, but the horror of using her taint still made her stomach churn. Praying the sailors mistook it for contemplation, she closed her eyes. Clearing her mind, she embraced the hateful thing. The ship fell away and she felt everything, every piece of the fabric of reality vibrating, humming and shaking around her. Closest there was the thrum of the crew, then was the murmur of the great ocean, beyond that was the slow mutter of the world itself, so faint it could have been the echo of a shadow. Suppressing a shudder, she stole a tiny shred of vigour from everything nearby. Gathering these stolen motes of existence together like a torch of life, she wielded them against the injury, repairing bone, rebuilding sinew, smoothing torn and pulped flesh. Finally she forced herself to stop, resisting the temptation to completely mend the wound. There was no point exposing herself needlessly. Cold sweat ran down her back. Her limbs ached. Her mouth was so dry it might have been full of dust. With an immense effort, she opened her eyes.

'It's hardly more than a scratch.' Even speaking took all her concentration.

'It's not! I felt it break,' the boy sobbed. 'I'm maimed.'

'Look, silly, it's just a bad cut.'

Lewis, one of the other sailors, laughed as he saw the hand. 'She's right! Only a little cut. With all that screaming I thought you'd been murdered!'

The men laughed and Charley blushed crimson.

James pushed through the crowd 'All right, men, back to work and be careful. No more accidents. Charley, you go and get that little nick sewn up.'

The boy gawped down at his hand in disbelief. 'Yes, Captain.'

'And try not to squeal at each stitch!' De Lacey called after him.

Chuckling to themselves, the men climbed back into the rigging and James and de Lacey returned to their watch and their pacing. Once no one was watching, Sophia staggered away towards her cabin, utterly spent.

18.

URIAH GAZED ACROSS the water towards his city for what must have been the hundredth time that morning and sighed. It was peculiar being an outcast in your own country. The *Palinurus* had arrived in Stormhaven four days ago and since then she had lain at rest, hopefully anonymous, among the flock of other foreign merchant ships in the Lizard. He was so close to his old life that if his glasses hadn't been lost, he figured he would have been able to see the roof of his office. At least the crew had fetched him a replacement pair from ashore. The lenses were cheap and his vision was blurred when he wore them, but it was better than being blind.

Fiora wasn't willing to risk his going ashore, so each day he waited, lonely, anxious, homesick and bored on a ship where only half a dozen of the crew spoke his language. Worse, so far the Tallowman's trail had proven elusive and each night the countessa had returned to the *Palinurus* tense and frustrated. At least she'd posted his letter to Moreau. That hardly guaranteed Sophia's safety, but he told himself it was something.

'Mr Blake,' the countessa called.

He hadn't seen her come back aboard and she didn't normally return till after sunset. 'Countessa.'

She gestured across the water. 'It must be hard to be this close, yes?'

'It's very hard.'

'I still miss my estates and I left them by choice.' She turned and looked him up and down. 'But, Mr Blake, it is time to end your exile. I need your help.'

'Yes?'

'I've still uncovered nothing of the Tallowman. Not even a whisper.' She pointed towards the city. 'And people are reluctant to speak to me because I am a foreigner. I need you to ask some questions for me.'

He ran a hand over his head. 'Ah, right, good. Who do I need to, um, interrogate?'

'Some people who live near the place where I found you.'

'What? The old blacksmiths?' he squeaked.

'Exactly.'

'When are we going?'

'As soon as you are ready. The boat is waiting.'

This time he didn't need to worry about the watchmen on the docks spotting him – his pulped face was the perfect disguise. He doubted even a close friend would recognise him now. His spectacular bruises and the countessa with her sword and pistol at her side got some looks, of course, but foreigners and their strange ways were common enough in Stormhaven that they didn't attract *too* much undue attention as they came ashore.

A little way inland from the docks, the countessa sat down at a rough stone bench outside a tannery and pretended to fiddle with her boot. 'How much further? I didn't come this way when I rescued you.'

It was hard for Uriah to tell. The Lizard was even more of a tangle than the Hill. 'Only a couple of hundred yards or so, I think.'

'Good. Are you all right?'

'I'll manage. Still weak.' He grimaced. 'And scared.'

'Stay calm. Breathe. The Tallowman should be long gone.'

'Is this really worth it?' He tried to swallow but his mouth was very dry. The streets of his home seemed brooding and weirdly oppressive. 'I doubt the neighbours will know much.'

'It is long odds.' She stood and motioned for him to follow her. 'But we've no choice. None of my other enquiries have turned anything up.'

A block away from the workshop they paused to let a convoy of wagons laden with coal rumble by. 'When will the Camar Shiem arrive?' he asked over the clatter of hooves and the cracking of the driver's whips.

'Your city watch should have sent word west by pegasus or pigeon as soon as they found Mr Otter had been killed. A band should arrive soon.'

'And then Sophia will be safe?' If she was still alive, he didn't add.

'Not safe, but her chances of survival will be far, far better.'

The question that had been bothering him since he had woken up on the *Palinurus* suddenly bubbled to the surface, uncalled for. 'What is the Tallowman?'

'What do you mean?'

'Well, when you speak about him, and alchemy, magic, you almost make him sound inhuman.'

She glanced at him, her expression unreadable, distant. 'That was certainly not my intention. They are a brotherhood of assassins, trained by the enemy from birth to be perfect, remorseless hunters.'

'Why are they called Tallowmen then?'

'They take their name from their appearance.' She grimaced. 'When they are not wearing another's face, their own countenance is like tallow or hot wax.'

'Why?'

'The alchemy they use to transform their appearance destroys their original visage.'

'Their face, what, melts?'

She nodded.

'Do they have other tricks, besides being able to change their faces?'

She studied him for a moment and then shrugged. 'I suppose you deserve that much. Yes. We fear them so much because many also carry a taint that is very unusual.'

That sounded ominous. 'What, ah, aspect does their taint take?'

'Like me, they can detect the use of the taint in others.'

The corpse-cold hand of fear encircled Uriah's heart. 'So if Sophia uses her taint he will know where she is?'

'It might. Thankfully they only seem to be able to detect the use of the taint within twenty leagues or so.'

A lump of coal fell from the last wagon as it passed and crashed down on the cobbles in front of them. They both took a step back. 'Still, twenty leagues!'

'You see why they are so dangerous.'

They rounded the last corner before the thugs' smithy and Uriah stopped in surprise. Bright sunlight poured into the street. The workshop was gone and all that remained where it had been were a few charcoaled beams and a pile of fire-blackened rubble. The buildings on either side were scorched but had been saved.

The countessa scanned the rooftops around them. 'To cover its tracks.'

'What now?'

'The plan is unchanged. You speak to the neighbours and see if they know anything. I'll keep a lookout.'

Uriah knocked on the door of the house across the road from the workshop and an elderly man, his beard stained yellow by pipe smoke, opened it. When Uriah questioned him about the fire the man squinted at him and grimaced. 'Keep to myself,' he wheezed. 'Mind my own business.'

'You didn't see anything?'

'Told you, I keep to myself. You should too.' The man slammed the door in his face.

When he knocked on the second door a tall woman with a squalling baby in her arms ducked under her doorframe and came outside to stand in the lane with him. 'Known them boys since they were lads. Always up to their necks in some nasty business or another.' She looked at the remains of the workshop and shook her head. 'Didn't imagine they'd end up like that though.'

'What happened?'

'The place went up like a tinderbox. Nothin' we could do. My husband helped save them other houses. We thought no one was home till the watch found their bones in the morning.'

'Were people suspicious?'

'Some say they were already dead when it went up.' She shrugged, opened her blouse and put the baby to her teat. 'I heard they'd suddenly come into plenty of coin. Doubt it was honest coin.'

'Anything else you can tell me?'

'Sorry, guv. Kept well enough away from them.'

'Thank you.' Uriah stopped himself. He couldn't just walk away. This wasn't the time for good manners. Sophia's safety might depend on what he could uncover. 'There must be something more? Anything?'

'Sure you want to know?' The woman frowned. 'Your face might be a mess, but you've still an accent like a gent.'

'They were the ones who messed it.'

'Fair enough then,' she dropped her voice to a gravelly whisper. 'I can't tell you any more myself, but go to the Jolly Widow down by the old Lizard after tenth bell and ask at the bar for an honest fishmonger. If it's worth knowing in Stormhaven, they know it. They might help for the right coin. Watch out though. You wouldn't be the first of the Jolly's patrons to end up face-down in the harbour.'

'Many thanks.'

'Just don't mention me.'

Once the woman had disappeared back inside, the countessa emerged from where she had been hidden.

'Hear that?'

She nodded.

'Was that helpful?' he asked.

'It's a start. The Tallowman will be wary now, but they might still know something.'

'What do we do until ten o'clock?'

'We'll head back to the *Palinurus*. There's little point spending more time ashore than we have to.'

'Good.' A spurt of relief coursed through him. He'd be glad to get out of the city. His city.

They'd hardly got fifty paces back towards the docks when the countess suddenly gave him a hard shove in the middle of his back. With a gasp of surprise and pain he stumbled forward just as a shattering retort barked out.

A hot wind brushed his face and something hammered into the shop-front beside him. A spray of masonry covered his face.

He turned to the countessa, mouth open in surprise.

She ignored him. Like magic a heavy pistol blossomed in her hand. In one smooth motion she raised the gun and fired. A dark shape crouched by a chimney above them screamed and something metal clattered down over slate tiles.

She took off at a sprint, leaving only a plume of gun smoke behind her. 'After him,' she shouted.

He stared after her. Someone had shot at them!

With a great effort he forced himself to take a first step and then another and another. Then he was running after her. Head craned skyward to search for the marksman, the countessa rounded a corner a hundred yards ahead of him. Uriah followed her grimly, desperate not to lose her. The street stretched a couple of blocks ahead. There was no sign of their attacker. He slowed. In this warren of intertwined gables, alleyways and twisting streets, the assassin could be anywhere. The blackguard could cover blocks leaping from roof to roof without ever touching the ground. To Uriah's left a crooked lane ran between two terraces. A family's washing hung out to dry across the space, obscuring the view.

He stopped.

One of the bed sheets was marked by a single bloody handprint.

'Countessa!' he yelled, and pointed down the lane. 'This way.'

Fiora skidded to a halt and then raced back past and disappeared through the screen of washing. 'Come on!'

He fought his way through the sheets and sprinted after her. Ahead, the laneway opened out onto a wide space with a dirty canal running down the middle of it. The road was busy with workmen and traffic and Uriah stopped beside the countessa, searching for their attacker.

'There!' She pointed directly across the canal to where a man was running along the far bank. His right hand was clutched to the bloody wreck of his shoulder and his left hand flapped uselessly by his side.

The countessa swore in Caladian.

Uriah looked up and down the canal. The still waterway was almost ten yards wide and impossible to jump. To their left on the towpath two draughthorses were coming from the direction the assassin had run, pulling a laden canal barge towards them. The only crossing he could see was a stone footbridge a couple of hundred yards to their right. The assassin was going to escape.

The countessa sprinted left. She raced past the startled horses and bounded across the intervening water to land on the barge. She danced and skipped across the cargo stowed on the barge's deck and then launched herself towards the far side of the canal and their quarry. The bargeman's startled shout alerted the assassin and he dodged out of the countessa's way so that she landed hard on the cobbles a yard or two behind him. Rolling back to her feet, she raced off after him.

Uriah followed her. He stumbled through the horses' leads and tackle and threw himself down onto the deck of the barge. Something barked his shin and threads of pain snaked out from his back.

'Maniacs!' the bargeman screamed at him.

'Sorry!' Forcing himself up, he lurched across the barge's laden deck and jumped over to the far bank. Missing his footing, he landed heavily by the side of the towpath. Quivering with the agony that throbbed up his spine, he trotted painfully in the direction Fiora had disappeared.

'Uriah!'

To his right, the countessa, sword in hand, had the assassin trapped in a kind of brick recess between two warehouses. Uriah looked up and down the canal. In the distance the bargeman had calmed his horses. The few remaining bystanders were living up to the Lizard's reputation and walking away, with as much affected disinterest as they could muster.

He stepped into the alcove.

The man who had tried to kill them looked nondescript. He was middle-aged, thin and badly shaven. His clothes were shabby and his boots scuffed and ragged. His face was pale and streaked with sweat, grime and blood. His good hand was still clutched to his shattered shoulder. Blood trickled between his fingers.

'How did you know I was in Stormhaven?' the countessa hissed.

The man blinked. 'Didn't know nuffin' about you, blackie. I was paid to wait for your purple-faced mate there.'

'Who paid you?'

The man shook his head grimly.

The countessa danced forward and her sword tip lanced into the man's thigh. He screeched and fell back against the dirty bricks.

'I said,' she whispered, 'who paid you?'

The man panted and licked his lips. 'Calls 'imself Mr Savage.'

'How much did he pay?'

'Two hundred crowns.'

'That's what my life was worth?' The warmth of anger crept up Uriah's neck. 'Two hundred crowns?'

The man shrugged wearily, the fight suddenly gone from him. 'Would 'ave done it for one hundred, but he offered two up front.'

'Where and when do you collect the coin?' the countessa asked.

'Got it all already.'

Uriah shook his head. 'I don't believe it. What'd stop you taking it and running?'

'Believe it,' the man muttered. 'Mr Savage paid me up front. He promised that if he found you'd showed up and I hadn't offed you it'd be bad for me, real bad. I believed him, too.'

The countessa shook the blood from the tip of her sword. 'Where did he hire you?'

'Place called the Rag and Bone. Bought a bunch of my mates too. He's got some of them waiting up by a place on King's Row, a few others by some lawyer's office and one by the south arsenal. That news is worth something, ain't it?'

She ignored that. 'How can you get in contact with this Mr Savage?'

'I can't.' The man shook his head. 'Said he'd find me if he needed me.'

'You swear.'

He nodded.

'I believe you.' Fiora stepped forward and plunged her sword into the man's chest. His eyes flashed wide and white and then he slid down the wall without a sound. The countessa jerked her blade free, briskly cleaned it on the dead man's trousers and then calmly slid it back into her scabbard.

'You can't...' Uriah fumbled for his words. 'He'd surrendered.'

She held up a hand. 'He shot at us in cold blood, for a Tallowman's gold. He got the only payment he deserved. Now, will this be reported to the watch?'

He looked down at the dead man.

'Uriah,' she snapped. 'The watch?'

'I don't know.' He took a deep breath. 'The Lizard is famously silent about brawls and murders – but it isn't every day a black woman is involved.'

'We better get straight back to the ship, then.'

Blood was slowly filling the gaps between the cobbles around the dead man. 'Was it worth it?'

'Worth it?'

'Killing him.'

'Yes. He'll do no more evil and now we know the Tallowman's name.' She turned him away from the corpse. 'Come, Uriah.'

He let her lead him away. 'We know he calls himself Mr Savage? Surely he will just invent another name?'

She shook her head. 'He can't.'

'But...'

'I can say no more. You will just need to trust me. Knowing his name is a great advantage.'

'Trust you?' He nodded slowly and took a deep, shuddering breath. 'I suppose you did save my life, Countessa.'

'No more Countessa, Uriah. You are a gentleman and now we have fought together, call me Fiora.'

They walked back out onto the road beside the canal and turned towards the harbour. He looked back over his shoulder one last time. It was impossible to tell a man had just died between those two forgettable buildings. It was a strange thing.

Weakened as he was by his injuries, the chase through the Lizard had exhausted Uriah and as soon as he was back on board he slunk away to his cabin. Sleep eluded him, though. Every time he closed his eyes he pictured the momentary surprise in the assassin's eyes as he had died. It had been so easy to kill him, so no-nonsense. Fiora had almost been casual about it. Killing him hadn't bothered her a jot. Indeed she'd obviously given it no more thought than a cat did when it killed a rat. That scared him. He was still thinking about that when his door banged open and Fiora herself burst into the cabin.

'Do you have an item that was owned or handled by Sophia?'

He sat up. 'Sorry?'

'Something linked to Sophia. Do you have something?'

'My handkerchief was a birthday present from her.'

'Give it to me.'

Caught up by her urgency, he wrenched it out of his pocket. 'Here you are.'

'Come with me.'

He stumbled after her until they reached the *Palinurus'* great cabin. The ship's captain, Scarrus – a small, heavily muscled, square-shouldered man

– was already there. He had a large chart spread out on the table in front of him.

'What's happening?' Uriah was suddenly very awake and very afraid.

'Someone just used a healing taint nearby. The odds are good it was Sophia,' Fiora replied.

'She's in the city?'

'Quiet. I'm trying to find her. Once these echoes fade she will be gone again.'

Fiora grasped the handkerchief and studied the chart like a musician looking for inspiration in a sheet of music. For a long time she didn't move and he turned to study Scarrus. The captain's ebony face was calm. If the little man was bothered by being in proximity to someone using the taint, he didn't show it.

In the distance the city bells chimed four o'clock.

Fiora suddenly slumped forward. Shaking in exhaustion, she lifted herself back upright and stabbed a finger onto the chart. 'Only a little power was used. But it was definitely Sophia and she is there.'

Uriah leant forward and his heart sank. Fiora had pointed to a spot due east of Stormhaven and a long way out to sea. 'That mark can't be right. She's not at sea.'

'It's right to within ten or so leagues,' said Fiora.

'Well she isn't coming back to Stormhaven then.' Scarrus shook his head. 'Not unless the captain of her ship is a fool. The Grand Trade Wind blows this time of year and he'd have to beat all the way home. It'd take an age.'

Uriah sat down heavily. 'He is no fool. He is the captain who captured one of your ships in Asare Roads.'

'Captain Faulkner of the *Inflexible*?' asked Fiora.

Uriah nodded.

'He's definitely no fool,' said Scarrus.

Fiora sighed. 'He must be when it comes to women.'

'I told her she had to come home when they went to sea,' said Uriah tiredly. Not that he was surprised. Sophia had always been far too headstrong. It was his fault for spoiling her so much.

Fiora studied the mark she had made on the map. 'It may still work out for the best. At least this keeps her out of the Tallowman's grasp. For now, anyway.' She turned to the captain. 'Scarrus, let us assume Uriah's daughter has decided to go along to hunt this leviathan. Where do you think that ship is headed?'

Scarrus considered the map for a moment. 'The Bastion Islands.'

'And has the leviathan been seen there?'

The captain nodded. 'According to the sailors I've spoken to ashore, that's where most of the attacks have taken place.'

'Well then, we'll head for the Bastion Islands and hope to find news of them there.'

'I'll get us under way.'

Uriah looked at her questioningly. 'What of your hunt for the Tallowman, Fiora?'

'Don't worry on my account, Uriah. The Tallowman will find your daughter. Now we might just get to her first.'

19.

THE TALLOWMAN STOOD at the window of the whore's garret and watched the heavily laden white pegasus drift down over the dark water of the bay. It smiled. The Royal Aerial Mail arrived more regularly than the seasons. That made intercepting the letters it carried even easier.

It turned from the window and stepped over what was left of the whore's body. Her spirit had been worn away by gallons of gin and a life of disappointments long ago and she had proven a most unsatisfactory meal. Nevertheless, her tiny, dirty room had at least provided the Tallowman with a place to bide its time. It would need to move today though; her corpse was starting to stink.

The morning after it had found the bill poster, it had paid some men to lie in wait for Uriah Blake should he and his mysterious rescuer return, and then it had borrowed a sailor's face and gone to his firm. They had described their master as indisposed, which it presumed was more socially acceptable than 'wanted for murder' and had referred it to the Drum and Monkey, a nearby public house. There it had found it was already too late – Captain Faulkner's boatswain had left for parts unknown. It couldn't risk trying to follow the boatswain, not on a hunch and not when it might easily pass Sophia on the road coming home. With the Camar Shiem certain to be on their way, time was priceless. It couldn't afford a gamble like that. Instead it had killed the whore and hidden away with her corpse. Since then it had simply walked into Stormhaven's General Post Office each day like clockwork and, wearing the face of the postmaster, it had stolen Uriah's letters.

The Tallowman stepped out of the garret and shut the door behind it. There was no point burning the place down; the death of a woman like her would go almost unnoticed and largely unremarked. The grand General Post Office was only a few minutes' walk away and soon it was inside and standing in front of its tame mail sorter.

''Ere you are, Mr Bobbin. All ready for you.'

The Tallowman pocketed Uriah's letters and pushed a coin into the man's ink-stained hand. 'Thank you, Eric.'

'Not a worry, sir.' The mailman beamed. If he had any concerns about handing over the letters, the face the Tallowman wore and the silver plum it paid him each day killed them.

Mail in hand and whistling a gratingly jaunty tune that the postmaster liked, it walked briskly back out of the busy post office. Outside it leant against one of the sandstone lions that guarded the post office's doors and checked its catch. Almost twenty letters! At least one of them must be useful. It was just lucky Realmsmen placed such childlike faith in their postal system – even the watch waited for the letters to be delivered before they confiscated them! It chuckled to itself as it turned the letters over and marked each of them by the sender's details. Most were business correspondence, but on the seventh in neat, orderly handwriting was written: *Capt. J Faulkner. Blue Moon Tavern. Waterford, Dercia.*

It smiled at the twelfth letter with even more pleasure. In flowing script was printed.

Miss Sophia Blake. The village of Waterford-on-Sea

It walked across the road to a nearby public house, ordered a pint it would never drink and sat down at the last empty table. It opened Sophia's letter last.

Dearest Father,

I hope my letter finds you well.

Unfortunately, you will not be happy with its contents. As I have no desire to keep you in suspense, I will say it simply. I have decided to accompany the ship to sea.

I appreciate you expressly forbade this. I also must emphasise that this decision was mine and mine alone. In fact, I expect Captain Faulkner to strenuously argue against my choice, when I tell him.

I only hope you are not too angry. I know you only wanted me to stay ashore for my own safety, but I believe this decision is the best one for our venture and, if I am to be honest, myself. You have always taught me to follow my instincts and do what is right – this is one of those times.

I will write to you from the Bastion Islands.

Isaladar keep you, Father.

Your lovingly disobedient daughter,

Sophia

Waterford Manor

The Tallowman reread the letter twice and then hissed with pleasure. The stupid girl still had no idea anything was amiss. She hadn't even realised that her father was in trouble, let alone that she herself was being hunted. Even better, she was unknowingly sailing away from the safety of the no doubt fast-approaching Camar Shiem. It couldn't have wished for more.

Crumpling up the pile of letters, the Tallowman threw them into the nearby fire. It stood and looked out the window. It was almost dark. That was good. It needed to contact its master and to do that it needed to create a conduit.

The urchin gurgled as his lifeblood dribbled out into the muck. The Tallowman stood in the mud of the canal and looked down at the dying child. Happily there was no way the noise of the child's dying could be heard over the happy chatter from the nearby tavern.

Kneeling down in the mud, it leant down over the child.

The boy's glazed eyes fluttered. 'Muf, is that you? A man hurt me real bad,' he sobbed.

The Tallowman reached into a thick leather pouch at its belt and removed a scrap of writhing, wriggling flesh the size of a large earthworm.

The seed-flesh responded to the smell of blood in the air and squirmed hungrily between the Tallowman's thumb and forefinger, reaching out towards the child's wound. The Tallowman forced the twitching worm-thing deep into the wound its knife had made in the child's belly. The boy cried out in agony.

'Master, I must speak with you,' the Tallowman whispered.

Putting a hand over the urchin's mouth, it watched intently. At first the child continued to moan and gurgle. Then, the noise muffled by the Tallowman's hand, he began to scream. Finally, the boy gave one last convulsion and lay still.

Squatting down in the mud it watched the dead child and waited. For a full minute the child lay motionless. Then slowly, moving like a poorly made puppet, the corpse sat up and turned its head jerkily towards where the Tallowman crouched. The terror was gone from the urchin's dead eyes now, replaced by a deep hatred.

'Have you harvested her?' asked the urchin's corpse.

The Tallowman bowed its head. 'I have not.'

'Then why do you summon me? My patience is not endless. You know using a conduit risks both our detection.'

'The girl is travelling by ship to the Bastion Islands.'

'Did I ask to be bothered with every little detail of your hunt?'

'I need more resources. I will most likely have to charter a vessel to follow her.'

'I am disappointed you do not have her already, Tallowman! And now you summon me to ask for more aid!' the corpse hissed.

'I am sorry, master,' replied the Tallowman. It threw itself forward and grovelled, prostrate in the stinking mud.

The corpse studied him. 'Go to 12 Hammersmith Road. Tell the man who opens the door that you have come for your dowry. He will give you what you need.'

'Thank you, master.' The Tallowman took a deep breath. 'I also thought that as the girl is going to the Bastion Islands the—'

'No!' hissed the urchin. 'Clever spiders do not tangle the webs they weave. You will do this yourself, Tallowman, and you will do it before the summer equinox.'

'Yes, master.'

The urchin's corpse coughed wearily and collapsed back into the mud. 'Remember, Tallowman, should you fail me, you know what awaits you,' it breathed.

The flickering lanterns gave the tavern a muted, underwater feel even at midday. The man eyed the Tallowman with a wild dog's wary curiosity. It wasn't surprised; even in a greasy harbour-side tavern, a mud-covered man with a bandaged face still got some looks. But it was better this way. It wouldn't be able to keep up the effort of wearing a face for the entire time they were at sea. They should see it in its rags from the start.

'Jacob Roberts?' it asked him, sitting down at the man's table.

'Depends on who wants to know,' the man said. Dagger-sharp eyes glittered above an impenetrable black beard.

'My name is Mr Savage and I hear you have a ship available for charter.'

Roberts nodded and pushed his lunch of pickled herring away. 'I'm only the mate, but I handle the business side of things for *Dead Reckoning*. What do you need a ship for?'

'Tell me about your vessel first.'

'*Reckoning* is a ship-rigged sloop. Navy-built for convoy work in the last war. She can outrun what she can't fight and is seaworthy to boot.'

'Sounds suitable. But my work is private in nature and I do not much like questions. Take my drift?'

'We are not by nature a curious crew, Mr Savage.'

'Good.' The Tallowman was used to employing these types of men. Every port had a few of them. They chopped and changed between merchant, smuggler, murderer and pirate as whim and opportunity required. 'Now how much do you charge a day?'

Roberts told him the price.

'I could almost buy my own ship for that!'

Roberts finished his beer and stood up. 'I suggest you do then, Mr Savage.'

The Tallowman waved for him to sit down. It couldn't afford to waste time looking for a ship. 'I will pay.'

'Good. Now where will your work take us?'

'The Bastion Islands.'

Fear glinted in the sailor's eyes. 'Haven't you heard? That's the devil fish's fucking lair!'

'The leviathan doesn't frighten me.' The Tallowman took a heavy purse from its belt and tipped the contents out. The heavy, old-fashioned gold coins clinked as they hit the tabletop. 'I will pay double if we leave tomorrow.'

The mate gathered the coins up and then glanced greedily around to make sure none of the other patrons had seen them. Happy they hadn't, Roberts studied one of the coins. 'These are Andiel marked! Where'd you get them?'

'Where I got the coin is my business.'

'Bad luck, Andiel coins.'

'Are you bothered by wives' tales? They're still gold. Melt them down if you fear their mark.'

'Fair enough, Mr Savage.'

'Do we have a deal then?'

'Pay two and a half my first quote and you're on. And don't tell anyone on the *Reckoning* about the extra half. That is our little secret.'

'Done.'

20.

AS *GAME BIRD* ploughed her way west south-west through a moderately heavy blue-grey sea, Faulkner found he was quite content with how she was handling. She leaked a little near the bow and was appallingly unwieldy compared to the *Inflexible*, but overall *Game Bird* was sailing well.

'They don't like these drills, do they?' Jenkins remarked as they watched the longboat running along through the heaving seas a few cable lengths astern.

'They never do, Boatswain. Remember how they used to groan back on *Larkspur*?'

Faulkner was one of the new school of captains. He was a firm believer in improving a crew by practice, practice and then more practice. Sailing drills, gun drills and whatever other drills he could dream up. In this case de Lacey and his watch had practised abandoning ship, a drill particularly appropriate for any vessel hunting the leviathan, he thought.

'I do. That grumbling dried up after that first cruise through Delago Bay. Nothing like a gaggle of prizes and pockets full of crowns to shut the whingers up.'

'True.' That had been a good cruise. 'At least this weather is about perfect. It's just what we needed to make a proper crew out of them.'

'The way they swung that boat out, why they almost looked like sailors,' Jenkins said.

For the first few days there had been some predictable fights and bickering between the two tribes of men: the merchantmen and the *Inflexibles*. But since this little storm had blown up they had been working well together. It always seemed to take a little rough weather or a brisk action to get a crew to knit together. They were almost ready to hunt this great fish. If he could just convince Sophia go ashore he would have counted himself a happy captain. Faulkner sighed and his eyes strayed to the hatch. For a moment he considered going below to see if she was all right before he shook his head to clear away those dangerous thoughts. His moment of weakness at the dance had been bad enough. Now, like some divine punishment for that lapse, he was stuck with her at sea. It was a horrible feeling having her life in his hands. He was sure his paternalism would have enraged her, but the terror that something might happen to her was more crushing than all the other pressures of his command combined. Why hadn't he simply bundled her ashore? How had she managed to talk her away aboard? Even thinking about it made him feel sick and nervy. He turned back to Jenkins. 'We'll recover the boat now. I imagine they're already wet through. See to shortening sail. Boscawen, take the wheel.'

Jenkins blew a long blast on his whistle and jogged forward. 'Shorten sail! Stand by to take in royals and flying jib! Man royal clewlines, weatherbraces, flying jib downhaul! Stand by royal halliards, flying jib halliards!' he roared.

Shielding his eyes against the spray, Faulkner turned back to the old whaler. 'I won't tell you your business, Boscawen. Just give them as much shelter on the lee as you can. We aren't all forever in and out of our boats like you whalers!'

By the time Faulkner had reached the group of men manning the davits, Jenkins had already begun to shorten sail and the *Game Bird* was slowing. Leaning over the side, Faulkner watched the angry sea as it slid along the side of the ship. 'Giovanni, get some more oil over the side.'

The Cartian sailor nodded and, taking a pail, slopped more oil onto the water. The oil spread quickly across the surface of the sea and the waves shrunk noticeably under its effect. Faulkner climbed a ratline and waved for de Lacey to approach.

The boat bumped alongside and Faulkner threw them down a line. 'Fancy a lift, gentlemen?'

'Would we? It's fit only for fishes down here!' de Lacey called up.

The men got the boat back aboard with an impressively sailor-like efficiency that made Faulkner smile. 'Well done, you handled that boat very fast and very clean, lads. Most handily done,' he told them.

A soaked and bedraggled de Lacey nodded. 'Thank you, Captain. Shall I dismiss the men?'

'I'll check the boat's supplies first.' As part of the drill the men had prepared the boat as if for a long journey. Faulkner climbed into the boat and began his review. The sea anchor was well stowed. The scuttlebutt was full of water and neatly sealed against the spray. The first locker held the matches, two bottles of rum and a supply of canvas, all tidily stowed and dry. But at the bread locker he stopped. It was empty. Unfortunately he wasn't surprised; stowing the bread had been Nagel's task.

If Faulkner had any time to spare he would have never taken Nagel to sea. The man was a weaselly looking fellow whose sallow and bitter face was perpetually framed by his lank blonde hair. During the repairs in Waterford he had seemed lazy. At sea he had proven insubordinate and sarcastic. He reminded Faulkner of the kind of stray dog that would snarl at your heels, only to slink away as soon as you turned to face it. He stood up in the boat. 'Mr Nagel, the bread locker is empty. I believe that was your responsibility.'

Nagel shifted uneasily, glancing to his few mates for support. 'I thought the lieutenant told me not to fill it.'

'I said no such thing,' said de Lacey.

'Why didn't you fill it, Nagel?' Faulkner asked.

'Why didn't I fill it?' Nagel's thin lip curled. 'We are all heartily sick of these drills, Captain. Man the gun. Reduce sail. Raise sail. Your drills have already hurt poor Charley. And then we have to launch a boat in this foul sea. Why should I have had to load up the bloody locker with your bread? We shouldn't even be going out when it's this rough. You'll drown us.'

Fury grabbed at Faulkner's jaw and only with a deep breath did he steady himself. If the *Game Bird* had been one of the king's ships Nagel would have already earned himself a dozen lashes. 'Firstly, you should have stowed the bread because it was an order and I expect my orders obeyed. Secondly, what if we had genuine cause to launch that boat tonight and we didn't check the supplies as they had been filled today? Would you want to be in the boat with no food? Would you want to draw straws?' The sailors nearby muttered angrily, they had all heard stories of what happened when men were trapped in an open boat with nothing to eat – cannibalism of the dead and worse. Nagel's snarl vanished like morning fog and he hung his head. 'Nagel?'

'Sorry, Captain,' the man spat through gritted teeth.

'I expect my orders followed. I don't issue them to amuse myself or torment my crew,' Faulkner turned to the rest of boat crew. 'That was still a first-class drill, lads. Square the boat away and then the lieutenant will issue all of you except Nagel an extra tot of rum.'

'Thank you, Cap'n,' the men chorused.

Turning, he walked back aft. 'Donald! Donald!' he called.

His servant appeared, muttering under his breath. 'Gale blowing and he expects me to trail him about like a mangy bloody…'

'That will be enough, thank you, Donald.'

'What is it then?'

'I've got an errand for you.'

Judging by her pitching and groaning, Sophia was sure *Game Bird* must be about to break apart at any moment. She scrunched her eyes even more tightly shut. She would have almost welcomed the sea's cold embrace. In fact, she would have welcomed any relief from the deep, burning exhaustion that her use of the taint always brought with it. Even the tiniest of splashes she had used on Charley had left her feeling like all her blood had been replaced by a mixture of bile and weariness. She missed her father and her home with an aching, almost consuming loneliness. Coming to sea seemed like a worse and worse idea with each groan of the ship. James still hadn't even bothered to speak to her since their fight.

A knock at the cabin door roused her from her half sleep. 'Miss Blake, are you decent?' called Donald.

'Yes,' she croaked.

The man bumped his way through the cramped door and handed her a flask. 'Take this ginger wine, miss. Captain Faulkner said it would help your sea sickness.'

'He did?'

'Yes, miss, he did. Well, his exact words were, "We can't have our benefactor's daughter dying from sea sickness, now can we? Donald, take his down to her immediately."'

She took a long pull from the flask. She was glad to have something to drink, even if she wasn't really seasick. 'That was very gentlemanly of him.'

'Oh yes. That is our captain, always quite the gentleman.' Donald shook his whiskered head sadly. 'You should have seen how hard he had me work back on old *Larkspur* or *Inflexible* whenever he entertained some ladies aboard. Polish this, Donald. Where's my best coat, Donald? Do not skimp on the wine, Donald. Shine the cutlery twice, Donald. I swear it vexed me half to death it did, Miss Blake.'

'And did Captain Faulkner often entertain when you were in the south?'

'He did. Aged me horrid.'

'I thought you would have usually been at sea.'

'Oh no, miss. The rascal that passed for the controller of our dockyards in Cartia considered it his duty to line his own pockets, not outfit the king's ships. So we spent a goodly amount of time ashore for want of spars and other stores.'

'So, Captain Faulkner had plenty of time to entertain these elegant southern ladies then, did he?'

'Must have cost him a fortune. He was quite famous for it.'

'He was, was he? Thank you for the drink, Donald. I am feeling well enough to get up now.'

The officer's wardroom was normally light and airy, but with the storm blowing and the grates shut it was grey and grim. It was empty except for Morgan. Sophia took a seat across the table from the carpenter.

The grizzled old man put down the intricate little model of a ship he had been working on and looked up with a smile. 'Feeling a bit better?'

'Much better, thank you.'

'It's not much fun, seasickness.'

'It's not.'

'Well don't let it upset you. Even Captain Faulkner used to be sick every time he went to sea.'

'James got seasick?'

'Aye, he used to get sick as a dog back when he was a mid. Even a little blow like this would have sent him green for a day or two.'

'That does make me feel better.'

'Now, miss, I did want to say how sorry I am for the confusion.'

'Confusion?'

'About your coming to sea. For some reason I just assumed you'd stay ashore. If I'd know you were coming with us I'd have made things more, ah, hospitable for a lady.'

A flutter of guilt ran through her. 'It's my fault. I should have spoken to you myself. Anyway, I have everything I need.' In an effort to change the subject she smiled and leant forward, studying the model the carpenter had been working on. 'It's beautiful, Morgan. You're very good.'

'When I've spent a quarter of my life whiling away quiet hours at sea, it would want to be.' He carefully put the model back in a straw-lined box beside him. 'So, Sophia, sickness aside, how've you found things these first few days?'

'It's nicer than I expected. I expected...' she trailed off.

'Don't mind me, girl, speak your mind.'

'I read so much about flogging, press-ganging and scurvy. I expected things to be grimmer aboard.'

Morgan considered that. 'Things will get nastier the longer we are at sea. And I have known captains who'd give the cat to any man who looked at them sideways. And things can get much worse than that. Why, back on *Queen Anne* we once came across a collier drifting on the tides, every man aboard her dead from the plague.' He frowned. 'Though I shouldn't speak of such things to a young lady. Yes, life at sea is tough. But what's it like to grow up in the slums of Mandor or Farron or Stormhaven? Rise before dawn to go to a dirty, back-breaking mill, come home after dark to a hovel, too tired to even lift your head to speak to your wife or brats.' He held up a hand. 'I'm not saying life aboard is comfortable, but the lads have food and steady pay. To men from the slums or to poor tenant farmers that means a lot.'

She had been exposed to enough to the worst of the cities to know that Morgan wasn't exaggerating. 'That makes sense.'

'And on the *Game Bird* we are lucky to have Captain Faulkner. A good captain goes a long way towards making a happy ship.'

'What's he like as a captain?'

'Driven, ruthless, kind, hard and fair. It's not chance that has made him successful.'

'Is that why we found this crew so easily for this hunt? Because of James?'

Morgan nodded. 'Aye, a good number of men came solely because of him. De Lacey, Jenkins and the majority of the *Inflexibles*, to be sure. But you shouldn't discount the bounty for this leviathan either. It's a king's ransom, after all.' He considered the question for another moment. 'Perhaps it'd be fair to say that one third of the men came directly out of loyalty to Faulkner, one third came for the money but only accepted the risk because Faulkner was the captain, and the final third came only for the coin.'

'So James is captain, but how do the watches work?'

'The carpenter wouldn't normally stand watch, but on the *Game Bird*...'

She and Morgan chatted away for some time about life at sea and it was almost dark when Sophia finally decided to go up on deck for her second round of arguments with James. The wind was still blowing hard and it tore at her hair. The sea was heavy and whitecaps tossed and heaved about *Game Bird*, vivid white in the gloom as they churned past.

Her eyes hadn't even grown accustomed to the gloom before James loomed up out of the dusk. 'Hello, you're looking a good deal better,' he said.

'I almost feel human again.'

'I feel for you. I used to get terribly seasick as a boy, not that you would believe it now!'

'So you have forgiven me for coming with you?' She had no desire to dance around the subject of their last fight.

'I was hoping now you've been sick I could talk you into going ashore at our next port?'

'No such luck.'

'Well then you're definitely not forgiven. I've just accepted that you're harder than an albatross to get rid of!'

'I'm glad you've accepted your fate.'

'I have. Anyway, if I'm stuck with you I'm glad you're up and about. We're stopping at Lord Morgans Island tomorrow and I thought you might like to meet my brother Tom. He's studying at the War Flying Colleague.'

'Your brother is training to be a flyer?'

'He is indeed.'

'How exciting! I'd love to meet him.'

21.

THE *PALINURUS* HAD almost reached the Bastion Islands when the storm caught her.

In the gentle and warm waters of her southern home the xebec danced across the surface of that azure ocean like a feather on the wind, but she was not built for the angry waters of these cold northern seas. As the storm began to batter them, Scarrus gave up any hope of reaching the safety of the islands and he turned the *Palinurus'* head to let her scud away before the wind. Although this reduced the pummelling impact of the waves, it had been terrible on Uriah's stomach as the *Palinurus* took on a terrible, shuddering yaw. In the end he had left the heaving, wet deck and retired to his damp and claustrophobic cabin to be alone with his sickness and worry.

In the middle of the second night of the storm, Uriah woke up and immediately knew something was wrong. Even as ignorant as he was of nautical matters, it was clear that the ship's movement had changed; the *Palinurus* was wading tiredly through the water, more submerged than afloat. As he threw on his clothes, fear tore away his drowsiness. He had to at least get up on deck. Getting trapped below decks as the ship sank would be worse than a nightmare.

In the companionway he met Marcellus. The big man's ebony skin was almost grey and he looked so far beyond exhaustion he could hardly stand.

'What's happened?' Uriah asked.

'We are flooding.'

'What, a leak?'

The big man nodded tiredly.

'Can I help?'

'Anyone would be welcome at the pumps.' Marcellus pointed him in the right direction and then stumbled off into the dark.

The hellish scene that confronted Uriah when he reached the pumps was like something produced by the fevered imagination of a master painter. The main pumps were below decks and set against the main mast. The only light in this claustrophobic space was cast by two storm lanterns. By their flickering glow he could just pick out the men bent to the backbreaking task of pumping. It was such hot work they were all at least stripped to the waist and many were naked. In the dark corners huddled the shapes of men who had clearly been too tired to even return to their quarters and had simply thrown themselves down on the deck when their spell was over. Not that they would have been getting much sleep – the plunging of the ship was too severe to allow the water to be funnelled out properly and it was simply being pumped up onto the deck to slop about before being carried overboard by the scuppers. The air was thick with the stench of salt water, vomit, sweat – and acrid, clinging fear.

With shaking fingers, Uriah stripped off his jacket and shirt and then watched for a moment to make sure he understood the pumps' operation. When he was confident he did, he stepped forward and tapped the closest sailor on the shoulder. The man looked around and said something to him in Caladian.

Uriah mimed working the pumps. 'I'll take over.'

The sailor nodded and stumbled away to collapse on the deck.

Within minutes his arms felt as if his muscles had been ripped out, flayed and crudely stitched back in, and his hands were blistered and bloody. The movement required to work the pumps also put terrible pressure on his old back injury and twisted his spine into a knot of pure, searing agony.

A thousand times he meant to stop, but each time he flagged, he thought of Sophia at the mercy of this Tallowman and worked on. After a time the pain took him over completely and he felt divorced from his body's suffering.

To keep the timing required to work the pumps and stop himself from falling asleep where he stood, he began to recite the complete works of Hamlyn to himself over and over, almost like a hymn or mantra.

'*A Knight of Mourning. The Drifter. Prince Isaladar. The Golden Ox…*'

On and on he went, mumbling the fifteen names. The sailors around him must have thought him mad, but he kept at it, murmuring and working. Working and murmuring.

Finally, mercifully, someone tapped on his shoulder and a sailor motioned him away. He let go of the bloody handle and reeled away to collapse in a corner like a poleaxed steer. A dark, smothering thing like sleep swallowed him.

Three more times he took his place at the pumps. Three more spells of endless pain and repetition. He was amazed that so much suffering could fit into one night. It was midway through his fourth spell when a man behind him shouted something in Caladian. The sailor working the pump next to Uriah's gave a hoarse cheer and collapsed wearily over the pump handle. Uriah turned around and saw Scarrus.

The little captain spotted Uriah and smiled. 'I didn't realise you were helping. We have patched the leak and you have pumped out enough water to keep us afloat. The storm seems to be finally dying too.'

'I can go?'

Scarrus smiled. 'With my thanks. Go try and get some sleep.'

Uriah was so tired he hardly remembered getting back to his cabin, but when he fell into bed he just lay there wide awake, too sore and exhausted to sleep. He tossed and turned for a while then got up and padded aft to the day cabin and let himself inside.

'Couldn't sleep?' Fiora asked.

Uriah started. Fiora was sitting on one of the benches that lined the sides of the great cabin and he hadn't noticed her when he entered. She looked as awful as he felt: her hair was in disarray and she was covered in tar.

'No. I thought I'd come up here and watch the sea at least,' he replied, sitting down.

'I was the same. There is no forcing sleep when you are this weary.'

'True.' He paused. 'What happened to you? I didn't see you pumping?'

'I was helping the men patching the leak.' She looked at his torn and blistered hands. 'You have my thanks. Scarrus tells me you worked like an ox.'

'No thanks required. I was working to save my own skin as well.'

She smiled and picked up a bottle from by her side. 'Try this. It is posca from one of my estates. It will relax you.'

'Posca?'

'A mixture of sour wine, vinegar and herbs.'

That sounded like a doubtful mix and he wasn't normally much of a drinker, but Uriah took a nip anyway. It was sharp and refreshing. 'Very nice.'

'You should see the estate where it is grown. The vines run almost all the way down to the shores of the bluest lake you will ever see and on a little island there are the most picturesque ruins. In the spring, Lucullus and I would boat out and...' She petered out and shook her head as if to throw off the weight of homesickness and grief. 'Enough nostalgia. What should we talk about while we wait for sleep to come and claim us?'

Uriah passed the bottle back to her. 'What are our plans now the ship is damaged?'

She took a long swig. 'The logical place for us is still Hazlewood.'

'The weather mages' island?'

'It's the only place in the islands where *Palinurus* can be repaired. I also think your daughter's ship will probably pass through the mage's town at some stage. That means that the Tallowman will probably go there as well.'

'Why do you think James will call in there?'

'The weather mages know these waters better than anyone. My guess is that Captain Faulkner will seek their counsel.'

'Will the Tallowman really be able to hunt Sophia while she is at sea?'

'Not at sea, no. But once it finds out she has come out here to hunt this leviathan – and I promise you it will somehow learn that much – it will wait for them in a town. In Hazlewood, probably.'

'It sounds invincible.'

'The Tallowman?' Fiora placed a hand on his hunched shoulder. 'Try not to dwell on it too much, Uriah. Worry does nothing but rust a blade before it is needed. You must take your mind off it.'

'Take my mind off the fact my daughter is being hunted? How?'

She stretched. 'Ask me anything else you would like.'

'Anything?'

'Anything. As long as I am not sworn to secrecy, I will answer it as best I can.'

'Then tell me what the taint is. What it really is.' His voice was barely audible over the insistent pattering of the rain against the stern windows. Although in his heart he had known Sophia carried the taint for years, he had never really dared ask anyone *what* it was.

She made a sound that was almost a chuckle.

'Is that one of the things you can't speak of?'

'No, I can speak of it. You have picked a question that would take a sphinx to answer correctly!'

'Sorry?'

'There are theories. But no one is really sure what the taint is, even if the fanatics argue like they do. You may as well ask me why the sun is hot or what causes the tides for all the chance I have of giving you the correct answer.'

'Ayscough argues that the tides are caused by our moons.'

'But that is only a theory!' she retorted.

'Well, tell me the different theories of the taint then. I'm a lawyer. I've spent my life trying to make sense of people's differing accounts of things.'

She threw up her hands. 'There is no beating you, Uriah. I will tell you all I remember.' She paused and collected her thoughts. 'I said no one truly understands what the taint is and that is true. But there are two main theories and most scholars of the taint adhere to one or the other.'

'Go on.'

'The first school is the most prevalent. Arrogantly, they call themselves the "Daemonic Realists". To cut a very long spiritual and scientific argument short, they believe that those with the taint are a kind of bridge between our plane and a plane inhabited by fiends, daemons and gods. They argue that some kind of daemonic power leaks through the tainted from this other realm and this is what grants them their power. They also believe this is why the tainted go mad. When enough of this daemonic ether has passed through a tainted person their mind simply fragments.' She stopped and took a swig of the posca.

'That doesn't sound particularly scientific or rational.' He was also reluctant to accept that Sophia was some kind of conduit for dark magic.

'No? Well, then you will most likely be an "Attributist". They argue that the taint is simply a trait, in the same way that my skin is black or you have freckles. For them the taint is nothing more. They hold that the Realists are little better than superstitious peasants trying to hide old hatreds behind a thin veneer of scholarship.'

'And what are you, Fiora? An Attributist?'

She grimaced. 'I believe neither theory in its entirety, but I lean towards the Realists.'

'You do?' Uriah was shocked. Did this intelligent, articulate woman really believe that some spirit realm full of daemons and hobgoblins reached out to somehow infect normal people? Every Realmsman knew that Caladians were spiritual and pious, but it still surprised him to hear her say it.

'The Attributists are trying to crush and batter an inherently illogical problem till it appears to fit their sense of the rational. If daemons are real, and I know they are, we are probably foolish to even try to understand their alien motives or existence.'

He stared at her. She was tired and dirty, but she wasn't mad. She seemed deeply intelligent and this was an issue she had obviously thought about in depth. 'So you really hold that some evil power bleeds into Sophia and creates her taint?'

Fiora shook her head. 'I don't believe all of the Realists' nonsense. But I do believe there is some interrelation between this other plane and the taint. Honestly, we are hardly even knowledgeable enough to bother talking about it. We don't even know where the taint begins!'

'Sorry?'

'I knew a man once. He was the best shot I have ever seen. If you threw a thousand oranges in the air he would hit *every single one of them* from twenty paces before they landed. It didn't matter what pistol he used, either. Unless the gun misfired, he would hit every single one of those thousand oranges.' Fiora spun the bottle in the air and caught it. 'Is that the taint?'

'Definitely.'

She nodded her agreement. 'I knew another man. He had been a duellist before he joined the Blessed Lance and he had practised with pistols for hundreds or maybe even thousands of hours. Out of his thousand oranges he would have hit eight hundred. That is incredible talent, but is that taint?'

'But a taint like Sophia's is clearly abnormal?'

Fiora nodded again. 'True, both your daughter and I are undoubtedly tainted. Neither of our aspects could be confused for anything other than the taint. But in many cases we still don't even know where the talent ends and taint starts. A genius composer or the taint? An incredible card player or the taint?' She pointed to the angry sea outside the stern windows. 'An uncanny understanding of the ocean or the taint?'

Uriah yawned again. 'Mm, that is complicated...' He desperately wanted to ask another question, but exhaustion rose up suddenly and swallowed him.

22.

DAWN FOUND THE *Game Bird* sheltering in one of Lord Morgans Island's numerous bays. Faulkner rose with the sun, shaved and washed, and then spent the morning watch checking over the ship. Although the storm had blown itself out overnight, the sunlight still looked like it was filtered through cheap green glass and scattered clouds dashed across the sky like lonely messengers running to distant shores. A few minor repairs were needed after the blow, but by seventh bell the crew were on their knees like men at prayer, the rasping of their holystones and the sound of their low singing hanging in the air as they scrubbed the decks.

Donald brought him his morning cup. 'Your coffee, sir.'

'Thank you, Donald.'

'There's no milk.'

'At all?'

'Our goat doesn't like being at sea.'

'Damn.' Faulkner grimaced. 'Well, it can't be helped.'

'Could I get another goat here? You and Lord de Lacey do like your coffee.'

'There isn't much here other than the fortress. But we'll make for Hazlewood next. You should be able to get one there.'

Donald looked shocked. 'That's the weather mages' island.'

'And?'

'I don't want to go ashore there!'

'I think you'll be safe, Donald.'

'You say that now, sir, but a bloody island packed full of tainted folks just ain't right.'

'Imagine it. We already have a ship's cat – if you annoy the weather mages enough you could become our ship's toad.'

'What has toads got to do with—' Realisation dawned and his servant's eyes narrowed. 'The tainted aren't for joking about, Captain.'

'You're right, I'm sorry. Now go and wake Sophia, we'll go ashore soon.'

Faulkner turned to study the island that was his little brother's temporary home. It was a wild, windblown place that was so much a part of the ocean that it was difficult in places to mark where restless sea ended and low chalk cliffs began. Above the scarred and pitted rocks lay a rolling blanket of dark green heather. In the far distance he could just make out a grey smudge that must have been the walls of the fortress.

His bitter black coffee was long cold by the time Sophia appeared on deck, but he had to concede the delay was worth it. Her cheeks glowed in the brisk morning air and her mane of red hair danced in the wind. She had picked a green-hooded cloak that he thought suited her marvellously. Spotting him, she threw him a strange little smile that plucked at something in his chest.

He walked down to greet her. 'Nice of you to finally join us.'

The men swung the pinnace out and then rowed them ashore.

'Excuse me, sir,' Lewis asked when they were halfway to shore, 'but the men were sayin' your little brother passed the Big Test and is a flyer now. That true?'

Faulkner nodded. 'It is.'

'You must be mighty proud.'

'I am.'

'Being a flyer is next best thing to being a sailor, right, Captain?' Simon ventured.

Faulkner chuckled. 'Yes, though even I have to admit it is perhaps a little more glamorous.'

They landed in a small, well-protected cove. Faulkner lifted Sophia ashore, who for once didn't brush off his offer of help, and then they clambered up the tall sand dune behind the beach. They found a small path at the top of the dunes and followed its snaking path across the island. Faulkner did his best to think of something to say, but every time he opened his mouth the words caught in his throat. They walked on in silence until they crested a small rise and the fortress came into view.

'I didn't realise it would be so big,' Sophia said. The ugly walls were made up of enormous triangular bastions and glacis, each shaped to cover its neighbour and survive the fire of heavy, modern guns. Even Faulkner dreaded to think what else the nation would have been able to do with all the money.

'The king built the fortress to cover our western approaches. Though they say he also hoped to quarantine our flyers from the plague.'

'It looks expensive.'

As they approached the closest gate, a sleepy-looking soldier in the grey uniform of the Royal Eastern Army came out to meet them. 'Who goes there?' he barked.

'Captain Faulkner. This is Miss Sophia Blake, my, ah, business partner.'

'No one ever comes to this gate,' the solider observed accusingly.

'We landed on the far side of the island and walked across the moor.' He turned to her. 'Soldiers, always so full of initiative,' he whispered.

Sophia put a hand to her mouth to hide a smile.

The soldier didn't seem to notice. 'Why are you here?'

'I hoped to visit my brother.'

'Faulkner? Wouldn't be Tom Faulkner's brother, would you?'

'The very same. May we come in?'

'Most visitors land at the port and go through that gate.'

'You did say that. Surely we don't have to walk all the way around to the port though?'

The trooper removed his battered shako and scratched his head. 'I'd better go and ask the sergeant.'

The soldier disappeared back inside the fortress, slamming the heavy gate behind him. Luckily they didn't have to wait long before his sergeant appeared. The sergeant was a huge man, broad of shoulder and a full head taller than even James. He looked them up and down for a moment and stroked an immense, curling blonde moustache. 'Sergeant Hacket at your service, Captain Faulkner.'

'Sergeant.' They shook hands.

Releasing his hand, the sergeant turned his attention to Sophia. 'Your wife, Captain?'

'My business partner, Miss Sophia Blake.'

If the sergeant thought that was unusual, he didn't give anything away. 'My pleasure, Miss Blake. A beautiful lady is always welcome on this god-forsaken island. Now, please come inside. We can't leave you both standing around.'

They followed the sergeant through the postern gate and into the fortress proper. Once through the dour, warlike walls, they were surprised to walk out onto sprawling playing fields. Directly in front of them a small group was playing cricket. Beyond the fields, in the centre of the huge ring created by the fortress walls, were the buildings of the school and garrison.

'Welcome to the Royal War Flying College.' The sergeant paused and thought for a moment. 'Now, if the memory serves, Tom has theory today.'

The buildings were well kept and the gardens immaculate, but the place looked somehow vacant. Other than the cricketers, only the odd student or soldier could be seen going about their business and the overall effect was one of well-kept emptiness. It reminded Faulkner of town on the morning of Saviours Day when everyone was at home with their family.

'Is it always this quiet, Sergeant?' Sophia asked.

The big man nodded. 'Since the Blackwing Plague, anyway.'

'Was it bad out here?'

'Very,' he confirmed. 'My father was stationed here back at the turn of the century with the East Lanark Regiment and when he was here the school was training about two-hundred-odd pegasi and perhaps fifty griffon.'

'And how many are you training now?'

'About thirty or so pegasi and only four griffons.'

'So few! There won't be any flyers left in a decade!' she said.

A shout went up from the game as one of the batsmen middled a ball and sent it racing towards them. Faulkner jogged a few paces ahead to intercept the shot.

'Idiot.' Sophia said, just loud enough for him to hear. 'It's hard to imagine what the world will be like with no flyers,' she said to the sergeant. 'One of my tutors argued that the civil war in Barraine is partly caused by the Blackwing Plague. Her theory was that without the constant stream of messages and communications that flyers used to carry between the electors, princes, dukes and bishops, they all became suspicious of each other and began to drift towards war.'

Faulkner snatched the ball up cleanly and hurled it back to the bowler in one smooth throw, eliciting an approving clap from the fielding team. He turned back to Sophia with a wide grin and was surprised when she grinned back at him.

'Handy work, sir.' Hacket said, before turning back to Sophia. 'If you ask me, miss, Barrainers have always been pretty enthusiastic about slaughtering each other. Still, your clever professor type might be right. Us sergeants only have to fight wars, not worry about what started 'em.'

Hacket led them inside an ornate building. Like the fortress outside, it was largely empty and their footsteps on the polished wood floors echoed up and down corridors. The sergeant briefly paused to talk to a servant and then motioned for them to follow him. Coming to the end of the long hallway they followed the soldier up a flight of stairs, before stopping in front of a plain wooden door on which hung a sign reading *Practical exams – Absolutely no entry – Quiet please*. The sergeant put a finger to his lips and then took out a large key, unlocked the door and opened it. 'Looks like we'll have to wait for your brother to finish.'

Faulkner and Sophia followed the big man through the door and out onto an internal balcony that wrapped around the edges of the first floor of a large hall. The roof above them was glass, like the top of a greenhouse, and the room bright and airy. A strange arrangement of rope and tackle spanned the open space. Standing at the edge of the balcony, Faulkner looked down. The centre of the ground floor below them was taken up by an intricate model of a seaport. It was so detailed that Faulkner could make out perfect little replica ships lying on the polished glass that stood in for water. The model was fenced in by large wooden boards so it could only be viewed from above.

'I recognise that place,' Faulkner whispered to Sophia. 'It's Taurenburg in Auerswald. I spent half my fifteenth year blockading that cold, tedious place on *Colossus*.'

Sophia put a hand on the sergeant's shoulder and stood on her toes to whisper to him. 'What are we waiting for, Sergeant?'

'You'll soon see, miss.'

Below them a door opened and a group of five men walked in. One was obviously a student and by the look of their robes the others were dons. Snatches of their conversation carried up to where Faulkner stood.

'Are you ready?' one of the teachers asked.

The student nodded nervously.

'We are only marking on ships. You may ignore the fortifications and such. Is that clear?'

'Yes, Master Hodge,' the boy replied nervously.

The teachers clustered around the young man and he was strapped into a kind of harness. The harness was then attached to the rope and tackle that spanned the room. The teachers stood back.

'Now remember, boy, just concentrate,' one of the masters said. He turned to the others and nodded. On his signal the three other dons grabbed a line and hauled away like common sailors. With an 'oomph' the boy was pulled up into the air until he was almost level with the balcony. The masters then pulled on their ropes and the boy bounced and swung over the top of the model. They let him have perhaps four seconds to take in the scene then dragged him onwards. On the far side the masters let him down and unclipped him from his harness.

'So Forbes, what did you see in the harbour?'

'Ah, there were about twenty sail of small coastal merchants and perhaps forty fishing ships.' The lad paused and licked his lips. 'Then there were three frigates... five, no four seventy-four-gun ships and three eighty-gun ships. Oh and that's right, there were two very large southern merchantmen under the fortress walls.'

Faulkner shook his head. 'I wouldn't want to lead a cutting out exhibition on that lad's advice.'

'Was he wrong?' Sophia asked

'He was, although it is a bit of a cheeky test. Those "two very large southern merchantmen" are actually both Caladian 74s. Although, Auserwaldian ally or not, I doubt you would ever catch a Caladian man of war so far north. They do hate our miserable climate.'

The sergeant's eyes widened. 'You aren't *that* Captain Faulkner, are you?'

'He is,' Sophia whispered.

'I'm sorry, sir, I just thought you were a common merchant sailor. Tom has never said anything about you being…'

Faulkner smiled. 'We Faulkners are keen to make our way in the world under our own sails.'

Sophia elbowed him in the ribs. 'Shhh, this must be him.'

Faulkner saw that the years had been good to Tom. His pimples had disappeared and while he was still thin, he was no longer gangly. It also seemed Tom had picked up a cavalryman's arrogant swagger from somewhere. Faulkner made a mental note to tease his little brother about that.

Like the student before him, the masters explained the exercise, strapped him into the harness and then hauled him up and over the model. On the other side they unclipped him and helped him out of the harness.

'You claimed this one was going to be hard, gentlemen,' Tom said.

The senior master sighed long-sufferingly. 'What ships did you see, Faulkner?'

'Oh, I should say there were about twenty-five-odd sail of smaller ships. Sloops and brigs mostly, though I did see some god-awful old carracks thrown in for good measure. Fifty-something fishing ships, mostly those herring busses the continental types love.' Tom paused and stepped out of the harness. 'Warships; there were three frigates, all from Auserwaldian yards. Then there were five 74s and three 80s, again all Auserwaldian-built. Lastly, and very impertinently, you had two Caladian 74s hidden away in the lee of the fortress, both of the *Pater Patria* class.'

'Good man,' Faulkner said under his breath.

The senior master looked somewhat deflated. 'You can go, Thomas… oh, and I believe Sergeant Hacket of the garrison is waiting for you upstairs.'

The younger Faulkner looked up to the balcony. 'I can't go shooting today, Hacket, I've got—' His face creased in a broad smile. 'James, you old devil! Ha, still checking I go to my lessons, are you?'

'I'll take you down to meet the young wastrel,' the sergeant said.

Once the sergeant had led them downstairs to meet Tom, the big soldier said his farewells and the three of them adjourned to a sheltered courtyard. The quad was bordered on all four sides by the sandstone facades of the school buildings and roofed by the intertwined branches of some gnarled old oaks and elms. They sat together on the grass under one particularly large tree and Faulkner took a bottle and some tin cups from his rucksack and passed them around. Sophia sat down across from him, leaning back against the rough bark of the oak.

'It's capital of you to come and see me, brother.' Tom poured himself some wine and took a big sip. 'Mmm, this is very nice claret too. So how goes your hunt? I almost thought you were joking when I got the letter.'

'We've only just started. But we have a ship and a gun. Tomorrow we'll start searching the islands,' Faulkner replied.

'Well, good luck killing the silly thing – it's making life thoroughly boring here!'

'Oh?'

'Normally we have plenty of visitors. Theatre companies, musicians and such. At the moment everyone is too scared to sail out here. We are pushing it to even get our supplies delivered, so it has been a very dull spring.'

Sophia smiled at him. 'That must be agony for you.'

'Oh it has.' He considered her for a moment. 'So, Sophia, how did you end up wandering around these dangerous oceans with my brother?'

'My father put up most of the money for the venture. I was sent along as his representative.'

'Isaladar bleeds, how progressive of him! Uriah is your father's name, is that right? Your family used to look after James when he was ashore in Stormhaven, didn't they?'

'That's right,' she nodded.

'So then you must be the red-haired beauty he always wrote about in his letters.'

Faulkner blushed. 'Don't tease the poor girl, Tom. And on the subject of parents, I've a present for ours.' He rummaged in his rucksack then took out a little box and opened it. 'It's a fire pine for their garden. Can you fly it up next time you visit them?'

Before the plague the Caladian emperors had kept entire plantations of this particular pine to feed their dragons. Although the dragons were all gone, the fruits were still a delicacy. The sapling had cost a small fortune.

'They'll love that. There can't be many in the entire Realm. The frost won't kill it?' asked Tom.

'Not according to the chap I bought it from.'

Tom took it and placed it carefully on the ground. 'Wasn't there a poem about these trees?'

'There is,' Sophia said. 'It's one of my favourites.'

Then from the sad west turning wearily,

I saw the pines against the white north sky,

Very beautiful, and still, and bending over

Their sharp black heads against a quiet sky.

She blushed. 'Sorry, that was pretentious.'

'Never apologise! Educated *and* beautiful – you don't have any sisters, do you?' Tom asked.

She was saved from having to reply when a fat man in blue coat and old-fashioned wig emerged from one of the buildings and waddled in their direction.

Tom glanced back over his shoulder. 'Oh dear, it's the commandant.'

'Captain Faulkner! As I live and breathe. What an honour,' the man puffed as he approached.

Rather disappointed at being discovered, Faulkner stood and doffed his hat. 'Knight Admiral Trollope, what a pleasure. I was just about to come and see you.'

'I should hope so, boy! We don't get nearly enough naval visitors out here. Soldiers are all well and good, but they do get a little dull,' the old admiral confided.

'Tom, perhaps you could show Sophia around while I speak to the admiral.'

The admiral beamed. 'That's a superb idea. Now come inside, Captain, I want to hear firsthand about the Asare Roads. A frigate capturing a third rate! I tell you, I almost choked on my port when I heard it!'

'It was a *small* third rate, Admiral,' Faulkner was saying as they passed out of earshot.

'So how long have you had him?' Sophia asked, patting the neck of Billy, Tom's pegasus. Almost luminously white, Billy stood slightly taller than a draught horse. Even at rest and with his enormous wings folded along his flanks, the pegasus radiated a look of nobility and speed.

'He's three now.'

'Why is he called Billy Ruffian?'

'Everyone calls theirs "Northwind" or "Dawnstar" and other pretentious bloody things like that. I thought "Billy Ruffian" had a nice ring to it.'

'So you named him then? You were already on the island when he was born?'

Tom nodded. 'When, and more importantly if, you qualify as a flyer they send you out here to the college. Then it is just a question of waiting. If there is a bad run of stillborns you might wait a year or two to receive a mount. I was lucky and only had to wait about ten months.'

'When do you graduate?'

'Assuming I pass exams, this Saviour's Day. Can't say I'm sorry either, it'll be nice to get out in the field.'

She rolled her eyes. 'You Faulkners are positively called to adventure, aren't you?'

'We are.' He laughed, but it echoed hollow and false in the airy stable. 'But even for us, hunting this leviathan in your little ship seems suicidal.'

Something about his sudden honesty caught her off-guard and a cold stab of fear slid through her. She had been so focused on her taint and her selfish decision to come to sea, it had been a while since she had thought about how incredibly dangerous the leviathan was. 'Do you think?'

Tom shrugged. 'James is the sailor, but yes, I'd hazard that hunting a beast that eats large ships in a small ship is quite suicidal.'

Quite suddenly she was very afraid. 'Could you ask him to give up this hunt, Tom?'

'Me?'

'I'm sure my father could square any debts we've incurred,' she said.

Tom laughed again. 'Telling my brother not to do something he has set his mind on is like telling a river to stop flowing. He's been like that since we were little.' He turned to fiddle with some tack. 'But what are you doing along? I'd expect him to risk his life as usual, but I can't imagine what under the sun he is doing letting you risk yours as well.'

'He didn't "let" me.'

Tom raised an eyebrow.

'I own the ship.'

'Well, sell it then. Make him give his mad scheme up.'

Billy whinnied quietly at the strain in his master's voice.

'I can't do that.' She shook her head. 'I won't do that.'

'Why?'

'He's bankrupt. This is his last chance.'

'Bankrupt is rather less permanent than dead.'

'I couldn't do it to him.'

He turned and looked at her with a very strange look on his face. 'So that's how it is?'

'It is.'

Tom didn't reply and they stood in awkward silence for a moment.

'So were you close as boys?' she asked in an effort to steer the conversation to calmer waters.

He seemed glad of the change of subject. 'Yes, back then we were always getting into one scrape or another. It was a very happy time.' He shook his head. 'I remember once we snuck down to the Royal Highway and, for reasons Isaladar only knows, threw rocks at the squire's coach. It's a wonder our behinds still aren't red from that thrashing! We were always in scrapes like that.'

'And I bet you two chased all those blonde northern girls together.'

'James went to sea when I was only eleven. At that point in our lives girls were alien, boring creatures who split their time equally between crying and telling tales.'

'I've been known to cry, but I never tattle.'

'She has had no need to tell tales – I doubt she has ever lost a fight,' said James from where he had been standing quietly by the stable door.

'And how long have you been there?' Sophia asked.

'Not long enough, by the look on your two guilty faces,' James replied. He stepped into the stable. 'Now I suppose I better let you show off this glorified horse of yours, Tom'.

As the shadows lengthened across the lawns, Tom walked them to the fortress gate. The young flyer kissed Sophia's hand gallantly and then waved them goodbye from the shade of the gatehouse.

'Did you like him?' the older Faulkner asked as they walked out across the moor.

'Very much. He will grow up to be a charming man.'

'Grow up? You're his age!'

'Women grow up much more quickly, James.' She kicked viciously at a rock on the path. 'It's so unfair!'

'Ah… unfair?' he asked, caught off-guard by her sudden anger.

'That's right, unfair! You're a sea captain and he is a flyer and the interesting parts of my life are already almost over!'

'Things are changing…' he ventured. It did seem unfair when she put it like that. If he was in her place he'd probably run mad with claustrophobia.

'What utter rot!' she said. 'What am I going to do? Sit on the Century Council?'

'Why not?'

'Don't be patronising.'

'Patronising?' He grabbed her hand and hauled her around to face him. 'Why not? You're as brilliant as any man I've served with. I'd rather one of you on the Century Council than ten Dukes of Mandor!'

'Swear that you mean it.'

'On my honour.'

'Then you don't wish you'd made me stay in Waterford?'

'What? No! Of course, I wish I had left you ashore as I'd rather keep the number of my friends potentially eaten by the leviathan as small as possible.'

Quite suddenly fat drops of rain began to fall around them. He took in a deep breath. The air was thickening with the smell of rain and to the west a downpour had already obscured the coastline on the far side of the island. 'I'm afraid it looks like we'll be getting wet.' He began to undo his coat to offer it to her.

'Keep your coat on, we can beat the storm to the boat if we run.'

'We'll be soaked before we get halfway.'

'I can make it. We Blakes are sportier than we look.'

He grinned and sized her up. 'Is that right, Sophia?'

'What? You can be gallant about my imaginary political career but as soon as it comes to anything physical I'm still a precious little flower to be protected? I bet I can beat you there too. You were puffing and wheezing like de Lacey on the way up and we only walked!'

'Puffing? Wheezing?'

'Yes, puffing.' She pantomimed it for him. 'But then I suppose you're getting old. And you drink too much!'

'Drink too much?'

'Yes! Drink too much.' She mimed that as well.

'You're on then. First to the boat,' he snapped.

Without another word, she turned and sprinted off towards where the *Game Bird*'s boat was waiting. The first thing he noticed was that she was fast, ominously fast. Realising he would be lucky to catch her, even without giving her a head start, he bounded off after her.

They hadn't even covered half the distance back to the boat before Faulkner was in trouble. Black spots floated in front of his eyes and the insides of his lungs felt like they had been roughly sanded. Worse, Sophia still had a good twenty yards lead and didn't seem to be slowing.

In front of them a nesting tern took flight and, surprised, Faulkner stumbled on a root that lay across the sandy path and almost lost his footing.

'Careful, James! Balance is often one of the first things to go with age!' Sophia called.

Without the breath to spare for a rejoinder, he put his head down and doggedly ran on after her. It began to pour as they crossed the last hundred or so yards of heather before the dunes and his eyes stung from the mixture of rain and sweat. Neither of them slowed down as they raced across a small stony stream. Sophia leapt nimbly from rock to rock while he lurched and staggered along behind her, barely able to look up to see where he was going.

Almost side by side they crested the last rise before the little cove and there below them, small as toys, were the men and the boat. Their pace slowed as they left the track and began to slip and slither down the face of the shifting dunes.

Faulkner was done. His last reserves were shot through and he began to prepare himself for the teasing he would have to endure at the bottom.

'We should have agreed on a prize, old man!' Sophia shouted.

Her gloating was what did it. He gathered his tired legs under him and leapt forward after her. Even with his arms outstretched she was almost too far ahead, but her cloak betrayed her and, as he crashed face down in the sand, his hand caught a corner of it and he jerked hard on the fabric. Sophia stumbled and fell. They tumbled down the face of the slope in a sandy avalanche. Over and over they went in a maelstrom of thrashing limbs and grit before they came to rest in a small hollow at the bottom.

They ended up entwined together, covered by a coating of damp sand. For a moment they lay together, the only noise the distant crashing of the surf and the rustle of sand slithering down the slope after them.

Faulkner started laughing, a deep belly laugh that shook his whole body.

Anger blazed in Sophia's eyes. 'You cheat! You dirty, dirty cheat! You tripped me because you knew I was going to win! You… you… you villain. I've sand everywhere!'

Faulkner continued to laugh as he looked down at her face. She was covered with sand and flushed with anger and incredibly beautiful. 'I'm not sorry…'

That didn't help. She began to punch his chest. 'Brute! Monster! Cheat! Trickster! Fraud! Rake!'

Faulkner felt as if his heart was expanding in his chest. He had a sudden thought that this might, somehow, be the most perfect moment of his life so far. He kissed her softly on the lips. For the briefest of moments, she stiffened under him, then her lips parted and she kissed him back insistently. Arms that had been hitting him coiled about him, hands grasping his hair, pulling him down towards her. Something like distilled exultation flowed through his veins and he hugged her tight.

'Captain Faulkner? Miss Blake? Are you all right? The lads reckon you fell,' called Jenkins loudly from somewhere close by in the dunes.

Faulkner gritted his teeth and thanked Isaladar he wasn't carrying his pistol. At that moment he would have been sorely tempted to use it on his faithful boatswain. He tore himself away from her.

'Just here, Jenkins,' he called out, with distinctly more kindness than he felt.

Sophia pushed him off her and smiled. 'And we are fine, Mr Jenkins, not hurt at all.'

23.

SOPHIA SAT IN her favourite spot by the chickens, enjoying the evening breeze on her face and the tune de Lacey was playing and doing her best not to think about James. The storm that had soaked them as they ran to the boat had passed while they were manoeuvring back out to sea, but the night sky was still cloudy and cool. The gentle wind that had carried the storm away was steady and true and the men of the watch had it easy. Those not on lookout or at the helm were clustered together smoking their long pipes and chatting quietly.

The gentle, haunting piece de Lacey had been playing trailed away to its mournful conclusion. As the last notes were swallowed by the murmuring of the waves, Sophia jumped down and walked aft. 'You're very good, de Lacey,' she said when she found him. She wasn't exaggerating. He played in an assured, almost doleful style completely at odds with the rakish character he normally affected.

'I'm glad someone aboard has a bit of taste.'

'I'm serious. I've heard worse from musicians who play for a living.'

'Thank you.' The young lord fumbled in his jacket for a cigar. 'I find it very relaxing. Playing, that is.'

'Did you ever consider becoming a musician?'

'No. I never did.'

'Did I just offend you?'

He chuckled. 'No. It was just a surprising question.'

'Surprising? How?'

'I could never be a musician,' he said musician like it was a dirty word. 'To touch my fiddle is to touch the body of my lover. To play is to have the world stand still and pure around me. I can make the hardest men cry like a sweet child as I play.' His lip curled in a sneer. 'What utter saccharine rot. Never have been able to stand fools like that.'

'Why? You play so well yourself.'

'Why?' His sneer twisted into a different expression, something self-mocking. 'Perhaps I am just jealous it was never a path I could explore.'

'I think you could have, you're easily good enough.'

'It was never a door that was open to me.' He smiled at her and lit his cigar.

'You're speaking in riddles, de Lacey. What do you mean?'

'My father, the current duke, lost his arm when he was a colonel in the lancers. My grandfather commanded the same regiment in General Alton's army. His great, great grandfather was killed defending Ararn the Conqueror when the king was unhorsed at Pike River. One of my other ancestors fought alongside Prince Isaladar himself during the Deluge. My family doesn't produce musicians, we serve the nation. It is what we do.'

'So, what? Because some of your ancestors were soldiers and aristocrats your course in life was charted out for you before you were even born?'

'Exactly.'

'That's horrible.'

He shrugged. 'It isn't that bad, actually.'

'How isn't it that bad?'

'For a start, if I had a choice between being a sailor or a musician, I'd probably pick sailor. It's just the not being able to pick that rather grates sometimes.'

'It's like being a well-treated slave!'

He laughed at that. 'Don't feel too sorry for me, Sophia. Men are all slaves to something and I'd much rather be the next Lord of the Lonely Isles than a pauper. Look at our Captain Faulkner, he is just as enslaved as I am and his father was only a bloody headmaster.'

'What do you mean he's enslaved?'

De Lacey gestured at the dark sea with his cigar. 'He's out here hunting this bloody fish, isn't he?'

'I thought he was hunting it because he was bankrupt?'

'He could have easily taken a plum job in a foreign navy to pay his debts. There is a lot less chance of getting eaten teaching some foreign lubbers to sail.'

'Why didn't he then?'

'Like I said, he's a slave. A slave to a nation that threw him ashore on half pay as soon as it was finished with him. The navy is thick with fools like us.'

They chatted on for a while about the navy and the implications of the peace. It was a depressing subject though for all de Lacey's joking, and Sophia soon made her excuses and headed below. Back in her cramped little cabin she shrugged out of her heavy cloak and sat down at the makeshift dressing table that Morgan had fashioned. She lit her lantern, picked up her novel and opened it. Four or five times she read the same paragraph, but the story couldn't hold her. It felt as if two utterly separate and competing emotions were warring for control of her.

The first was the joyous blossoming of what she knew now was love. The last weeks she had shared with James had stripped away the gentleness of her childish infatuation and her feelings had blossomed into something larger, deeper and hotter. If she'd had any lingering doubts, their dance at Waterford and their kiss that afternoon had thoroughly snuffed them out. She closed her book and put it down. She shut her eyes and tried to recapture the moment of their kiss, attempting to hold onto it all, forever. The tilt of his head, the flash of fire in his eyes and the set of his jaw as he laughed, even the memory of it made her feel somehow simultaneously weak and ferocious. When she opened her eyes again, the flash of desire she saw reflected in her little mirror almost shocked her.

But something darker bubbled and writhed below the surface as well and tonight it threatened to drag her down into its grasp. It was hard to fight, especially as this despair was as true and solid as cold stone and her happiness was as false as a drunk's. She had seen the hunger in James' eyes when he had kissed her but his longing sprang from his knowing only a part of her. When James found out the truth he would be revolted. She wasn't a serving girl to be elevated from despair to happiness by a simple kiss. Her stain was darker than soot and far, far more permanent than grease. She knew how the taint corrupted a person, how it drove one to madness and worse. Perhaps de Lacey was right? Maybe everyone was beholden to something, and just as duty dominated and enslaved the two men, the taint would always control her destiny. Looking up at the timbers of the deck above, she angrily scrubbed her half-formed tears away.

She wasn't a slave to her taint. Not yet, anyway. She wasn't going to sulk until *Game Bird* returned to Stormhaven. While they were still at sea she would do what she wanted. There was no point wasting her last days of freedom. She had to cram all her life into this summer and autumn.

She tied her hair back, artfully undid her top button and walked out of her cabin.

Faulkner was lying on his makeshift cot reading when Sophia stepped into his cabin without knocking.

'I was bored. I hope I'm not interrupting,' she said.

'Ah, no. Not interrupting.'

'When I saw the lantern was burning, I thought you'd be looking at charts or something.' She shut the door behind her.

'No, no charts tonight. I needed a rest from them.' He frowned at the closed door. 'Charts and leviathans are all I see when I shut my eyes these days.'

She pulled the chair out and sat at his table. 'What are you reading?'

'Callimachus, *The Collapse of the Republic*.' Was it strictly appropriate to have a young lady you had recently kissed in your cabin in the middle of the night? Especially when she was wearing a man's shirt that appeared to have come half unbuttoned?

'I've always thought Callimachus was Lysander's poor cousin.'

He gestured to a little battered locker. 'Well there are other books in there if you want something to read.'

She opened the locker and looked through his small library. 'Ah! Raleigh's *Pirates of the Sunset Isles*. I used to love this when I was a girl.'

'You recommended it to me.'

'Did you like it?'

'It's a great story.'

'It is, isn't it?'

'If only real pirates measured up to Raleigh's ideal.'

'Pirates don't meet with your approval?' she asked.

'I've never quite understood the romantic appeal of men who make their career out of murdering the weak and running from anything approaching a straight fight.'

Her gaze fell on his sword leaning in the corner. She put the book down and drew the sabre from its scabbard. The blade flashed in the lamplight. 'They don't have your sense of daring?'

'I don't think adding the sea and a parrot to a robber makes a hero.'

'But adding a sword to a sailor does?' She swung the sword dramatically.

'For Isaladar's sake, don't touch the blade! Donald will never let me hear the end of it if he has to clean your paw marks off it.' He stood up. The cabin felt even smaller than usual and Sophia seemed very close.

She carefully held the blade up in front of her face and read out the inscription. '"*Captain James Faulkner. For His Zealous & Active Service during the capture of the enemy vessel* Conte di Agrippa, *On The 13t. Of Jany, 634.*"' She threw a hand to her head in mock swoon. 'I think I've found my hero. I'm sure no pirate has ever been so zealous or so active!'

'It wasn't as exciting as it sounds.'

'And what is this inscription?' she asked pointing to some more engravings on the pommel.

'It's Classical Caladian. I can't remember the exact text, but it claims that the hilt contains a splinter of the lance Prince Isaladar used to kill the Great Wyrm.'

'Does it?'

'I imagine that if you got all the alleged pieces of the Golden Lance together in one place you'd have enough timber to construct an eighty-gun ship.'

'The cynical, superfluous hero.' She flourished the sword again. 'Lock up your daughters!'

'Careful! With a stroke like that you're more risk to yourself and the furniture than any foe!'

'Our hero is a swashbuckling sword fighter, too! James, how have you remained a bachelor?'

He sighed and ignored that last part. 'I'm no swordsman. I've all the grace of a woodcutter when I fight! But here, at least let me show you how to stand before you do yourself a mischief.'

He moved to stand close behind her. Guiltily, he admired the elegant lines of her long, graceful neck. Her hair smelled of the ocean and the sun.

He took her warm hand in his. 'Keep this hand holding the blade forward. Put your right leg forward a bit as well. That's about it. And now set your left leg. There, that's about as much as I actually know. From here I just hack away till the action is over.'

'I wish I had a sword.'

'Take this one. I'm forever tripping over the silly thing anyway.'

She turned so she could look at him. 'I couldn't, James.'

'Of course you could. Here, I want you to have it. At the Asare Roads I just used an old cutlass and some pistols Donald threw me at the last moment when we were about to board.'

'Perhaps if I just keep it till we are finished with this fish.'

'I'd like that.'

They stood in silence for a long moment.

'So what happens now?' she asked at last, leaning towards him.

His heart was beating very fast and he took an involuntary half step back. 'We are stopping at Hazlewood to speak with the weather mages.'

She looked up, eyes suddenly wide. 'But they're tainted!'

'They are, but they also know this part of the ocean better than anyone living or dead.'

'You don't fear the tainted?'

'Well, I wouldn't want to live next door to one of them,' he chuckled, 'what with the chance of them running mad and bringing down the mother of all storms on my head or setting their neighbours afire. I am more than happy to quickly seek out their help though.'

Sophia blanched like he had sworn a vile oath.

'Did I offend you?'

'No. I am getting a terrible headache, James. I need to lie down.' She slid his sword back into its scabbard and threw it back in the corner. It slid to the deck. 'I can't take your silly sword, James. You keep it.'

'Sophia, it was only a joke.' He stepped towards her. His stupid mouth! 'I didn't mean to upset you.'

She didn't reply. Face pale as fresh canvas, she stepped out of the cabin and slammed the door behind her.

He thought about following her, but the strength of her reaction stopped him. He blew out the lantern and lay down on his cot. Even though he had no watches that night, it took him an age to fall asleep.

Faulkner stepped out onto the deck and looked about, blinking owlishly in the morning sunshine. Even as tired and low as he was, he couldn't help but be impressed by the scene that greeted him.

The village of Hazlewood was directly to starboard, cupped in the palm of rolling hills, its whitewashed walls and red-tiled roofs picturesque against the blues of the bay and the sky above. The village only got a fleeting glance as to larboard the view was simply spectacular. What once had been granite cliffs now, through hundreds of years' work and vast expense, had been reshaped into an awe-inspiring work of architecture. Faulkner's eye followed the countless sweeping arches as they flowed to meet elegant sea towers or sturdy bastions. The Basilica of the Seafarer, home of the Weather Mages Guild, was a fortress and cathedral hacked right out of the bones of the island. As if the splendour of the fortress-cathedral wasn't enough, above the cliff stood the towering statue of King Isaladar, one hundred feet of bronze and stone, shining and magnificent in the morning sun. In its hands the plate-armoured statue clasped the famous lance that, through some arcane trick, shone brightly at night like a lighthouse. At the statue's feet the Great Wyrm that the young god had slain sprawled in intricately carved horror down the cliff face.

De Lacey strolled over from where he had been overseeing the launching of boats. 'It certainly is something, isn't it? Which is more than I can say for you, Faulkner, you look like death warmed up.'

'Just tired; I couldn't sleep. A situation not much helped by the infernal scratching of your fiddle, I might add.'

'It was a boring watch. I had to amuse myself somehow.'

'No sign of the leviathan?'

'Not a jot, though we did see some wreckage just before dawn.'

'Maybe your bloody playing is annoying enough to ward off even monsters of the deep?'

'Great artists are never appreciated in their own lifetime, Faulkner.'

Faulkner had no reply for that, so he turned his attention to the small group of sailors clustered together by the main mast. They were all dressed in their Sunday best, ready to go ashore. 'Did you forget to tell the rest of them they could have the day in Hazlewood town?'

'I told them, but it seems their usual desire to indulge in debauchery is outweighed by their terror of an island full of the tainted.'

'Jenkins!' he called.

The boatswain appeared with a tin of paint in one hand and a brush in the other. 'Yes, sir?'

'I take it you aren't going ashore then?'

'What? With all them tainted on that bloody island?' The big red-headed man shook his head and looked at Faulkner like he was insane. 'I may not be a clever cove but I am cleverer than that.'

'Well, if you and nine tenths of the crew are going to cower here on the ship, we may as well put you to work. I'll have you dry out the canvas.'

'Want it loosed to the buntline or bowline?'

The bay was a natural anchorage and the wind was only light. It also seemed unlikely the weather mages would let a storm rage on their very doorstep. 'Do it by the bowline, just watch her if the wind picks up.'

'Righto, sir. And what do you want me to do if you don't come back?'

Faulkner sighed. 'Are you joking?'

'They are *tainted.*'

'In the unlikely event we aren't back by eight, you can send a boat ashore to look for us.'

'Eight it is.' The boatswain headed forward to see to the drying of the canvas.

'Now that's taken care of and we are nice and safe, let's get ourselves ashore,' de Lacey said.

Faulkner turned and looked around the deck. 'You there, Lewis, you aren't going ashore?'

Lewis' fat face crinkled into a frown. 'The wife'd kill me if she found out.'

'What about you, Simon?' Faulkner called. 'I've yet to see you pass up a drink.'

'I'll stay.' Simon stroked his huge nose nervously. 'Not enough grog in the Realm to get me ashore on that island, Captain.'

Faulkner gave up and walked down to the boats. The few men who had elected to risk taking their day's leave took the whaler and the pinnace and rowed towards shore. Faulkner spent a moment double checking that Jenkins had things in hand and then shinnied down the side of the *Game Bird* to join de Lacey in the dinghy. The young lord was already lounging languidly in the bow of the small boat smoking one of his cigars, so Faulkner took off his jacket, picked up the oars and pushed off the ship's side. The little boat rocked gently as his first few strokes cut the ultramarine water.

'I would have thought Sophia would come ashore, it being one of the most famous places in the country and what not,' said de Lacey, between puffs. 'Can't picture her being scared of the tainted.'

'She wasn't interested,' Faulkner replied. He had no desire to tell de Lacey that when he had knocked on her cabin door that morning she had said she had no desire whatsoever to go ashore with him again, ever.

'Then I take it your rather foul mood means you two squabbled again?'

'If you're going to smoke that disgusting thing, you can at least try not to blow the smoke all over me.' Instantly regretting his snappishness he concentrated on his next few strokes of the oars. 'Yes, we had a disagreement last night.'

De Lacey puffed a smoke ring out over the water. 'A serious disagreement?'

'I made a boorish joke about the tainted.'

'Not serious then.'

'She seemed fairly upset.'

De Lacey flicked his now spent cigar off into the bay and watched it spin down into the water. 'If she had to listen to one of your witticisms then I'm not surprised.'

'Very helpful.'

His friend grinned. 'I shouldn't worry. Unless her mother was secretly tainted or something, in which case you'd be better off avoiding her anyway, she'll be fine by sunset. Just remember in future that despite her tender age she has already risen far past our immature level of wardroom banter.'

'Thanks.'

'What about you? I've never seen you mooning about like this before.'

'Mooning?'

'Mooning. In fact if I was a betting man, which of course I am, I'd say you're in deep trouble.'

Faulkner grimaced. No doubt the entire ship knew. Isaladar only knew what kind of gossip was doing the rounds of the lower decks. 'I do have some feelings for her.'

'You have *feelings* for her? Isaladar's blood, man, you sound like one of my mother's dreadful novels.'

Faulkner gritted his teeth and concentrated on not belting his friend on the head with an oar. 'I like her. A great deal.'

'And have you thought to mention this to her?'

'We partially kissed the other day.'

De Lacey took out another cigar and lit it. 'Leaving aside the question of how you can partially kiss someone, bravo! I haven't given you enough credit.'

'It wasn't bad form?'

'All's fair as they say. Also let me add that a cynical observer might conclude that Miss Blake came to sea for the singular purpose of being kissed.'

'Her father—'

De Lacey cut him off. 'James, considering in the past you have been able to convince grown men to follow you to almost certain death in storms of shot and shell, sometimes you can be phenomenally bad at gauging motivations. Do you seriously propose to tell me that her father, by all accounts a loving, sensible and level-headed father, told his only daughter to go to sea to participate in a fairly suicidal hunt for a sea monster?'

Faulkner had never considered Sophia would disobey her father, but it did sound unlikely when phrased like that. 'Not even to oversee financial matters?'

'What financial matters? The ship is purchased and provisioned. We have the gun. The cost of the few supplies we might need during our expedition would be pocket change to the Mr Blakes of the Realm. I wouldn't imagine any potential savings on nails and biscuits would be worth the risk of his only child ending up lunch for some ancient primordial terror.' He kicked his boots up on the gunwales and the boat rocked sharply. 'So if he didn't send her, which he didn't, then why did she come? I doubt it was just for the excitement of a voyage in our cramped and fragrant little tub.'

Faulkner gave up. Normally their arguments went on for some time, but in this case he found he wanted to believe his friend and that took most of the fun out of it. 'Assuming you're right, what should I do then, oh wise one?'

'As I like Sophia, most of my normal reprehensible sets of tactics are out of the question. But let's consider the matter anyway.' He held up a hand and ticked off one finger. 'By the sound of it you're probably smitten.' He ticked off another finger. 'If I'm right, which I am, she is smitten as well.' He ticked off a third finger. 'So, considering that despite you being a bloody idiot you're also one of the nation's most eligible bachelors, all you really need to do is ask yourself one selfish question.'

'Which is?'

'In my not inconsiderable experience there are three types of loves. One type makes you feel worse than you really are. By that I mean meaner, grubbier, angrier, more jealous, nastier and generally low. It goes without saying this type is to be avoided. The second type is by far the most common. They leave you as you are and you think of yourself in exactly the same light as before they came into your life; you're neither ignobled nor ennobled by their love. The final lover is one who, by their very presence, seems to change, lift and improve everything about you and the days you pass through. The sun is brighter, wine is cooler, passion is stronger and you are a better person yourself. Or at least it feels that way, which is just as good.'

'That is fairly self-absorbed.'

'Honest is the word. You can thank me later. There should be no martyrs when it comes to love. Now in which category is Sophia?'

'The latter by a sea mile.'

'Then considering she is also attractive, kind, intelligent and brave, I strongly suggest as soon as we are back from our little jaunt, you apologise to her for your terrible sense of humour and then tell her how you feel.'

'And if she doesn't accept my apology?' asked Faulkner

'Give her a stiff drink and try again.'

'You're a bad man.'

'But it is such good fun.' De Lacey yawned, stubbed out his second cigar on the outside of the hull and pulled his hat down over his face. 'I'm having a nap, wake me up when we reach shore.'

The dinghy grounded gently. They jumped ashore, dragged the boat above the high water mark and then trudged through the sand towards Hazlewood. The village's fishing boats were drawn up against the sea wall and Faulkner paused to study them as they passed. The wood of their upturned hulls was bone-dry. 'This one hasn't been to sea for months. Nor has that one.'

'The leviathan?' asked de Lacey.

He nodded. 'I think they mostly fish cod in these parts and the leviathan would make ocean fishing just about a death sentence. Must make life hard for the village.'

'Someone should really think about killing that fish.'

Leaving the fishing boats behind them, they walked up into the village proper. From across the bay the village had been pretty, but on closer inspection Hazlewood was all peeling paint and boarded-up windows. The men of the village sat around on street corners in listless little groups.

'Nothing is quite as depressing a sight as a sailor cast ashore against his will,' Faulkner said quietly.

'Indeed. Which is why I am thoroughly glad you talked the money out of Mr Blake. Or that could be us,' de Lacey replied. 'Although obviously we'd be better dressed.'

A tall, thin and grey-haired woman in the robes of a village official left the shade of a building and walked across the leaf-strewn cobbles to meet them. 'Are you the captain of the ship in the bay?' she asked as she approached

'I am Captain Faulkner and this is my lieu— my first mate, de Lacey.'

'I am Mayoress Wiggins and I just wanted to thank you for sending your men ashore.'

'That isn't the response I normally get when I send a mob of unruly sailors into a town.'

A ghost of a smile touched the woman's weary eyes. 'In the past we did our share of complaining about drunken sailors. In these hard days we will take any coin we can get. People were afraid enough of coming here when it was just the mages, now with this leviathan stalking the sea we are lucky to see a ship a month.'

'If it's any consolation our lads are sure to spend all the coin they have,' said de Lacey.

'It will all be welcome.' She paused and looked them up and down.

'Now, if you are here to hire a mage, I will save you a walk up the cliff. They're not taking contracts at the moment.'

'No?' Faulkner glanced up at the great statue. 'I thought they were honour-bound to help any Realmish sailor who can pay?'

'Too many of them have been killed by this beast. They say they can't risk losing any more brothers or sisters. They'll still work for the navy or the Crown, but they will take no more private contracts. Sorry to disappoint you.'

'I am not disappointed, Mrs Wiggins. I only came here to seek their advice.'

'Oh?'

'We are hunting the leviathan.'

The mayoress blinked. 'The leviathan? In that little bark? Captain, you are madder than a basilisk in the noonday sun.'

'I've been told that before.'

'You're not joking?'

He shook his head. 'We mean to kill it. Or do our best, anyway.'

'I'll take you to the mages myself then. If you two are really hunting the leviathan you are mad enough you might miss the path.' She led them briskly through the twisting and turning streets of Hazlewood and then up the hillside along an overgrown cobbled road that snaked between rambling heather and stunted hawthorn.

'Has there ever been a sighting of a leviathan in these parts before?' Faulkner asked as they crossed a bridge over a swift-flowing rivulet.

She shook her head. 'We had a pair of kraken attack some ships back in the winter of '14 but we've never even heard of anything like this. Not even in folklore or old sea shanties.'

'Any theories on why it has suddenly appeared?' asked de Lacey between laboured gasps.

'You don't look well, boy,' Mrs Wiggins slowed her pace for him. 'And yes, there are plenty of theories, but they are nothing more than the foolishnesses of old fishermen with too much time on their hands and rum in their bellies.'

'I still wouldn't mind hearing them, Mrs Wiggins. Sailors often have some sense buried in our nonsense,' Faulkner said.

'It's the normal rubbish. At the cleverer end of the scale I have heard it said that the beast may have just taken a set against boats in the same way some dogs hate birds or bearded men.'

'And at the sillier end?'

'They talk about the devil fish having been sent up from the depths to punish us for harbouring the tainted.'

'What's your opinion?'

The mayoress stooped, picked up a rock and threw it off the path. 'If old age has taught me anything it's that nature does what she does. I didn't ask the storm why it drowned my dear husband, so why should I ask this fish why it took my youngest son? I'd bet this monster will eventually die or disappear and we'll still be none the wiser as to why it did what it did.'

Ahead of them, rising above the foliage, the vaulted spires of the mages' home loomed into view. The heather soon gave way to the bare cliff top and then they were only separated from the cathedral by a deep chasm in the rock. The gulf was spanned by an impossibly thin bridge, guarded at either end by bronze statues of Isaladar's companions General Toman and Queen Elizabet. Far below the sea surged and crashed against jagged rocks.

She stopped. 'Impressive, isn't it?'

'It certainly is,' Faulkner replied. Sophia would have appreciated it.

'I'll leave you here then.'

'When you get down, could you send someone out to our ship?'

'We might be poor but I'll take no charity, Captain Faulkner.'

'This is no gift. We could do with a goat for a start. Send a boat out to the *Game Bird* and ask for a man called Donald. He'll work out what we need and pay for it.'

'You are a decent man, Captain Faulkner. Travel safe and hunt well. I'll pray to the Seafarer for you.' Turning, she walked briskly back down the mountain and disappeared out of sight.

Faulkner turned to where a puce de Lacey had slumped down in the shade cast by the tall statue of Queen Elizabet. 'Come on, lobster, we're almost there.'

Standing up, de Lacey pointed down toward the bay. 'When it rains it pours,' he wheezed. Another ship was dropping anchor near the *Game Bird*.

'Hopefully they'll spend some crowns as well. The place needs it.'

De Lacey squinted down at the ship. 'It's one of those ugly sloops we made for convoy work. I always forget we sold some of them into private hands.'

'We can talk ships later. I want to get this over with.' Faulkner looked across the bridge. 'You ready?'

'Ready to go into an enormous cave-cum-cathedral packed full of the bloody tainted?' De Lacey straightened his sword and brushed an invisible speck of dust from his jacket. 'As ready as I'll ever be.'

'If anyone can tell us about this leviathan it'll be them.' Faulkner put a foot onto the bridge. 'We'll be fine. It'll be worth it.'

'So I keep telling myself,' de Lacey muttered.

24.

'IT GLADDENS A man's heart, doesn't it?' Marcellus asked.

'Even a sailor's heart?' Uriah replied. The green hills of Hazlewood had felt like dearly missed old friends when they had slowly coalesced out of the morning haze. While Fiora and Scarrus' rough repairs had stopped most of the leak, the *Palinurus*' pumps still had to be used a couple of times a day to keep her afloat. More than once Uriah had caught Captain Scarrus casting nervous looks at the barometer or a suspicious cloud formation on the horizon. Thankfully, the weather had taken pity on them and soon they would be getting the repairs they needed at Hazlewood. Better than that, he might even have news of Sophia's whereabouts. He was almost happy.

'I am no sailor, Uriah. No more than a man who lives in a barn is a horse. I served the countessa long before she took to this nautical life.'

'How long have you been at sea?'

Marcellus turned and looked astern to make sure no one was listening. 'The countessa bought this ship almost straight after her son was murdered. We have been almost solidly at sea since.'

'Oh.'

'It is hard on my family back home…' He shrugged as if to say, 'what choice do I have?'

Uriah heard his name called from somewhere astern. He stepped out from behind the foremast and waved. 'Up here, Fiora.'

'There you are.' She strode across the deck to join them. 'I've just spoken to Scarrus and, considering the state of the ship, he isn't confident we can safely make harbour with this wind. Our charts show a sheltered cove on this side of the island, so we'll anchor there to wait for a change in the weather. In the meantime I'll take you and a few other men and we'll walk overland to Hazlewood town.'

'Walk?'

'It's only about ten miles.'

'That's not too bad. It'll be nice to stretch my legs.'

She turned to Marcellus. 'I don't want to look like a foreign war party so I am only taking five men ashore. I'll leave you to choose them.'

The big man nodded. 'Countessa.'

'Are you ready, Uriah?' she asked.

'I suppose I'd better change into my clothes. I look frightening enough with my face in this mess without dressing like a pirate,' Uriah said.

She laughed. 'You could never look like a pirate.'

Strangely that hurt his pride. 'I think I almost look fierce.'

'I meant that as a compliment. The world has more than enough savages.'

'Thank you, Countessa.'

'I've told you a thousand times, call me Fiora.' She turned to go. 'And make sure you bring the pistol I gave you.'

'The pistol?' He ran a hand over his bristly scalp. 'The Tallowman might be here already?'

'Probably not.' She opened both hands and held them out before her like balanced scales. 'But we lost time running before that storm and, as you saw in Stormhaven, it has a long reach.'

The Tallowman studied the other ship anchored in the bay. It was a small vessel, a brig or a bark perhaps, and it was going nowhere in a hurry as its full spread of canvas was set out to dry. The name painted below the little ship's stern windows read *Game Bird*. It turned to the first mate, Roberts. 'Could that ship be hunting the leviathan?'

'So that's what yar lookin' for, is it?'

The time they had spent together hadn't left the Tallowman completely happy with the mate as a choice of henchman. Roberts was vicious and greedy, which was good, but he was also intelligent and curious, and those traits didn't suit at all.

It decided not to lie. 'Yes. I am looking for a girl. I am told she is on a ship hunting the beast.'

'Well that bark ain't your ship then, Mr Savage. That ship would throw less weight with its broadside than I shit out after breakfast. You'd have to be mad to even go near the devil fish in that little tub. Fuck knows what they're even doing out here.'

The other vessel did look far, far too tiny to hunt the leviathan. The Tallowman shrugged in disappointment; it was still positive this Faulkner would visit Hazlewood at some point. It just had to hope he hadn't already been and gone.

'I'll go ashore now, Mr Roberts.'

'What about the crew?'

'They can stay aboard. You and a dozen men can come with me.'

'Right. Can't say I like the idea though.' Roberts shuddered. 'Not with all them fucking tainted types on the island.'

'The weather mages? You've nothing to fear from those sanctimonious mice.'

They rowed ashore in one of the longboats. The Tallowman and Roberts then stood together on Hazlewood beach while the *Dead Reckonings* hauled their boat up onto the sand. 'The crew of that other ship are already ashore?' the Tallowman asked, pointing to the boats drawn up on the beach nearby.

'Some of 'em anyway. Probably got the day's leave.'

With their boat dragged safely past the tide mark, the *Dead Reckonings* came wandering up the beach, talking amongst themselves. 'Lucky bastards. Even if she was captain's wife she'd be at least good to look at...' a sailor was saying as they came back within earshot.

'And did you see those fookin' teats?' a pasty-faced sailor asked, holding his own broad chest to mime breasts.

'I've always liked redheads too,' a third sailor agreed. 'They're screamers in the hammock.'

The Tallowman spun to face them. '*What* did you just say?'

The dozen sailors took a step backwards, almost as one.

'Speak up,' it hissed.

The *Dead Reckonings* shuffled another nervous step back towards the water. Finally, his hands shaking, one of them stepped a half pace towards the Tallowman. 'Sorry, Mr Savage. We meant no disrespect. Me and the lads were just havin' a laugh...'

'I am not angry. You said something about a red-haired girl.'

'We saw one. On that ship out there.'

'What? On that ship?'

'I swears it.'

The Tallowman narrowed its eyes and studied the *Game Bird*. Its deck crawled with men at work, but it couldn't see a red-haired girl. If the sailors had really seen her, she had gone below now. 'How sure are you?'

'Oh, very sure, Mr Savage. We all saw her. Didn't we, lads?'

The sailors nodded eagerly, sensing they might be out of trouble.

The Tallowman stood quietly for a moment, its methodical mind working. When it finally spoke its whispered voice was thick pleasure. 'Mr Roberts, take the men to whatever passes for a tavern in this poxy village. If you encounter any crew of this *Game Bird*, buy them some drinks and get them talking. I will meet you there.'

'Might I ask what you're going to do, Mr Savage?'

'You may not.'

'Your country isn't living up to its name today,' Fiora observed.

They followed a winding path that threaded its lazy way across the forested spine of the island. The dappled spring sun was warm, birds sang in the trees above, and it was incredibly good to be back on dry land.

'Oh?'

'The Realm of the Mists.'

'No, it certainly isn't, is it? But that name is from long before we called these lands home.'

'I always forget. What was this kingdom called again?' She struggled for the name. 'Dercia?'

Uriah nodded.

'And how long ago did you invade?'

Uriah was in too cheerful a mood to point out the Realm considered it unification. 'It was during the reign of Ararn the Conqueror, about two hundred years ago.'

'Barely a heartbeat in my part of the world.'

He smiled at her. 'We can't all hail from the cradle of Circillian civilisation.'

'And this entire island belongs to the weather mages?'

He shifted his pistol as the annoying thing was digging into his leg again. 'Yes, Ararn gave it to the mages as a royal estate. Mind you, they were already here.'

'It's funny how every nation is different.'

'How so?'

'In my country a person with the taint still fears that a church-led mob will rip them from their bed in the dead of night and take them to the stake. Here they have this island gifted by the Crown,' she said.

'We might be better to the tainted, but we still have our weaknesses and prejudices.'

'Like how you hide your women away?'

'That, and we assume every foreigner is a thief or a brigand. Oh, and we do our best to keep our poor classes oppressed and poorly educated.'

Fiora brushed a branch out of her way. 'Well, as a Caladian I can hardly comment. I would be – how do you say it? Throwing stones in a glass house. We still hold that men and women can be owned as property.'

'Slavery! At least we got rid of that, along with feudalism. The thought of owning people as a possession turns my stomach.'

'Yes. If only we ruled the world.'

'Sorry.' Uriah laughed. 'I find I am getting more and more pompous in my old age.'

'Wise, my friend, not pompous.'

Ahead of them Marcellus had stopped and was leaning against the trunk of a tree, his musket cradled loosely in his big arms. 'We should be about halfway to the village, Countessa.'

Fiora nodded. 'Good.'

The Tallowman spent almost an hour exploring Hazlewood and preparing for the hunt. By the time it had finished it wasn't happy. Not only did the town boast half a dozen volunteer constables but a company of Eastern Foot were also garrisoned in an old walled house at the edge of the village.

That displeased the Tallowman no end. The constables it could deal with easily, but thirty hardened soldiers who had probably spent most of their adult lives fighting against the druids in the north? That was too much, even for it. The existence of the weather mages complicated matters even further. They claimed to be peaceful these days, but who knew what tricks they had up their self-righteous sleeves? Even if the mages were toothless, it clearly wasn't going to be able to risk a direct attack on the girl's ship.

It made its way to the tavern. The place was not much different from the ones the Tallowman had frequented in Stormhaven. The once-white-washed roof was stained almost black by years of soot and grime, and a long bar ran along one wall. Roughly cut benches dotted a floor covered with rushes that smelled a few weeks old. Roberts was sitting at a table with two sailors the Tallowman didn't recognise – *Game Birds*, hopefully. Ignoring the looks elicited by its bandaged face, it crossed to them and sat down at the chipped and stained table. The mate looked up and his eyes gleamed with more than just drink. 'Nagel, this is the man I was telling you about, Mr Savage.'

The Tallowman held out its hand. 'Mr Nagel.'

'Just Nagel is just fine, Mr Savage, I ain't no gentleman.' The ugly sailor ignored its outstretched hand. 'What happened to your face?'

'The pox,' it answered curtly. 'I take it you and Mr Roberts have made friends?'

Roberts smiled broadly, showing his yellow teeth between his beard. 'Why, Mr Savage, Nagel and I've known each other for many a year.'

Nagel nodded in agreement.

'We even sailed together a while back on the run down to Iperus. 'Til our dear old captain took it into his head that Mr Nagel had somewhat sticky fingers.'

'I never stole nuffin'.'

The Tallowman gave what it hoped was a placating nod. 'I'm sure you didn't, Nagel. Now you're one of the crew of the *Game Bird?*'

'Unfortunately.'

'And is there a red-haired girl aboard?'

'There is. Pretty sure she's the captain's little trollop. Hope you weren't married or nothing.' Nagel took a long swig from his beer and chuckled. 'Though with a face like yours I can see why she'd wander.'

'We're not married.' Its mouth was dry with desire. 'What's her name?'

'Sophia Blake.'

The Tallowman stood and walked quickly to the bar. The grey-whiskered publican looked up apprehensively at its approach. 'I need somewhere to talk. In private.' It rolled a gold crown across the bar.

'You could have just asked.' The man caught and deftly pocketed the coin. 'Go through that door into the courtyard. I'll make sure no one bothers you.'

The Tallowman returned to the table. 'Roberts and Nagel, come and join me in the courtyard.' He turned to the other *Game Bird*. 'What was your name?'

The younger sailor looked up blearily. He was almost dead drunk. 'Clarke.'

The Tallowman pressed some more coins into the lad's hand. 'Buy yourself some drinks while we speak to your friend.'

Outside, they sat at a weathered table under the single sickly tree.

'I don't see how I can help,' Nagel whined.

The Tallowman held up a hand to quiet him. 'Do you like Captain Faulkner?'

'Captain Faulkner? That fancy navy boy can go fuck his mother.'

'You're a good judge of character then, Nagel.' It carefully pulled out the Camar Shiem badge it had taken off Mr Otter's corpse and dangled it in front of them. 'Do you know what this is?'

Nagel's eyes widened.

'Isaladar's fucking cock,' Roberts breathed.

'That's right. I am Camar Shiem.' It slipped the medallion back inside its shirt. 'Captain Faulkner is not hunting this leviathan. That is nothing but a convenient lie. He is out amongst these islands because he is being controlled by Sophia Blake. A tainted girl who is dangerous, unregistered and on the run after she murdered her own father.' It paused to let that sink in for a moment. 'Didn't you wonder why he is out here meeting the weather mages? He is trying to blackmail them into helping his tainted mistress. Like all criminals, the tainted stick together.'

'Typical.' Nagel looked up, obviously eager to accept its story. 'The big hero prances around like his shit don't stink, but secretly he is fucking some *tainted* harlot. Disgusting.'

'How much do you like Clarke?'

'Clarke? I don't. Not really. He's just someone to drink with. Got less of a pike up his arse than all them navy tars is all.'

'Good. I am going to take his place aboard.' This was perfect. Once on the *Game Bird* it could bide its time, waiting close to its prey. Lurking like a basilisk circling a desert oasis.

Nagel shook his head. 'That ain't ever goin' to work. Faulkner and his fucking boatswain are certainly going to spot a new face on board.'

'Wait here,' the Tallowman hissed. It stood and walked into the far corner of the courtyard where they wouldn't be able to see the horror of its change. Once it was done the Tallowman removed its blood-soaked bandages and walked back to face them. The two sailors gasped with a mixture of revulsion and amazement when they saw it now wore Clarke's face.

Nagel half stood at the table. 'Fuck me.'

'We Camar Shiem have many tools to use in our battle against the enemy.' It threw its heavy purse down on the table. 'If you get me on board the *Game Bird* that much is yours, Nagel. If we get the tainted bitch off the ship alive, I'll pay you tenfold and more.'

Nagel looked at the purse and then sat back down. 'How do I know you'll pay?'

'I am Camar Shiem.'

Leaving Nagel to mull the proposition over, the Tallowman led Roberts away from the table so they could talk alone. 'Get the sailor Clarke dead drunk and then separate him from the rest of his crew. If you aren't prepared to kill him, sneak him back to the *Dead Reckoning* and lock him below. No one must see him. Is that clear?' it asked.

'Crystal, Mr Savage.'

'Good, now go.'

Back at the table, Nagel had opened the purse and discovered the gold inside. The fool was turning the coins over avariciously in his hands.

'Are you up for it, Nagel?' it asked.

'I am, Mr Savage. It's not just the money either, I can't wait to see

Faulkner's fucking face when we pull it off.' He paused. 'And helping the Camar Shiem is an honour too.'

'Good. Now what time are we due back at the boats?'

'Five sharp.'

'Fine. I will meet you back here at half past four. If I am late, wait for me. Speak to anyone of what we've discussed and our deal is off. And I *will* get my gold back. Piece by piece if I have to.'

Nagel nodded slowly then snatched up the purse and scurried back into the tavern.

After he was gone, the Tallowman sat at the table and thought. It viewed the prospect of having to contact its master again with an almost equal mixture of hatred and fear, but for the plan that was taking shape in its cold mind to work it desperately needed more help. It had just about steeled itself to make contact when the door to the courtyard flew open and Roberts stumbled back into the courtyard.

'Is that you, Mr Savage?'

'Of course it is, idiot. You should be taking care of Clarke.'

'I thought considerin' the business we are involved in, you might want to hear this.'

'What?'

'Some lubber was just telling the tapman that some strange foreign ship landed on the far side of the island. Some of the crew are walking over here on foot. A shepherd saw 'em.'

The Tallowman drew in a sharp breath. It couldn't be the real Camar Shiem, could it? Not this far from Stormhaven? Surely even they couldn't work this fast? 'Did he say what these strangers looked like?'

'That's why I came and got you. Bloody strange thing it is: they said they were blackies and that they was led by a woman, if you can believe that.'

'Blackies? Men and women with black skin?'

Roberts nodded.

Rage slipped into the Tallowman's belly and writhed around like an eel. Countessa Fiora Varzi. It had to be! It slapped the table hard enough that wood splintered under the force of its blow. If anyone was tenacious enough to follow it all the way from Caladia it was her. She must have been the one to rescue Uriah Blake back in Stormhaven, too. It should have killed her in Caladia after it killed her son. It should have known she was too dangerous to leave alive. How many of its kind had she already destroyed? The Tallowman knew of at least one and not many mortals could boast that. It grabbed the mate by the arm and pulled him close. 'Listen well, Roberts, and I will tell you how you are going to make your fortune.'

25.

A CHUBBY, BROWN-HAIRED man dressed in the blue monastic robes of a weather mage was waiting for them on the far side of the bridge. Although his smile was welcoming, a heavy musket was strapped across his back. 'Captain Faulkner, we've been expecting you. I am Brother Barnes.' Barnes laughed at his expression of shock. 'Don't look so frightened, we are not prophets, gentlemen. The taint of weather weaving is a singularity. Word was sent up from the town when your men came ashore.'

Faulkner did his best to force a smile. 'It's a pleasure to meet you, Brother Barnes.' He shook the man's hand. 'This is my friend and associate, Lord de Lacey.'

They shook hands as well.

'Now come, let us get you out of the sun,' said the brother. 'Lord de Lacey looks quite tired.'

'I am,' de Lacey agreed. 'The path up from the village was murder.'

'I don't mean to pry,' said Faulkner as they followed the brother through a cavernous portal carved into the rock face. 'But you just mentioned you have a singularity. What does that mean?'

'It is our taint that is the singularity, Captain Faulkner,' said the brother, as he unstrapped his musket and carefully placed it on a rack just inside the doors. He shut the heavy carved iron door behind them and motioned for them to follow as he set off down what looked like a surprisingly airy and well-lit corridor leading off into the heart of the cliff. 'And what that means is that a weather mage only has the one aspect to their taint.'

'So no reading minds or setting things on fire as a side business?' de Lacey asked, exchanging a look with Faulkner before hurrying after Barnes.

Faulkner cast one last, nervous look at the closed door behind them and then followed after the mage.

'Exactly, there has never been a recorded case of a weather mage having dual aspects,' said the brother.

'I didn't realise anyone could carry more than one type of taint,' Faulkner said as he caught up with the pair.

'It is rare. We count the fact that our taint is a singularity as something of a blessing. It is one of the reasons our guild is tolerated. Common – that is to say, untainted – folk are much relieved to know we can't read the future or scry out their darkest desires.' The weather mage paused as they reached a branch in the corridor. 'Now, considering you are such famous guests, the councillor asked me to offer you a tour of our home before I take you to meet her. Would you like that?'

Being entombed inside a rocky labyrinth packed full of the tainted made Faulkner more than a little uncomfortable, but it also wasn't every day you were offered a tour around a wonder of the world. His curiosity and manners won out, just. 'Thank you, we'd like that very much.'

He wasn't sorry he took up the offer. They drank cool Gelanian wine from crystal glasses on a balcony suspended out over the bay on impossibly elegant buttresses; they emerged from passageways hollowed out of the core of the island into great domed amphitheatres or sunny atriums full of vegetables and flowers; they looked out over the bay through windows that boasted more glass than the average village; they browsed through a library that Faulkner had only seen surpassed in size by the Royal Library in Drania itself – and he was positive that many of the pictures that adorned the wall were by some of the great masters.

When he remarked on the splendour the brother nodded. 'Much of the money that we earn from protecting the merchant ships goes to the maintenance of the basilica. We are something of a collective.'

'Do you stay here forever?' de Lacey asked.

'We are not prisoners. Nor are we sworn to the order for life like the Camar Shiem, if that's what you mean. I visit my family once every couple of years. But yes, most of us see out our lives here.'

'You prefer that?' Faulkner asked.

'Most do, Captain. I certainly find my visits home nerve-wracking. No one would ever say anything to me, but I hate the feeling of frightened and suspicious eyes on me. It makes me feel like a rabid hound or a hunted man. Here in the basilica, among our own kind, we are free from that judgement. This is the only place I really feel at home now.' He motioned for them to follow him again. 'Come. I still have much to show you.'

'What is that, Brother?' de Lacey asked. Through a wide bay of windows cut into the rock, a squat, ugly tower was just visible. The tower didn't face the bay but rather sat out in the ocean proper, only joined to the basilica itself by a long, windswept breakwater. It looked heavily fortified and not nearly as elegant as the rest of the weather mages' home.

'It is nothing,' the mage replied, beckoning them once more.

'It looks like a fortress.'

Faulkner followed his friend's gaze. 'I can't imagine why you'd bother. What fleet would attack an island populated by men and women who can control the weather?'

'It is no fortress.'

'What is it then?' de Lacey asked.

'It is the asylum where we care for my brothers and sisters driven mad by their taint. It looks fortified because it is,' the mage said sadly. 'Those walls are warded to stand against powers almost unimaginable. If my broken brothers and sisters ever escaped that miserable tower they could raise a storm powerful enough to sink this island. Caring for them and keeping them from harming their countrymen is a large part of our duty.'

Faulkner stepped back from the window. 'We didn't mean to pry, Brother.'

'It is no secret. The madness is simply something no one tainted likes to speak of or be reminded about.' The mage set off down the corridor, as if eager to get away from the sight of the tower. 'I will take you to the councillor now.'

Brother Barnes led them up a long spiral staircase that burrowed up through the rock.

'Is it always this quiet?' asked de Lacey.

Barnes drew in a sudden breath. 'No. It... it is the leviathan.'

'The leviathan?'

'It has taken almost thirty of our brothers and sisters.'

'Thirty!'

The mage nodded. 'We are in mourning'

Faulkner was shocked. 'That many?'

'Perhaps even more; some are still at sea and are late returning home.' The brother's voice wavered. 'It has been terribly hard. Our job is to steer ships safely out and back to the wildest corners of the world's six oceans and we expect to lose friends every now and then… but this… this leviathan… I still can hardly believe some of them are gone.'

'I am sorry I brought it up.' De Lacey put an awkward hand on the man's shoulder. 'My manners have forsaken me today.'

'You weren't to know.'

At the top of the stairs the mage swung open a simple wooden door to reveal rolling green fields drenched by the fat noonday sun. 'Here we part, gentlemen. I have a class to teach. Down that path you will find the councillor under a big old oak.'

Faulkner doffed his hat. 'Thank you for the tour. It was breathtaking.'

They left the tower behind and walked across the warm, grassy fields that blanketed the top of the cliffs. They followed the path and soon came upon the majestic oak the brother had described.

A raven-haired woman rose from where she had been sitting cross-legged under the tree and came to meet them. She was perhaps forty and her cool blue eyes were curious as she studied them. 'Captain Faulkner. The man come to kill the leviathan.' Her voice was as clipped and cultured as he had expected from a family as aristocratic as the de Alberns. 'I am Councillor Alice de Albern.'

'A pleasure to meet you, Councillor. This is Lord de Lacey.'

She nodded and turned to his friend. 'A pleasure, Lord de Lacey. How are your parents?'

'My mother is well. My father and I do not currently correspond, but last I heard he was well.'

'Ah. Well give your mother my regards. We went to school together and I have always thought very highly of that most patient woman.'

'I will.'

'Now, Captain Faulkner, how can I help you?'

'I'd hoped to see what you knew of this leviathan.'

She nodded.

'As long as we aren't interrupting,' he added.

'I always have time for the navy, Captain. We are just so short of teachers at the moment I was helping teach Albert myself.' At the mention of his name, a freckled boy of about five poked his head out nervously from behind her skirts.

Faulkner knelt down. 'Hello, Albert. What have you been learning today?'

The boy gestured out to sea. Some miles offshore a waterspout was weaving its way drunkenly across the otherwise calm surface of the water. Faulkner started in surprise. He had seen a spout like that once before, but that had been in the heart of a black-as-the-night storm, not in the middle of a calm and sunny day. Nerves fluttered in his guts. It wasn't right for anyone to hold that kind of power over the elements, especially not a child. 'Is that safe?' he asked.

The councillor smiled. 'We do check the ocean is empty first, don't we, Albert?'

The boy nodded and whispered something to the councillor. She smiled again. 'I am sorry to impose, Lord de Lacey, but Albert is very interested in the navy and he wondered if you'd tell him the story of your action in the Asare Roads. Could you indulge him while Captain Faulkner and I confer?'

De Lacey forced a thin smile. 'I'd love to.'

They walked away from the oak along the edge of the cliff. 'I'm not sure how much I can aid you, Captain,' the councillor said.

'Any information could help.'

'If you have read the papers then you know as much as I do. The beast generally sinks each ship in one or two strikes. It then circles around and devours any survivors.'

'I did my research.'

'Then what do you need from me?'

Faulkner looked out over the ocean. Without the boy's attention keeping it alive, the vicious little storm had almost entirely dissipated. A patch of disturbed water was all that marked were it had been. 'Prior to this leviathan rearing its ugly head, how many ships would have sailed through these waters in any given month?'

'The Bastion Isleands?'

He nodded.

'I couldn't tell you exactly.' Her brow furrowed. 'Thousands if you count fishing ships and smaller vessels.'

High above them a lark began to sing its high, clear song. Faulkner had always liked the lark. Such a plain bird on the ground, but its song was so beautiful when it was on the wing. 'Brother Barnes said that as many as thirty of your guild had been killed. Is that correct?'

'Twenty-nine brothers and sisters have been killed. Seven are missing or late.'

'Does that strike you as a lot?'

'Of course it does!' she snapped. 'I have known many of the dead since they were in swaddling clothes.'

'Sorry, that was incredibly tactless.' He took off his hat, ran a hand through his hair and tried to collect his thoughts. 'Thousands of ships sail these seas in any given season and thus far less than one hundred have been sunk by this beast, as far as we know. What portion of ships passing through the islands hires your services?'

'Not many. Obviously we serve the Crown at our pleasure, but only the richest merchants can generally pay, although we occasional offer our services for free if the cause is a good one.'

'So what, one in twenty merchant captains might employ a mage?'

'It would be closer to one in fifty I would estimate.'

'But a full third of the ships destroyed have carried one of your mages.'

'Isaladar!'

He nodded.

Her eyes widened in dismay. 'How could I have missed that? How could I have been so blind?'

'It is a good deal easier for me to be logical when it isn't the people I grew up with being killed.'

'If only I had realised earlier...'

'Nothing like this has happened in the history of well, um, history.' He shook his head. 'It's hard to step back and look at the entire puzzle.'

'When did you realise?'

He spread his hands. 'It was only when Brother Barnes told me about the number of mages who had been killed that it began to fall into place.'

'Does our aspect somehow attract it?'

'I'm no expert on your tai— sorry, aspect, but yes, I think it must.'

'Our order had sailed a good part of the globe for almost five hundred years, but we have never seen anything in the ocean like this!' She looked out to sea almost accusingly.

'I don't think anyone has seen anything like this leviathan before.'

'What should I do then, Captain Faulkner? I am a teacher first and a politician second. This is far, far outside of my field.'

'I am no expert on sea monsters either, but my advice would be to call in every single favour you're owed to try to have this beast killed. The king, the navy, Isaladar's blood – even the Iron Brotherhood if you can manage it.' He cleared his throat. 'I'd contact the Camar Shiem as well.'

'The Camar Shiem? Surely you don't think…?'

'I've no idea. But you aren't in a position to discount any possibilities.'

'And what are you going to do?'

'Me? I'll continue my own hunt.'

'In that little bark?'

'Yes.'

'That's madness.'

'I prefer to think of it as long odds.'

'Sail back to Stormhaven, Captain Faulkner. You have already done us and the nation a great service just by delivering this warning. I'll see you are well rewarded.'

'I can't just go home. I've seen what this beast is doing out here.'

'Of course you can.'

'I can't.'

'Why?'

'Why? We are safe here in the Realm because for three hundred years the navy has not baulked at any fight. Seventy years ago they shot Admiral Lockwood on his own quarterdeck as a reminder to the rest of us that the nation would rather we fight and lose than run. That is the simple school I was raised in. I freely admit I started out on this hunt driven by greed and my desire to win the reward, but now I'm out here I can't just walk away. That would be something very close to cowardice.'

'There is nothing I can say to change your mind?'

'No.'

'Is there anything I can do to help?'

For a moment he considered asking her to take in Sophia, but he couldn't bring himself to maroon her amongst the tainted. That, and the thought of bodily dragging her kicking and screaming off *Game Bird* like some kidnapper was highly unappealing. 'No, I think I have everything I need.'

The two of them turned and began to walk back to the gnarled oak. 'I will be praying that Isaladar keeps you safe, Captain Faulkner.'

'I am not a deeply religious man, Councillor, but I'll take what help I can get.'

Above them the lark had reached the top of its ascent and it glided inland, singing its soaring song as it went.

26.

'HOT WORK.' URIAH took out a handkerchief and, careful to avoid the bruising around his eyes, mopped his brow again. After a couple of miles the trees had given way to rolling, flower-dusted fields. Now and then they disturbed the odd flock of sheep or a rabbit. Once they saw a shepherd's hut in the distance, but otherwise this part of the island seemed almost empty of human habitation.

'This is a pleasant winter's day in my homeland.' The hike hardly appeared to have tired Fiora. She still walked with all the tight, controlled elegance of a cat.

'I'd hate to see your summers.'

'You would. Only cockatrice and snakes venture out at noon.'

They had gone on a little further and were splashing across a wide, clear stream when Fiora cleared her throat and glanced at him. 'I hope this isn't impertinent, Uriah, but I have been meaning to ask you something.'

It took Uriah a moment to realise her expression was nervousness. 'Go on.'

'How did you deal with the discovery of Sophia's taint? It must have been very difficult for someone who is not tainted themselves.'

'Well, it was.' He stepped from rock to mossy rock, trying unsuccessfully not to wet his feet in the stream. 'Other than when Mary died, it was the most shocking experience of my life.'

Fiora helped him up onto the far bank. 'Tell me if I am prying, but how did you actually find out?'

'It's not prying.' He paused to shake the water out of his silver-buckled shoes. 'When Sophia was only nine or ten I was away on business and she found a stray kitten. Sophia, being Sophia, adopted it. I have never liked cats, but by the time I got home from Drania she was so attached to it that I could hardly send the blasted thing away. She pampered that cat.' He smiled at the memory. 'She even made the unfortunate thing wear bonnets and ride in her little pram. But she'd only had it for a year or so when it got mauled by our neighbour's wolfhound, an ill-set beast I had never much liked. Poor Sophia found the cat on the way home from school. The little thing was torn to shreds. I should have put it out of its misery, but I didn't have the stomach to do it and Sophia disappeared into her room with the dying cat in one of her mother's hat boxes.'

'And in the morning the cat was healed?' Fiora guessed.

'Yes. In the morning Mary took Sophia's favourite breakfast up to her while I got out a shovel to bury the cat. Instead, my wife found Sophia pale, cold and almost at death's door, with the cat lying next to her, fit as a fiddle and without a scratch on it. It took Sophia almost half a year to recover her full strength and for the rest of its life that cat followed her everywhere like a lapdog. It also slaughtered a good portion of the local bird population and brought them to her as offerings.'

'Did you ever speak to her about it?' Fiora asked.

'Stupidly, we didn't. We struck that foolish impasse children and parents sometimes reach, where neither side is sensible enough to reveal or admit they both know something.'

'It is a hard thing to talk about.'

'Well I wish I had,' he said. 'My cowardice in not confronting this taint might still cost Sophia her life.'

'You handled the discovery better than I did with my son and I am tainted myself.'

'Oh I don't know, Fi—'

Something shrieked past his ear. A split second later a sharp crack reverberated across the tranquil fields. He looked around dumbfounded. He remembered that noise from Stormhaven. Musket fire!

He turned to run, lost his balance, tumbled backwards down the slope and splashed down into the cold water of the stream. Above him Fiora's pistol barked out a reply. *Deus pascit corvos! Deus pascit corvos!* she roared.

A second and a third musket roared and a ball ricocheted off a stone close by with a crack. Behind him someone screamed in long wavering shrieks. Uriah scrambled along the streambed on all fours, desperate to put as much space between himself and the sounds of the fighting as he could. The rocks tore at his knees and elbows. In his panic he hardly noticed.

A heavy hand fell on his shoulder and he was thrown headlong into a bush by the side of the water. Branches cracked under his weight, thorns scratched his face and he tasted sap in his mouth. He scrabbled at the pistol on his belt but he couldn't get it free. Opening his eyes he saw Marcellus. The big man crouched down near him and held a finger to his lips. 'Lie still. It's the running rabbit that gets shot.'

'Sorry.' With shaking hands he worked his pistol free. 'I lost my head.'

'It's all right.'

The two of them huddled in the lee of the bank, watching and waiting. Around them they echoed the occasional crash of a shot and more screams.

'Are we winning?' Uriah whispered.

'If the countessa is still alive, we are.'

Uriah nodded and crouched still, watching as a yellow ladybird climbed sedately along a branch in front of his face, serenely unaware of the maelstrom of violence swirling around it. Marcellus' sudden sharp intake of breath jerked Uriah from his reverie. He followed the big man's gaze to where three men were advancing in their direction down the stream, muskets at the ready. They were dirty, unshaven and dressed in a mess of tattered and brightly coloured clothes; sailors by the look of them.

He gathered his feet under him, ready to run back to the way he had come but Marcellus held him down. 'If you run now, you die. Stay hidden. When they get closer use your pistol. Then run.'

Without waiting for an answer, Marcellus raised his musket to his shoulder and fired. The sailor on the left's head popped open like a smashed melon. Bone and blood splattered down into the waters of the stream around the dead man. The report of the shot set Uriah's ears ringing. Marcellus threw down the musket and stepped into the middle of the stream.

'*Cunnus!*' the big man screamed at them, as he fumbled for the pistol in his sash.

One of the remaining two sailors, a massive, black-bearded villain, raised his musket and fired. The ball caught Marcellus in the throat with a wet thwack and he clutched at his neck and toppled back into the water like a felled tree. Marcellus thrashed once, gasped out a choking gurgle and then lay still. His face lolled towards Uriah and dark, almost blue blood bubbled from his mouth and mixed with the pools of water in the stream.

Uriah crouched down behind his bush, breath rasping thunderously loud in his ears. The acrid taste of powder filled his mouth. He held the pistol so tightly his fingers felt like they would break. The two remaining sailors paused for a moment and checked their mate. Seeing he was dead, the bigger man stopped to reload his musket while the other one slunk up the stream bed towards where Uriah was hiding.

Uriah watched the man come, nerves fraying under the pressure of the sailor's steady advance. The sailor was still twenty yards away when his resolve broke. He raised his pistol and pulled the trigger. The gun barked and kicked savagely in his hand.

The sailor ducked his head and then grinned. His shot had missed.

The man Uriah had missed raised his musket to his shoulder. 'Look what we 'ave 'ere,' he called back over his shoulder.

Uriah stared down the barrel of the gun. It yawned in front before him like the entrance to hell. He told his legs to move but they remained bunched under him, as dead as he soon would be.

With a hoarse war cry, Fiora crashed through the bushes behind Uriah and leapt through the air, swooping down on the closest sailor like a great bird of prey. The man tried to turn, but he was too slow. Fiora's sword took him just above the left eye and the force of her blow threw his corpse against the far bank.

The huge black-bearded sailor paused, ramrod in one hand, musket in the other. Trapped halfway through reloading he stared at the countessa. Then, with a grunt of terror, he threw down his gun and sprinted back down the stream. Fiora dropped her sword and calmly picked up the blood-splattered musket off the sailor she had just killed up.

She put the musket to her shoulder.

The sailor scrambled up the bank, his feet slipping in the sandy earth.

Fiora fired.

The big man threw up a hand and screamed in agony. But he didn't drop. He lurched up and over the top of the slope and was away into the bushes.

'*Mentulam Caco*,' she snarled. Picking up her sword she turned back to him. 'Drop that pistol and follow me.'

'What?'

'Drop the pistol and follow me.'

He nodded dumbly, let the pistol fall into the bloody water and clambered to his feet. Without waiting to see if he was following, Fiora turned and jogged down the stream. He stumbled after her. After a couple of hundred yards they picked up another of the *Palinurus'* crew. Although Fiora waved for the sailor to follow them, she didn't stop. She led them up out of the stream and back across the meadows towards the distant ship. They ran and ran and ran until Uriah's back burned and the wounds on his face were burning hot and crushingly heavy. Finally they reached a small wooded valley and Fiora stopped. Uriah fell to his knees and was immediately, noisily sick. Beside him the single surviving sailor sank down against the trunk of a tree. The man's left wrist was a bloody mess where it had been shattered by a musket ball or cutlass blow.

Even Fiora looked tired now. She was still standing straight and tall, but she was drenched with sweat and her chest was rising and falling like a bellows as she tried to catch her breath. Her face and arms were covered in a thick splattering of blood and gore. She drew her sword and advanced on the other survivor. For a mad moment Uriah thought she would kill him, but instead they talked quietly for a moment. Apparently satisfied with the man's responses to her questions, she turned and walked towards Uriah. Her eyes were hard.

'Marcellus died because of me,' Uriah said. When he shut his eyes all he could picture was that dark blood as it poured out of Marcellus' mouth.

'Marcellus died because of the Tallowman.'

'That's not true. He sacrificed himself for me.' He wished he could cry or scream. Instead he was just numb.

'He did. He was a good man.'

'He died because of me,' he murmured again.

'You can mourn the dead later,' she snapped. 'Listen to me. Answer these questions carefully or I will kill you.'

'Kill me? What are you talking about, Fiora?'

'Tallowmen love to take the place of those they have killed on the battlefield.'

'What?'

'Answer these questions or I will kill you.'

'Fiora!'

She ignored his shout and raised her sword till it was an inch from his neck. The blade was still flecked with blood. 'What was your wife's name?'

'Mary.'

'What drink did we share after the storm?'

'Posca?'

'Who did Sophia rescue when she was a child?'

'A kitten.'

'Good.' She cleaned her sword on the grass and then slid it back into its scabbard. 'It wouldn't be the first time a Tallowman has sprung an ambush so it could take a dead man's place after the action.'

'The Tallowman attacked us?'

'What other explanation is there? Yours is a peaceful country.' She nodded. 'They were most likely its henchman. I don't think he was back there.'

'What now?' he asked as she helped him up.

'We head back to the *Palinurus*.'

'But Sophia! We have to go on to the village.'

Fiora shook her head. 'To go into the town with the Tallowman alerted would be suicide. Anyone we meet might be the beast. It would pick us off like lambs.'

'But what about my daughter?' The thought that she might only be a few miles away but unreachable was agonising. 'We can't just leave her in its clutches.'

'What else can I do? There are three of us left. Of that three, one is crippled and you, you will not fight.'

'But—'

'Enough.' She cut him off with a sharp chopping gesture. 'We are returning to the ship.'

It took the Tallowman a long time to find what it needed. Villages were rarely good hunting grounds: unlike larger towns where urchins, whores, the mad and the weak were always ripe for the picking, villages tended to look after their own. Luckily it finally found an old shepherd dozing in the shade under an apple tree on the edge of town. It was in too much of a hurry to even bother waking him. Instead it simply slipped its knife into the old man's belly as he slept and quickly pressed one of its burrowing worms deep into the wound. It didn't even pause to savour his last flickers of terror.

It sat near the old man's corpse and wondered if this shepherd's pathetically frail body was even strong enough to hold communion. If the corpse failed, that would not make the Tallowman at all happy. Its pouch only held two more of the seed-worms and it needed to save them. Thankfully, the corpse finally gave a shudder and lurched upright in the long spring grass. The Tallowman started, torn between relief that it had worked and terror at its masters approach.

The hermit's dead face, beard matted with blood, stared at the Tallowman.

'Have you harvested the girl?'

'I haven't, master. Not yet.'

'What? My host is dying and I still have much to do,' the corpse hissed.

'I am so sorry, master. But I don't have her yet,' the Tallowman whimpered. 'But I almost do. I just need your help.'

'Help?' The corpse bared the few brown teeth the old shepherd had left. 'More help? You were summoned to help feed me. Your task in this cursed realm was to harvest one old man and one girl, both unaware of their peril. Even this simple chore has proved impossible for you! Have you forgotten why you were made?'

'I would never forget what I am! You are mighty and I am but a pitiful creature! If you do this one little thing then I promise the girl will be yours.'

When the corpse spoke again its words came slowly, as if controlling itself was an effort. 'If I had any other option I would destroy you now, Tallowman. I would scatter your soul like so much chaff and then I would strip what was left and drink your essence. But, as you were the only tool sent to help me, I will consider your request.'

De Lacey let out a long breath. 'That wasn't too bad.'

'It wasn't,' Faulkner agreed. 'I still wouldn't be tainted though, not for all the gold in Drania. That asylum tower out in the ocean! It mustn't be much fun trudging through life wondering when madness might suddenly claim you.'

'Nerve-wracking,' de Lacey agreed.

Faulkner shook his head to clear it of thoughts of the taint and all that came with it. 'Let's start back down to the village. If we are early we can always just stop for a beer.'

'Did you find out anything useful?'

'I did. I think our leviathan has been drawn to attack the weather mages somehow. That is, at least when they're at sea.'

'Are you joking?'

Faulkner shook his head. 'A full third of the vessels sunk carried weather mages.'

'That many?'

'I think so. A hundred or so ships sunk for thirty mages killed.'

'Isaladar's blood, those numbers stink, don't they?'

'They do. Have you ever heard of a predator being, ah, drawn to the tainted before?'

'No. They say most large beasts avoid the taint.'

'This leviathan certainly isn't "most beasts", is it?'

'No.' De Lacey ducked under a gnarled overhanging branch. He snapped off a twig and slowly broke it into smaller pieces. 'The more I hear, the more I can't shake the feeling that it is somehow intelligent. Properly intelligent.'

Faulkner opened his mouth to tell his friend that the leviathan was no different from a whale, shark or kraken – an ancient and powerful animal, but an animal nonetheless, but he couldn't. 'I know what you mean,' he said finally.

De Lacey stopped and cocked his head. 'Did you just hear shots?'

Faulkner shrugged. 'Their soup could probably do with some rabbit now they can't fish.'

'True.'

De Lacey got so out of breath heading back down the hill it was almost five by the time they reached the village. Although they hurried down to the boats, they needn't have bothered. Typically, Nagel and his mate Clarke were still nowhere to be found. It was almost twenty past five and all the other sailors were long back from the village's tavern when the two malingerers finally appeared.

'I don't like to be kept waiting, gentlemen,' Faulkner barked as they got close.

Nagel surprised him by almost grovelling. 'Sorry, sir, we got lost. We'll be more careful in the future.'

'Much more careful, sir. Won't happen again,' agreed Clarke, doffing his hat with a strange, alien little gesture.

Faulkner looked them up and down. He had already punished Nagel once and they both did seem to be genuinely contrite and, surprisingly, not too drunk. Perhaps Nagel was finally starting to fit in. 'Just don't let it happen again.'

'Thank you, Captain,' the two men chorused as they raced down to the waiting pinnace.

'I wouldn't want to be one of Clarke's mess mates,' whispered de Lacey as they pushed the dinghy back into the water. 'Never noticed it before, but the man stinks like the grave.'

27.

'LIFE CAN'T BE that bad, Sophia,' said de Lacey. He left his position by the helmsman to come and stand alongside her at the rail. The morning breeze was only a caress and the sky was a high, empty blue. James had taken them back out to sea at first light and astern Hazlewood was already only a dull smudge against the horizon.

'I look that grim, do I?'

'Oh yes.' De Lacey looked her up and down rudely. 'You look about as happy as a lieutenant who just got told his next post is with the press gang.'

'I'm just tired.'

'Everyone seems to be saying that lately.'

'Perhaps everyone is just tired, my lord.'

He took out a cigar and lit it. 'Perhaps.'

She liked de Lacey and enjoyed his company, but the man was far too clever and far, far too nosy for his own good. 'I'm just in a bad mood.'

'Would you like to talk about it?'

'Not particularly.'

'Did you and Faulkner talk last night, after his watch?'

'We didn't,' she snapped. 'I also said I didn't want to talk about it.'

'I'm going to give you some advice,' her friend said. 'Whether or not you follow it is your prerogative.'

'Aren't you meant to be on watch?'

'It'll be fine. Noblemen have always been good at doing two things at once. Comes from all those years spent oppressing the serfs at the same time as we were robbing them. Now as for the advice, it is quite simple. Duty, which we spoke about the other day, is one thing, but self-denial of one's, ah, finer feelings is an endeavour better left to nuns, monks and martyrs. Life is far too short not to chase what you desire.'

She didn't realise her girlish fancy for James had been that obvious and she blushed at the realisation that all the crew probably knew. She must be a laughing stock. 'De Lacey, you have no idea what you're talking about,' she lied.

'I'm not an idiot, Sophia.'

The sudden noise of men's voices raised in argument interrupted them.

De Lacey, swore, flicked his cigar over the side and jogged forward. 'You men there, stand fast!'

'You're needed on deck,' Donald hissed into Faulkner ear.

'Leviathan?' Having stood the middle and morning watches Faulkner had been deeply asleep, but he sprang from his cot like he had been scalded. 'Leviathan?'

'No, an argument amongst the men.'

'Serious?'

'Pretty serious, Captain. I believe the new man, Boscawen, raised a hand to Morgan.'

'Hit him?'

Donald shook his head. 'No, Captain. But still, to raise a hand…'

'Mmm,' Faulkner agreed distractedly. He rubbed the sleep from his eyes and then threw on his shirt. 'Which jacket is my most dignified, Donald?' The excitement and fear that always came with the prospect of an action slid away and last night's unhappiness crowded back in its place. He had followed de Lacey's advice and tried to talk to Sophia but she had quite literally slammed her cabin door his face.

'The blue one, sir.'

'I don't look like I am pretending to still be a naval officer, do I?'

'No, Captain. You look very serious, very stern.'

'Good.' He shrugged his way into the coat, strapped on his sword and put on his hat. He looked at himself in the mirror and scowled. Perhaps he had been too gentle, too forgiving with this new crew.

On deck he strode over to where de Lacey, Morgan and Boscawen stood. Morgan and Boscawen were still red-faced and obviously angry.

De Lacey lifted his hat and saluted impeccably. 'Captain Faulkner.'

'What happened?'

'Morgan was not happy with Boscawen's stock lashing. He asked Boscawen to redo it three times. They argued and Boscawen raised a fist, but did not strike Morgan.'

Faulkner turned to the two men. 'Do either of you dispute this account?'

Morgan shook his head. 'That is the truth of it, Captain.'

'Boscawen?' Faulkner asked.

The ex-whaler looked up, eyes still bright with anger. 'That's about it, Captain.'

'I will see you in my cabin then, Boscawen.'

Back down below and safely away from the prying eyes of the crew, Faulkner sat at the small desk they had built to fit the space in the stern cabin not taken up by the gun and considered his options. On a warship he was acutely aware of what power he could wield and utterly confident in his ability to both control and inspire the men. But finding a balance between fairness and obedience on the *Game Bird* had proved harder. The ship was neither merchantman nor man of war but a mixture of both – and there was the rub. Too hard on them and he would have an unhappy and rebellious crew. Too lax and they would be tardy, lazy and easy meat for the leviathan. A sudden and even more painful than usual longing for the navy flooded through him.

The door opened and Boscawen entered, clutching his hat before him.

He motioned for the whaler to stand in front of his desk. 'Boscawen, this seems fairly clear-cut. Do you have anything to say?'

'That was the third time I did that stock lashing and it was perfect each time, Captain.'

Faulkner was inclined to believe the whaler. Morgan was a fastidious man who only liked things done exactly his way, but discipline was discipline. 'Boscawen, you're probably the most natural sailor on this ship, but I don't want naturally gifted men. I want men who'll toe the line and work together. Raising your hand to any man on my ship is inexcusable, regardless of perceived provocation.'

'I understand, Captain.'

'Because you're an old hand, I will give you a choice.'

The whaler blinked in confusion. 'A choice, Captain?'

'I understand how hard it can be to fit into a new ship when you have been at sea for so long. Isaladar knows it has taken me some time to adapt to all this.' He made an expansive gesture taking in the entire ship. 'So, in deference to your age and experience, I will be happy to put you ashore at the next port with enough money to tide you over till you get another berth. If you wish it, anyway.'

'That wouldn't do at all.'

'Are you sure?'

'I'll stay.' Boscawen nodded. 'I've still got a debt owing to the leviathan.'

Faulkner nodded. 'I thought so. But it'll be half a dozen from the cat then. I can't have my crew threatening their officers.'

'The cat it will be then, sir.'

'Very good. Go and tell Mr Jenkins you're to be flogged at sixth bell this afternoon.'

Boscawen nodded and left. The sound of the man's footsteps had hardly died when Sophia stormed into the cabin.

'I assumed you'd be eavesdropping,' he said.

'You can't have that old man flogged, James!'

'I can.'

'You can't!'

'I can and I will.'

'That's barbaric!' She shook her head and a strand of her hair burst free, as if liberated by her fury. 'Barbaric.'

'You've been ill-mannered enough to refuse to speak to me for more than a day and now you burst into my cabin to call me barbaric,' snarled Faulkner.

'This has nothing to do with us! Thrashing that old man to prove a point is disgraceful.'

'It isn't to prove a bloody point.' He flung his chair back and stood up behind the desk. 'It's to maintain some discipline on this Isaladar-forsaken ship!'

'Discipline? Discipline? If you treat men like dogs, James, what will they act like?' Her eyes were blazing now. 'Dogs!'

'Don't be so dramatic.'

'Dramatic! I wouldn't be surprised if this crew mutinied. Not the way you tyrannise them with all your drills and punishments.'

'Don't you dare lecture me on the running of this ship.' A cold part of him noted that he was shouting, but he was too far gone to stop now. 'You might own this ship but by god I am its captain.'

'It's undemocratic.'

'Undemocratic?' He laughed at that. 'And how long did your beloved Cartian Republic run their fleet like a democracy for? Six months! And what happened the first time that most democratic fleet went to sea? One of their seventy-fours ran aground in the harbour mouth and another sprang a leak and sank. Sank! A ship's crew needs a firm hand. A ship's crew needs discipline.'

'You're no better than a fat old nobleman making excuses as to why the working man can't have the vote!'

'And you're a spoilt brat who knows nothing of the real world!'

'No wonder the oppressed in our nation talk of revolution.'

'Now you talk revolution? Get out, Sophia. I won't listen to another second of this seditious rot!'

'Good. I feel sick looking at your cruel face anyway!' She slammed the door behind her.

Faulkner sank back down into his chair, his hands shaking. A mixture of anger and tiredness as heavy as a cannonball twisted and turned in his guts.

Just before the sixth bell Faulkner came back up on deck. Boscawen's mess mates stripped the old whaler to the waist and chained him to the grate. Jenkins took his place a few paces behind Boscawen, the cat held loosely in his big hands. The crew were drawn up in a half circle, faces as grim as men at a friend's funeral. Sophia was nowhere to seen, but he was sure she was watching, disapprovingly, from some hidden vantage point. She'd probably write about his savagery in some radical pamphlet when they got home.

Despite the forbidding mood, Faulkner still found it all strangely informal. Where were the lines of marines in their dark blue coats? Where was the grim, rolling cadence of their drums? He felt naked with no orders to be read or charges to be laid. The utter power and absolute weakness of a merchant captain's position was suddenly very real. He cleared his throat and stepped forward. 'Boscawen raised a hand insubordinately against one of this ship's officers. Considering Boscawen only threatened the officer and his offence was in the heat of the moment, the penalty is to be six lashes. When you're ready, Mr Jenkins.'

The boatswain leant forward and slipped a bit of hard leather between Boscawen's teeth and then stepped back into position and flexed his wide shoulders. Jenkins raised his tattooed arm slowly and then the cat whipped through the air.

Crack.

Boscawen grunted in pain.

'One,' counted de Lacey.

Jenkins swung again. As it cut through the air the cat flicked a thin spray of Boscawen's blood across the deck.

Crack.

'Two.'

Crack.

'Three.'

The whaler moaned and his head lolled about on his shoulders.

Thwack.

'Four.'

Rivulets of sweat and rivers of blood trickled down the whaler's back.

Thwack.

'Five.'

Thwack.

'Six,' said de Lacey.

'Very good, Mr Jenkins.' Faulkner turned to the crew. 'Now I will have no more unruliness from any of you. Boscawen's mess mates, help him down and see to his wounds.'

'That's never much fun,' observed de Lacey under his breath as the crew dispersed.

'It certainly isn't.' Despite having once been given a round dozen himself, Faulkner had still never got used to it. 'Shall we have a drink?'

Before de Lacey could answer, a great shout of dismay from the men by the larboard side interrupted him. In three brisk strides he and de Lacey were at the rail.

'There! See?' asked Giovanni, pointing excitedly to the far distance. Faulkner shaded his eyes and searched the horizon. A sail! The ship was a great southerner and she was cracking along under a noble spread of canvas, probably eager to get her rich cargo home after a long voyage out to the colonies. It took him another moment to realise why the crew had cried out. A league or so behind the southerner there was a great, boiling disturbance in the water. Fear settled on Faulkner like a cold and heavy cloak. He snapped open his glass and trained it on the frothing ocean. There, in the heart of the spray and the churning water, he saw it.

The leviathan!

His hand shook a little and his heart fluttered and kicked. Viewed through his glass, the beast was more terrible than his nightmare. Its hide was a pockmarked mess of grey scale, streaked with lines of rope and canvas ripped from its victims. Its dorsal fins were torn and leathery parodies of wings. Its cavernous mouth could swallow a longboat whole. He fought his terror down.

'Beat to quarters,' he barked. 'De Lacey, you have the gun.'

Around him the men scrambled to take their places at the ship's battle stations. Glass locked to his eye, Faulkner watched helplessly as the unstoppable avalanche of water and gnashing teeth ran the flying southerner down like she was riding at anchor. Easily overhauling the ship, the leviathan tore into her stern with the fury of a dozen broadsides. The southerner's main mast fell slowly overboard almost immediately, tearing sails and rigging down with it. The impact was brutal enough that the sound of the leviathan's blow carried faintly over the miles and miles of water.

'Mr Jenkins,' he called back over his shoulder. 'See you get Boscawen into a boat.' He didn't want the injured man left behind if the Leviathan came after the *Game Bird*.

He put the telescope back up to his eye. The southerner was settling by the stern and it was obvious she had already taken her death blow. There was no sign of the leviathan, although an ugly mess of angry water marked where it must have dived back down into the depths. He fumbled for his pocket watch. The dying southerner was, what, six nautical miles away? The leviathan's speed was harder to calculate. The thing was incredibly fast though and it must have been making a least twenty, twenty-five knots when it hit the southerner. That meant it could be on them within the quarter hour. He checked the time again and slid the watch back into his pocket. 'Sing out as soon as you spot it,' he called up to the lookouts.

'There! Half a mile astern of the merchantman,' a man in the tops shouted back only seconds later. It seemed the leviathan wasn't finished with its original prey. It slashed back across the heaving water and tore into the ship again, almost completely stoving in her stern this time. Through his glass Faulkner could just make out the crew of the doomed ship scurrying about the listing deck, still desperately trying to swing out the boats. He had to admire their resolve. Most crews would have panicked long ago.

Her holds already filled with seawater, the ruined ship raised her bow and began to slip beneath the waves. Still not content, the leviathan threw itself up out of the water and crashed down on the deck, smashing timber and bodies apart with pitiless ease. A great lash of its tail caught a hapless sailor and the poor fellow tumbled through the air to splash down into the ocean a full hundred yards from the ship. Faulkner could take no more. Snapping the glass shut, he turned his back on the terrible spectacle. 'Mr Jenkins!' He took a deep breath and mustered the courage he needed to give the order. 'I'm going below to take command of the gun. I'll have you make full sail towards the southerner's last position, thank you.'

For almost two hours he and de Lacey crouched by the cannon. Slow matches hissing in hand, they stared out astern at the grey sea and tried not to blink, imagining in every wave, in every uprising of the swell and in every crest of spray, the great beast bubbling up from the depths to shatter the *Game Bird*.

But the leviathan didn't come for them.

Finally, knees groaning in protest, Faulkner stood up and extinguished his match in the bucket of sand. 'It seems we're out of luck.'

'Luck.' De Lacey gave a short, ugly laugh.

'At least now we've seen the thing.'

'We have.' Hands shaking a little, de Lacey took a cigar from his jacket and lit it with the end of his slow match. 'Did you realise it was that, um, brutal?'

'No.' Faulkner had seen de Lacey's courage in action too many times to patronise his friend. 'I mean, you read the accounts, but to see the thing actually sink a ship. Isaladar's blood, it's a murderer.'

'Reckon our gun is powerful enough to kill it?'

Faulkner glanced down at the enormous cannon and tried to picture the leviathan alongside it. It'd be like a heavy musket killing an elephant. 'Yes. I think it is. But we'll have to hold fire till it is right on top of us,' he said. Leaving de Lacey in command of the gun, he went back up on deck.

The men on watch were scared, silent and on edge. The gallows humour and cheery willingness to get to grips with the enemy that was usually present before an action with an enemy ship were completely absent now. He couldn't blame them. The empty ocean and complete absence of the leviathan was more terrifying than a fleet of enemy ships. Where had the beast gone? Had the destruction of the southerner satiated its terrible hunger? Or maybe it simply hadn't noticed them? Whatever the case, once it had finished devouring the southerner's crew, the leviathan had dived back down into the grave-black depths and simply disappeared.

Making slow headway in the gentle breeze, they sailed up to where the great southerner had sunk. By the time they reached the spot there was almost nothing left. He walked to the side and looked overboard. A few splintered timbers, a broken spar and the odd barrel was all that marked the site of the splendid ship's doom.

'Captain,' Nagel snarled suddenly, close behind him.

He turned. There were about a dozen sailors behind Nagel. He looked from face to face. All of them were new men he hadn't sailed with before. They were also the ship's malingerers and complainers. 'Yes?'

'We want out, Captain,' Nagel said. There was a muttering of agreement from the men behind him. 'We all saw what the leviathan did. It'll tear this little bark apart. This hunt is nothing but glory-blinded madness.' The sailors spread out into a threatening semi-circle, trapping him against the side of the ship.

'Tread carefully, Nagel.' Faulkner said, forcing his words out. 'You're only a point or two away from mutiny.'

'Is it mutiny if a captain is mad?' one of the sailors, Clarke perhaps, asked in a stage whisper.

'Talk all you want about madness. But you all knew what you signed on for. Every one of you knew the dangers.' He gripped the hilt of his sword tightly and took a step towards Nagel's sailors. They shied back, like wolves from a stag at bay. 'I gave all of you the chance to leave in Waterford. None of you took it. Now you're on the books and you'll have to stick it out like men.' He raised his voice. 'What we just saw was a terrible thing, a horrifying thing. But take heart and don't let it be claimed that Realmsmen are scared of anything that sails on or lurks beneath these seas. *Our* seas!'

'Flowery words, but some of us have families back ashore,' snarled Nagel.

'And by the terms of your contracts they will be generously provided for if you don't return.'

'We still don't like it.'

'And I do?' He took another step forward and Nagel and his mates backed away again. 'Do I like that an oversized fish is driving us from our own seas? Do I like it that sailors like you and I are being slaughtered in their thousands? Of course I don't. But what kind of man would I be to run snivelling home at my first sight of the beast?'

'But we're scared, Captain,' one of the men said.

'And so am I and I'd bet so was Isaladar when he confronted the Great Wyrm. But he still dug in his spurs, slammed down his visor and killed the monstrous thing. Just like we're going to kill this beast.'

'You really think we can?' one of the men asked.

'Think we can?' He forced out a laugh. 'Why else would I be here? Do I look like a man tired of life? Of course we can kill the leviathan. I've already been thinking about how I'll spend my share of the bounty when I get home.'

'But you saw what happened…'

'She didn't have a sting in her tail though, did she?'

'We all right here, Captain Faulkner?' Jenkins called. Behind the half-moon of men encircling him, his boatswain was standing by the main mast with a group of almost twenty *Inflexibles*. The *Inflexibles* had armed themselves with a wicked mixture of hammers, boat hooks, mallets and crowbars.

'I think we're finished.' One after the other, he looked each of Nagel's mates in the eye. Less than half of them even met his gaze. 'Unless there was there anything else, Nagel?'

Nagel looked over his shoulder at the *Inflexibles,* gulped and then looked to Clarke for support. The younger sailor offered him none. 'No, Captain,' Nagel replied.

'All right then, you fucking sea lawyers.' Jenkins cuffed a man over the ear and forced his way into the half circle. 'Back to work. Time to earn your bleeding pay for once, you lazy bastards.'

Simon slapped the hammer he was carrying against his palm 'Go on, Nagel, just say something. Anything.'

None of them said anything. The men broke up and shuffled back to their stations. Although he only got a brief glimpse of the young man's face as he walked away, Faulkner could have sworn Clarke almost looked amused.

'Sorry, sir. Had no idea they would be that nervy,' Jenkins said quietly.

'Neither did I, but between that first sight of the beast and Nagel fanning their fears, I suppose it's no wonder.'

'I don't like that man.'

'Nagel? No, nor do I. Pity we need him and his mates now. We don't have the time to return to Stormhaven and sign on more crew and I don't want us shorthanded if I can help it.'

'We'll need to watch him then. Dogs like him always bite the hand that feeds 'em.'

'Let's hope Nagel only barks. But you're right, we need to be careful. I'll give pistols to a few of the more reliable men tonight.'

'Aye. Can't hurt.' Jenkins spat over the side. 'Reckon trouble to Nagel is like flame to a moth.'

'We might need to watch Clarke as well.' Faulkner realised he was still holding his sword hilt tightly and he let go. 'I'd thought him a harmless enough lad, but lately he's had a very sullen air about him.'

'Boy stinks like a carcass, too.'

28.

SOPHIA SAT ALONE in the bow of *Game Bird*. The last few days had left her feeling utterly wrung out and she had taken to leaving her cabin at night to lurk here by the bow. At sea James posted his lookouts aloft, so at night in a calm weather she could almost guarantee she'd be left alone to brood. With one hand on a line, she leant forward so she could better watch a small sea wyvern as it flew alongside the ship, pale and lonely in the night. She admired the ease with which the lizard cut through the air on its silent wings. She wished she was like the little beast. Free from her shame. Free to explore the great oceans and wander where she wanted. Free from the pain of human contact.

Her and James' race and then kiss on Lord Morgans Island had been one of the most sublime moments of her life. Everything had fallen away and she had been so buoyant, so free and, like some moonstruck teenage dairy-maid, she had been so swallowed in that moment that, for the first time in as long as she could remember, she had been stupid enough to almost forget her taint. Then James had made his joke and the weight of the truth had come crashing back down on her. How could one silly, meaningless kiss change anything? She was a clock ticking down towards madness. As if that sadness wasn't enough, then she'd started their stupid fight over Boscawen. She knew she'd no right telling him how to run the ship but that horrible situation had provided her with the opportunity to finally be furious at the unfairness of it all and, by proxy, at him. She kicked her bare feet out over the side of the ship and the cold spray splashed her toes.

A flash of movement in the shadows made her turn her head. A strong arm encircled her waist and a hard, calloused hand clamped over her mouth.

The man dragged her down into the shadows beneath the anchors. She tried to scream. She tried to claw at her attacker but he was far too strong and he pinned her down against the cold timbers of the deck.

Through the web of rigging above her, the light of the cold moons shone down on her uncaringly.

The Tallowman smiled with Clarke's face.

Morgan and another man lay at its feet, their blood mingled on its heavy boat hook. Another one of Faulkner's tame men, Pincher, had also been by the wheel, but the Tallowman had recognised in Pincher a born killer. So it had used its knife on him and Pincher's corpse now floated face down somewhere in *Game Bird's* wake.

Nagel slunk across the deck.

'The other two?' the Tallowman hissed. The *Inflexibles* Giovanni and Peter had also been on watch.

'Trussed up like hogs for market.'

'Good.'

'Should I kill 'em?'

'No.' They might have to serve as bargaining chips later. It gestured to where Morgan and Simon lay. 'Tie the four of them up together. Are all our men up on deck?'

'Aye.'

'Good. Once you've tied up the other two, bring the men here. I want to speak to them. And remember, if we need to fight...'

'You've told me. Kill anyone except the girl.'

The man smelled of salt and tar. Hand still clamped firmly over her mouth, the figure raised himself up off her with his free arm. The moonlight lit his face and she saw it was the whaler, Boscawen.

'Please be quiet,' he whispered. 'In a second I'm goin' to take my hand off your mouth. If you scream I am a dead man and you are in deep strife. Understood?'

She nodded.

'Make a noise and we are both done for,' the whaler croaked as he released her.

Free of Boscawen's grasp, she slithered away from him until she was crouched underneath one of the anchors, panting in fear like a fox at bay. 'What on earth are you doing, Boscawen?' she hissed. 'If this is some sailor's stupid joke…' Sweat was cold and prickly on her back against the bitter iron of the anchor.

'This is no joke, Miss Blake.' The whaler wasn't even watching her. He had slunk forward to crouch near the foremast. He motioned for her to follow him.

Against her better judgement, she did. 'What?'

'Look,' he murmured under his breath, pointing astern.

She leant around the mast. Near the main hatch a group of about a dozen men were clustered together. They had armed themselves with a motley collection of weapons. One or two even had pistols.

As she watched, Clarke climbed up onto a barrel. 'You've done well.' His whispered speech carried very faintly to them over the creaking of the ship and the murmur of the sea. 'But it is still a long way to the Cold Barrens. We still have to trap the others down below like the rats they are.'

'I'm not keen on this, Clarke. I only wanted out of the hunt. I didn't want this,' said a sailor. The man gestured to a number dark shapes on the deck. 'We should just take a boat and go.'

Her heart lurched as she realised the utterly still shapes were bodies.

'And since when are you calling the shots for Nagel, Clarkey?' another sailor muttered.

'Since now, Boardman,' Clarke replied. He drew something out of his tunic. 'Nagel and I lied to you a little when we were organising this.' He held the thing out and it caught the lantern light. It looked like an amulet or locket of some kind. 'There are far more important things at stake tonight than our just own skins.'

The men gasped. 'Camar Shiem,' they whispered, almost as one.

'I am Camar Shiem,' Clarke nodded. 'And the fate of the nation depends on this ship being brought under our control.'

'Believe it or not, lads, but there are worse things than leviathans in these parts,' added Nagel. 'We are going to save ourselves and do the nation service in the bargain.'

The ship's goat brayed quietly and Sophia ducked back behind the mast, her heart pounding. But Nagel's men paid it no attention and she leant forward again.

Clarke had his chest puffed out now like some conquering tyrant. 'We are going to deal with the officers next. Each of them, from the captain down, is guilty of tainted perversion.' He reached into a bulging purse, took out a handful of gold and held it out to them. 'And like any common criminals they have bounties on their head. Any man who kills one of the dogs will get a bounty of one hundred crowns. It's two hundred for the man who cuts down the captain. He's the worst of them.'

'That's right, two hundred. A fortune,' Nagel whispered to them.

But they were going too fast and the sailors were confused. 'What? The captain's tainted?'

'That's fucking right he is. Why else did he sneak in his visit to those dirty weather mages?' Nagel gestured to Clarke. 'Why else would a Camar Shiem come huntin' him?'

The men gasped and whispered among themselves.

'I understand this is a shock,' Clarke forged on. 'But it is the truth. Harden your hearts against his evil and let's get to this brave work.'

Sophia had heard enough and she crawled back into the welcoming shadows at the bow. She felt sick and weak. Had she brought this down on them? Had the dreaded Camar Shiem come all this way to hunt her?

Boscawen slithered across the deck to crouch near her.

'The Camar Shiem,' she said.

The old whaler snorted quietly. 'That man Clarke is no more Camar Shiem than I am the Emperor of all Barraine.'

'What?'

He shrugged. 'The Camar Shiem usually travel in groups and Clarke is alone. Plus we stopped at Hazlewood, which has a garrison of soldiers. If he really was Camar Shiem he could have snapped his fingers and had them take over the *Game Bird* quicker than lightnin'. If he really is one of the king's servants, why would he want to try the long odds of mutiny at sea with only a bunch of miscreants for help?

'You're sure he is lying?'

He nodded. 'Good as sure.'

'But—'

'Do you really believe Captain Faulkner is a criminal?' Boscawen shook his head. 'Not only is the man straight as a die, but he's spent half his life in the navy. Do you really reckon he's managed to hide away a taint for the ten long years he's served on the king's ships?'

She took a deep breath and forced her breathing to slow. 'You might be right.'

'They're not Camar Shiem,' Boscawen said firmly. 'Clarke sniffed around me a few nights back, I guess he was checkin' my loyalty. He certainly didn't sound like one of the king's men then.' Boscawen grimaced. 'Wish I had told the boatswain now. I thought Clarke was just looking for an ear to whine into.'

'If he isn't Camar Shiem then who is he?'

'Pirate or slaver would be my guess. Does it matter? Whoever he is, he isn't the righteous man he claims.' The whaler frowned. 'He and Nagel are playing those fools like a fiddle.'

'If you said "no" to him then how did you escape?'

'This isn't my watch. I couldn't sleep 'cause of my back, so I came up on deck to take the air. When I saw it all start I figured there wasn't much I could to help and hid up here.'

'You didn't consider joining them? After James had you flogged?'

Boscawen shook his head. 'I got what I deserved. If a man had raised his fist to one of my officers I would have given him three times what I got.'

She peered back down the deck to where Clarke had finished his speech. He had apparently won they men over as the armed mutineers were spreading out across the deck. 'We need to warn James. They'll murder him.' Her initial fear had changed into a rushing, boiling thing that demanded action.

'Aye. But how?'

She peered back astern. The mutineers were alert and had the deck and hatchways well guarded. She wouldn't get five yards sternwards before she was spotted. But she had to do something. She could make a din. But what would that achieve? She'd be captured and James would walk straight into the mutineers' trap. No, somehow she had to warn him herself. She glanced hopefully up into the rigging, but a mutineer was already perched high up there. She couldn't shinny along the sides of the ship's hull, they had that watched too. How could she warn them without also alerting the mutineers? She searched the bow for something, anything that could help. There were chains, block, tackle, canvas, pots of paint, a bucket of lime and rope, yards and yards of rope, but almost nothing of use.

She had almost given up when the flickering of the idea came to her. She turned back to the huge coil of rope. Carefully, she looked over the side. Cold water slid along the side of the ship like liquid tar, swallowing any lantern light that fell upon its hungry surface.

'I've an idea.'

'Go on,' Boscawen whispered.

When she had finished outlining her plan, the whaler looked sceptical.

'I can't swim,' he muttered.

'None of you idiotic sailors can. I am going to do that part of it.'

He almost choked. 'What? Absolutely not.'

'I am.'

'The leviathan's lurking in these waters!'

She snorted quietly. 'I heard what it did to that ship the other day. I'm in no more danger in the water than on *Game Bird*.'

'But, but, it's positively indecent.'

'That I can't argue with. But a bit of indecency is better than a bit of drowning and a lot of murder. So unless you come up with a better idea in the next moment or two, I am doing it.'

Boscawen gestured at the black sea and shook his head. 'You can't.'

'I can. Now pull yourself together.'

He shook his head. 'You're a brave one, Miss Blake.'

'I haven't done anything yet. Now turn away while I undress.' She stripped off her clothes until she was completely naked except for the little whistle James had given her so long ago. Shivering, she lifted her arms. 'Now tie that rope around me. Make sure it's tight.'

Doing his best not to look at her and to touch her as little as possible, he did as he was told. 'How's that?'

It was tight enough that it hurt. 'Perfect. Now repeat the plan back to me.'

'You'll climb over the bow and down into the water. Then you'll swim along the side, deep enough under that the villain on watch won't spot you. I play out the rope till you are getting towed along only a few yards behind the stern windows. From there you can hopefully attract one of the officer's attention.'

'Perfect.' She grinned. It was the grin of a gambler with her family fortune on the table and the final card about to fall. 'Now let's get started before I lose my nerve.'

She climbed carefully over the beakhead and then down the bow until she was only a foot above the bow wave. From the deck the *Game Bird*'s pace had looked sedate, but down here, just above the bumping, restless ocean, it seemed like the ship was flying along. For an endless moment she froze, sickness clutching at the back of her throat and her heart fluttering in her chest like a wounded bird. It was obvious there was no easy way to do it. Ahead of the ship the little wyvern still drifted along on the night breeze.

She shut her eyes and plunged down into the sea. The cold water hit her like a hammer blow and tore the air from her lungs. The bow wave picked her up and slammed her into the ship's timbers. She grunted in pain as her hands and knees were gashed by the barnacles that coated the hull. The swell almost tore her free, but her fingertips closed on the ship's prow. The ocean washed over her. Her mouth and nose were full of freezing seawater. Battered by the pull of the sea, her hands and arms burned with the effort of clinging to the ship. She couldn't hang on much longer. If she was wrenched free the mutineers would certainly spot her. With a grunt of effort, she lifted her head out of the water and took a spluttering breath. She managed to twist her feet up under her and she crouched against the bow of the ship, held in place by the press of icy water against her. Boscawen let a couple of dozen yards of rope slither down into the water beside her. Another wave hit her and almost shook her free again. She couldn't wait.

She pushed free of the ship and kicked down into the coal black depths. Down and down she swam until the water pressed on her, loud and cold and heavy.

The rope was agonisingly tight about her chest.

Every part of her being screamed at her to swim back up into the moonlight, but she fought the panic down and forced herself to swim deeper and deeper and deeper.

Her lungs felt like they would burst, but she swam on. She rolled on her back and opened her eyes. *Game Bird's* hull was still sliding past above her, timbers ghost white in the moonlight. She swam on. Spots floated before her eyes and the iron taste of blood was in her mouth. Her hair floated around her face like a madwoman's shroud. She kicked out her leaden legs and swam on.

Finally, she broke the surface and sucked down an immense gulp of air. Pulling against the drag of the rope, she turned back to face the ship and hunched her shoulders, waiting for a pistol ball to tear into her. The shot never came. Sophia blinked the seawater out of her eyes and looked up. There was no sign of any mutineers and above her the stern windows shone, golden and welcoming, out over the ocean. She had made it! She was past the entire length of the *Game Bird* and the first part of her gamble had paid off. Crying with the pain and the effort of it, she grabbed the slippery rope and, hand over torn and bloody hand, she dragged herself through the water towards the stern of the ship.

29.

THEY RAISED THEIR glasses to the toast of the day. 'Our ships at sea.'

Only de Lacey and Jenkins were dining with him tonight as Morgan had the watch and Sophia was still doing her absolute best to keep away from him. Of course avoiding anyone completely was impossible on a ship of *Game Bird*'s size but their few accidental meetings had been silent, awkward affairs.

He put his glass down. 'So what do we have tonight, Donald?'

'A pork pie and then some syllabub for dessert, Captain.' Donald revealed the splendid pie. 'Though I expect it will be wretched. What with the wretched hearth on this wretched little ship.'

'She is a little ship, Donald, but hardly wretched,' de Lacey replied.

'You wouldn't say that if you had to use the rotten—' Donald's grumbling was cut off as the man left the cabin, slamming the door behind himself.

Faulkner picked up the fine bone-handled knife, stood and began to cut the pie. 'So, cheery old Donald aside, how have you two found the mood of the crew?'

Jenkins held out his plate and took a piece of pie. 'Still some mutterin', Captain. But they're better, calmed down a bit.'

'What about that Clarke?'

De Lacey shrugged. 'He's up to something. Always seems to be slinking about, but you can never quite catch him at anything.'

'Well, it wouldn't do to judge the man guilty without evidence.' Faulkner served de Lacey and himself and then sat back down. Mindful of his own foul mood, he groped around for a safe topic of conversation, preferably something naval and technical that de Lacey and Jenkins would talk about all night. 'Now to digress, what did you two make of Brooke's idea to fit *Imperious* out solely with carronades?'

That got de Lacey and Jenkins talking and Faulkner was able to sit back and eat and drink without being called to add much to the conversation. Once they had finished with dinner, they retired to one of the parts of the great stern cabin not taken up by the gun to drink their port in peace, safe from Donald's scolding and complaining.

'Faulkner?' de Lacey asked.

'Sorry. What were you saying?' Faulkner had been leaning against the stern windows, wondering if he should go and try to talk to Sophia again.

De Lacey sighed. 'Jenkins asked if you thought Mayfield should have pursued the Coalition Fleet at St Sebastian?'

'St Sebastian?' Faulkner stifled a yawn and threw down the rest of his glass. 'I've always been a bit suspicious of some of the criticism directed at Mayfield. It's a good deal easier to say you'd have ordered a general chase from your soft armchair by the warm fire than it is to actually do so on the quarterdeck.' Jenkins and de Lacey chuckled at that. 'And Lord Mayfield was mindful that at least five of his captains were unreliable political appointments.'

'Oh?' asked Jenkins.

'Ah, Jenkins, so shielded from the politics of the navy and the weight of command,' de Lacey said. 'Fraser, Macmillan, Gordon, Birdwood, Holloway, de Gardon and Hart were all promoted more for their Conventionist sympathies than for any particular merit as officers. And that's seven, isn't it?'

Faulkner nodded. 'I didn't include Hart or Birdwood. Political appointments they may have been, but they turned out to be capable, gallant officers for all that. But rotten captains or not, if Mayfield hadn't been deprived of his flying eyes I believe he would have given the order to chase.'

De Lacey groaned theatrically and grinned. 'Oh, I should have known. It always comes to this!'

De Lacey's great uncle had been attached to Mayfield's fleet and he and his griffon, Stormrider, had driven off the two Coalition pegasi, killing one of them in the process. Then, to the eternal shame of the de Lacey family, he had ignored his orders to stay with the fleet and had impetuously chased after the survivor like some foolish hussar.

'You asked.' Faulkner paused and cocked his head. 'I could have sworn I just heard a whistle.'

'Doubt it.' Jenkins reached inside his shirt and drew out his. 'This is the only one aboard.'

'I must be hearing things. What was I saying? Oh yes, without de Lacey's rash relative's stup—' He stopped again. The shriek had been louder this time. 'That was definitely a whistle. Isaladar's blood, it'd be a cruel joke if we collided with the only other ship on these lonely seas! I'd better go up on deck.'

He stood up, but before he could take a step away from the window he caught sight of something out of the corner of his eye. For the briefest of moments he had seen something pale and more constant than a wave in the *Game Bird's* wake. He put a hand against the glass to kill the reflection from the lanterns and put his nose against the windows. There was definitely something there. Fumbling for the latch he threw the window open to get a better look.

'Isaladar's blood!' he swore. 'Sophia!'

His heart leapt like a fired gun and he blinked to clear away the apparition. When he opened his eyes again she was still there. It really was Sophia. His drink-fuddled mind scrambled to catch up with what he was seeing. She was barely able to keep her head above waves, but it was definitely Sophia looking up at him from the black ocean below. 'Sophia's fallen overboard!' he barked.

Jenkins and de Lacey leapt to their feet, scattering glasses and bottles across the cabin.

Hanging halfway out of the window, Faulkner turned back to them. 'De Lacey, helm over, yards braced up and have the sheets let go. Jenkins, swing out a boat like your life depends on it.' He ripped off his coat and began to kick off his boots.

'Stop them, James! You have to stop them,' Sophia called.

That was when he saw the rope tied about her. 'Stop there,' he called back into the cabin. He leant as far out the window as he could, until he was only hanging on by his fingernails. 'What's happening?' he called down.

'Nagel and Clarke have mutinied.' A wave crashed over her, but she fought her way back to the surface, still clinging gamely to the rope. 'They mean to murder you and take the ship.' Another wave forced her under.

He gritted his teeth and fought down the urge to ask a thousand stupid questions. He kicked his left boot off and climbed up on the windowsill.

'No! Take the ship back.'

'I can't leave you.'

'Do it! I can hold on. Stop the mutiny.'

'Sophia…'

'I'll be all right.'

She was right. If it was mutiny he needed to be on deck. 'I'll be back for you.' Tearing himself away, he turned back to de Lacey and Jenkins. 'It's mutiny.' Blood thundered in his temples, loud with drink, fright and fury. 'We need to work quickly or Sophia will drown.'

'Who?' Jenkins growled.

'Nagel and a few others.'

'There's a surprise,' said de Lacey.

Faulkner tore off his shirt, he'd seen enough men die from fabric carried into a wound. 'Arm yourselves with whatever you can find.'

Faulkner and de Lacey took a knife and a pistol each while Jenkins liberated two heavy hatchets from the toolbox under the muzzle of the great gun.

'We've no time for manoeuvring,' he began. 'We'll climb out the windows and then go up and over the stern. They won't expect that.'

'What then?' de Lacey asked.

'It sounds like most of the crew aren't involved with the mutineers, so once we're into the fight we make as much noise as we can. Hopefully that'll get a few of the *Inflexibiles* up on deck.'

Jenkins tested the edge of one his hatchets on his forearm. 'How do you feel about killin'?'

'No slaughter once they've struck their colours, but if it is mutiny kill anyone who is armed and still in the fight.'

'Easy enough, Captain.'

'More mercy than they would have shown us,' de Lacey agreed.

Faulkner tucked the pistol into his belt. 'Questions?'

They shook their heads.

'Let's get to it then.' Faulkner put his knife between his teeth and clambered out of the window. He forced himself not to look down at Sophia. The other two followed him, silent as spectres in the night.

Nagel grinned to himself. He was almost rich. He'd never have to go back to sea on some leaky, stinking tub again. He'd never have some uppity gentleman with a rod up his arse push him around. He was going to spend the rest of his life lost in a delirious haze of gin and doxies.

'Are we ready?' he whispered.

The other mutineers nodded, fearful, savage and eager in the moonlight. They were armed with heavy planks, nails and hammers. Once Nagel, Clarke and a few of the other keener men had done in the officers, they were going to nail the hatches closed. The crew down below might still try to take the ship back, but with their officers dead and no easy access to the upper decks, they would be easy meat for the armed and prepared mutineers.

'Nagel, I 'eard something,' a man whispered from behind him.

It was Hesser, the Auserwaldian sailor Nagel had posted on watch by the stern. 'And what did you hear?'

'It sounded like a whistle.'

'Did you spot this phantom whistler, Hesser?'

'No, I figured I should come and tell you.'

Nagel looked about for direction. Clarke was up towards the bow overseeing the preparations there. He considered asking for orders but he had already worked out that Clarke, or whoever he really was, hated being interrupted. 'Take Howard and go and check then.'

'Can I take a pistol, Nagel?' Howard whined.

Nagel drew one from his belt and handed it over. 'Bring it straight fucking back. We've got our bounties to earn.'

'I swear I 'eard a whistle,' Hesser said as he and Howard reached the stern.

'Another ship?'

'Sounded too close for a ship.'

Howard laughed his flat, barking laugh. 'What is it then, you superstitious foreign bastard? A sea witch?'

Jenkins vaulted the rail and landed on the deck between the two sailors. 'It's worse,' the boatswain snarled.

The mutineers froze, mouths sagging open in horror.

Jenkins's first blow caught Hesser between the eyes, split the man's head and splattered his brain across the deck. His second swipe crunched into Howard's throat. The force of the blow lifted the mutineer's body up and over the lee rail to tumble down into the ocean below.

'Fuck!' a man screamed somewhere forwards.

Faulkner and de Lacey leapt over the rail and followed Jenkins into the melee.

Faulkner landed amongst a pack of mutineers trying to overwhelm Jenkins. Fighting like an animal, he lashed out with his knife and it tore into something. Flesh, timber or cloth, he couldn't tell.

'*Inflexibles*! *Inflexibles*! Mutiny!' he bellowed.

A man, Morrow, reared up before him and Faulkner shot him at such point blank range the man's dying gasp was burned onto his vision by the muzzle flash. He blinked, but his night vision was gone. A flutter in the shadows warned him but before he could get around something hit him across the shoulder and agony lanced through him, raw, hot, prickling and cold. He screamed in pain and rolled away. Tebbit, a big sailor and one of Nagel's closest mates, advanced on him, a heavy mallet raised. Faulkner's knife glinted and flashed in the moonlight between them, trying to keep the bigger man back.

'Looking forward to beat your fuckin' brains out!' Tebbit snarled as he swung the mallet again.

The mutineer was too slow. Faulkner threw himself forward inside the man's ponderous swing. Although the handle of Tebbit's mallet caught him a vicious blow on the hip, the heavy head of the weapon only splintered the timbers of the deck. The stench of the man's acrid sweat filled Faulkner's nostrils. He rammed his knife into the mutineer's belly.

Tebbit let out an inhuman screech.

Once, twice, three times more Faulkner rammed the blade home. His hands were slippery with warm blood. Screaming like a dying pig, the big mutineer dropped the mallet and caught him up in a crushing grip. Even wounded as he was, Tebbit was incredibly strong. He lurched forward and crashed Faulkner into the mast. Lights exploded before Faulkner's eyes, his ribs creaked and his heart thundered like it would burst. With the strength of desperation, he worked his knife hand free and stabbed the blade home again, higher this time. The blade crunched on bone and then slid into something thick and sinewy. Tebbit's eyes popped open and then he fell back, dragging Faulkner down with him.

Faulkner thrashed his way free of the corpse's clutches. His hand closed on his knife, but the blade was lodged deeply in bone and the hilt was slick with blood; he couldn't wrench it out. He looked over his shoulder. Clarke was advancing on him through the shadows, a boat hook raised and his cold eyes murderous. Feet slipping on the blood-wet timbers, Faulkner pulled desperately at the knife, but still couldn't free it. He raised an arm uselessly, waiting for Clarke to strike. But the blow never came. De Lacey was suddenly there, behind Clarke. The young lord's pistol barked. Clarke collapsed like he was boneless and his boat hook clattered across the deck.

Faulkner sat up, his hands shaking so much he could no longer even grip the knife handle. De Lacey's pistol shot had set the back of the Clarke's jacket smoking in the breeze. 'Thanks,' Faulkner croaked.

De Lacey dragged him back to his feet. 'Put it on my account.'

Faulkner picked up the dead sailor's mallet and turned to rejoin the fight, only to find it was all over. At the sound of the fighting, the loyal sailors had come boiling up from below decks and the few mutineers still alive looked cowed and utterly defeated.

Faulkner dropped the mallet and set off across the deck at a lurching sprint. 'De Lacey, you have the watch. Jenkins! Jenkins!'

The big boatswain loomed up out the gloom, eyes wide with the fury of battle and his hatchets dripping blood. 'Yes, sir?'

'Sophia's still in the water. Get that boat away!' By the wheel, Giuseppe leant over one of the cowering mutineers, his knife glinting in the moonlight. 'No, Giuseppe, they're finished!' Faulkner shouted.

The Cartian shrugged and delivered a savage kick to the man's head instead, laying him out on the deck cold.

Faulkner turned and spied Boscawen, a bloody chain still clasped in the whaler's big hands. 'You've got the wheel, Boscawen.'

Without waiting for a reply, Faulkner vaulted the capstan. He landed heavily and without regaining his balance he threw himself up and over the stern rail.

For a mad, endless moment he hung there, suspended in thin air behind the ship.

Then the ocean came up to meet him.

He landed inelegantly and the savage impact forced freezing water into his nose and mouth. The momentum of his plunge forced him down deep underwater. He fought down a momentary flutter of panic when he realised just how badly the blow to his shoulder had hurt him. Finding he could still just move the arm he kicked and thrashed his way back to the surface. He spat out a mouthful of seawater and sucked in a deep breath.

'Sophia! Sophia!'

He swam up to the crest of a small wave and spotted her by the trailing of the rope. Her long red hair was floating out across the black water and her body rippled ghostly white in the light cast by the ship. His heart lurched. Although she was still towed along by the rope about her waist, her head was down and her arms lay limp in the water. He struck out towards her, dragging himself closer with every last jot of his strength. Every time he got near her, the rope attached to *Game Bird* would drag her forward through the water and out of his grasp.

He spluttered as he swallowed another mouthful of water and thrashed up the face of a little wave after her. On the other side he threw himself down into the trough, stretching out after her, reaching out with everything he had till he felt like he might fly apart with the effort of it. His arms closed around her waist. Treading water he held her tightly with his good arm. With his injured arm he lifted her head out of the water and laid her on his shoulder.

In a futile gesture he patted her back. For a long moment the only sound was the lapping of the waves around them and the distant commotion on the ship.

Then she coughed weakly. 'You came.'

Faulkner wasn't sure if he wanted to laugh or cry. He held her tightly. 'I promised I would, didn't I?'

She draped her arms around his neck.

Then the longboat was there beside them. Strong hands reached down and dragged Sophia out of the water and into the boat. Moments later he had been dragged aboard as well. As he lay gasping in the bottom of the boat, the men began to see to Sophia.

'Isaladar's blood, she's not got clothes on,' Simon said, sounding more terrified than Faulkner had ever heard him.

'What do we do?' asked Patrick.

'Shove out of the way,' Lewis said. 'Poor lass saved our lives and you lot are panicked she's not got clothes on. It's not hard to tell why you two aren't married.'

'But what do we do?' Patrick repeated.

'Find something to cover her up with, you twits!'

The men frantically searched the boat until Simon found a length of sail. 'Will this do?'

Lewis sighed. 'It'll have to, won't it?'

When the boat bumped back alongside *Game Bird* they placed Sophia in the boatswain's chair and hoisted her gently aboard. When she was safely up on deck Jenkins handed Faulkner a flask. He took it and drank a long swig. Whisky.

'Thanks.'

'You all right, Captain?' the big man asked.

'Battered and bruised, but I've taken worse before. You?'

'It'd take more than a few raggedy-arse mutineers to crack this skull.' Jenkins grabbed the chair as it swung back down.

'If you seriously believe you're getting me into that you're going to be disappointed.'

'With your hurt arm…'

'The day I am carried up onto the deck of my own ship I will be wrapped up in an ensign.' At the top of a roll of the swell he stepped from the boat and onto the side of the *Game Bird*. Grunting in pain, he inched his way slowly up onto the deck.

'Welcome back aboard, Captain,' de Lacey said.

He looked about. 'Sophia?'

'Bundled up in blankets and sent down to her cabin. Looks like she'll be fine.' De Lacey handed him a clean shirt.

'Did she arrange that on her own?'

De Lacey shook his head. 'I gather Boscawen helped her.'

'Our whaler? And after I'd flogged him as well. See he gets some extra grog.'

'I will.'

'What is our butcher's bill?'

'Pincher's gone, thrown overboard, I'd wager. A few others are feeling sore and sorry down below, but they'll live.'

'Pincher was a fine hand, but if he was the only man we lost we got off damn lightly.' Donald brought Faulkner a bucket of clean water and he took it gratefully. Although the ocean had washed most of the blood away, he still scrubbed hard at his face and hands before gingerly pulling a shirt on. 'What of the mutineers?'

De Lacey shrugged. 'Six of them are still alive, but that number includes Clarke and he won't survive the night.'

'Where are they now?'

'In irons below. What do you want done with them?'

'I'll decide in the morning.'

De Lacey picked up the bucket and threw the water over the side. 'Righto. You get below. Jenkins and I had the next watches anyway.'

Faulkner shook his head. 'I'll stand this watch.'

'Get some sleep, you're more knocked about than us. Your shoulder already looks like a side of meat.' De Lacey held out his hands palms up, in a vaguely angelic gesture. 'Not being able to catch my breath after the brawl was the worst that happened to me tonight. Didn't take a scratch.'

'Thank you, de Lacey, but I'll stay on deck.'

His friend shook his head. 'Go below, James. The danger is passed.'

'I'd rather stay.'

'Go. The ship has probably never been safer. Our troublemakers are all either dead or in irons.'

30.

FAULKNER LOOKED DOWN at his cold, hard cot and sighed. As always after an action he was flat, battered and deflated. But tonight his melancholy was even heavier than usual. Mutiny, that hateful word! Mutiny was something that happened to other captains, to fools, tartars and drunks and other men who deserved it. Other than the unnecessary loss of your ship, there was no more damning indictment of a captain. Yet tonight it happened to him: more than a dozen of his crew had hated him enough to risk their lives trying to take over the ship. Intellectually he knew it was partly that they had been so spooked by the leviathan that terror had reduced them to little better than wild animals, but a creeping weight of disappointment and shame still lay under his heart, heavy and cold. How could he have let it come to blood? He'd always fancied that he had a way with his crews.

With a grunt of pain, he rolled back his bedclothes. Lying down and going to sleep was the easiest thing he could have done but instead he turned around and hobbled back down the companionway. At Sophia's door he raised his good arm and knocked sharply on the bulkhead.

'Yes?' she called.

'It's me, Faulkner. May I come in?'

'Just a minute.'

He stood there, his palm against the cool timbers of the ship for what felt like an hour. He should have just gone to sleep.

'All right, come in.'

Sophia was sitting up in his old cot, wrapped in a swathe of blankets. She was still a little pale and her hair hung damp about her face, but otherwise she seemed none the worse for wear. Indeed, he couldn't remember ever seeing anything quite so beautiful. 'I just wanted to, ah, well, are you all right?'

'Just a little cold.' She grimaced. 'I think I've spat out all the sea water I swallowed.'

'To throw yourself into the ocean like that – that was just about the bravest thing I've seen.'

She blushed. 'Really?'

He nodded. 'Really.'

'And you came in after me.'

'I said I would.'

She smiled up at him. 'You did.'

'I have a question though.' He dragged the single chair across the cabin so he could sit next to the bed. 'Where on earth did you find the whistle?'

She reached under the covers she had tucked up to her chin and brought it out. He saw she wore it around her neck on a chain like a locket. 'You don't remember?'

'Should I?'

Sophia smiled a peculiar little smile. 'You gave it to me the day you left to go south.'

He laughed as it came back to him. 'Of course.' She had always pestered him to get her one. He'd had no money at the time and in the end he had swiped the whistle from the *Colossus'* nasty old boatswain.

'And do you remember what you told me when you gave it to me?'

He shook his head. He remembered the day though. It had been pouring with rain and leaving had been just about the hardest thing he had ever done.

'You told me, "If you're ever in trouble, blow it and I will come."' She turned the whistle over in her hands and it glinted in the lantern light. 'I blew it plenty of times over the next few years, but you never came.'

'Sorry,' he said.

'Don't be. Perhaps wanting you to come back just didn't count as trouble.'

Faulkner fought down an almost indescribably strong urge to grab her, kiss her. Instead he dragged his gaze away from those drowning eyes and stared intently at the knotted timbers of the bulkhead. He was master of the ship and she was his patron's only daughter. 'I was a very serious young man.'

'I still liked you.'

Suddenly he felt very hot. He gulped and searched about for a safer topic. 'I've been meaning to say how sorry I was for offending you the other day with my joke about the taint. I've spent far too much time in the company of other rude, boisterous and boorish men.'

'You meant no harm. I shouldn't have been so precious.'

'Thank you.' He fumbled for the right words. 'You saved our lives. You saved the ship. Half my heroes couldn't boast that.' He stood up. 'I suppose I should let you get some sleep. I just wanted to check you had recovered from your swim.' Without thinking, he reached for the chair with his injured arm and grimaced.

She sat up in bed and held out a hand. 'You're hurt. Come here.'

'It's nothing.'

'It wasn't a question, James. Come here.'

She gestured for him sit down on the edge of the cot. Against his better judgement, he did as he was told. He heard her rearrange the blankets and then felt the warmth of her against his back. She reached around him, undid the buttons of his shirt and then tenderly drew it down over his shoulders. She gasped when she saw where the first blow had caught him. 'James! Your back is almost black!'

'Can't say I'm surprised. Hurt like the blazes at the time.'

She ran her fingers over his back and then up into his hair. 'But you still threw yourself into the ocean for me.'

What was left of his resolve splintered under that touch. 'I'd throw myself into worse things than the ocean for you.' He turned and she flowed into his arms, warm and soft and insistent. He kissed her, gently at first and then more and more passionately as something boiling and perfect burst into flame inside him. She was naked under her blankets and he ran a hand along her side, marvelling at the feel of her skin. She shivered in pleasure as he touched her and wrapped herself around him. His arm hurt and he didn't care. He gently cupped her breast.

He broke their kiss and pulled away, but only half-heartedly. 'I can't. We shouldn't.'

She shrugged her shoulders and the blanket fell away. 'Shut up, James.'

He made the mistake of meeting her eyes and he drowned.

He woke near dawn and for a long, warm moment he lay still listening to her breathing and to the creaking of the ship. Finally he gently disentangled himself from her embrace. Trying not to wake her, he sat up.

'Don't go,' she muttered sleepily.

'I need to go up on deck.' He brushed aside her tousled hair and kissed her temple. 'I'll only be twenty yards away.'

'That's twenty too far.'

The temptation to stay was almost implacable, but he fought it down. He stepped out of bed and leant down to kiss her again. She looked so young. A pang of guilt ran through him. 'I hope I wasn't too rough?'

'Don't be silly.' She smiled up at him.

'I, ah, should be going.'

'James,' she called as he stepped out into the companionway. 'Don't you dare worry about me.'

He shut the door behind him and took a deep breath. He'd never experienced such a queer mixture of guilt and exultation. Forcing the sheepish grin from his face he straightened his shirt and then made his way up on deck. No sign of the fight remained. The sun was warm, the blood had been washed away and everything was put back in its proper place. It was hard to believe that men had fought and died here only hours before.

'Can I fetch you anything, sir?' asked Donald, appearing almost instantly by his side.

'No, thank you.' Faulkner took a deep breath and looked around. Despite almost losing his life and his ship, he felt almost content. 'Actually, fetch Jenkins.'

'How's the knock, Captain?' called Jenkins as he ambled over.

'Just a little sore, thank you, Boatswain.'

The big man smiled. 'Glad to hear it.' If the boatswain already knew about his night with Sophia he wasn't letting on. 'You wanted me?'

Faulkner nodded. 'I'll see to the mutineers now.'

Donald had brought him his coffee and he had time to drink it before, one by one, the surviving mutineers were pushed and kicked up into the light. The five of them then huddled together against the lee rail, blinking pitifully in the sunshine. Jenkins and Giovanni emerged last, carrying the unconscious Clarke on a stretcher. Somehow he had survived the night after all.

'My old father used to say about mutineers,' Donald whispered darkly, 'that the best you can give 'em is a long drop and a short rope.'

Faulkner smiled. 'I see the apple fell close to the tree then, Donald.'

Morgan left the group of sailors guarding the prisoners and hobbled over. 'I'm so sorry, Captain. Can't believe I let these hog-grubbers catch me unawares.'

'Don't be stupid, they would have just as likely snapped me up. You just had the misfortune to be standing watch. You aren't too hurt?'

'Neck's a bit stiff, but twenty years ago I would have hardly felt it.'

'Glad you're still with us. Now, excuse me, I'd better deal with these wretches.'

The mutineers reminded him of dogs who had been kicked once too often. Not one of them looked up to meet his gaze. He considered them one at a time: Farrant, Gould, Scammel, Jordan and lastly, and of course unhurt, Nagel. He was oddly pleased that none of them were men that he had counted as reliable. 'I'm not surprised you're alive, Nagel,' he said. 'You don't strike me as a man much suited for a straight fight.'

'Just fucking hang us, you dog,' Nagel snarled, his face contorted in hatred. 'I'll have none of your speeches.'

The youngest mutineer, Jordan, sobbed quietly into his dirty sleeve.

Faulkner turned away from the filthy, broken men and unexpectedly caught Sophia's gaze. She had come up on deck without his realising and with the morning sun behind her, her hair shone. Something lurched inside him. He smiled at her and then turned back to the Nagel. 'There'll be no hangings, though you richly deserve it. You'll have one of the long boats, some supplies and a compass. The ocean and the leviathan can decide if you live or die.'

Jordan threw himself on the deck at Faulkner's feet. 'Oh thank you, thank you! I didn't ever really want to be a part of it. I had to think of my aged mother. Who'd have taken care of her if that fish et me?'

'Don't make the mistake of taking this as a mercy. I'll still report you to the first magistrate I come across. But this isn't a man of war and I just haven't the heart to hang you myself.' He turned his back on them. 'Jenkins, get the boat over the side and get them in it. I'd like these wretches off my ship as quickly as possible.'

'And what of this one?' the boatswain asked, pointing to where Clarke lay on the stretcher.

The sailor's breath came in shallow gasps and his pulse was little more than a flutter at his neck. He was so close to death that his face almost seemed to be melting away. Faulkner shrugged. With no surgeon aboard there was no one on *Game Bird* who could save him. 'Put him in the boat as well. He'll have as much chance with them as he would with us.'

'Very good.'

Faulkner looked about for Donald. Predictably, his servant was slinking away. 'Donald! I want two weeks' supplies on that yawl before it is away.'

'Two weeks' supplies! Two weeks? I'd rather cast it over the side for the bleedin' gulls and wyverns! Had my way, I'd give them a knife and let them murdering buggers sort out amongst themselves who was food and who wasn't.'

'I'm sure you would. But starvation in an open boat is too cruel a death even for them.'

Sophia watched the sailors swarm about the deck. For once, James was not helping. Instead he stood off to one side looking wan and hurt. Without meaning to she gathered her taint. The world slowed and the sunlight flashing on the waves reached out to swallow her, painfully bright. The noise of the ocean roared in her ears. In panic she released her grip and let the taint flow back out into the world. She couldn't use it now. James was only injured. As much as she hated to leave him like this, in a week or two he would only be bruised and a little sore.

'What are they doing, Morgan?' she asked to distract herself.

'By the look of it, the captain means to cast them adrift in the yawl.'

'He's letting them go?'

'Looks like it.'

'They almost killed you. They did kill Pincher.'

'Aye.'

'Aren't you angry?'

'No.' The carpenter shrugged. 'Adrift in that little boat they will do us no more harm.'

'But what about Nagel? That man is mean as a hungry manticore.' How and when had she grown so bloodthirsty? A day before she'd been disgusted that Boscawen had been flogged.

'I wouldn't worry, my girl. I've known men like Nagel. He'll meet his end by rope or knife long before there is a grey hair on your head.' He touched the ugly bruise on the side of his head gingerly.

'Isaladar, I didn't even ask! How are you, Morgan?'

'My pride is hurt more than anything. What about you? That was a spirited thing you did.'

'I'm fine, only a few scrapes.' She blushed.

'You are a fiery one, Miss Blake.' He chuckled. 'Almost drowned last night and here you are looking the very picture of health next morning! Me, I'm stiff as a plank. Think I am getting far too old for all this.'

'Too old? I can't believe that.'

'You are kind lass, but I am. Ten years ago those lubbers would've never got me.' He shook his head. 'I'm gettin' tired and too old for brawling. I suppose I might buy a pretty little ship like this if we kill that big fish and sail the coastal waters up to Oldfort. See more of my grandchildren. Maybe make a sailor of one of them.'

Below them, the mutineers had been loaded into the boat and they were hurriedly shoving off from the *Game Bird*'s side, as if worried James would change his mind. From up in the rigging a sailor spat down on the mutineers and Sophia averted her gaze from the ugly scene and went below.

Sophia burst into his cabin without knocking and Faulkner jumped and put a smudged kink in the course he had been charting through the islands. Once the mutineers had been dealt with he had retreated below deck to map their route, a task he had always found strangely relaxing.

'Morning, Sophia,' he said. It was hard not to admire how she looked in her sailor's outfit.

She sat on the edge of the chart table in her no-nonsense way. 'James.'

'How are you?' he asked, at a loss for anything more intelligent to say.

'Fine. How are you?'

'I'm, ah, fine.'

'You look worried half to death.'

'Well, I've a lot of worries.'

'Such as?'

'Such as how we will make the watches work with a dozen less crew. Such as whether or not our gun is really powerful enough to kill this leviathan.' He mustered his courage. 'Such as a certain Sophia.'

'Why are you worried about me?'

'I… I feel like I might have taken advantage of you. And advantage of my position.'

'Ha.'

'Ha, what?'

'Ha, don't flatter yourself, James. I took advantage of you. I own the ship and you're my employee.'

'I'm not joking.'

'Nor am I. I feel very guilty that I exploited one of my staff.' She leant forward and kissed him. 'Most unbecoming.'

He kissed her back gently. 'Unfortunately that wasn't my only Sophia-based worry. I'm also being selfish.'

'Selfish?'

Well, yes. There's something else I've been meaning to ask you for a long time.'

'This sounds serious.'

'Since Waterford I've had the strangest feeling that you're keeping something from me. Something significant…' He faltered, embarrassed at his foolishness. 'Have you?'

She bit her lip. 'Why did you have to ask that?'

'Because I have to know.'

She sat back down on the table, her shoulders stooped. 'I've a favour to ask of you and if you feel any regard for me whatsoever you will grant me it.'

'Go on.'

'Don't ask me that question again while we are on *Game Bird*. Just let me enjoy this time with you,' her voice wavered. 'The second we are home

ashore in Stormhaven ask me that question again and I will tell you everything.' She turned back to him. Tears shone on her cheeks.

Something leaden and cold settled in Faulkner's belly. 'Another man?'

'A thousand times, no.'

'And you are serious, you really refuse to tell me? Until we are
back ashore?'

She nodded.

'You won't tell me anything? Not even a hint?'

She shook her head. 'Only that it isn't another man.'

'Please tell me.'

She shook her head. 'I can't.'

'I hate this.'

She came and sat in his lap. 'I hate it too, James.' She kissed him gently
and he tasted the salt of her tears. 'I hate it more than anything.'

They kissed again for a long time. He ran a hand up her long neck and
into her thick hair and the tenderness faded away, replaced by a thing hotter
and more urgent. She moaned gently in pleasure as he ran his other hand up
under her shirt to brush one of her nipples with his thumb. She slipped out
of his grasp and sat on the edge of the table, pulled off her boots and then
her clothes melted away.

'You always teased me for being too skinny.'

He reached for her. 'You could still eat more.'

She slapped his hand away. 'Don't tease.' A look of concern settled on
her face. 'Do you think I'm beautiful?'

Leaning forward, he kissed her belly and ran a hand gently along the
curve of her back. 'Are you beautiful?' he asked as they sank down onto the
cool timbers of the deck together. '"I have heard the song of the blossoms
and the old chant of the sea, and seen strange lands from under the arched
white sails of ships; but the loveliest things of beauty God ever has showed to
me are her voice, and her hair, and eyes, and the dear red curve of her lips."'

Afterwards, as the sweat cooled on their bodies, they lay tangled together
amongst the mess of clothes they had scattered around them.

They had talked and talked and talked. Their conversation had been
of nothing and of everything. The youth they had shared so long ago in

Stormhaven, politics, the navy, the places James had visited, her father, his family, and everything else in between. She had laughed till her sides hurt when he had described to her how he had ruined the Archon of Cartia's ball by accidentally releasing all his monkeys. She had sobbed and he had held her while she talked about her mother's death.

The only thing they had avoided talking about was the future, keeping away from that topic like it was the sun and they were vampires of fable. She could tell how much not-knowing consumed him but, thankfully, he didn't press the issue. Finally he had fallen asleep.

As he slept, Sophia ran a finger gently along the line of his jaw and marvelled at the change their intimacy had wrought in him. Since he had come aboard *Game Bird* in Waterford he had never completely lost that aura of command, even when they had been alone. His back was always straight and his jaw had that hard set to it that reminded her that his school-yards had been bloody battles and open seas. It was only as they had made love that the mask fell away and she saw the kindly boy who had stayed with them as a midshipman. Asleep with her lying on his chest the change was even more profound. As his eyelids fluttered and his chest rose and fell gently with each breath, he looked more like a poet or a painter than a famous fighting captain.

She ghosted her hand over the angry scar on his shoulder. How long ago had it happened? Eight years? She could still see where each splinter had hit him. She left the scar alone, lest she was tempted to heal it away, and explored down his arm and across the backs of his big hands with her fin-gertips. She couldn't help but blush at how she'd writhed and moaned under their touch. She prided herself on being more modern than the girls her own age, but she still was almost ashamed at some of the licentious things she had told him to do to her.

She prayed they never killed the leviathan. Selfishly she was terrified they'd kill it and return home early. If they failed to find the beast at all, they'd have more time together and she could always convince her father to void James' debts before she went away into whatever dark monastery or asylum awaited her. She squirmed forward a little and kissed James gently on the cheek.

His eyes fluttered open for a moment. 'I love you, Sophia,' he murmured.

She stifled a gasp.

He should have said anything but that. Anything but those words of promise, of future happiness and of days shared. There was nothing she could say. She feigned sleep and Faulkner's words fell away unanswered.

Once she was sure he was asleep again she cried.

31.

URIAH SAT ON a damp rock and watched the frantic activity around the ship. As soon as they were safely back to the *Palinurus,* Fiora had swung into action. With the port of Hazlewood denied to them, she had elected to repair the *Palinurus* on the beach. With the tide at its peak they had towed the ship carefully into the shallow water and braced her in place, and when the ocean had crawled back out the *Palinurus* had been left marooned on the sand like a stranded whale. With the damaged hull exposed, the crew had set to repairing the timberwork and plugging the leak as best they could.

How long ago was that? Four days? Five? The crew had worked tirelessly through each day and then, when the sun went down, they went on by the light of the moons and their flickering torches. Scarrus was down there now, scurrying back and forth, urging the men on with a kind word here and a cuff there. Not that they needed much encouragement. The crew were so terrified that they worked with the grinding, unrelenting effort of machines in a mill, pausing only to drink a quick sip of wine or cast a suspicious glance up at the dark hills of the island. Hills they were sure hid a watching Tallowman.

Fiora must have feared the same thing. Having seen the work on the ship started, she had gathered together ten of the crew and established a picket line around the beached ship. Even though she must have been exhausted from her days on watch, she was still out there with them somewhere, searching for their faceless foe. Uriah was beginning to understand the true power of the Tallowman. Although he had sat in this one place in clear sight of the crew for hours, each man that passed cast him a suspicious look. He didn't blame them. How could misgivings not fester when you faced a monster like the Tallowman? He grunted and flicked a long tongue of black weed off the rock. That such evil walked abroad in the world twisted everything safe and pleasant he had believed in until it felt cheap and meaningless.

A figure detached itself from the press of sailors by the ship and began to walk towards him. In torchlight it took him a moment to realise it was Doctor Celsus.

'And how are you, Mr Blake?' asked the little man.

Uriah opened his mouth to release a pleasant lie but it died on his lips. 'I feel very low, Doctor. Very low indeed.'

The doctor climbed up onto the rock and sat down next to him. 'I am not at all surprised. It has been a miserable few days.'

'And I ran when we were ambushed. Did you know that? I ran and Marcellus was killed because of my cowardice.'

'Any man can run if he suffers a nervous shock.'

'Cowards run.'

'No. The great Thirteenth Legion ran when they were ambushed in their first action. Then they went on to break every foe they fought for the next twenty years. They even killed one of Demetrius' dragons.'

'I am a lawyer, not a legionary. What good am I doing out here on this wild ocean?'

'What good? You are trying to save your child. There is nothing better than that.'

'All I've achieved so far is to get a good man killed.'

'You must be careful to not let your sorrow at Marcellus' death master you. He was an experienced fighter and knew the path he walked.'

'If I had helped in the fight we might have won. Sophia could be safe by now.'

The doctor retrieved a bottle from within his coat, took out the cork and offered it. 'Or you might have been killed. It is all very well for educated men to sit in their richly appointed houses and say that "every man thinks meanly of himself for not having been a soldier" but it is another thing entirely to see people slaughtered and to watch life needlessly destroyed. Men like us were raised to repudiate violence.'

'But if half Fiora's stories are true this is a fight against an utter evil.'

Uriah took a swig and spluttered. It was a hard spirit he didn't recognise. 'I wish I had stood up when I was needed.'

'It is not over yet, Uriah. If you must pick a battle to lose, it is better to lose the first than the last.'

'And you really think we can win the last battle do you, Doctor?'

'It will not be easy. Tallowmen certainly do not die without taking their pound of flesh. The countessa has killed one before though, so there is always some hope.'

'Fiora killed one? How?'

'Back in '31 we tracked one of the creatures to a boarding house in a small city near Misenum in the south of Caladia. After a week or so of observation we eventually found that we could get into the house's wine cellar from the sewers. When the Tallowman was away, we filled the cellar with gunpowder. When it came back…' The doctor flicked his fingers out to imitate an explosion.

'That was well done!'

'It was well done.' The doctor took the bottle back and swallowed a long gulp. 'Except the family who owned the boarding house was at home that night. Even now I still hear their screams…' Celsus looked down into the bottle. 'A Tallowman always takes his pound of flesh.'

'That's terrible!'

'All war is terrible and this is the most terrible of wars.' The doctor stood up. 'Now go and get some rest. Making yourself exhausted worrying about being useless is not time well spent.'

It took them another two long and weary days to repair the ship's damaged hull. Not only was it physically brutal labour but the fear of the Tallowman continued to eat away at them. Tempers frayed and even normally placid or cheery men had snapped and fought amongst themselves. Fiora and Scarrus had only just been able to keep the crew together and Uriah was convinced that if they'd been any closer to home, many would have already deserted.

When they finally finished the repairs, the crew had been so keen to escape the hated island that they almost leapt at the task of towing the ship back out into the open water. Then, when the damaged *Palinurus* had finally spread her sails and caught the wind, Uriah could have sworn he'd heard a collective sigh of relief run through the crew. As the distant hills of Hazlewood melted into the evening fog, he, Fiora, Doctor Celsus and Captain Scarrus gathered around the long table in the *Palinurus*' great cabin.

'So, Scarrus, what is the state of the ship?' Fiora asked. As usual, they spoke in Circillian for his benefit.

'The repairs are as good as we can manage without a dockyard.' Scarrus rubbed at his bloodshot eyes. 'She will be fine as long as the weather holds, but she won't ride out another storm. Poor *Palinurus* wasn't built for these grim northern seas.'

'You have done all I asked and more.' She studied the chart on the table. 'We'll hug the islands as much as we can and seek a sheltered shore if it looks likely to storm. That should also help us avoid this leviathan.'

'Thank you.' The captain sat down and yawned. 'That will help.'

'And what is our plan?' Uriah asked.

'Now the Tallowman has the advantage over us, there is only one course for us to take. We'll sail these islands and stop any ship we meet. It will take luck, but we just might meet Sophia and her ship. Or the Tallowman.'

Uriah blinked. 'That's it? We just sail around hoping to meet her?'

'Do you have any other suggestions?'

'No.' He felt like shouting, screaming or crying, or doing all three simultaneously. 'But I thought you'd have an idea.'

'I am not a magician.'

'So we just pray the Tallowman doesn't find her first? Or hasn't already?'

'Yes.'

'This is lunacy.' A sob bubbled up from deep in his chest. Tears pricked at his eyes and he ran his hands over the bristly regrowth on his skull. 'Lunacy.'

Fiora leant forward across the table. For a second he thought she might slap him and he shied back from her. 'This wallowing in despair won't help your daughter. Unless you have a better idea, it is what it is. Show some backbone.'

He stared at her, at a loss for anything to say and transfixed by her glare.

Celsus coughed to interrupt. 'You forget, Uriah, we still have one significant advantage.'

'Which is?'

'If, Samaryan willing, your daughter uses her taint again, the countessa will know exactly where she is.'

He almost choked at that. 'I never thought I'd be willing her to use her taint.'

The first week of their hunt was exhausting after the frenzied days of repairs. The course Scarrus had chosen snaked in and out of rocks, reefs, shoals and bars and therefore called for endless changes of sail. Each time the crew climbed aloft they went a little more slowly and even Uriah could tell each change was a little sloppier than the last. The sailors also no longer sang as they worked. He was sure the crew weren't being disobedient, they were merely exhausted and scared.

Their search had so far turned up nothing of the either the Tallowman or Sophia. All that had punctuated their lonely days had been the occasional ship sighting; each vessel scurrying along under the weight of as much canvas as she could carry from the transitory safety of one shallows to another. Every ship's story had always been the same and none of their Frightened captains knew anything of Faulkner, Sophia or a ship hunting the leviathan. The only good news was that they had seen nothing of the leviathan either.

As their aimless sailing dragged on, Uriah found himself sinking deeper and deeper into depression. With each passing day he became more convinced that their search was hopeless and that this Tallowman thing already had Sophia. He saw little of Fiora. She was not obviously unkind, but the few times he bumped into her he was sure the corner of her mouth twisted into the faintest of sneers. They almost never spoke. She always seemed either to be at the helm of the ship or training with her remaining men at arms. She hardly ever seemed to sleep and her eyes burned with a dark intensity.

With nothing useful to do, Uriah spent the majority of his time with Celsus. Most nights they would sit together in the doctor's book-lined cabin, playing chess and talking into the small hours. The little doctor had just crushed Uriah with a very strong rook and knight middle game and was setting the board back up when something about the futility of their endlessly repeated games struck Uriah. 'Can I ask you a question?' he asked.

Celsus looked up from the drink he was pouring. 'All we do is ask each other questions and tell stories.'

'This is a more, ah, serious question.'

'Ask it.'

'Well, ever since I discovered Sophia was being pursued, I've been swept along and never once have I actually stopped to ask why.'

'Why what?'

'Why is this Tallowman going to such lengths to capture my daughter? I understand she is tainted, but so are hundreds or even thousands of other people scattered about the Realm. They can't all be being hunted. It would be in the papers.'

The doctor took a sip of his wine. 'That is a good question.'

'Let me guess. You are sworn not to answer it?'

'I suppose I can give you an answer, now that you have come this far. Be warned, though, you will not like my theory. Your question touches on why the countessa has me along in the first place. Of course I treat the sick and wounded in her party, but my role is more involved than that.'

'Oh?'

'In the last century or so, our enemy has turned to science and anatomy to further its cause.'

'Go on.'

'How much do you know about fiends?'

'Fiends? Like the Duke of Andiel?'

'No, the duke is not a fiend. He is something older and even more terrible. Ignore your Duke of Andiel for now. He is an unfathomable terror beyond the comprehension of modern scientific minds.' Celsus drained his wine in one gulp. 'I will start from the start. Daemons exist.'

Uriah raised an eyebrow.

'Look as doubtful as you wish, my friend. They do. I have had the misfortune to encounter two of them.'

'Daemons?' Uriah asked.

'Yes, exactly.'

'As in the malevolent spirits of children's stories?'

'The same. Now, as you just observed, they are spirit creatures.'

'Daemons?'

'Yes, Uriah, daemons! Beasts of magic, imagination and aether. They are powerful beings of nightmare, but are also entirely unsuited to survival in our plane. A daemon in our world is like a kraken or shark washed up on a beach – a mighty creature, but one out of its place and quickly drowning in our thin air. Yes?'

'I'm not convinced you aren't mad, but I follow your analogy.'

Celsus waved that comment away. 'Fiends on the other hand are a physical construct. An unholy mixture. An intentional and hideous forging together of daemonic and animal flesh. A process that, thankfully, our enemy only discovered in the last few decades and still seems to be perfecting.'

Uriah's mouth was suddenly dry as a desert grave. 'You are saying people, what? *Grow* these things?'

'Make, not grow.'

'Make? How?'

'The process is complicated in the extreme. In simplest terms, a weak daemon is summoned, caught, distilled and then' – the little doctor made a cutting gesture – 'sewn into animal flesh. If the process is undertaken correctly, the animal and daemon tissue merges to create a fiend. This weakens the daemon terribly, but its connection to mortal flesh lets it survive in our plane for much longer.'

Uriah gulped. 'Is this only done to animals or to men also? To humans?'

The doctor made the holy sign of Samaryan. 'Both, although fiends are more commonly created from animals. A man's soul must be truly evil and degenerate not to choose honest death over amalgamation with a daemon. Even our enemy has trouble finding many such ruins of men.'

Uriah poured himself a good dash of wine and drank it all down. 'And what is a fiend's mind like once this… this amalgamation has taken place? Man or daemon?'

'They seem to be a fusion of both parent parts, tied together in one intellect. The two egos mixed as perfectly as water and wine.'

'Why would anyone do that?'

'To make a weapon.' Celsus sighed. 'Even if daemons could survive in our world, they are capricious and inherently uncontrollable beings. They are just as likely to destroy their summoner or follow some obscure agenda of their own as do their summoner's bidding. While much, much weaker, a fiend is controllable. A terrible and terrifying arcane weapon of flesh and blood.'

Realisation dawned on Uriah and he poured himself another glass of wine. The wounds on his face throbbed as he drank it down, but the wine killed some of his terror. 'The Tallowman is a fiend then, isn't it?'

'It is, of a kind.' The lantern rocked with the movement of the ship and a shadow danced across Celsus' brown skin.

'Fiora told me they are men.'

'It was once a man, but no longer.' Celsus shook his head. 'We tell that lie to those not yet ready for a story full daemons and other planes.'

'But even if true, then what does all this horrific madness have to do with Sophia?'

'Ah yes.' Celsus held up one bony finger. 'Although the merging with mortal flesh lets the resulting thing survive for far longer in our plane than it would as a raw daemon, the creation is still a failing construct. It seems the daemon's touch is anathema to life and, even when weakened and contained, it quickly corrupts any corporeal flesh that holds it. Of course our enemy has worked tirelessly to correct this process but they have been largely unsuccessful. Even the weakest fiend, that is to say the one that carries the least daemon within it, will still fail within a few years.'

'So all fiends are dying?'

'Essentially.'

Uriah looked down at the chess pieces. 'They need Sophia's taint to sustain a fiend, don't they?'

'I believe so, Uriah. When the enemy goes to the great trouble of summoning a powerful daemon and then binding it as a fiend, the last thing they want is their construct expiring within a season. If they had Sophia or others like her they could vastly extend a friend's lifespan.'

'My beautiful Sophia. That is, it is,' he struggled for words, 'it is beyond evil.'

'I did say you would not like this theory.'

They came across the castaway just before midday the next day. The *Palinurus* was threading her way down the channel between the rocky, pine-covered shores of Dogwood and Coffin islands when the lookout spotted a man floating in the water clinging to a spar. Fiora swung out a boat and they soon had the sailor back aboard. As they carried him gently up onto the deck Uriah gasped at the sight of him. The skin hung off his face, hands and upper torso in long white ribbons. The flesh beneath was pulped and bloody.

Celsus took one look at the man and ordered him taken below.

Uriah and Fiora followed the doctor down and then stood waiting in the cramped companionway outside the little cockpit Celsus used as his surgery. As the silence stretched on, Uriah opened his mouth to ask Fiora what she thought had happened before one look at the scowl on her face relegated him to silence. Instead they waited by the shut door in an awkward, unpleasant quiet that was broken only the once when the castaway screamed.

Eventually the doctor emerged, looking grim. 'I have bled him, but he still won't last long.'

'What happened to him?' Fiora asked.

'I don't know. He is delirious from his burns, too confused to speak to me coherently.' Celsus turned to Uriah. 'Perhaps you might speak to him? He is a Realmsman and might be more likely to speak to one of his countrymen.'

Uriah nodded and stepped inside. A dish full of drawn blood lay on the timbers next to the cot, the blood vibrant red in the lamplight. The injured man lay on the cot, his breath shallow and his wounds even worse than Uriah had first thought. The sickly sweet smell of suppurations already hung thick in the air. The poor boy wasn't more than twenty years old. Fiora followed him into the cabin and stood quietly to one side.

'Hello, lad,' Uriah said.

'Hello, sir.' The boy coughed and his swollen eyes flickered open for a second. 'Who are you?'

'Uriah Blake from Stormhaven.'

'It's nice to hear that accent. Name's Jack Williams.' He coughed again. 'I was surprised to be picked up by a ship of blackies. Not that I was sorry to see you.'

Uriah pointed to Fiora. 'This is the Countessa Varzi. It is her ship.'

Jack coughed again. The horrible sound was somehow both wet and rasping. 'Thank you, Countessa. I was getting cursed lonely on my own in the water.'

'It is nothing.' Fiora bowed graciously. 'Ask him what happened,' she whispered in Uriah's ear.

'What happened, Jack? How did you come to be in the water?'

'It was the devil fish, sir.'

'The leviathan?'

'Aye. It tore us up like matchwood. Killed all me mates.'

'And your burns?'

Jack laughed at that. The laugh was a shrill thing, very close to madness. 'Once he saw the leviathan was destroying the boats in the water and murdering all his men, Hayes, that proud old bugger, set off the magazine. Tried to take the leviathan down with us.'

Uriah's eyes widened. 'Hayes? As in Captain Hayes of the *Tonnant?* You are a *Tonnant?*'

'Was, sir, was,' he coughed again. 'That leviathan sunk *Meteor* quicker than you'd believe and then came back for us.'

Uriah was dumbfounded. The *Tonnant* had been a 74, a battleship with a crew of almost seven hundred men and boys, and the *Meteor* was a large modern frigate with a crew of maybe two hundred and fifty. That meant almost a thousand men were dead, far more than had been lost winning the great victory at the Iron Cape. Through his practice, he knew plenty of the men who had perished. Captain Hayes to speak to; dear fat Yorrick, flag lieutenant on *Tonnant* and only recently married; Barkley, the clever purser on *Meteor*. He must have had at least twenty of them over for dinner at one time or another.

'Were you the only survivor, Jack?' he asked.

'Don't rightly know, Mr Blake. When *Tonnant* blew up I was knocked about pretty bad. I woke up alone in the water, clinging to that spar.'

Uriah carefully took the lad's ruined hand.

'Did I tell you how very lonely it was in the water on my own? For some reason, I just kept remembering this little dog I used to have as a boy. Bounce was his name. He always cheered me up when I was a little squeaker. Did you ever have a pup, Mr Blake?'

Uriah tried to fight down the thickness in his throat. 'My daughter always wanted one, but I never let her get one.'

'Oh that's all right, sir. Doesn't do for a father to give his children everything they want.' He coughed again for what seemed like an age. 'I'm dying ain't I, Mr Blake?'

'I'm sorry, Jack.'

'I'm very tired,' he whispered. 'Just please sink me in the shallows. I don't want that monster fish getting my body.'

'We will, Jack, in the shallows.'

The young sailor nodded, gave out a long, shuddering breath and died.

That afternoon, Scarrus took the *Palinurus* into the shallow waters off the appropriately named Coffin Island. They carried the sailor's canvas-wrapped body up onto the deck and laid it on the pale wooden timbers of the deck. The crew clustered around in silence. In the distance, gulls squawked and called.

'You should say some words, Uriah,' Celsus said.

Uriah looked up, surprised. 'I'm not a priest.'

Scarrus motioned him forward. 'The doctor is right, Uriah, it is better that you should speak.'

Uriah looked around. Fiora met his gaze and nodded curtly.

He drew a deep breath. 'Ah, Prince Isaladar, we commit this man, Jack Williams, to your eternal care.' He thought back to Mary's funeral, trying to remember the words the priest had used then. 'May he walk by your side in the Great Kingdom you now rule. May you, ah, wipe away the tears of those that remain behind.' Uriah faltered there for a moment. 'I didn't know this boy for more than a moment, but he died in the service of his nation and I suppose that is worth something at the great reckoning. Isaladar take care of his eternal soul, and, ah, we commit this body to the deep.'

Fiora nodded. '*Media vita in morte sumus.*'

They lifted the grate upon which the corpse lay and, with a rattle from the cannonballs that weighted it down, the body bumped over the side and splashed into the grey water. After a moment's silence a word from Scarrus sent the assembled crew back to their duties around the ship. Within minutes the ship was under sail again. Uriah walked aft to where Fiora stood at the stern rail, watching the dark, forested shores of the island with an unreadable look on her face. 'What are we doing now?' he asked.

'Doing? We'll continue south into this god-forsaken island chain. The Tallowman lurks somewhere close. I can almost feel it.'

'And what about the navy?'

'What about them?'

'Surely we need to warn them? About the leviathan attacking men of war.'

'We can't afford the time.' She shook her head.

'What?'

'Your navy can fend for itself.'

'A thousand men were killed, Countessa. A thousand!' Uriah was shocked. He had just assumed they would return to raise the alarm. 'We have to head back north and warn the fleet.'

'Don't presume to tell me what to do, Uriah.'

'We have to do something!'

'If it was my daughter the Tallowman was hunting, I would not be so quick to abandon the chase.'

'The chase? This is hardly a chase! What chance do we even have of just bumping into my daughter or the Tallowman on these unpathed waters?' A warmth crept up from under Uriah's collar. 'Warning the navy is a difference we can actually make!'

'You are a fool.' Anger flashed in her eyes. 'This mindless fish is nothing. Nothing! Someone will kill it and in ten years it will be nothing but a fireside story.'

'A fireside story? It just sank two men of war!'

'Don't be so naive, Uriah. Leviathan, kraken, roc – the world is full of beasts, but a single Tallowman can break nations. And what will it do to Sophia should it catch her?'

'Do you think it's easy for me to argue we should sail away and abandon my daughter?' He set his shoulders like he was attacking a ruck. 'But the leviathan just killed a village's worth of men. Each of them was a father, or a son, or a brother to someone. If we don't do something it will kill thousands more!'

'We continue the hunt for the Tallowman.'

'Fiora!'

'This point is not open for discussion.'

'But heading back to warn the navy will only take a few days. Days!'

'In a few days your daughter may be dead.'

'You think I don't know that? But warning the navy is a million times more productive than this madness.' He was shouting now.

'You didn't call it madness when I offered you a place on the *Palinurus*.'

'Then I only had one choice. Now we have two. Either we continue this useless game of blind man's bluff across the great ocean or we can save countless men's lives.'

'I will not leave the hunt. I will not leave your daughter.'

Something cracked inside Uriah and anger coursed through him. He would do anything for Sophia, but he was a logical man and the choice between aimlessly wandering the ocean and making an active, useful effort to save thousands of lives seemed like no choice at all. 'Fiora! Listen to me! You aren't doing this for me, or for Sophia, and you are lying to yourself if you believe you are. You want to revenge yourself on this Tallowman. That's all! Your son is dead and his death may or may not have been your fault, but he is dead. Giving up everything you once believed in to chase his killer won't bring him back and it may well besmirch his memory.

'That was ill-mannered, Uriah.' Her hand went to her sword hilt. 'Even for a Realmsman.'

'This is not the time to be well-mannered!' he roared. 'I've spent all my bloody life being well-mannered, but right now my countrymen are being butchered, and I'm far, far from home and my face has been smashed to pieces and I only just found out my daughter is probably being hunted down so she can be used to keep some monster alive. For Isaladar's sake, you need to listen to me! Remember why you began this fight. I care about Sophia more than life itself, but I will not just stand by while this leviathan continues its slaughter! I will not!'

Her eyes went wide. 'What did you say?'

He paused, chest heaving. 'Remember why you began this fight.'

'Before that.'

'About Sophia being hunted to sustain a fiend?'

She took a few steps down the deck. 'Celsus!'

'Please, Countessa, you mustn't punish him.' He held a hand out after her. 'I am the girl's father. I had a right to know.'

'I don't want to punish him.'

Summoned by one of the crew, the little doctor's head appeared in the hatchway. 'Countessa?' he asked nervously.

'Do you have a book of zoology in that messy cabin of yours?'

'Zoology? I have a few.' He paused, caught by the strangeness of the request. 'Ah, do you need one for any particular reason, Countessa?'

'I need a description of the leviathan.'

The doctor considered that. 'Chatel's noble work briefly touches on the beast.'

'Fetch it. Quickly.'

The doctor disappeared back down below.

'I'm sorry I spoke to you so rudely, Countessa,' Uriah said. The passing of his sudden anger had left him indescribably tired and wrung out.

'Those words were hard words, Uriah, but I needed to hear them.' She turned away and looked out over the ocean. 'I had lost sight of the oath I once swore. Worse, I might have been blind to one of our enemy's schemes.'

Celsus soon reappeared on the deck, staggering under the weight of an enormous leather-bound tome. 'I found it.'

'What does it say?' she asked.

The doctor reread the passage. 'Nothing very useful. Chatel states they are one of the hardest animals in the world to study because they rarely, if ever, come up to the shallows.' He scanned the text. 'He hypothesises they feed on the whale, sea dragon and kraken of the depths. Nothing is known of their reproductive cycle or life span. Let me see... ah yes, many ancient cultures considered that if one of their corpses ever came to the surface it was a very ill omen.'

'They are creatures of the depths?' Fiora asked.

'So it seems.'

She blinked. 'Great Samaryan.'

Uriah shuddered. 'It can't be, can it?'

'I believe it is.'

'This leviathan is one of these half-daemon fiend things?'

'I've been a fool.' She nodded slowly. 'The beast's behaviour is so focused, so driven.'

'Do you think it might have *wanted* the navy to come hunting it?'

'Probably.'

'Why?'

'The single biggest barrier to any physical attack on the Circillian nations will always be our navies. And your navy is the strongest of them by far.' She turned to the little doctor. 'What do you think, Celsus? Is it possible?'

'Catching a leviathan to use as the host for a fiend would be incredibly difficult.' The doctor clutched the book to his chest. 'But it rings true. We know during the war in the south they made fiends of manticores, elephants, lions and rhinoceros.'

'So then the Tallowman is here to – what? To keep this leviathan fiend thing supplied?' Uriah asked.

Celsus nodded.

'Like its personal dockyard.' Uriah struggled for an analogy, something to help him make sense of it all. 'Except the leviathan doesn't use up spars, canvas, powder and ropes like a fleet would, it consumes tainted. Tainted like my daughter.'

'I fear you're right.' She put a hand on his shoulder. 'The Great Enemy long ago used up all those with your daughter's particular aspect in their homeland and now they must hunt in more distant pastures. That is also why the Tallowman would have killed my son, so it could feed his taint to this leviathan as the beast travelled north. Tallowman are often slaved to a great fiend and forced to feed their endless hungers.'

She turned and called in Caladian to the sailor in command of the watch. With a groan the *Palinurus* turned in the channel, her bows swinging round to face north. As the *Palinurus* settled on her new course, Fiora turned back to them, her face grim. 'I just hope your navy will take the word of a foreigner and a wanted murderer.'

32.

THE SEAS WERE up and the little boat was tossed about mercilessly. At the top of each rolling grey ridge of swell, the mirrored sky stretched away to the lonely horizon, then the bow would fall and the boat would skid and plough its way down into the trough until their entire world was nothing but the blue-green face of the next wave and the white flapping sail.

Crouched in the yawl, by the body of the dying thing-that-was-Clarke, Nagel looked astern at the men clustered together by the tiller and knew he wouldn't survive the night. Farrant, Gould and Scammel had all been wounded during the fighting back on *Game Bird*, and Jordan was so confused and broken by their sudden exile that he had been rendered almost mute. For now the four men were thankfully silent, drenched and dejected. What little spark of intelligence they still showed was all directed into keeping the boat afloat. Soon, though, their anger would burn through their despair and bewilderment and then they would turn on him. Nagel couldn't blame them; he would've done the same. He had promised the mutineers freedom and a fortune, but instead half of them had been killed and the survivors were wanted men. He looked down into the scuppers where the wounded Clarke lay and shuddered at the sight of him. Even if the other four forgave him for the mutiny's failure and the death of their mates, once they got a look at Clarke's face it would be enough to seal his fate. They were violent, amoral men, but they'd never forgive him for tricking them into the service of some occult terror. And occult the thing-that-was-Clarke was. In the hours since they'd left *Game Bird*, its face had collapsed until Clarke's features had completely sloughed away. Now its countenance was a featureless mass of flesh the colour of melted wax and its only identifiable features were cold black eyes and a snake's lipless mouth. Even the thought that this ruthless thing was a Camar Shiem knight-monk in the service of Isaladar now seemed laughable.

'What now, Nagel?' asked Scammel finally.

'We make for the Cold Barrens and meet up with Clarke's mates.'

'But they gave us more than enough food to make Stormhaven,' whimpered Jordan.

Scammel nodded. 'Aye, and Clarke will be dead long before we reach the Barrens.'

Nagel ignored the older sailor. 'Then what, Jordan? We wait till Faulkner finds a magistrate and we end up dancing a jig at the end of the rope? Wake up, *boy* – he mightn't have had the balls to kill us, but do you really reckon he'll forget that we mutinied and murdered one of his beloved fucking *Inflexibles*!'

Jordan began to cry quietly.

'We're heading for the Barrens,' Nagel said.

The men nodded their heads, their first brief flutter of fight snuffed out. The buggers had rebelled against their officers but were lost without them. Nagel could have spat on them. They were pathetic; they hated authority but were too fucking gutless to survive without it.

He looked down at Clarke's body and for the thousandth time thought about throwing the thing into the sea. But he couldn't shake the terrible thought that if he tried to heave it overboard it would reach out with its last strength and drag him down with it. Instead, he pulled the tarpaulin up to hide the horror that was its face.

They sailed on towards the Cold Barrens for the remainder of the bitter and wet day. As the sun set the wind died away. The seas quietened as well, as if flattened by the weight of the darkness drawn across them.

Sometime after dark Nagel managed to fall asleep, uncomfortably draped over the boat's side. His dreams, when they came, were red. The fight on the deck of *Game Bird* raged for hours and a slick of blood coated the deck like warm red snow. He knew the officers were winning, but he was rooted to the spot, pissing himself again and still too scared to join in the fighting, even in his dream.

He jerked upright. His mouth was dry and his tongue heavy. The night was still black. He scrabbled for his bottle of rum and held it out in front of him as an improvised club. He was sure they'd finally come to cut his throat. 'Back, you dogs,' he hissed.

But there was no one there.

From astern came a wet cracking noise, like something tearing at damp timber. He could just see movement. A hunched shape down in the scuppers was tearing something apart with short, sharp motions. He whimpered.

Warm urine ran down the inside of his leg.

'Shut up, Nagel, we're trying to get some shut-eye,' Scammel murmured.

'I'd only just got to sleep too,' Gould grumbled.

'And what is that fucking noise?' asked Scammel. He turned to face the tiller and the hardened sailor's hands flew to his mouth in a pantomime gesture of terror. 'Oh god... Oh no... Oh Isaladar's... Oh Isaladar... Oh Isaladar... he's... he's eating Jordan.'

There was pandemonium.

The creature that had worn Clarke's face rose up from where it had been feasting on Jordan's corpse and, with one savage swing of an oar, smashed in Scammel's skull. With a screech it leapt forward, cracking bones and pulping flesh with each stroke. Blood splattered the limp sail. Finally, the oar broke with a resounding crack and Nagel watched, frozen, as the creature rammed the splintered stump into Farrant's belly and then tore the dying sailor's throat out with its teeth.

Nagel shut his eyes and waited for the beast to end him. But the blow never came and he lay there for what seemed like hours, leaning out as far as he could over the bow of the boat with his eyes screwed shut. He couldn't close his ears though and he was forced to listen as the beast feasted. First came the wet slurping and tearing as it ripped at the dead men's flesh, then a set of terrible, rending cracks followed as it tore at their bones. Finally, there was an animal-like gnawing as it feasted on what he was sure must be their hearts.

After an age the noises stopped.

He still didn't move.

Nagel remained frozen where he was, ignoring the agonising cramps that clawed at his back and his legs. When he finally opened his eyes, he immediately threw up over the side. The yawl looked like a charnel house.

The bottom of the sail was dark with gore. Blood slopped, ankle-deep, in the bottom of the boat. The remains of the dead men lay scattered around the boat, white and naked in the moonlight. A few pieces were still recognisable: an arm here, a leg there and, directly in front of Nagel, a torso with its ribcage peeled open like some perverse mockery of a flower.

The thing was leaning with its back against the small mast like it was resting. It was covered in a thick dark coat of what must have been blood. Its cold eyes met his.

'What are you?' Nagel whispered.

It laughed.

'What are you?' he asked again.

'I am the hunter, I am doubt, I am hatred, I am malevolence, all clothed in human skin. I am a Tallowman.' It studied him. 'And because you remind me of the man I once was, I will give you a choice, Nagel. Listen carefully. I will make this offer only once. Do you understand?'

He managed to nod. 'I understand.'

'You may either join them.' It gestured towards the bloody leavings scattered about the boat. 'Or you may serve me.'

'Please, please, please, please let me serve you.'

As the night retreated and a pale and sickly sun rose in the east, Nagel's raw terror slowly faded and a wary curiosity grew in its place. Although it was clear the creature did not kill indiscriminately, he still treated it like a coiled snake and made sure he did nothing to enrage it.

The creature, the Tallowman, proved more than happy enough to talk to him and over the next few long days he gradually pieced together a few things. The creature, or Mr Savage, as it asked to be called, was the servant of some funny-sounding foreign power. It wanted Sophia Blake because the little bitch was tainted and that meant the creature's master could use her. More than that Mr Savage would not say and Nagel couldn't guess.

As time passed, Mr Savage seemed to slowly recover. At dusk of their third day in the boat, it suddenly gasped, fished in the filthy bottom of the boat and then held aloft a misshapen pistol ball in triumph. It claimed its body had forced the piece of shot back out.

'You said you were made?' Nagel asked, as he stared at the bloody piece of lead. 'Could I ever be like you?'

'You could.'

'Would you consider it? If I served you well?' The thought of having the same strength and cunning as Mr Savage was intoxicating.

'You would no longer be human.'

Nagel laughed. 'Human ain't really working out for me, is it?'

'It didn't for me, either.'

On the morning of their sixth day in the boat, they reached the Cold Barrens and soon found the bay where Mr Savage's ship, *Dead Reckoning*, was waiting. When they spotted the ship, Mr Savage ripped some clean canvas from the edge of the sail and re-bandaged its face.

When the little boat bumped alongside the sloop, it turned to him.

'I am still weak, Nagel, but I must hurry. I will need to be rash. Support me and I will reward you,' it whispered.

Up on *Dead Reckoning*'s deck they were met by a blustering, red-faced old drunk who Nagel assumed was the captain.

'Well, if it isn't Mr Savage. I suppose getting half my men killed wasn't enough for you, was it? Was it!'

'The men who went ashore on Hazlewood are all dead?' the Tallowman asked.

'Apart from Roberts. And he will be shortly.'

'What happened to them?'

'How'd I know, Mr Savage?'

'What happened to Roberts then?'

'Shot through the back. We can't get the ball out. Your gold is all well and good, but I've no need for this... this slaughter!'

'Where is Roberts?'

'Down in his cabin. And let me tell you, Mr Savage, it is only because Roberts is so damn sure you can do something for his wound that I waited here. I would've gladly left you.' The man puffed himself up like a little rooster. 'I might not be the best captain, but at least I look after my people.'

'I will see Roberts,' it said.

'Fine, but I'm coming. I've learned better than to leave my people alone with you, gold or no.'

They followed the captain down to Roberts' cramped cabin. Roberts himself was lying face down and naked on his cot, groaning incoherently. Nagel had been in enough street fights and scrapes to know Roberts wouldn't live long. The musket ball had taken him high in the back and the wound was already puffy and suppurating a thick yellow pus. The thick, sickly sweet stench of infection hung in the air. Bloody knives and other tools that the crew must have used to try to get the ball out littered a little table. It was a miracle the mate had lived this long.

The Tallowman kneeled near Roberts. 'Can you hear me?'

The big man slowly raised his grey and sweaty face towards the Tallowman. 'It was that fucking black bitch that shot me.'

'She is dangerous. I told you to kill her first. Now listen to me: what would you do to not die?'

The captain backed away into a corner. 'I don't like this…'

'Shut up, fatty,' Nagel snarled.

'What would you be prepared to do to not die?' it asked again.

'I'd do anything just to end this fucking pain.'

'Good.' It turned to the table and studied the blood-spattered surgical tools.

'Know surgery, do you?' Nagel asked.

'Butchery is more my thing.' Mr Savage snatched up a wicked knife, turned and slammed the heavy blade into the captain's stomach. The man vomited up a choking squeal and slid to the deck, eyes wide in agony and terror. It drew the knife back out with a wet squelch and turned to Nagel. 'Cover his mouth, I don't want to listen to his screaming.'

Nagel did as he was told.

The Tallowman reached into a pouch at its belt and carefully took something out. Nagel only saw the thing fleetingly. It had the colour and appearance of an earthworm, but thicker, and it writhed viciously in the Tallowman's hand like it was trying to get free. Mr Savage pressed the worm-thing down into Roberts' wound. The mate squealed out in agony as the creature burrowed its way down into him.

Nagel threw up on the captain's legs.

The Tallowman sighed. 'Pull yourself together.' It stepped back from Roberts. 'Now we wait.'

At first Roberts groaned and writhed. Then he screamed and thrashed about. Finally he shrieked and convulsed like he was having a fit. Nagel pushed himself further into the corner, vainly trying to shelter behind the dying captain. Eventually Roberts gave one last mighty kick and lay still.

'Now we will see what kind of man Roberts was,' the Tallowman said. 'Death or damnation. What do you think he chose, Nagel?'

'I… I… I don't know.'

Roberts slowly rolled over and sat up.

'Damnation,' the Tallowman hissed.

The man's skin was corpse-white. Thick black veins tracked out from around his vacant eyes, extending like some mad spiderweb out over his body. The muscles on his arms, legs and chest writhed and twitched, like rodents were wriggling about beneath his skin.

The thing-that-had-been-Roberts turned its head slowly towards the Tallowman. 'This body is dying already,' it said.

'I had no choice.'

'I must feed,' Roberts hissed.

'That has been prepared.' It gestured towards Nagel and the dying captain.

Roberts rose slowly from the bed and walked stiffly towards him. Nagel scrabbled to get away, unable to get purchase on the blood- and vomit-slick planks. The Tallowman grabbed his arm and pulled him out the way. 'Not this one, he is our servant. You may have the captain.'

'One is not enough. I am weak.'

The Tallowman opened the door and shoved Nagel out of the cabin. 'One will have to be enough for now. As you eat I will tell you of the girl I am hunting. If we harvest her all our hungers will be sated.'

'Good. I won't return to the shade.'

The Tallowman turned back to him. 'Nagel, now prove yourself to me,' it ordered. 'Take command of this ship and get us underway. Head for *Game Bird*'s last location. Roberts and I will be up on deck shortly and we will deal with any crew who refuse your orders.'

Before Nagel could reply, it slammed the door shut.

So they began their hunt for *Game Bird*. As the days of lonely islands and empty sea dragged on, both Roberts and the Tallowman seemed to steadily weaken. By the end of the third day on *Dead Reckoning*, the Tallowman was almost as weak as it had been immediately after it had been shot. Roberts was in an even worse state and could hardly lift its head. Just when Nagel had finally decided that both creatures were definitely going die and he should start planning his escape, the Tallowman had found the strength to totter about the ship and find him.

Although stinking of death and barely able to stand, its voice was still steady. 'Within the hour we'll pass by a fishing village. You will row us ashore.'

'Us?'

'Roberts and I.'

Nagel wasn't stupid enough to argue and he was soon rowing across the black expanse of ocean with his two companions silent in the bows. Spying a small cove only a few hundred yards from the village, he pulled the boat ashore and then dragged Roberts and the Tallowman up onto the beach. The village was so close he could smell cooking and wood smoke, even over the stench of the two dying things.

'What should I do now?' he whispered.

'You wait here,' the Tallowman hissed.

It and Roberts had then clambered slowly to their feet and disappeared into the dunes, stumbling and lurching slowly towards the village.

Nagel had waited, shivering in the cold spring air by the boat. For a long time all he could hear was the hiss of the surf and the calls of night birds. Then came a scream, a gut-wrenching, dying scream, and the night's quiet exploded into a cacophony of shouting, more screams and finally, a single pistol shot.

After that there was silence, a terrifying, empty silence.

Slowly a glow coloured the sky. The village was burning.

When Roberts and the Tallowman loomed back up out of the gloom he saw that all their weakness was gone and the two of them now walked upright and strong, like ancient predators of the night. 'Are we finished?' Nagel asked, throat tight with fear.

Roberts laughed. 'Those fisher folk are fucking finished. We've just begun.'

They were both so covered in blood it looked like they had bathed in it. Chunks of flesh and hair clung to their lips, cheeks and chins. Nagel rowed them back out to *Dead Reckoning* and then, shaking with terror, snuck away down to the powder magazine to hide.

33.

SOPHIA LEANT BACK against the sun-warmed timber of the mast and smiled indulgently at James and de Lacey. The fools were both peering through their glasses at a distant smudge on the horizon that they had somehow decided was a ship captained by a friend of theirs.

Their hunting amongst the isles had yielded no more signs of the leviathan and once the shock of the mutiny had passed anyway, the crew had settled into a surprisingly content rhythm. The ship's few troublemakers had mostly gravitated to Clarke and Nagel and the defeat of the mutiny had worked like the lancing of a boil. Since then, even though the reduced crew had to work much harder, *Game Bird* was a far happier ship. They were alert and wary, of course, with lookouts always aloft and a team of men always ready by the great gun, but they were definitely cheerier. As the days wore on, Sophia found she thought less and less of the leviathan and came to simply enjoy this languorous time aboard.

On a ship as small as *Game Bird*, the crew must have known about her and James' affair, but they had taken it in their stride. Only Donald had proven bothersome. Whenever he passed her in the companionways or caught her alone in a cabin he would mutter under his breath about young girls going to ruin. Finally her patience had worn through and she had explained to him in great detail exactly what would happen to his long nose if he continued to put it in her business. Since then he had treated her with exquisite courtesy. Only her nights were sometimes unhappy. When James was on watch she was left alone with her thoughts and then the creeping, sneaking claws of despair came slinking back into her heart. Fighting down the familiar tendrils of those gloomy thoughts of the taint, she pushed off the mast and joined the men at the rail. 'At this distance there is no way you can tell even what type of ship that is,' she said, 'let alone who's her captain.'

'We can,' de Lacey said.

'Reveal your dark arts then.'

Faulkner handed her his glass. 'Have a look.'

She held the telescope up to her eye and a tiny ship, blurred by the irregularities of the lenses, sprang into focus. The distant vessel was running through the water at a great pace with a rolling bow wave thrown out before her and a mountain of pure white canvas up aloft. 'What am I supposed to have noticed?'

Faulkner's hand brushed her hip. Their game in public was to accidentally touch as much as possible. It was pathetic and she adored it. 'Her larger mizzen and longer gaff gives it away,' he said. 'As does the absence of a spritsail topsail.'

It still looked exactly like every other ship. 'Gives what away?'

'That she's a frigate of the *Captain* class,' Faulkner said.

'Or maybe one of the very last *Tigers*,' de Lacey added.

'Fine then.' She sighed. 'I'll concede that you two savants have a vague idea of what type of ship it is, but I don't believe you can tell who the captain is.'

'Picking the captain is easier than picking the ship,' Faulkner said a little smugly. 'See, she has almost everything aloft: royals, studdingsails, skysails, the whole lot. He probably has his crew lining the rail holding out their handkerchiefs and blowing into them as well.'

'And I presume that arrangement of canvas and rope speaks to you naval men as clearly as the footsteps of a family member?' she asked.

'Definitely,' agreed de Lacey. 'It'd have to be Adair in *Minotaur*. He goes everywhere like the Duke of Andiel is chasing him. He's the nightmare of dockyards far and wide. Consumes more cordage than half the rest of the fleet. Bloody superb sailor, though.'

'Are we going to say "hello" as he comes past? We should be able to get our old tub across his bows before he passes,' she said.

She caught James and de Lacey glancing at each other.

'We wouldn't want to bother him,' James muttered.

'He's probably in a hurry,' de Lacey agreed.

She tried not to laugh. 'You said he is always hurrying!'

De Lacey coughed. 'He could be carrying orders.'

James nodded. 'It'd be a shame to waste his time.'

'Most remiss of us,' de Lacey agreed.

Sophia narrowed her eyes and stared closely at them. 'You two are just embarrassed to be seen by one of your brother officers out of your pompous uniforms and on our nice little ship.' They squirmed under her gaze. 'Aren't you?'

'Embarrassed? Nonsense, pure nonsense,' de Lacey spluttered, blushing a deep crimson. He looked around a little wildly. 'I have been meaning to check the gun crew. I'll leave you and Miss Blake to finish this discussion.'

Once de Lacey had escaped she fixed James with her gaze. 'I'm right, aren't I? You two are like the girls at the ball with last year's dresses!'

'Well, I, ah…' He looked skyward. 'That is to say, our situation is a little, ah, irregular.'

'And we wouldn't want to be irregular, would we, James?' she asked.

He laughed. 'We can't all fly as courageously in the face of convention as you.'

Behind them the *Game Bird*'s bell rang, ending James' watch and summoning Jenkins to begin his.

'Dinner time?' she asked.

'Thankfully. I'm famished.'

'You're always famished.'

'That's because I work so hard.'

She rolled her eyes and they headed below decks together. It was only her, James, de Lacey and Morgan at the table tonight. It was a little mean to think it, but Sophia always felt a flutter of relief when Jenkins had the watch and missed their meals. Their boatswain was a loyal man, but he could also be somewhat intimidating company.

Their supplies, supplemented by the extras from Hazlewood, were still holding up so the dinner was an affair of pleasant food and even more pleasant company. After the meal was finished and Donald had cleared away the plates they lingered on at the table, content to chat and finish the wine. De Lacey lit one of his cigars and James stood on his chair and opened the grate. Almost immediately the sea air grabbed at the pall of smoke and whipped it away into the night. His stiffness from the blow he'd taken during the mutiny was almost gone now.

'What's the most amazing thing each of you have seen in your travels?' she asked as James climbed back down.

'I met an honest dockyard comptroller once,' James said, and the men laughed.

She sighed. 'It was a serious question.'

'You're very curious, aren't you, Sophia?' observed de Lacey through another plume of smoke.

'You would be too if you'd spent most of your life trapped in parlours and sitting rooms.'

'Fair enough.' The young lord thought for a moment. 'What do you think, Faulkner? The Sea Gate at Scogolio?'

James' gaze was suddenly thousands of miles away. 'The Sea Gate. Bronze doors, large enough to take a galliass, looming up above us; merchant ships from distant shores scurrying back and forth through the great portal; the great arcane device that works the doors glowing like a second sun.' Beneath the table James surreptitiously laid a hand on her leg. 'It was definitely impressive. But personally Scogolio was nothing compared to the eclipse on *Colossus*.'

'An eclipse?' Sophia asked.

'A proper one, too,' Morgan said.

De Lacey took a long pull on his cigar. 'It was terrifying when it happened – one minute we were sailing along in bright sunshine and then *bang*' – he snapped his fingers – 'suddenly it was as black as the Lord of the North's waistcoat. The men thought we were cursed. Poor Barry had a daemon's own work stopping them from panicking.'

'Aye,' Morgan agreed. 'And despite the officers warning them, a few fools still looked up at it and blinded themselves, or went over the side.'

James drained his glass. 'I'd forgotten that.'

She turned to the carpenter. 'And what about you, Morgan? You've been at sea for longer than these two braggarts put together, surely you have seen something wondrous.'

'We all know Morgan's sad and magnificent story,' laughed James.

'Well I haven't heard it.' She pinched his hand, hard. 'What happened, Morgan?'

Morgan smiled at her. 'It was a long time ago now and by the sound of it these lads have probably heard my little story far too many times. But I'll tell it again.' He topped up his wine. 'I was carpenter's mate on *Ararn the Conqueror* when it happened. It was during the Blackwing Plague, not that we knew what to call it back then. Anyway, we were returning from blockade duty and we were just off the Caladian Horn when we spotted something strange in the water ahead.'

'What did you see?' she asked.

'A great dragon floating dead in the water, like a small island. It was,' he turned to James, 'how do I say it again?'

'Regina Caelorum.'

'That's right. *Regina Caelorum.* The last Imperial Dragon. Poor thing had died from the plague and was bobbing in the sea like so much flotsam. The rider, if that's what you call 'em, was still alive, clinging onto the beast's body. Saddest thing I ever saw.' Morgan paused. 'But I was also a little glad the thing was dead, to be honest. Those dragons could make short work of a man of war when they had a mind to.'

'What did you do with him?' Sophia asked.

'The dragon?'

'No, the rider.'

'Wasn't a him. Rider was some Caladian princess. Can't remember her name, but she told our captain she had been trying to get somewhere remote to save her dragon. Quarantine it or whatever. Poor beast must have been sick before it even took off and it died before they could get back to shore.'

'What happened then?'

He shrugged. 'We put her ashore on a Caladian-held island and that was that.'

'To have seen the death of the last dragon!' She paused. 'But weren't you at war, shouldn't you have ransomed the princess or something?'

James grinned at her. 'The navy isn't in the business of kidnapping princess.'

'Why?'

'It's not really our thing.'

'But surely she would have been a useful bargaining chip or something?'

'A bargaining chip? We aren't bloody slavers, Sophia!'

'I'll never understand your navy's silly code.' Sophia sighed. 'You applaud the cleverness of a man who fires grapeshot into a packed deck and kills a horde of enemy sailors, then next minute you go and return captured princesses.'

'It's hardly silly. We fight against other sailors busy trying to kill us. None of this burning towns or sacking villages that the army goes in for.'

De Lacey chuckled, coughed for a long moment and then blew out another thick puff of smoke. 'That, and we always make sure we look after any ladies present, don't we, James? Or do they look after us? I can never remember.'

Faulkner yawned, closed the lantern and turned away from the chart he had spread out over the grate. As the sun had set, Jenkins had anchored them in one of Knifeback Island's rocky inlets. It was almost dawn now and the night was so foggy that the cliffs above them were only just visible as indistinct and brooding shapes through the gloom. They were so close to shore that the quiet calls of the birds nesting on the rocks floated down to him. After seeing firsthand the destructive power and speed of the leviathan, Faulkner had decided that they'd anchor at night as often as was possible. He figured the less sailing they did in the dark the better, as even the slightest delay spotting the leviathan would be the end of them. Of course he had no idea how shallow the oversized fish could come, but *Game Bird*'s tiny draft meant she could get in fiendishly close to shore where hopefully the jagged reefs of Knifeback Island would keep the beast at bay. Their nightly stops also meant a reduced watch, which gave the smaller crew more sleep. Tonight he had taken both the middle and morning watches to give Jenkins, de Lacey and Morgan some proper rest.

With a groan he turned back to the chart and unshuttered his little lantern. He had found this last bit of sailing entirely frustrating. This bumbling around trying to get hunted just did not suit him at all. Even during his independent cruises as master and commander of *Larkspur* and then *Inflexible* there had always been a purpose, an objective. Even if there wasn't a prize to snatch up, there were always sails on the horizon to chase down and enemy ports to snoop about. He surveyed the winding course marked across the chart and grimaced. This sailing, on the other hand, was just so damned aimless. As there was nothing he could do to attract the beast or even predict where it might strike, they had basically just been blundering around the islands like a drunken sailor looking to get in a fist fight with a footpad. He just had to hope that it attacked them before they ran out of coin and he had to return to Stormhaven.

Stormhaven! He looked guiltily at the large icon marking Stormhaven on his chart. The less he thought about heading home the better. For a start he'd have to tell Sophia about his mountain of debts and, while the thought of that conversation was horrible enough, it paled into insignificance when he considered how awful his next meeting with Uriah would be. Faulkner wouldn't be surprised if the poor man demanded the satisfaction of pistols at twenty yards – he deserved it. He closed his eyes and pictured Sophia's smile and her temper and her kindness and her intelligence and the way she moved beneath him and knew he'd do it all again, even with the prospect of the pistols at the end. He sighed. Maybe he was just a rake. The only even slightly positive thing about returning home was that he'd have gotten Sophia home in one piece.

He glanced east to where the first pink branches of dawn were slowly seeping across the night sky. Thank Isaladar, they'd soon be under way. Even aimless sailing was better than lying at anchor in the dark.

They were tacking in a tight channel under the iron-grey cliffs of Knifeback Island when the lookout's cry came. Fear bubbled into Faulkner's guts. It was the ever-reliable Patrick who had sounded the alarm.

'Boscawen, you have the helm.'

'Aye, aye.'

'Morgan! Man the gun. Don't fire till you smell the stink of its breath. Jenkins, Jenkins!' he bellowed. The boatswain pushed through the press of sailors. 'Make as much sail as she will carry, then get the men down out of the tops as quick as you can.'

Satisfied all was in hand, he motioned for de Lacey to follow him and then clambered aloft. On reaching the top spar of the main mast he crouched next to Patrick. A few seconds later de Lacey, wheezing with the effort of the climb, joined them. Below them doll-sized men scurried about the deck.

Faulkner fumbled for his telescope. 'Where is it?'

'There,' Patrick replied, pointing ahead.

Faulkner raised his glass to his eye and scanned the black water. He jumped a little when he spotted the enormous grey shape lying low in the water a few miles ahead.

'The leviathan?' de Lacey panted.

'Can't tell at this distance. Something big, though.'

They crouched in silence as *Game Bird* inexorably bore down on the shape. When they were finally close enough, Faulkner raised his heavy glass again and a mixture of disappointment and relief flooded through him. It was the corpse of a whale turtle. They were massive creatures, half as big again as a blue whale and so heavily armoured the most desperate whalers generally ignored them, despite the oil they carried. This one had been ripped apart. The savage red gashes in its armoured belly were visible even at this distance.

He handed de Lacey the telescope. 'All clear. False alarm,' he shouted down to the deck.

His friend whistled. 'Lords of the bloody North. Think the leviathan did that?'

'I doubt anything else could.'

'Sorry, sir,' muttered Patrick. 'I was sure that was the devil fish.'

'It doesn't matter.' He clapped the lookout on the shoulder. 'It was well spotted – I'd rather a hundred false alarms than a real sight of the thing goes unreported.'

De Lacey nodded in agreement. 'Speaking of drills, do you care for a race? First down to the deck? Like when we were on *Glorious*.'

Faulkner laughed. 'I used to win every time.'

'That was before you got old and decrepit!'

'I beat you up here, didn't I?'

'I wasn't trying.'

'So a wager then?' Faulkner asked.

'I thought you were destitute?'

'I'll pay you off once we kill the leviathan.'

'I'll hold you to that,' replied de Lacey, as he threw himself off the spar.

'Cheat!' Faulkner shouted. He plunged off the mast after his friend and after a short fall caught hold of the futtock shroud. For a dizzying moment deck and sun-flecked ocean whirled beneath his feet. With a grunt of effort, he swung himself around and dropped down onto the shroud. The lime creaked and bounced under his weight. Wrapping his legs about the rope he slithered down it. He was so caught up in the excitement that he dropped the last few yards down onto the deck and landed with a bone-jarring crash.

Picking himself up, he looked around and cursed. De Lacey had still beaten him back to the deck by a yard or so. 'That's a damn sight harder on the legs than it was ten years ago!'

De Lacey turned to face him. His friend's face was white as canvas and his lips were red with frothy blood. 'I don't really feel quite the thing, James,' the young lord said. He swayed for a moment and then collapsed to the deck.

Sophia watched the sailors carry de Lacey tenderly below. They were incredibly gentle, almost maternal with him. The old *Inflexibles* especially had all seen death enough to recognise its face now. They laid him on his cot and she waited outside the cabin while Faulkner talked to Morgan.

'What is it? Consumption?' James asked.

'Not sure.' Morgan tucked the blanket around de Lacey's shoulder. 'Not good, though.'

James looked down at this friend. 'Set a course for Lord Morgans Island.'

'Aye, that'd be the closest physician that isn't half hedge-mage.' The old carpenter backed out of the cabin and hurried away, as if worried the sickness was contagious.

She squeezed into the tiny cabin and took his hand. 'James?'

'What do you think it is?' His look of utter helplessness made her heart lurch.

'I don't know, darling.'

'Do you think he is dying?'

'I don't know.' She looked down at de Lacey. He already looked like a corpse. His lips were blue and if not for the faint rattling of his breath, she would have guessed he had already died. 'He could be.'

'In battle, storm or wreck you almost expect it.' A tear trickled down his face. 'But not like this. Not sickness. He deserves better.'

'He does,' she took him in her arms and his body shuddered with long sobs. 'What can I do, James?'

'Just sit here with me a while.'

Towards evening de Lacey woke and, although he still looked wraith-like, he was able to sit up in bed. They decided that the sea air would do him good and Morgan and James arranged for his cot to be carried up on deck. When James finally had to leave de Lacey's side to take the watch, Sophia stayed with him.

'Sunset could have been nicer,' he wheezed. To the west the sun was being dragged under by a school of iron-grey clouds.

'There's always tomorrow,' Sophia replied, hating the inanity of her reply.

'At least tomorrow.' He nodded. With a wheezing groan he sank further back into his pillows. 'Something has been wrong since my last winter in the south, Sophia. There's been great weight in my chest. Clutching at my lungs.' His voice was very quiet. 'I've felt it growing, strangling my breath.'

She took his cold hand. 'I'm sorry.'

He smiled. 'I most regret leaving things as they are with my father. Still hate the man, but it does seem a pity to sneak out during the second act.'

'You might still put things to rights.'

'I won't. This is canker.' He chuckled. 'I read up on it back in Stormhaven.'

'You knew you were sick?'

'I did.'

'Why didn't you do something?'

'Nothing to do. Canker in the lungs is always fatal.'

'But you still came to sea?'

'Why not? This mad hunt seemed the perfect employment for a dying man. That and Faulkner needs someone to look after him. Outside of naval matters, the man's a bloody fool.' De Lacey held his handkerchief to his mouth and coughed. When he took it away again the fabric was speckled with blood. 'You will, won't you? Look after him that is? He loves you.'

She couldn't bring herself to answer that.

She sat with de Lacey till he fell asleep and they carried him back below. By that point she was so tired and wrung out she retired to her own cabin. When James finally got off watch he came and lay down beside her. It was clear he didn't want to speak and she simply held him until he eventually fell asleep. After that she simply lay awake next to him, enjoying his presence, his smell and the feel of his body next to her for the last time.

When the first fingers of light tracked their way across the wood above her, she rubbed at her eyes and tried to still the nerves that fluttered in her belly. She knew there was no decision to make. She rolled out of bed and pulled on her clothes. James murmured her name, but she forced herself on. She shut the door slowly behind her and then pressed her forehead against it. 'I'm sorry I didn't tell you,' she whispered.

She crossed the companionway to de Lacey's cabin. The deck was cold beneath her feet as she opened the door. De Lacey's breathing was even more laboured than it had been the previous afternoon. Whispering a quiet prayer, she gently took hold of his icy wrist and let a trickle of taint seep into him. The young lord's self-diagnosis had been right. The thing sat heavy, cold and hungry across his chest. She could feel it eating and spreading even now. A cruel weed that's rampant growth somehow also repudiated all life.

She readied herself. She flexed her limbs and tried to brace herself against the agony that was to come. She had never healed a hurt this vast, this infectious, this intertwined with its host.

She began.

The walls of bone and flesh that held her fell away and the true world sprang into achingly sharp focus. Close by, only just beyond the nebulous melding of her and de Lacey, was the strong, sturdy presence of James and his love for her was dazzling.

Past him, surrounding and protecting her, was the steady presence of the crew and the ship. Then there was the ocean, bustling with all the weight of life it contained. Beyond that, to the west, like boils on the face of the world, shimmered two shades of unlife – demolishers and destroyers. Those mere flickering candles of darkness were nothing compared to the rolling, boiling well of evil that lurked deep beneath the waters away to the south, however. The leviathan! Desperation, hunger and fury given mortal form. She shied away from it.

Gathering up her taint, she began to work. She purged his lungs first, burning away the scum and rebuilding what was left. By the time she had finished she was already agonisingly tired. Her vision flickered and blurred as the taint burned away at her.

But there was more of it, the canker had crawled and snaked its way through his body, growing and multiplying as it went. It riddled his bones and some of its tendrils had even penetrated his brain, turning yet more of the body's essence against itself.

She wanted to give up. Her own heart laboured and strained under the pressure.

Sophia carried on, searching down the last branches of the poisonous vine and melting it wherever she found it.

She caressed life back into existence once the poison weed was gone.

An eternity later she was done.

She went to pull her taint back but something blacker than obsidian boiled up after it, an ancient monolith of oil and darkness. It came after her like a beast rushing at a closing fortress gate. A dizzying array of images – red of blood, white of splintered bone, unfathomable shapes and dimensions hammered at her. Her mind strained, writhed and buckled as the alien thing battered her.

She remained herself, just.

Then it was suddenly gone and her taint slithered safely back inside.

She crashed back down into her exhausted shell of a body. Unable to even hold herself up she collapsed to the deck and pulled a chair down on top of her. With an enormous effort, she rolled onto her back. She was wet and cold with sweat and vomit.

'What?' De Lacey slowly sat up in his cot. He looked dazed, but his breathing was effortless. 'Sophia?'

'The taint!' Faulkner whispered in horror, from where he stood at the open cabin door. 'You're tainted.' Before she could even think about mustering the strength to reply he had reeled away from her like he had been shot.

34.

URIAH TOOK A sip of his lime juice and shuddered. 'I think I'd rather the scurvy.'

Fiora had taken a break from her early morning fighting practice to sit by his side in *Palinurus'* bow and share an unappetising breakfast of stale biscuits washed down with lime juice. The meagre meal was somewhat made up for by the fantastically stark view of dark blue ocean and pale dawn sky framing the distant islands.

'You'd be singing a different song if your teeth fell out,' Fiora replied.

'I suppose so. I've lost enough teeth for one year.' He sighed and ran a hand along his lumpy jawline. 'This horrid concoction it is then.' Since their argument about warning the navy, he and Fiora had been getting along surprisingly well. At her core Fiora was a Caladian aristocrat and, for all the lip service she paid cold logic, and for all she emphasised the savagery and barbarity of her secret war, she was just as proud, honourable and warlike as her ancestors who had carved out their Empire. Her exposure to this Great Enemy and the death of her son had hardened her, but a broad steel stroke of martial chivalry still ran right through her. It was this martial pride that had brought them back to even footing. He might have been flattering himself, but he guessed she had realised that while he couldn't boast her hot bravery in battle, he did carry a quieter courage of conviction and strongly held ethics.

'So is this how your normal mornings are, Uriah?' Fiora asked.

'What? Up with the dawn to watch a foreign noble practise sword fighting and pistol shooting? Followed by a breakfast of hard tack and lime juice?' He smiled and shook his head ruefully. 'No, not quite.'

'What is your normal routine then?'

His past life had been staid in retrospect, boring even, and he glanced at her to make sure she wasn't teasing. 'Most mornings I would get up at six. I'd wash and then have some breakfast and read the morning paper. If Sophia wasn't lying lazily in bed, we'd talk about what our days had in store. Then I'd walk down to the office in time to be at my desk by just after the eighth bell.'

'So that's the routine of a lawyer in the Realm?'

'A prize agent, anyway. And you? What does a normal day look like for a countessa fighting a secret war?'

She grimaced. 'My normal day has more in common with yours than you might think, Uriah.'

'Oh.'

'The majority of my time is spent buried under mountains of parchment.'

'I thought you'd be out and about searching out ancient holy weapons or hunting down the enemy or something?'

'That is very rare.' She gestured up at the broad blue sky. 'I don't spend enough time outside. My work for the Blessed Lance is mostly scribe's work. For every hour I spend stalking our enemies, I spend months and months collating reports from our agents, managing our treasury or documenting past operations. It is boring, unromantic work in the main.'

'But like staff work for an army, I suppose, that is just as important as the actual fighting.'

'It—' Fiora stopped abruptly. Her eyes suddenly went wide and a violent spasm shook her. Her tin cup clattered to the deck. She fell back and a great convulsive jolt shook her so her feet drummed on the deck.

'Fiora!' He grabbed her shoulders and looked around for help. Then, as quickly as it had started, the fit subsided. 'Great Isaladar, are you all right?'

'Sophia,' she croaked. A dribble of spit ran from the corner of her mouth.

'What happened to her?'

'She just used her taint.' Fiora struggled to get her breath. 'A huge amount of it. Close by.'

His heart fluttered with fear and excitement. 'Are you sure?'

'It was your daughter.' Fiora let him help her back up into a sitting position. Her skin was almost white and she was shaking. 'For a moment I thought her power would break me.'

As the leviathan swam languidly through the shallows it peered up through the green water towards the coppered bottom of the warship it was going to destroy. This was a little luxury it allowed itself, a moment of anticipation before each kill.

It opened and closed its massive jaws. It hoped they launched a longboat. That was the worst thing about this enormous shell. One death at a time wasn't enough for it to enjoy, but twenty sailors dying together in the one boat released just enough of a spurt of terror and despair for it to savour.

Suddenly, the great fish stiffened like a snake that had been trodden on. It thrashed and writhed for a moment before it steadied itself. For the first time since it had been captured in its current prison of flesh and scale, true pleasure coursed through it. The warship forgotten, it rolled onto its back and plunged down into the coal-black depths. All its calm was gone now and it tore at the water like a salmon climbing rapids. Turning north, it raced towards where the distant essence of the girl's power still resonated through the cold water.

As it went, the thing gathered its taint and threw its dark mind out before it.

'Nagel!' Although the Tallowman's cry was muffled by the powder magazine's heavy door, it was still loud enough to wake him.

Nagel scrambled to his feet and knocked over one of the barrels of powder. He quickly stood it back upright and then hurried to meet his master. He knew better than to keep the thing waiting.

'Where have you been?' it asked.

'Ch... ch... checking the powder was well stowed.'

'I will speak to you in my cabin.'

Nagel followed it aft. The few crew members they passed quickly looked as busy and as oblivious to the Tallowman's passing as they possibly could. After it had killed the captain, the Tallowman had moved into the dead man's cabin. Appropriately, the place already stank of decay. Nagel shut the door behind them.

The Tallowman perched itself like some great vulture on the edge of the captain's table. 'You have been hiding.'

Nagel opened his mouth to lie and then thought better of it. 'I have.'

'You fear us?'

'Yes, I mean, no.'

'Spit it out. Which is it, Nagel?'

'I would only fear you if I failed you, Mr Savage. But Roberts, he looks addled as a mad dog.'

'Roberts is an unfortunate necessity.'

'A necessity?'

'Yes. I wouldn't have made it if I didn't need this ship. What I did to Roberts is as much a curse as a gift.'

Nagel smiled. That was good to hear, he'd been a little jealous of Roberts. 'So if you get a chance, you will make me like you?'

'I—' Without warning, the Tallowman stiffened and crashed to the deck. Nagel backed away. He looked around but the cabin was still empty. Should he run? At his feet the Tallowman writhed on the deck and moaned. The horrible sound was low, almost sensual. After an endless moment its shaking stopped as suddenly as it had started. As the tremors died the Tallowman clambered slowly back to its feet. 'We are saved, Nagel,' it murmured.

'We are?'

'The whore is close. She just used her taint, the fool. She is incredibly powerful and' – it flicked its tongue across its thin white lips – 'delicious.'

'You know where *Game Bird* is?'

'I do.'

The cabin door crashed open and Roberts lurched into the room.

'What is this?' Roberts howled, pointing at its own chest. 'I did not give you permission to raise up a fiend.' Roberts was always frightening, but now it had expanded and an aura of darkness seemed to flicker about his edges like smoke about a fire. A new and keener fear gripped Nagel, almost smothering him.

The Tallowman threw itself down before him. 'The task you gave me required it.'

'This' – it pointed to its chest again – 'is a waste. A travesty of our art.'

'I had no choice.'

'Fool,' Roberts hissed. 'We will add this crime to your reckoning.'

'Yes, master.'

'Did you feel the one we hunt? The girl?'

'Yes, master.'

'She is even more powerful than we dreamed.'

'I know, master,' the Tallowman whined. 'I will capture her for you.'

'You have already failed me too many times.' Roberts shook its head. 'An opportunity this perfect will never come again. I will destroy her ship and kill her companions. You will then pluck her from the water.'

The Tallowman looked up in shock. 'But if she drowns or is killed…'

'Then much of what we could have harvested from her will be lost.'

'Please, master, no! Leave it to me, let me capture her, she is too precious to waste.'

'No!' Roberts screamed. 'Your promises are worthless, Tallowman. Just pray she is still alive when you find her.'

'Yes, master.'

The dark weight of presence left the cabin and Roberts stumbled and almost fell. Nagel shuddered in relief.

Steadying itself, Roberts stared around the cabin, its eyes wide, looking for its invisible assailant. 'What the fuck was that?' The black veins on its face throbbed. 'It was in my head.'

'That,' the Tallowman said slowly, 'was my master. I am surprised you survived direct communion with it.'

Scarrus studied the chart laid out before him on the table. 'So, Countessa, the girl was about thirty miles away due north-east and heading north-west, is that correct?'

'That's about right.'

'Then that will put them on the other side of this.' He read the name off the chart. 'Dogwood Island.'

'Can we catch them?' Uriah asked.

Scarrus nodded. 'Aye, we can. This gentle weather is perfect for the *Palinurus*. As long as the wind stays light, she'll run down any northern tub.

If we can just thread a safe channel through these reefs here' – he stabbed a finger at the map – 'we'll have them a little after dawn.'

'Very good.' Although she was still wan, Fiora looked pleased. 'See that the men sleep well. I want them armed, fed and ready for action an hour before sunrise.'

Scarrus nodded and left to see to the preparations.

'We can expect more trouble?' Uriah asked.

'We can. The Tallowman will have her location now as well.'

'But I thought it only had a limited ability to scry out the tainted?'

'It does. But the small amount of taint she used near Stormhaven was like a murmur in a crowded room. What she used today was a cathedral bell ringing during a silent winter's night. If it is within a hundred miles, even a creature as clumsy as the Tallowman will have marked her location.'

Uriah experienced a strange flicker of pride. 'She is that powerful?'

'Untrained, loud and wasteful, but incredibly, incredibly powerful. I can see why the enemy hunts her so tirelessly.'

'So now it is just a race to get to her before it does?' Uriah said.

'It is, my friend.'

35.

FAULKNER FELT HOLLOWED out.

De Lacey was cured. Sophia was tainted.

Those two thoughts spun around and around inside him like two great suns orbiting each other. That was what Sophia had been hiding. Not a betrothed, or a debt, or a parlour room secret. The taint.

He rifled through his trunks until he found his bottle of whisky. He reefed out the cork, took a long swig and then sat down on the deck, with the cool of metal of the great gun against his back.

Sophia was tainted. She seemed so perfect, so happy, but under it all bubbled the taint.

When he was a boy one of his family's neighbours had hidden his taint from the world. One cold night something in him had broken and the cursed fellow had lit himself on fire and run screaming through the streets, immolating all he touched until he threw himself into the freezing ocean. Faulkner shuddered and took another swig. Was that what awaited Sophia? Would she splinter apart like his neighbour had? Transformed in one random moment from a kind and beautiful woman into mindless engine of destruction?

In a way he couldn't blame her for keeping the secret. To reveal the taint was to commit social suicide. How many people would ask a tainted into their home? One in twenty? How many mothers would leave a tainted alone with their child? Not one in a hundred. He would have never let her come along if he had known her secret. He spun the bottle up in the air and let it tumble back into his lap. But he had let her come and then he had fallen in love with her.

Where did that leave them?

He laughed bitterly. To think he had been worried there might be another man.

He sat thinking in the darkened cabin for a long time. Until, in the cold hour just before dawn, he fell into a fitful doze.

'I thought this would be all gone.' De Lacey leant forward and picked up the bottle of whisky.

Faulkner started. He had been drifting, unable to tell where wakeful despair and dreaming nightmare began and ended. 'I was tempted to,' he said groggily. The cabin was awash with grey light, dawn must have snuck in.

'I can imagine.'

'How are you?' he asked.

'Me? I've never felt so damn well. I could reef the mainsail on my own and not break a sweat.'

'I'm so glad.' That at least was the truth.

'So am I.' De Lacey smiled wryly. 'I have a lot to live for, you know. The prospect of dying was most unappetising. Knowing I'm going to see out the year is going to take some getting used to.' He turned and put the bottle gently down on the small writing table. 'So, the taint. Sophia is tainted.'

'The taint,' Faulkner agreed. The word filled the room and hung in the air like powder smoke after a broadside.

'What are you going to do?'

'What can I do?'

'So that's it, then?'

'It is. You know how the navy feels about the tainted.'

De Lacey picked the bottle back up and took a swig. 'So you'll just walk away?'

'What can I do?'

'What rot are—'

From above them the frantic rattle of the drum beating to quarters cut de Lacey off in midsentence.

'Leeeviathaaan!' a lookout screamed somewhere above.

'Take command of the gun,' Faulkner barked.

Scrambling to his feet, Faulkner snatched his sword belt, buckled it on and then sprinted out of the cabin and scrambled up out of the main hatch. Reaching the deck, he jogged to the taffrail.

The beast was already on the surface only half a dozen cable lengths behind them, a rolling mess of teeth and torn water; a living, moving reef of scale, fangs and muscle. It looked even bigger than he remembered. For a mad moment he wondered if it'd simply swallow the *Game Bird* whole. His mouth went dry and vomit scalded the back of his throat. 'Isaladar's blood,' he whispered. His heart thundered in his chest like a cannon loose below decks during a tempest. 'You men, down on the deck. Now!' he yelled at the sailors up aloft in the rigging.

'What course?' called Jenkins from the wheel.

Thankfully the course he had charted had them near to Dogwood Island. 'Put us as close to the shore as you can. If we end up having a swim, I'd rather it be as short as possible.' Jenkins nodded and swung the wheel over. With a groan, the *Game Bird*'s bow swung towards the stony, unwelcoming island shore.

Walking down towards where the sailors had gathered in the waists, Faulkner raised his voice. 'This is it, lads, this is what we came to sea for – it's time to kill the beast. Look after your mates and keep your heads. You all know what you have to do. Today will be a day we can boast about when we are old and grey. Now go!'

The men let out a frightened, ragged cheer and jogged to their stations.

He glanced back aloft and frowned. Some men were still working their way down. There was no point hurrying them though, they'd all seen what happened to the poor southerner's masts when the beast hit her. He put a hand on his sword hilt and walked back to stand next to Jenkins and Simon by the wheel. 'Big bastard, isn't he?'

Simon spat on the deck. 'Ugly as he is big.'

Jenkins nodded. 'Aye.'

For the first time in all the years he had known him, Faulkner thought he detected a hint of fear in his boatswain's voice. Turning back aft, he forced himself to watch the leviathan as it scythed through the water towards them. Even though their plan depended on getting the monster in close, it was still terrifying to watch it eat up the fathoms between them.

He held onto his sword so tightly the wire on the hilt dug into his hand.

The beast's stench, a mixture of saltwater and decay, filled his nostrils. He forced himself to stand calm and upright.

'Isaladar's fucking blood,' a man just forward of them whimpered.

'Quiet there,' Faulkner barked.

The beast was close now, less than a cable's length away. He could see its teeth quite clearly. Each fang was taller than a man, jagged and splintered. Its mouth snapped open and closed, eager to smash wood and pulp flesh. An anchor and its chain were tangled in its fangs.

'Fire, de Lacey,' he muttered.

The great foaming wave the beast cast before it rocked *Game Bird*.

The putrid warmth of its breath swept over the deck like a foul wind.

The gun roared.

The concussion of its blast hammered up through Faulkner's feet and made his teeth rattle. The muzzle flash was hot on his face, even from his sheltered position on deck. Through a gap in the smoke, he saw the huge stone ball catch the leviathan just above its left eye and blow away a wagon-sized globule of flesh and scale. Faulkner watched, transfixed, as the huge lump spiralled away lazily to splash down into the sea. Black blood pumped from the terrible wound and the leviathan shrieked in rage, or agony, or both. But it didn't slow.

It hit the *Game Bird* a monstrous blow dead astern.

Faulkner was hurled to the deck as the impact threw the ship forward. Timbers cracked and splintered and from deep in her belly the *Game Bird* groaned like a dying animal. With a rending crash the foremast broke. A man screamed as he tumbled down with it until his cry was cut off as he hit the deck with a wet *thwack*.

Still shrieking, the leviathan rolled on to its back and plunged back down into the depths. The mighty kick of its tail drenched the entire weather deck with spray.

Faulkner shrugged off a fallen line and scrambled back to his feet. Jenkins was somehow still on his feet by the wheel. 'Don't bother with that, the rudder's gone!' Faulkner yelled over the din. 'Get the boats free! Even *Game Bird* won't last long after that hit.'

'Aye, aye, Cap'n.' Jenkins let go of the useless wheel and began gathering together some of the stunned crew.

There was nothing more for him to do on deck. With the rudder gone and the gun fired, the *Game Bird* was lamed and had lost her sting. Faulkner plunged down the main hatch. The space below was in an even worse state of confusion. The deck was thick with a carpet of supplies and possessions shaken loose by the impact. Beams and planks had been splintered and lay at crazy angles, blocking passageways and bulkheads. 'Up on deck, all of you, up on deck!' he shouted. 'Everyone up on deck!' Forcing his way through the bedlam of panicked men trying to escape, he clambered down to the hold. In the flickering light of the lanterns he saw that water already sloshed there, waist-deep. 'Forget repairs, Morgan,' he screamed down into the dark. 'She won't last long enough for it to matter. Get your men up on deck.'

The carpenter's frightened face appeared from the gloom. 'Aye, aye.'

'And for Isaladar's sake, make sure you and Jenkins keep the men out of the water for as long as you can. It'd swallow a boat in one gulp.'

Leaving Morgan, Faulkner clambered aft towards the gun. When he reached the great cabin, he almost wept at the havoc there. The stern windows had been completely smashed in and the deck was carpeted in splintered wood and broken glass. The cannon had been wrenched free from its carriage and lay askew on the deck. Beams from the deck above had also fallen across the top of the gun, making it difficult to even get to. A dead man, Smith, lay beside the cannon, a dark pool spreading from the ruin of his head.

The rest of the gun crew were clustered at the back of the cabin, ashen and silent.

A shaken de Lacey was looking at the mess in helpless anguish. 'Sorry.'

'Don't be, you hit it. Thought you'd killed the blighter for a moment,' he said. 'Now help me clear this wreckage off the gun. It'll soon be back to finish us off.'

'We can't fire it again. We've checked,' de Lacey gestured at the gun helplessly. 'And even if we could, the recoil would pulp every man in here.'

Faulkner took a deep breath and fought down the urge to scream at his friend. 'You're right. Take the gun crew and go up on deck. Take command. Send Morgan and a few men down here with crowbars.'

De Lacey saluted. 'Very good, Captain.'

'And for Isaladar's sake, make sure someone gets Sophia into a boat.'

He waited for his friend to leave. There was no way Morgan would have time to clear the gun, but he couldn't just leave his crew to be slaughtered either. He studied the wreck. Even though the cannon had been torn free of its carriage and lay askew on the deck, it was still pointing roughly astern. He leapt into the wreckage and began kicking the mess out of the way. He didn't bother looking for the swab. He'd have to risk a misfire. He snatched up a silk bag of gunpowder and jammed it into the gun's ornate, snarling mouth, cursing as the hot metal burned his hands. He grabbed the ramrod, threw himself down amongst the debris and hammered the powder bag up into the belly of the gun.

Below him he could hear the urgent rushing gurgle of water pouring into the hold, even over the sound of the pandemonium up on deck.

Still on hands and knees, he looked out through the ruin of the stern.

Still no sign of the leviathan.

Faulkner couldn't find the cloth wadding amongst the chaos. He'd have to do without that as well. Ignoring the splinters of wood and glass that tore his hands and knees, he scrabbled across the cabin to where the gun's heavy stone balls lay. He grabbed at one, but it slipped through his bloody fingers. On the second attempt he managed to drag it back to the mouth of the gun. With a grunt of effort, he heaved the ball into the barrel. With one hand holding the cannonball in place, he searched around behind him in the glass and splinters for the ramrod. His hand closed on it and he braced himself to roll the ball up to lie against the powder. He left the rod inside the gun, with any luck it'd help stop the unwadded ball from just rolling out. Standing back up, he began searching amongst the wreckage again. Finally in a corner, partially hidden by a fallen board, he found the slow match still spluttering and hissing spitefully.

Game Bird groaned again and settled by the stern. A river of broken glass slid down the tilting deck and poured out through the holes in the stern.

He approached the gun. The carriage was broken and the shot was incredibly badly packed, but if he waited till the beast was right on top of them then it might not matter. All he needed was to find a tiny gap in the wreckage blocking the touchhole, so he could use the match to fire the gun.

A hoarse cry of terror from above made Faulkner look astern. The leviathan had burst back up to the surface. His stomach lurched. It was like standing at the bottom of a valley watching the avalanche come down on top of you.

He heaved at the timbers covering the gun. Although he strained till his muscles felt like they'd tear and pain radiated out from his injured shoulder, he couldn't get the match anywhere near the touchhole.

He screamed in frustration.

He glanced astern. The beast was halfway through its furious charge.

He grabbed the timbers again and pushed and pulled, but no matter what he did, he couldn't move the beam enough to slide the match in under it.

A panicked man leapt overboard with a splash.

'I can lift it,' said Boscawen from the doorway. Without waiting for an answer, the old whaler crossed the room and gripped the heaviest piece of wreckage covering the gun.

'If I fire it like this, the gun will kill you,' Faulkner said.

Bracing his feet wide apart, the whaler lifted the beams an inch off the gun.

'It will kill you, Boscawen.'

'I heard you.' The muscles at the base of Boscawen's neck quivered like taut ropes. 'But I wouldn't count myself much of a man to falter now. You see, what I left out of the story I told you was that I was captain of the *Clermont* and my dear wife and two young lads were aboard.' Sweat ran down his face in rivulets. 'So strike that match when it's close, Captain Faulkner. Send the beast back to its maker.'

Faulkner faced the leviathan. Above the froth of churned water its milky eyes stared at them. The massive gun looked utterly impotent before it. Surely it couldn't possibly kill this ancient, primordial beast?

He turned back to the whaler. 'You're a brave man.'

'I'm not brave.' With a bestial roar of effort the whaler heaved the heavy beam another inch off the gun. 'I'm going to see my wife and boys.'

The leviathan snapped its great maw open. Its stench flooded the cabin.

Faulkner jammed the match down into the precious space Boscawen had made under the beam. Hidden by timbers, the match hissed and sparked. Faulkner frantically jiggled it back and forth over what he hoped was the touchhole.

The leviathan screamed like a great bird of prey.

The cannon barked out a thunderous retort and flew back across the cabin like a maddened beast. Boscawen caught the full force of the recoil and the impact tore him apart. Faulkner almost managed to dodge clear, but a piece of wreckage still caught him with a blow like a lightning bolt.

With a moan, Faulkner picked himself up. He shook his head in a futile attempt to clear the deafening ringing from his ears and gasped for air. The room was full of smoke. He staggered across to where the gun had thrown Boscawen. The whaler's body was pulped almost beyond recognition and the timbers around his corpse were drenched with blood.

Hand clutched to his injured side, Faulkner crawled up the ladder and out onto the weather deck, which looked like a forest after the passing of a tempest. The main mast lay across the deck, wrapped in a funeral shroud of twisted rigging and torn canvas. All that was left of the other two were their splintered stumps. Poor *Game Bird* was so far down by the stern now that water already lapped hungrily over the deck. She wouldn't swim much longer. Faulkner hobbled towards the rail.

'Here, Faulkner,' cried de Lacey. 'Nice of you to save me the trouble of coming back aboard to look for you.' His friend was perched in the prow of the longboat bobbing alongside. In the stern Jenkins worked the heavy oar forcing the boat closer, while behind de Lacey, Morgan was trying to drag a swimming man into the boat. Further out the other boats bobbed around the sinking *Game Bird*. It looked like they had got all of them away.

He looked astern and a flicker of exultation cut through his pain and fear. The enormous corpse of the leviathan lay on its back in the water with its pale grey belly exposed to the sky. A thin ribbon of smoke curled away from a cavernous wound between its eyes.

They had killed the thing!

'Sophia?' he called.

'We put her in the first boat,' de Lacey shouted back.

Satisfied, Faulkner knelt down and placed a bloody hand on the tilting deck. 'Thank you.' As if in answer *Game Bird* let out a great shudder as the gun tore itself free and smashed its way out through what was left of the stern. 'Thank you,' he said again.

'She's about to go!' Jenkins yelled.

The boatswain was right. From beneath his feet came a long, low sigh as the last air bubbled from the hold. Faulkner stumbled forward at a half run then jumped over the intervening water and crashed down awkwardly in the bow of the longboat. The pain hunched him over for a moment. Once it had passed, he looked back at the corpse of the great fish. 'We killed the bloody leviathan.' He shook his head. 'We actually killed the thing.'

With a groan of effort Morgan heaved Simon up out of the water and aboard the boat.

'We did.' De Lacey laughed. 'And I might even live long enough to spend my share of the money.'

Simon spat out a mouthful of water and looked around blearily. 'You won't if we don't get clear of poor old *Game Bird*.'

The men pulled hard on the oars and they slid away from their dying ship. They were only just clear when the *Game Bird* let out a last mournful sigh and slid beneath the iron-grey seas.

36.

URIAH ROSE BEFORE dawn. He washed thoroughly in cold seawater and then dressed carefully. The weight of the coming day lay like a lead cloak upon him. To pass the time, he sat on his sea chest and took apart and then cleaned the pistol Fiora had given him. Once he had wasted as much time as he could, he went up on deck.

Although the eastern horizon was already pregnant with the colours of the coming sunrise, it was still dark. The breeze was brisk and the *Palinurus* was cutting along quickly through the choppy sea. The crew were clustered together shoulder to shoulder in the bow. It took him a moment to realise they were praying together. He joined them. Scarrus was leading the service, his baritone voice low and almost serene. Although the foreign words were alien to him and he was unable to join in the refrains, Uriah's nerves calmed a little.

'Samaryan, I have never believed in you,' he whispered. 'But I never believed in evil either. Now that I have discovered true evil, I wonder if something as foolishly perfect as you might be true as well. If you are, please send your martial son Isaladar to look after my daughter. She deserves so much better than to die at the hands of an evil she knows nothing about.'

The service ended and, feeling a little foolish, guilty and gullible, he walked aft to the wheel.

Fiora was already there. 'Are you all right?'

'Just nerves. I always had nerves before kickoff.'

'Kickoff?'

'I always had nerves before I played rugby.'

She shook her head. 'You Realmsmen and your games. Just remember what I told you after the storm: "worry only rusts the blade before it is needed".'

'I just hope this time I can be braver if it comes to a fight.' He looked back at their wake. 'We seem to be making good speed.'

'We are. But we still have the reefs and shoals around Dogwood Island to navigate.'

'Can we do it?'

Scarrus joined them and took the wheel. 'Aye, but can we do it fast enough to intercept your daughter's ship? That is the question.'

Nagel looked up again at the massive spread of canvas the *Dead Reckoning* was carrying and swallowed nervously. 'I don't think we should be cracking on this fast. Not until daylight.'

'Shut up, Nagel,' growled Roberts.

Nagel shut up. If they tore the bottom right out of her, it wouldn't be his fault.

'So if we catch this girl, we will be able to heal this body?' Roberts asked.

'Correct,' the Tallowman replied.

'And then the fucking life won't just leak out of me?'

'That's right.' It peered ahead into the murky dawn. 'Is that the island?'

Nagel took out his spyglass. It took a moment for him to see it. A dark smudge ahead, Dogwood Island. 'That's it.'

'Good.'

'Open the arms locker, Nagel.' Roberts pressed a key into his hand. 'See the men take what they want.'

'Yes, Roberts.'

'And remember, Nagel,' the Tallowman called after him. 'They can kill who they want, but if one of them even injures the girl, then the life of every single man on this ship is forfeit. And that includes you.'

'What did he say?' asked Uriah, looking over the side of the *Palinurus* to where the leadsman had his sounding line in the water.

'Three fathoms beneath us,' Fiora explained.

'Can't we go any faster?' Since they had entered the labyrinth of reefs and shoals around Dogwood Island their pace had been painfully slow.

Scarrus shook his head. '*Palinurus* draws a little over one fathom of water herself. We don't have much honest ocean beneath us.'

'Besides,' said Fiora, 'we made very good time this morning. We should still meet Sophia's ship as it passes the northern tip of the island.'

'And the Tallowman?'

She shrugged. 'It will be coming.'

'Strange sail ahead!'

'And what do you mean strange, you whoreson?' Roberts roared up at the lookout.

'Foreign. Never seen nothin' like her. She's two points off the port bow, if you want to 'ave a look yourself.'

Nagel snapped open his glass. The ship was just visible through the morning fog. Nagel had never seen anything like it either. It was long and low with a strangely overhanging bow and stern. It was lateen-sailed, like some lubber foreigners favoured.

'Well?' the Tallowman asked.

Nagel shrugged. 'It looks like some southern merchant ship. No fucking idea what it is doing this far north, but it ain't the ship we're looking for.'

'It's her, isn't it?' Roberts hissed. 'The one who shot me?'

The Tallowman looked at Roberts for a long moment as if deciding if it should lie. 'Yes,' it said finally. 'Countessa Varzi.'

Roberts gave an inarticulate roar of rage, threw the helmsman out of the away and swung the wheel over until the *Dead Reckoning's* bow pointed directly at the other ship. 'Man the guns!' it screamed.

Nagel gulped. 'It's shoaling water ahead, Roberts. You can't go in there – not at this rate of knots.'

'Fuck you, Nagel. *Dead Reckoning* is goin' to rip her pretty little ship apart.'

'You'll kill us all!'

'Shut it, Nagel, or you'll swim.'

Nagel turned to the Tallowman. 'Mr Savage…'

It shook its head. 'A chance to kill that meddling bitch is worth the risk. But make the longboat ready, we will have to go after the girl in that if *Dead Reckoning* is sunk.'

Although Uriah had no idea what the lookout had screamed, he followed the man's outstretched arm and started in shock. A ship had burst from a fog bank only a few hundred yards off their beam and was bearing down on them with acres and acres of canvas aloft. Scarrus and Fiora took one look at the strange ship and then ran aft, shouting to the crew as they went.

'The Tallowman,' he whispered to himself. It must be.

The other vessel was making directly for them and, with most of the *Palinurus'* sails reefed and lifeless, they were helpless.

The other ship's bow chasers roared and a ball whined angrily past Uriah's head.

Around him the crew ran out *Palinurus'* few light guns.

Fiora barked an order and their pitiful few cannons crashed out at broadside.

When the smoke cleared Uriah saw that although the bow of their attacker was splintered and pierced in a half dozen places, their broadside had done nothing to slow the other ship.

Slowly it dawned on him that the enemy vessel meant to ram them.

The deck bucked as they fired again. Still the other ship came on undaunted. Even to Uriah it was obvious their gunfire would never stop her. Their only hope was that she ran aground.

Uriah stood frozen at the side, begging a rock to tear the guts out of the Tallowman's ship. But it came on inexorably, throwing a massive bow wave as it closed. Now he could clearly pick out the details of the ugly sloop. Its stained and unpainted sides, the two anchors tied across the bows, the leering figurehead, and the damage Fiora's firing had inflicted. He could even see men scurrying around her deck. The name *Dead Reckoning* was marked on the bow in cracked and yellowed paint. He blinked. It was mesmerising watching hundreds of tonnes of ship come to murder you.

'Back, you fool,' snapped Celsus, dragging him away from the rail. 'Can't you see they mean to ram us? It must be the Tallowman. No other captain would—'

A shadow fell across them and *Dead Reckoning* hammered into the *Palinurus* hard amidships. The deck under their feet bucked and buckled. Uriah was picked up and slammed down against the edge of a hatch. Pain exploded from his back. Heavy timbers screamed in protest. With an agonising shriek the *Dead Reckoning's* bluff bow ground and splintered their way along the *Palinurus'* flank. All around him men were screaming.

Through a jagged hole torn in the deck, Uriah found himself staring down all the way into the *Palinurus'* torn belly. A black sailor stared back up at him, his mouth open in helpless terror. Then the water swallowed him.

'Fire! Fire!' a hoarse Realmish voice on the other ship screamed.

The *Dead Reckoning's* broadside roared.

The world spun. Ship. Water. Sky. Ship. Water.

The water rose up to swallow him.

Nagel laughed hysterically.

The tops and the bow were all but wrecked, the beakhead was stoved in and the figurehead gone, but somehow it looked like they just might swim. Even better, the *Dead Reckoning* had broken the flimsy foreign ship in half. Astern the xebec's two shattered pieces were already slipping beneath the waves. Plenty of the blackies were already in the water and he could just hear their screams over the creaking and groaning of the *Dead Reckoning*. Fucking foreigners, couldn't be trusted to do or make anything right.

Roberts snatched up a musket and rushed to the stern rail. It frantically searched the water behind them but, judging by its roar of frustration, it couldn't find what it was looking for. Snarling in anger, it finally contented itself with shooting a random swimmer.

'Will our ship sink?' the Tallowman asked.

Nagel shrugged. 'Depends on how badly we're holed below.'

'Go and check.'

Dark and cold water was pouring in through a few leaks near the bow but, with some repairs and some pumping, he thought the *Dead Reckoning* might survive. He went back up on deck and reported his findings to the Tallowman. He was finishing his account when the Tallowman gave a strange little shudder and almost fell.

'Whore use her taint again?' Roberts said.

'No.' The Tallowman shook its head. 'Now go and clean the ship up, Roberts. I want it to look as normal as possible, as quickly as possible.'

'Nagel, go and cl—'

Nagel turned to do as he was told, but the Tallowman's crushing grip on his wrist stopped him.

'I told you to do it, Roberts. Now go, you've had your fun.'

Roberts stared at the Tallowman for a moment and then stalked off towards the bow.

'What just 'appened?' Nagel asked once it was gone.

'My master was just destroyed,' the Tallowman whispered. 'The link broke.'

'What? How?'

'I've no idea. But the Leviathan is destroyed and my master banished.'

Nagel gaped at it. 'Your master was the Leviathan?'

'As far as you are concerned, yes.'

'That giant fish was your master?'

'That's what I just said.'

'And it is dead? Killed?'

'The Leviathan is killed. My master is banished.'

'So it's over?' It was too much for Nagel to take in. 'All this was for nothin'?'

'Yes.'

'What'll become of us, then?'

'We have failed. We will have to try to…' The Tallowman blinked. 'No. No. No. Don't you see? We are free. I am free. The Impervious Obligation is broken. I owe no master anything. I am free!'

'Free?'

'Free! If we can capture and drain this girl ourselves, we don't have to share what we harvest from her.' The Tallowman leant forward, its tongue flicking about the edges of its mouth. 'We could live like the Lords of Andiel – beholden to no man, no conscience, no ethics, no false morality and best of all, no masters. Free of all petty human obligations.'

Uriah shuddered and vomited up a gutful of cold seawater onto the sand.

'Thank Samaryan,' said Celsus.

Uriah tried desperately to vomit again, but nothing came up. He gingerly sat up and looked around. A few bedraggled survivors were huddled together on a thin strip of grey sand, just out of the reach of the pounding breakers.

'You saved me?' he croaked.

Celsus shook his head. 'I can't swim. You carried me on your back all the way in. You passed out when we reached the shallows.'

A dim memory of the endless swim came back to him. 'Fiora?'

'Here.' She was sitting on the sand behind him, wet but unhurt.

'Scarrus?' he asked.

'Dead,' she said. 'They shot him when he was swimming.'

He absorbed that. 'What do we do now?'

'Do, Uriah? Do?' She sneered at him. 'My ship is sunk and most of my men drowned. We don't do anything. The hangman has kicked out the bucket. The Tallowman has won.'

'Well.' Uriah slowly stood up and brushed the sand off his face. 'I'm not just waiting here.'

Fiora didn't move. 'And what are you going to do?'

'I am going to the north-west corner of the island. Sophia's ship might spot me as it passes. I'm not just giving up. We've come this far.'

'They'll be long gone.' She plunged both her hands into the sand. 'It's over, Uriah.'

'It isn't.'

'It is.'

'In what year did Demetrius sack Levestar?'

'He didn't sack Levestar.'

'That's right. When all your senators, all your legates and all your tribunes had fled south, Sertorius beat him with two legions made up of boys and old men.'

A ghost of a smile touched her lips. 'The old men were the veterans of Magnus Mucianus' Thirteenth Legion.'

Uriah held out a hand. 'Even so.'

His hand hung in empty air, the wind bitterly cold between his fingers.

'Even so.' She grasped his hand and pulled herself to her feet.

'So, are you coming?'

Fiora straightened her sword belt. 'I am.' She turned to Celsus. 'Will you be all right?'

The doctor nodded sadly. 'Very few of our wounded made the shore, so I have little to do.'

37.

DOGWOOD ISLAND WAS a barren place, its shore a battleline between hungry breaker and jagged rock. The *Game Birds* and their captain knew their business though, and within a half hour they had found a sheltered sandy bay and got themselves and their few supplies safely ashore.

By then Faulkner's euphoria had been replaced by a mood even blacker than his customary after-action melancholy. His side ached and he had a blinding headache, but even worse was that he had lost his ship. He'd known *Game Bird* may well be sunk, but he had still never lost a ship under his command before and, like all captains, he had kept a part of his spirit in *Game Bird's* timbers and now he felt adrift and disorientated. As if that wasn't enough to leave him feeling low, the spectre of Sophia's taint also hung over him like the blackest thunderhead. He desperately wanted to stop, to rest, to give himself some time to think. But the first few hours after a shipwreck were always the hardest. He knew of more than one crew who had survived the actual wreck had lost their lives afterwards as discipline collapsed.

When he called the *Game Birds* to work, they came willingly enough and quickly moved the supplies they had salvaged from *Game Bird* and her boats under the lee of the cliffs. As they worked, the men called out to each other merrily and clapped one another on the back. Sailors were stoic about death, and to most of the old tars a few lost mates was fair enough payment for the fortune they had each just won. Satisfied the men had things in hand, Faulkner walked back down the beach. 'Who did we lose?' he asked de Lacey.

'Smith, Brown and Francis dead. Mellor's missing and Harris has a badly broken leg.'

'Boscawen's dead too. He lifted those timbers off the gun so I could fire it. The recoil killed him.'

'A brave act.'

'It was.'

'How are you?' de Lacey asked.

'Even more battered than before.' He poked at his side. 'Nothing broken though. You?'

'Never been better.'

Morgan came ambling up. 'I've rigged Miss Blake and Harris a set of tents. That should keep them out of this cold wind.'

'Good work, Morgan. How did we do with supplies?'

'Oh, pretty well. Plenty of bread, meat and water.'

Faulkner nodded. 'Good. I'll send the longboat to Lord Morgans Island and the pinnace down to Hazlewood to get us help. I'd also like to keep a week's rations here, just in case some weather comes up and we can't get off the island. Do we have supplies for that?'

'We might need to tighten our belts, but we'll manage.'

'Do you want to pick crews for the boats now?' de Lacey asked.

Faulkner shook his head. 'No. I'll let the men have a rest first. As you're feeling so fresh and new, you can take Jenkins and some unhurt men up that ridge behind us and have a look about. I don't remember seeing one on my chart, but there might be a whaling station or something on this blasted rock. That'd save us a wet trip in an open boat.'

'Your brother's school is only a few miles away as well. One of them flyers might spot them,' Morgan added.

'Good idea, I'll take some kindling and a tinderbox. A fire might attract the interest of one of their flights,' de Lacey said.

Once they'd gathered a few supplies, De Lacey and Jenkins took half a dozen unhurt sailors and scrambled up the rocky slope behind their makeshift camp. They moved quickly, eager to get up and back as quickly as possible. Inland, the island became even more desolate than by the shore and soon they were climbing over bare slopes of contorted rock. Despite de Lacey's newly restored strength it was still hard going, and when they reached a small shelf of flat stone halfway up the incline they stopped and de Lacey passed around a canteen. To the west the upper slopes of the island still blocked their view. To the east the ocean was empty except for the floating corpse of the leviathan.

'What are you lads goin' to spend your coin on?' Jenkins asked, once he'd caught his breath.

Lewis chuckled. 'I'll buy a house for the wife. Put her near her parents.'

'It's in the bank with mine,' Patrick said.

'I'd never trust a banker.' Hook-Nose Simon spat. 'I'm going to buy me a tavern.'

The men laughed at that.

'What?'

'You'll piss away plenty of bloody money in taverns. But you ain't buying one,' said Jenkins.

'I'll win this time. My luck is in.'

The men laughed again.

'And what about you, Lieutenant?' asked Giuseppe.

'Me?' de Lacey looked up. 'I'll cover my debts, spend some on drink, gambling, women and horses, and then waste the rest.' He stood up and screwed the cork back into the canteen. 'Come on. The quicker we get off this cold blasted hell of an island the better.'

'Especially with this freezing bloody easterly picking up,' Jenkins said.

The other men got up and they began trudging onwards up the slope.

'You won't believe this!' said Morgan.

Faulkner looked up. 'Oh?'

'A ship!'

Faulkner followed his carpenter's gesture. Sure enough, the sloop they had seen back at Hazlewood was making its way into the little bay. 'Our luck is certainly in.' He grabbed the lip of a barrel and hauled himself painfully to his feet. 'I suppose I should go and meet them then.'

Donald appeared at his side. 'Here you are, sir, your hat and good blue coat.'

Faulkner raised an eyebrow. 'The ship was sinking and you saved my hat and coat?'

'And the bowl the Archon of Cartia gave you.'

'So hat, coat and ugly glass bowl. No sextant or ship's log?'

'The bowl is crystal, sir, not glass.'

He sighed. 'Thank you, Donald. You'll have to help me into my coat, though.'

De Lacey watched the ship round the point and drop anchor in the little sound. The sloop looked like she had been in some kind of accident since they saw her at Hazlewood though – her bow and rigging was in terrible disarray.

'Well that's a bloody climb wasted,' Simon muttered.

'Should we hurry down?' Jenkins asked.

De Lacey shook his head. 'No, it'll take them a while to get the others aboard anyway. We can take our time.'

They watched as the sloop swung out two boats.

'That was fast work.' Jenkins whistled appreciatively. 'I doubt many of you buggers would have done it that seamanlike.'

'They're probably bloody smugglers. Smugglers are always in and out of little boats,' Simon complained.

De Lacey watched as Faulkner hobbled down the beach to meet their rescuers. The other ship definitely must have been in some kind of scrape. Even from this distance he could see that one of the men in the lead boat was heavily bandaged. Could the leviathan have attacked it, too?

As the boats kissed the beach, Faulkner stepped forward and doffed his hat. De Lacey rolled his eyes. His friend was always so bloody formal.

'Something doesn't look—' Jenkins muttered to himself.

A giant bearded man stood up in the bow of the first boat, drew a pistol and calmly shot Faulkner in the head.

Faulkner tottered forward and fell face-first on the shale.

The faint echo of the shot reached them a few seconds later.

Roberts roared, hurled away its pistol, grabbed its axe and led the men of the *Dead Reckoning* ashore. Three of the braver *Game Birds* stood and faced Roberts. It hacked them down effortlessly, roaring with laugher as its blows splintered bone and sliced through flesh.

With that little skirmish, the fight was over.

The *Game Birds* were already shocked by the murder of their captain and the impact of Roberts' ferocious charge broke them. They scattered like rabbits with a wyvern circling above. Although few fell to speculative shots from the *Dead Reckonings*, the majority escaped into the rocky hills behind the makeshift camp.

The Tallowman strode up the beach behind Roberts, nodding in satisfaction. Before its master had died the girl's ship had been sunk and it seemed that most of the crew had survived. If the girl had survived as well then things couldn't have gone more perfectly. 'Tear this place apart. Find her,' it hissed.

Roberts strode up, grinning through its blood-splattered beard. 'I am going to chase the ones that ran.'

'No. Stay here until we have the girl.'

Roberts growled with barely contained rage but did as it was told.

They began to search the camp.

Sophia's eyes flickered open. She was lying on solid, unmoving earth. She blinked again. The ceiling above her was canvas and it wasn't a sail. A tent? What had happened? How long had she been unconscious?

Healing de Lacey had hollowed her out to a point where it was almost beyond her body's capacity to keep her heart beating. It had been so close. Had the canker infected one more organ or had its grip on his body been that tiny bit stronger, Sophia knew she would have emptied out her life force trying to heal him. She had never tried to heal anyone that ill before and it was terrifying to discover that she could have simply extinguished herself. Although she had survived, the healing process had still left her so weak that even the thought of crying out for help was impossibly difficult.

Somewhere close by she could hear James speaking to Donald. The look of disgust that had contorted his face when he had looked at her was still etched on her mind's eye. The depth of his revulsion had been even worse than she had expected. He had looked like he would vomit.

The crack of a gunshot cut through her sluggish thoughts.

More shots rang out. Men screamed and shouted.

Her heart raced unevenly and she struggled to get up. Her arms and legs wouldn't obey her. Her muscles felt like they had melted away. The canvas above her was suddenly torn away and the flood of grey light made her blink.

'I've got her!' An ugly man leant over her and grinned. 'I've got her!'

Then Morgan was there, a heavy boathook in his big hands. 'Get away from her, dog!' He smashed the hook across the man's head and the ugly sailor fell without a sound.

Dropping the hook, Morgan reached for her.

A gun barked and a bright flower of blood blossomed in the middle of Morgan's broad chest. The carpenter clutched at his wound and collapsed beside her. His wide, terrified eyes met hers and his lips moved, but she couldn't make out what he was saying. His warm and bloody hand touched hers and something cold pressed into her palm. She closed her fist around it. He tried to say something again, shuddered for a long moment and then lay still.

A man, his face completely covered by bandages, loomed over her, a smoking pistol clutched in his hand. 'You have no idea how happy I am to see you, Sophia,' he hissed.

Rough hands grabbed her and she was bound, gagged and blindfolded. Once she was trussed up, she was roughly hoisted up on a man's shoulders. Although the men patted her down roughly, they didn't find Morgan's tiny knife that she held so tightly.

Uriah and Fiora set off north across Dogwood Island, scrambling up and down endless gullies and ridges of loose shale. Within minutes their hands and knees were bloodied by the unforgiving stones. They were negotiating another torturous climb when Fiora held a hand out to stop him.

'I heard a shot,' she said.

All he could hear was the clatter of rocks their climbing had disrupted. 'I think you are mi—' A distant rattle of musketry cut him off.

Fiora drew her sword and increased her pace up the bluff. 'It seems you have kept us in the fight, Uriah.'

'We go in together,' de Lacey said. 'No calling out till we are among them. Once we are at it we give no quarter and ask for none.'

The men nodded.

'If you don't have a knife, take a rock. Brain the first of the bastards you come across and take his weapon,' Jenkins added.

De Lacey took his boatswain's advice and grabbed a heavy fist-sized stone. 'Let's go.'

They raced back down the hill, stumbling and slipping as they went.

They had only gone a few hundred yards when they rounded a sharp bend in a little valley and almost collided with a man and a woman who had just slid down into the same depression. The sailors fanned out around the strangers, ready to attack.

Something about the pair gave him pause. 'Wait.' De Lacey called.

The woman was black and wore a man's trousers and a hard leather jacket. She held an old-fashioned sabre with the confidence of a seasoned soldier. If the odds stacked against the pair bothered her, she didn't show it.

Simon edged towards them. 'Wait!' de Lacey barked. Despite the foreign woman's unusual appearance, it was the man who had caught his attention. He was a Realmsmen, tall and gaunt, and with a face mottled by fading bruises. His hair had once been shaven, but it was now growing back in ugly clumps. De Lacey gasped. 'Mr Blake? Uriah Blake?'

The man squinted in his direction and his mouth fell open in shock 'Lieutenant Lord de Lacey!' Uriah turned to his strange companion. 'What luck, Fiora, this is one of Captain Faulkner's officers. Lieutenant de Lacey, this is the Countessa Fiora Varzi.'

The black woman nodded.

'What on earth are you doing here?' De Lacey struggled for calm, but it was slipping away like a faint breeze. 'And why did I just see half my crew murdered?'

The woman and Uriah glanced at each other.

'Fiora would be best to answer that question.'

'We don't care who answers it,' Jenkins rumbled. 'Just make it fucking quick.'

'Yes, of course. But before she starts, let me assure you, as mad as this story will sound, it is all true.' Uriah nodded to her. 'Fiora.'

She sheathed her sword. 'Lord de Lacey, I am sure you understand the need for haste. I will explain quickly. Detail can wait.' She quickly outlined a strange story of a beast, a Tallowman, and its hunting of Sophia. At the end she turned to Uriah. 'I am sorry to reveal her secret, Uriah.'

'I already knew,' de Lacey said.

The sailors behind him muttered.

'Yes, she is tainted. Doesn't change anything,' de Lacey snapped at them. He looked the foreign woman up and down and did his best to digest the rest of what she had just told him. 'I won't lie, I understand only a third of you just said, Countessa. But if you're enemies of the men that killed Faulkner, well, that will do for now.'

Uriah paled. 'James is dead?'

De Lacey blinked away his tears and nodded. 'They shot him.'

'Isaladar wept. The poor boy—'

'Did you have a plan? For the attack?' the woman interrupted.

'Plan? I thought we'd go down there, surprise them and then kill as many as we can.'

'Simple, good. I'll lead the attack.' She drew her sword again. 'Who is your best fighter?'

De Lacey nodded towards Jenkins.

'Will you cover my left?' she asked.

'Gladly,' Jenkins replied.

'Some men are sneakin' down towards the beach,' the lookout said.

'Give me the glass.' Taking the man's telescope the Tallowman turned and scanned the rocky hillsides. After a few sweeps of the barren ridge it spotted them. They appeared to be a group of *Game Birds* who had somehow come to be led by the bitch Varzi. It snarled in rage and the strength of its grip cracked one of the lenses in the telescope. Would that woman never die?

'Roberts!'

Roberts came lumbering up the beach, its beard matted with fresh blood. 'I was feeding.'

'Your countessa is still alive.'

'What?'

'I thought exactly the same thing.' The Tallowman pointed up the hill. 'She is slinking down that little valley there. Take a few of your men and kill her.'

Roberts didn't bother to answer. It just pounded up the beach, screaming in rage and waving its axe in the air.

'I'll leave a boat for you,' the Tallowman yelled after its departing back.

Roberts didn't answer, or even slow.

With a shrug, the Tallowman climbed aboard its waiting boat. 'Cast off and take me back to the ship.' Sitting down, it smiled at the sight of Sophia Blake lying tied and bound in the scuppers. Sometimes fortune couldn't be more kind. Its master was gone and the girl was in its grasp – nothing could have been more perfect. When they were halfway back to the *Dead Reckoning* it shuffled aft. 'As soon as we get back to the ship, find Nagel,' it said to the man at the tiller. 'Have him weigh anchor and set a course for Levestar.'

'What about Roberts?'

'Do you really want to share our ship with that thing all the way to the Free City?'

'Right.' The man nodded, 'I'll find Nagel.'

38.

LED BY FIORA, the *Game Birds* charged over the last rise before the beach. The *Dead Reckonings* greeted them with a ragged volley of musketry and, although the range was long, a lucky shot still tore away most of Lewis' face. The man's body bounced down the slope and de Lacey had to leap over the tumbling corpse to avoid it tripping him. Yards ahead of him, the countessa flew down the hillside, bounding from rock to rock with a dancer's grace.

'*Deus pascit corvos! Deus pascit corvos!*' she shouted.

The giant black-bearded man who had shot Faulkner was leading the *Dead Reckonings*. He raised an axe and screamed a challenge up at them. Blood coated the man's face and beard. The skin of his arms was white except for where impossibly dark veins writhed. De Lacey noted with detached surprise that the countessa had been telling the truth – whatever the huge fellow was, he was no longer human. An apparition like that should have terrified the *Game Birds,* but they had just seen their captain killed and they thundered. A foolhardy *Dead Reckoning* dashed up the hill to meet them on his own. The countessa brushed the clumsy swing of the man's musket aside and her sabre tore his throat away. Yelling in fury, a bunch of his mates charged her.

'The bearded one is mine! Leave the big one for me!' she yelled, hacking her way towards him.

Jenkins reached the *Dead Reckonings* just after her. One of them crashed the butt of his musket into the boatswain's shoulder, but Jenkins shook off the blow and crunched his rock down on the sailor's head. The man collapsed like he was boneless. A second sailor came at him. Jenkins dodged and jabbed with his stone, crushing the man's fingers against own musket.

The sailor screamed and dropped the weapon. A *Dead Reckoning* drew a pistol and levelled it at Jenkins' back. De Lacey couldn't possibly reach the man in time to stop him firing, so he threw the stone he was carrying. The heavy rock caught the sailor squarely on the side of the face. Teeth and blood sprayed from the man's mouth and he went down like well-hit stumps.

A man with a knife rushed at de Lacey. He tried to dodge out of the way, but the *Dead Reckoning* still caught him a raking blow to the side of the head. An inferno of pain roared around his ear. The young lord screamed in agony and threw himself at the man. His weight unbalanced the sailor and they fell down entwined onto the rocks and then rolled down the jagged slope until a boulder stopped them with a jarring crash. The other man was stronger and he ended up astride de Lacey's chest. De Lacey caught the man's knife arm with his right hand. The man hammered at his face and chest with his free fist and de Lacey's vision began to blur. The man snarled and the knife inched its way down towards de Lacey's eyes. Then blood suddenly drenched de Lacey's face and clogged his eyes. The sailor sagged down on top of him. He opened his eyes. Giovanni had grabbed the *Dead Reckoning* by his hair and cut the man's throat from ear to ear.

Giovanni kicked the body to one side and de Lacey scrambled out from under it.

He spat out a mouthful of the other man's blood. 'Thanks.'

Giovanni grinned fiercely and hauled him to his feet. 'It's nothing.'

De Lacey snatched up the dead man's knife and looked around. The only live *Dead Reckonings* were fleeing towards the distant surf. One hand clutched to the injured side of his head, he clambered to his feet and to check on his *Game Birds*. Lewis was dead and Simon had a nasty wound in his upper arm.

'You going to live, Simon?' de Lacey asked.

'I'll live.' The sailor took his hand off the wound and grimaced down at it. 'Can't believe they didn't get more of us. Them pirates must spend more time on their fancy costumes than on their bleedin' shootin'.'

Jenkins shook his head in wonderment. 'Helped that woman got about a dozen of them.'

De Lacey glanced up and down the slope surveying the dead and the dying. 'Where is our foreign noblewoman and Mr Blake?' he asked.

The fiend wielded its axe with such force that even the most graceful parry made her sword quiver in her grasp. It was also shockingly fast. It threw its enormous axe about like the weapon was a feather. The moment she made even the slightest mistake she would die. For the first time since Lucullus had died she was suddenly very afraid.

But she knew what she had to do.

She parried another swipe and danced a couple of yards back up the ridge and away from the rest of the melee. She rocked under another dazzlingly fast blow and scrambled a few more vital yards towards the top of the slope.

It rushed after her with a mindless shriek of rage and she parried again.

By the time they had almost reached the top of the little incline, she had managed to nick it a couple of times. Not that the cuts mattered; a fiend wouldn't even feel those small wounds.

Reaching the stony plateau above the beach, she rode out another bone-jarring parry and skipped away again. With some yards between them she was finally able to study it. Both her guesses had been correct. The fiend had been made from the man she had shot back on Hazlewood and the injury she had done him then was too severe even for a daemon to heal. The thing had been dying from the second it was born. This information wouldn't be enough to save her life – her arms were already leaden and her sabre weighed a tonne – but, if she could sell her life dearly enough, she might just weaken it enough for the surviving Realmsmen overpower it.

It lunged at her. She glanced away a blow that should have torn her in two and pirouetted away. 'You are an aberration, fiend.' She ducked back further out of its reach. 'The wound I gave you on Hazlewood is too cruel for even your cursed flesh to survive. Your master birthed you knowing you wouldn't see another spring.'

'No!'

'You can feel the life leaking from you. Soon you will return to the shade.'

The thing roared and rushed at her. She jumped its blow and the thing's axe struck a galaxy of sparks from the rocks where she had been standing. 'What did the Tallowman promise you?' she shouted. 'Was it an early grave and eternal damnation?'

'We have the girl. She will heal me,' it snarled.

'Sophia Blake? Her power won't help you.' It swung again and the blow almost wrenched her sword from her hand. 'You, fiend, you are a bucket with a hole in the bottom of it. No matter how much water you pour in, it will still just run straight out again.'

'No!' it bellowed! 'No!'

'Oh yes, fiend…' Behind the fiend Uriah stumbled up onto the little plateau and started sprinting towards them. She faltered. What did the fool mean to do? He didn't even have a weapon drawn. She rushed on, hoping it hadn't noticed her pause. 'The Tallowman has played you. How does that feel?'

It snarled and leapt forward. This time she met its blow head-on with a jarring two-handed parry. She had to keep it facing her. The thing would simply tear Uriah apart. She disengaged and unleashed a flurry of cuts at its face. It batted them away with a chuckle.

It grinned down at her. 'You're tired, bitch.'

It finally heard the pounding of Uriah's shambling run.

It spun to face this new threat; its axe raised to parry a blow from a sword. Instead Uriah leapt towards it in a diving tackle. Roberts brought its axe crashing down, but the blow was timed to kill an attacking swordsman and instead caught only rock. Uriah's shoulder slammed into Roberts' belly and the air exploded from the thing's lungs. The beast was so strong it only took a staggering half a step back.

That half step was all Fiora's needed.

She leapt forward even as the thing's axe whipped back around in an attempt to blindly block her blow. Her sabre hacked into Roberts' neck just above the shoulder and, driven by all her remaining strength, the blow sliced through muscle, sinew and bone with ease. Blood fountained into the air and the fiend's head tumbled from its shoulders. Its headless corpse collapsed between her and Uriah.

'What' – she fell panting to her knees – 'kind of stupidity was that?'

'Stupidity? That was a perfect tackle. Textbook.' Uriah groaned, picked himself gingerly up and wiped the thing's blood off his face with his sleeve. 'Nice work with its head, by the way. Now, shall we go and rescue my daughter?'

39.

'ISALADAR'S BLOOD, HE'S alive,' someone said a long, long way away.

His face was wet and cold.

'He can't be,' another voice replied.

He was so tired. Why couldn't they just let him rest? Instead they rolled him over and poured something, rum, into his mouth. The spirit burned his throat going down and he spluttered. He opened his eyes. Blurred shapes move about above him.

'What happened?' he croaked.

'Isaladar's blood! He's alive, he's really alive.'

'What happened?' he asked again.

'You got shot in the head.' Jenkins' face swam into focus. 'Got you a glancing blow. Still left a nasty gash by the looks of it.'

'Shot?' Faulkner put a hand to the side of his head and then held it out in front of his face. His fingers were red with blood and matted with hair. Pain sent bright lights flashing behind his eyes and his vision blurred. 'Get me up.'

They did. He stood with his hands on his knees. The world spun around him and he was violently, nosily sick. When he looked back up a blood-soaked de Lacey had appeared and was staring down at him, incredulous.

'Merciful Isaladar, you are bloody alive,' his friend said.

'What the blazes happened to your ear?'

'Cut off, apparently.'

'Cut off?'

'In the fight.'

'Are you all right?'

'I'll live.'

'What happened?' Faulkner looked around groggily. Bodies littered the churned and bloody sand.

'The crew of the other boat attacked us. They were after Sophia.'

'Sophia? Where is she?'

'They took her.' De Lacey's shoulders slumped and he pointed out to sea. 'We were too late to stop them.'

In the distance the sloop was already miles off shore and fast disappearing into the east. 'Why Sophia?'

'Something to do with her taint.'

'Her taint?'

'I don't really understand the full of it, Faulkner, and Uriah is so distraught he can hardly talk. The black woman he arrived with can explain it though, she seems to understand things.'

'Black woman? Uriah?' Getting shot must have scrambled his brain. 'Uriah Blake is back in Stormhaven, de Lacey.'

'The woman will explain. Can you walk?'

Faulkner gingerly took a step forward. 'I think so. Just get ready to catch me.'

With Guiseppe and Jenkins' help, de Lacey led him up the beach to the ruins of their camp where, sure enough, Uriah Blake sat, looking so disconsolate he could hardly raise his head. Standing over him was an armed, regal-looking black woman.

De Lacey nodded to her. 'This is, ah, the Countessa Galliate. Countessa, this is Captain Faulkner.'

'Call me, Fiora. I thought you were dead?'

Faulkner shook his head. 'I have a thick skull, it seems. Now, Fiora, de Lacey tells me you can explain what the devil is going on here?'

'I can, but first call someone to see to your wound before you bleed to death.'

While Donald bandaged up his head, Faulkner sat on the edge of a barrel and listened to the woman's tale. When she had finished he tried to collect his fragmented thoughts from under the blinding headache that smothered them. It was almost too much to swallow. Leviathans eating the tainted along with ships? Otherworldly horrors roaming the Realm dressed like men? He really must have gone mad. 'So you'd have me believe that Sophia has been kidnapped by some kind of daemon that means to feed on her?'

'It is a fiend, not a daemon, but otherwise you are correct,' Fiora agreed.

'That is a fairly large story to choke down in one sitting.' He turned to where Uriah sat in the sand, deep in his misery. 'Uriah. Can you vouch for any of this?'

Uriah looked up, his eyes red and puffy. 'I can. All of it.'

Faulkner met Fiora's gaze. Something in her hardness and her calmness reminded him of Admiral Barry on the quarterdeck.

'Oh, and just in case you've still any doubts, the countessa killed some daemon kind of thing up the ridge as well,' de Lacey added. 'Didn't she, Jenkins?'

'Foul thing.' Jenkins spat on the ground. 'Rotting on the inside but strong as an ox. Dark work it was.'

Simon made the sign of the holy lance. 'Evil bastard.'

That did it. If he had gone insane then the insanity was convincing enough that he should at least conduct himself like a captain. 'Is Sophia likely to be still alive?' he swallowed down his terror. 'Or will they have killed her already?'

Fiora shook her head. 'She is almost certainly alive. Luckily she has just drained herself. I believe it will probably need to let her recover much of her strength before it can harvest her.'

'They'd be running for the Imperial Free City of Levestar then.' The sloop was now little more than a smudge under the washed-out mid-morning sun. How was it still only morning? 'That's the only major city on the continent's coast in that direction. It is also big and more than half lawless.'

She nodded. 'Levestar has long been a favoured base for our enemy.'

'Where are you anchored, Countessa?' Faulkner looked about for his sword. 'A stern chase is a long chase but that sloop's rigging was pretty knocked about. With a bit of luck we'll catch them well before they reach the Free City.'

'My ship was sunk.'

'Your ship was sunk,' he said. His headache pulsed behind his eye and he wondered if helpless rage would drive him into apoplexy. 'Ready the pinnace,' he said. At least it boasted a sail.

'The pinnace will never catch that sloop,' de Lacey said.

'I know.' A great sob forced its way past his lips. 'But I have to do something.'

'Faulkner. It's over.' De Lacey took his arm and lead him a few yards away from the group. 'It's over.'

'We can't just leave her to this… this thing.'

'I know, but going in the pinnace is madness.'

'I have to.'

'Faulkner, I owe Sophia my life.' Tears glistened on de Lacey's cheeks. 'But on the open sea against an alert crew you'd have about as much chance in that pinnace as a sparrow would against a pegasus. That's if you could even catch *Dead Reckoning*, which you couldn't.'

'A pegasus?'

Faulkner strode back to the ragged little group.

'Donald,' he snapped. 'Make the pinnace ready for sea.'

Donald had seen him furious often enough not to bother with any questions. His servant gathered together some unhurt *Game Birds* and sprinted down the beach.

'Jenkins. Find Morgan. Tell him I want that boat back in the water within five minutes.'

'Morgan's dead. Shot through the heart,' Jenkins said.

'Oh.' He fought his tears down. Mourning was for after an action. 'Then who is the best small boat sailor still alive?'

'Charley,' Jenkins answered immediately. 'Raced 'em as a squeaker.'

'I want him in the boat immediately then. You as well, de Lacey. And Uriah and Fiora, you two can tell me about this Tallowman as we go.'

'The five of us are going after the Tallowman's ship?' Fiora looked confused. 'In that little boat?'

'My brother is at school nearby. I mean to borrow his pegasus.'

'Your brother is a flyer?'

He nodded.

She looked doubtful, but she still helped Uriah up and they trotted down to the pinnace.

Faulkner worked quickly. He rifled through their supplies until he found the biscuits. He wolfed a big handful down hungrily and then washed them down with a good pull of water and a long swig of rum. Thankfully, though his guts rebelled, he just managed to hold the mixture down. He knew he'd need all the strength he could get later. As the burn from the cheap spirit warmed his belly, he buckled on his sword, picked up a heavy oilskin and then jogged down the beach towards the waiting boat. 'Jenkins, you've got command of the camp,' he shouted back over his shoulder. 'I'll have a ship sent here as soon as I can.'

'Make the bastards pay,' his boatswain called after him.

De Lacey caught him halfway down the beach. 'May I speak to you, James, as a friend?'

'Make it quick.'

'I think I know your plan. You are throwing your life away. Leaving Sophia to that thing is the cruellest thing imaginable, but killing yourself into the bargain won't help.'

'I have to try, de Lacey.'

His friend almost looked wild. 'Have to? You don't have to do anything. If we had even the slightest chance to save her I'd beg you to take it. But this? This is insanity!'

Faulkner pulled on the heavy coat. The pain from his arms and his shoulder and his ribs and his head made him sweat 'I love her.'

'Love her? Back on *Game Bird* you said it was over.'

'What are you talking about? I meant my career, de Lacey, that's what is over. When the Admiralty finds out I love a tainted girl, they'll never let me hold a sea-going command again. But I love her. So that's that.'

'Oh...'

'Exactly.'

'I'm not going to talk you out of this then, am I?'

'No.'

De Lacey sighed. 'Let's get going then,'

The pinnace flew across the restless channel between Dogwood and Lord Morgans Island. Charley was a superb sailor. The lad could pick the fickle movements of the sea and the wind perfectly. Although Faulkner buzzed with nerves and terror, he knew there was nothing he could do to make Charley sail faster and he clambered forward to sit down near Uriah and Fiora. 'Would you like to hear the plan?' he shouted over the crack of the sail.

They nodded.

'I'm going to convince my brother to take me after them on his pegasus. In the unlikely event I spot the *Dead Reckoning* I'm going to drop into the ocean ahead of them, board the ship as it passes and then find Sophia.'

'That plan is a death sentence,' Fiora said. She studied him for a moment, her dark eyes unreadable. 'I will take your place, Captain Faulkner.'

'You won't.'

'I have a score to settle and I know far more about fighting the Great Enemy.'

'I've no doubt of that, Countessa. But how much do you know of ocean tides and how a sloop will handle in conditions like this? Can you predict where our little pinnace will be in thirty seconds? In a minute? In ten minutes? In half a bell? Because if you can't then you'd drown long before you even get to think about fighting this Tallowman.'

'It still should be me. You're wounded.'

'I'll be the one going. This isn't a discussion.'

'Captain—'

'It's going to be me. That's final.'

She looked for a moment like she would argue, but then she nodded. 'You are placing a very large bet on very, very long odds.'

'It's better than Sophia having no chance at all.'

'Is what you are planning even possible?' Uriah asked. 'I mean technically? Can you board a ship in mid-ocean like that?'

'With some luck, yes.'

'Should you be doing this, James?' Uriah looked at the cloudy sky, then back to him and then to the sky again. 'It sounds like you are taking suicide. I'll never forgive myself for saying this but I would understand if you didn't try.'

'I am going. That's the end of it.' He stumbled for the words. 'Uriah, I've fallen in love with your daughter, so you see my desire to rescue her is somewhat selfish.' He blushed at his own dramatics. 'I can hardly imagine living without Sophia.'

'You love her?'

'I do.'

'Oh.'

'I'm sorry.'

'I am an old fool. I suppose I should have expected it when she went to sea against my instructions. You two were always so close.'

'I am sorry, Uriah, I mean it. Especially that I didn't look after her better. Sophia never should have come to sea in the first place.'

'She wouldn't be alive if she hadn't gone with you,' Uriah said simply.

Fiora nodded. 'She'd be long dead.'

'Thank you, I think.' He coughed awkwardly. 'Now, Fiora, how dangerous is this Tallowman? Really?'

'They are deadly. Even your Camar Shiem never send less than ten of their number to hunt one. I know of no man living who could stand against one alone, even if he carried a holy artefact.'

'Then I'd better do my best to avoid the thing,' he said. 'I've never been much of a fighter and I'm rather short of saint's fingerbones and holy water.'

'A wise course, Captain. If it knows you are aboard its ship, you will surely die.'

'So with that out of the way, do we all agree to my plan?'

Fiora and Uriah nodded.

'In that case I need to try to sleep.' Faulkner pulled his oilskin tight around himself and lay down in the water that sloped around in the bottom of the boat. 'Wake me when you see land.'

40.

CHARLEY BROUGHT THE boat neatly into the same bay where *Game Bird* had anchored those few endless weeks ago. When the water was still chest-deep Faulkner leapt overboard and ploughed his way ashore through surf. His long sleep had cleared some of his headache and exhaustion, but his clothes were waterlogged and heavy and each lurching step across the sand was a little agony. By the time he got off the sand, his body was a mass of aches but he ran on, hunched over like a cripple. Wounded and tired as he was, Fiora, de Lacey and Uriah soon caught up with him and the little group crossed the miles of moorland to the fortress at a shuffling, painful jog.

Sergeant Hacket was on duty by the gate. The big soldier must have seen them approaching because as they got close he emerged from the gatehouse, his musket cradled in his arms

'Who goes there?' the sergeant barked.

The countessa, who had been leading the group, coasted to a stop and Faulkner limped past her. 'It's me, Sergeant. James Faulkner.'

The giant sergeant looked them up and down. 'And judging by the state of you, some trouble's afoot. I'll have one of my men fetch the commandant.'

'No, please don't get the admiral.' Faulkner tried to catch his breath. 'But can you send someone to get my brother? Please?'

'Your brother?'

'Please.'

Hacket considered them for a moment and then nodded. 'I'll go myself. Let yourself into that guardhouse there. I've another four hours of my watch to go, so you'll be left alone. Help yourself to the stew on the stove.'

The giant soldier disappeared into the fortress and the four of them shuffled into the soot-stained little room and sat down at the battered little table.

'Will he bring other guards, James?' Uriah asked.

Faulkner shuffled his seat closer to the fire. His wet clothes lay cold and crushingly heavy on his back. 'We'd better hope not.'

'If he does, I can't see Admiral Trollope approving of Faulkner's little junket,' added de Lacey.

After that they sat waiting in silence, until the door banged open and Tom stepped into the room, grinning from ear to ear. 'James! Don't tell me you have killed the leviath—' the smile dribbled off his face. 'Isaladar's holy bloody lance, what happened to you lot?'

'We've been rather knocked around.' Faulkner stood up slowly. 'Sit down, Tom. You may as well come inside too, Sergeant Hacket.'

'You sure, Captain?' Hacket asked. 'Don't mean to pry into your business.'

'Quite sure. I'd rather you hear what I have to say.' He drew a deep breath. 'Time is literally running out, so I will be quick.' Half of the story was still a muddle in his own mind and in places de Lacey, Uriah or the countessa corrected him. 'Does that makes sense, Tom?' he asked once they were done.

'Not really. But I think I got the essence of it.' The young flyer began to pace back and forth. 'Poor Sophia! We have to do something. But what? No ship would catch this Tallowman's sloop now, not with this head start anyway.'

'You believe our story? Just like that?' de Lacey asked.

'James and I are brothers. That and I doubt you cut your ear off as part of a prank,' Tom said. 'So what are we going to do then, James?'

'That's why I am here. Can I speak to you outside?'

Tom nodded and they stepped out into the afternoon sun.

'I need Billy's help,' Faulkner said.

'Of course. But why?'

'We're going to go after them.'

'After them? Even if we do spot them, what good'll it do? The quickest frigate in the world couldn't catch them before they reach Levestar.'

'If we spot them I am going to try to board their ship in mid-ocean.'

'Board them mid-ocean?' Tom whistled quietly. 'All right.'

'All right? No complaints? No arguing?'

'I said "all right".'

'I don't want you to risk your career and your life rashly, Tom. Think about it.'

'There's nothing to think about.' His little brother shrugged. 'If we do nothing, Sophia dies. Horrifically. So let's get to it.'

'Thank you.' They shook hands. 'I'll tell the others.'

Hacket let them into the fortress and with Tom leading the way they snuck through the school to the stone stables where Billy was kept. Tom unlocked a small side door and motioned them inside. Thankfully no grooms were to be seen. In his stall, Billy whinnied quietly at the sight of his master.

'All right, we need to work quickly,' Tom said. 'The hard part will be getting Billy into his harness. Who rides a horse fairly often?'

De Lacey, Fiora and Uriah held up their hands.

'You three can help me get him ready then. James, you've always been a god-awful rider – can you go into that back room and find my flying kit? It's in a trunk with my name on it.'

The back room was full of tack and it took Faulkner some time to find his brother's chest. By the time he returned Billy was almost into his harness and Tom was buzzing around, checking the others' work.

'Does it kick?' Uriah asked.

Tom looked horrified. 'It's a he, not an it, and no, *he* does not kick.'

Billy snorted in agreement.

When the harness was finally on, Tom left a nervous Uriah holding the reins and began to struggle into his bulky leather flying kit. 'There are plenty more suits back there, James,' he called. 'Take one your size. I'll be in so much trouble anyway, a bit of extra stealing shouldn't matter.'

'A tonne of wool-lined leather is hardly suitable attire for a man about to drop into the ocean.'

'You'll be damnedly cold aloft then.'

'I imagine so.'

There was a sudden commotion at the other end of the stables and a rather plump young man with curly brown hair burst into the room.

Tom looked up. 'Oh, it's you, Alexander.'

The newcomer's eyes went wide. 'I thought I saw something suspicious happening down here. And how unsurprising that you should be involved, Thomas Faulkner.'

'Who's this little tyrant?' de Lacey asked.

'Alexander is a prefect,' Tom said, as if that explained everything.

Alexander's gaze roamed the stable and then fixed on Billy. 'You're stealing your pegasus!'

'I'm only borrowing him, Alexander.' Tom pulled himself up into the saddle. 'Don't get a bee in your bonnet.'

'I always knew you were trouble. I'll see you expelled for this!'

'Could you move the honourable prefect out of the way, Lord de Lacey?'

De Lacey drew a pistol and motioned Alexander towards a small storage room.

'My father sits on the Century Council. I'll have your head for this!'

'As my father owns a good deal of the Century Council and already despises me, we can have them talk it over.' De Lacey shoved the prefect into the little room, slammed the door shut and then locked it.

'Thank you, de Lacey. Now, James, time to come aboard.' Tom leant forward and helped him up into the saddle. 'Right, now that clips there, that clips there. And this does up here.' He ran an eye over the buckles. 'That should stop you falling. Until you want to anyway.'

'Before I jump I just unclip myself?'

'Exactly. And by the holy bloody lance make sure you do, or you'll get towed along like an anchor. And that wouldn't be good for either of us.' Tom turned back around to face forward. 'Open the doors.'

Fiora, Uriah and de Lacey swung the doors open and the afternoon sunlight flooded the room.

'Tally ho!' Tom dug in his heels and Billy shot out of the open doors like a racehorse, with their companion's shouts of good luck echoing in their wake. Faulkner desperately clutched onto his harness as Billy tore across the cricket field snorting and tossing his head. Someone shouted a warning or a curse at them, but by the time Faulkner looked up the man was far behind. Billy went from canter to full gallop and unfolded his mighty wings. Muscles as thick as cables tensed and rippled along the pegasus' sides.

Crack! The pegasus beat his wings. The noise was like a gunshot.

Crack. They were airborne. The thunder of the gallop vanished and was replaced by the shriek of the wind as the grass slid by beneath them.

Crack. Billy carried them up over the towering wall of the fortress. The freezing wind cut straight through Faulkner's wet clothes. Below them the school buildings looked tiny, insignificant. Their pace made the fastest frigate seem slovenly. Faulkner had left his stomach somewhere far below. Tom turned Billy's head and they swung out over the ocean, still gaining height. Faulkner held onto his straps till his fingers ached. The ocean beneath them looked miles away and behind them Lord Morgans Island was already shrinking away.

'Are you all right, James?' Tom yelled back over the rushing wind.

'Yes.'

Crack. Billy beat his wings again. Their tempo was more leisurely now, but they were still whipping along at a ferocious speed.

'When I say we have to head home, we have to head home,' Tom shouted. 'Billy can only stay aloft for so long and I'm not going to drown all three of us.'

'It will be dark soon anyway.'

'We've a few hours yet.'

Faulkner leant forward. 'Do we even have a chance of finding *Dead Reckoning*?'

'It's a wild gamble.' His brother starred down at the empty sea far below. 'The first thing they teach us is that the ocean is a big place.'

41.

'WILL WE REACH Levestar in this state?' the Tallowman asked.

At the bottom of the ladder water slopped about in the depths of the hold. Nagel wasn't exactly sure if they'd sink, not that he wanted the Tallowman to realise that. The leak had certainly got worse, but he didn't think it was gaining on the pumps. 'We should be fine.'

'Can we go any faster?'

Nagel shook his head. 'Not into this easterly and not with that mast damaged we can't.'

'Could another ship catch us?'

'No fucking chance, even if they guess where we're bound. Not with this head start on the open ocean.'

The Tallowman smiled grimly. 'Roberts most likely butchered them all anyway.'

'How long will this process with the girl take once we get there?'

'You're eager to cast off your humanity, aren't you, Nagel? If all goes to plan it should only take four days.'

'Then what?'

'Then what? Then we drain the taint out of her and devour it.'

'I meant, what do we do?'

'Do?'

'You know, once we eat her or whatever. What's the plan then?'

'Perhaps we might copy the Dukes of Andiel. Find a small backwoods kingdom or island and dominate it. We could rule over a small population like undying tyrants.'

Nagel smiled. 'I like the sound of that.'

'I thought you would. Now, let's check on the source of our salvation.'

Sophia was tied and bound on the captain's swinging cot. The hood had been removed and her hair was in disarray. Her hands were tied behind her back. Aboard *Game Bird* she had always seemed so confident, so in control. Now she just looked scared. Nagel felt a stirring in his loins. What a piece of meat.

The Tallowman looked at him. 'You hunger for her?'

'That Faulkner had taste in his bitches, I'll give him that.'

'I have delicate equipment to prepare.' The Tallowman shrugged. 'Just don't kill her.'

Nagel grinned. 'You sure?'

'Soon you'll feel no such weak desires of the human flesh. You might as well indulge them one last time.'

Faulkner couldn't stop his teeth chattering and he hadn't been able to feel his hands for at least an hour. He was also fast losing hope. All afternoon they had flown a weaving path across the Tallowman's likely course and had seen nothing but empty ocean. Now the water below them was shrouded in twilight and, though Tom hadn't said anything yet, Faulkner thought he could feel Billy tiring under them. He was tiring as well; the mad energy that had propelled him last night and that morning was slowly fading, and pain, despair and crushing weariness was creeping in its place. Perhaps it had been insanity even to hope. What chance had they ever really had of finding a ship that didn't want to be found on this trackless ocean? He blinked away his tears and forced himself to keep methodically scanning the empty waters.

Billy reached the end of one of his south-eastern long runs and banked steeply into his next leg. Again, Faulkner fought the mad feeling he was about to fall and snatched at the back of his little brother's harness. Only this time, as the ocean yawed and swung crazily below, he saw something, a solid smudge of gray on the white waves.

'Tom! Tom!'

His brother gave him the thumbs-up and turned Billy so they could look straight down without his enormous wingspan blocking the view.

Faulkner blinked in amazement. There it was. Almost directly below them the ugly sloop was forging its way eastward through the gloom. He shut his eyes. When he opened them the ship was still there, just as real as before.

'Is that them?' his brother shouted.

'It is! It is!'

'Yes!' Tom leant forward and patted Billy's flanks. 'Shall I take you down?'

'Not yet.'

Once he'd determined the sloop's heading, Faulkner worked out a primitive system to make sure Tom dropped him in the right spot. A light tap on either of his brother's shoulders meant steer one point in that direction, a squeeze two points.

Squirming in his harness, he kicked off his heavy boots and then carefully undid his sword and tied it to his saddle. He unclipped himself and then cast off his heavy oilskin and watched it twist and flutter down towards the dark water. Without his coat the cold was even more savage and it took him five goes to clip his harness back on. With shaking hands, he strapped his sword across his back.

'Let's go,' he shouted.

Billy folded his wings and they plummeted downwards. They fell faster and faster until the freezing wind tore stinging tears from his eyes. The ocean rose to meet them. Faulkner raised a hand in a futile gesture of protection but the crash never came, and at the last instant Billy opened his wings, flattened out and shot along above the waves like a sea eagle. They were so low sea spray lashed him. They overtook the *Dead Reckoning* in a wide sweeping turn that hugged the waves, to avoid the prying eyes of any lookouts. In moments they were well ahead of the ship.

'Ready?' Tom yelled.

'Pop up!'

Tom yanked on the reigns and Billy zoomed up above the waves, giving Faulkner one last look at the Tallowman's ship. Tom had done well, incredibly well. They were almost perfectly on the sloop's course. He tapped Tom's right shoulder once and Billy banked ever so slightly to starboard. Faulkner began to count to ten. If he went too early or too late the ship would simply pass him by and leave him to drown.

'One.' He unclipped his main binding.

'Two.'

'Three.'

'Four.' He undid his right leg strap.

Billy flared his wings. Tom must have been bleeding off speed so the drop didn't kill him. He forced himself to slow his count.

'Five.' 'Six.' 'Seven.' He loosened the straps across his chest and shrugged his way out of them.

'Eight.' His frozen fingers fumbled with his left leg strap. He couldn't get it open.

'Nine.' The water was flying past below, a blur of white and black.

He wanted to throw up. He kicked his leg free.

'Ten. Thanks, Tom!'

He rolled backwards off Billy and for a mad moment his entire world was a spinning kaleidoscope of white wings, black ocean and grey sky.

The he smashed down into the sea.

Sophia had thought Nagel would rape her as soon as the bandaged man had left. Instead he had just leered at her for what seemed an age before turning and walking out. On the threshold, he paused. 'I'll be back for you, bitch. Try and get wet for me.' He slammed the door behind him.

As soon as he was gone, Sophia began to work at the ropes with Morgan's little knife. Her hands were soon slick with blood from where she had cut herself, but the rope began to fray. She knew she'd never be able to escape, not when she was still so weak she could hardly stand. But she could at least cut her own throat and deny these evil men whatever it was they wanted from her. The rope was cut almost three quarters of the way through when the door banged open and Nagel staggered back into the cabin. His eyes were wide and he stank of rum.

He threw his pistol belt onto the table. 'Are you ready, princess?'

She feigned unconsciousness, but her little knife still worked furiously at the rope beneath her.

'Faulkner could definitely pick them, I'll give 'im that,' Nagel slurred as he staggered across the room. Leaning forward, he ran a hand roughly up the inside of her leg. With his other hand he reefed her shirt open. She struggled not to let the pain and fear and revulsion show on her face.

'I'm gonna enjoy this,' he said.

He was panting like an animal. He clumsily straddled her and began to fumble with his own pants. The rope holding her hands parted. Above her

Nagel had got his pants down and was leering at her like a mad dog. She wrenched the hand with the knife out from under her and plunged the tiny blade into Nagel's side.

He screamed and writhed on the blade. 'You fucking bitch!'

She yanked the knife free and stabbed him again.

He raised a fist to smash in her face.

Time slowed and the taint tugged at her, calling through the flow of blood.

She looked up at him. She hated him more than she had ever hated anything in her life. She hated him till it burned with a savage, consuming fury. The blood from his shallow wound flowed warm and wet over her hand. She closed her eyes and opened herself up to that taint. But she didn't reach into herself, she didn't grip the world. Instead she reached into him. Into Nagel.

On some distant level the collection of matter that made up his body resisted, but she smashed through its pitiful defences. Now he was exposed. His life throbbed before her in the dark. She reached into him and tore away great chunks of that life and dragged them down into her.

He wailed.

She tore more life out of him.

And more.

And more.

Nagel's heart faltered and then stopped.

He was hollowed out. Empty.

Her taint collapsed and slid back into her.

She opened her eyes and screamed. Nagel still sat astride her, but something worse than death had caught him. His hair was white and his skin sallow, wrinkled and marked with liver spots. Teeth had fallen from his mouth like a rotten hail. He had aged fifty years and more in the seconds her eyes had been shut.

She hurled the ancient corpse off her and scrambled out of the cot.

She held her hands up in front of her face. They were still bloody, but under the gore her cuts and nicks were gone. The sickness that healing de Lacey had left her with was gone too. She was stronger, fitter and more alert than she had ever been in her life. In destroying Nagel she had healed herself.

She threw up.

Down in the hold, the Tallowman was standing in the ankle-deep water, carefully removing its tools from one of its sealed trunks. One by one, it gently brushed straw off the polished metal and then tenderly laid them on a nearby table.

As it leant into the trunk to retrieve a particularly favoured bone saw, it gave a deep shudder and lurched upright. It laughed out loud.

'Sophia Blake, another surprise! And to think we thought your kind had all died out aeons ago.'

Faulkner burst back up to the surface and spat out a mouthful of seawater. His head wound had reopened under his bandages and blood mixed with water trickled down his face. At the top of the next wave he twisted in the water. There was no sign of the *Dead Reckoning*. All he could see stretching off to the horizon was shifting ocean.

He floated down into a trough and then up the face of the next wave.

Still nothing but the empty, mocking ocean.

Had he miscalculated his jump?

He wouldn't have had to drop far off the ship's course for it to pass him by in the gloom. Or they could have changed course suddenly. Or perhaps his impact with the water had dazed him so badly the ship had already passed him by?

He swam and swam and swam.

The weight of his sword was dragging him under, making it hard to even lift his head.

His legs felt waterlogged and his lungs burned.

He swam through another full circle but all he could see was black, restless water. He had never been so lonely. He was going to drown and his dying was going to doom Sophia as well. He raised his voice in a scream. The vast ocean swallowed the sound.

Then he saw it.

A set of staysails, set to run close to the wind.

He bobbed up to the top of the next wave and there was *Dead Reckoning*, almost running straight at him. He struck out towards the oncoming ship. When it finally reared above him, he surfed down the face of a wave and banged against the timbers of her side. His fingers tore at the hull, but he couldn't get purchase. The ship battered him out of the way and forced the air from his lungs. He scrabbled uselessly at the wood, hoping for a lead or a toehold as it slipped past.

Ahead he could already see the stern. Soon the ship would have passed him by and it would all be over. He slapped at the timbers again, but still couldn't get a grip. Something bumped against his shoulder. He snatched at it with his left hand and it slipped through his fingers. He spun in the water and threw out his right hand. It closed on good, honest rope.

The sea grabbed at him and almost shook him free but he got his other hand onto the line. Grunting with effort, he dragged himself up out of the water until his toes found purchase on the lip of one of the closed gun ports. Shaking with exhaustion and cold, he rested against the side of the hull, safe from the seawater rushing along just below him.

Once he'd got a little of his strength and breath back, Faulkner caught hold of the gunwale and, quivering with the effort, dragged himself up enough to peer over it.

The deck was almost deserted. Near him two men stood by the ship's wheel. Forward by the bow a group of four sailors were still working to clear away the damage that the sloop had suffered when it rammed Fiora's ship. Where was the rest of the crew, then? He frowned. Surely there should have been more than six men on deck?

Or perhaps the Tallowman had hardly any crew left alive? Faulkner quickly did the calculations. Fiora and her men had killed about ten of the cutthroats on Hazlewood and then another dozen or so had been killed on Dogwood that morning. With that many of the crew missing the Tallowman would struggle to even work the ship, let alone stand proper watches. This was no trap. There just weren't many *Dead Reckonings* left alive.

He crawled silently up over the rail. Crouching in the shadows near the stern he slid his sword free from its scabbard.

He skipped across the deck towards the wheel. If the *Dead Reckoning* was a foreign warship he would have screamed out a war cry, but the Tallowman's henchmen didn't deserve one. Holding his sabre tightly with both hands he all but cut the closest sailor in half with a vicious swing. The second man leapt back, eyes white and wide in terror. Faulkner sprang after him and his heavy blade caught the *Dead Reckoning* just above the ear with and shattered his skull. Warm blood splattered the deck.

Panting, Faulkner knelt near the men's bodies and studied the *Dead Reckonings* by the bow. The working party was still busily repairing the damage, oblivious to the fact their mates had just been killed.

Placing his sword on the deck he braced the wheel to prevent it from swinging about too freely and attracting attention and then heaved the two bodies overboard. The deck was still covered in blood and shit, but there was nothing he could do about that.

Picking his sword back up he stalked towards the main hatch, willing the men at the bow not to turn in his direction.

Deciding the mystery of what this other hideous, vampiric taint was could wait, Sophia wiped her mouth and quickly repaired her torn clothes. Ignoring Nagel's corpse, she walked to the table and picked up his pistol. It was loaded. Maybe she could at least kill the bandaged man before she died. That would help make her death meaningful.

A shadow moved across the light that spilled under the door and she froze. Whoever had come to check on her was moving almost silently. Someone must have heard Nagel's scream and come for her. She cocked the pistol and blew out the cabin's little lantern. Gun held tightly in her shaking hands, she backed into the corner out sight of the door, squeezing as far back into the shadows as she could.

The door swung open and a bare-chested man carrying a naked sword padded into the cabin. The man knelt down by Nagel's corpse and the light from the companionway played across him and revealed that bandages swathed his head. Her heart thudded painfully. Mr Savage! The one who had killed Morgan. A great bubble of hatred expanded inside her and she raised her pistol and trained it on the back of the man's head.

Her finger tightened on the trigger.

The ship rocked in the swell and the lamp in the corridor outside swung, casting a pattern of light that danced across the man's bruised back. She blinked. She recognised those bruises and the old scar across the man's shoulder.

'James?' she whispered.

'Sophia?' He spun around. 'Isaladar's blood, don't shoot!'

The hand holding the pistol fell limply to her side. Tears ran down her face. 'James?'

He caught her around the waist with his free hand and pulled her to him.

She threw her arms around his cold chest. 'For a moment when I saw that body in the dark…' he said.

'He was going to rape me. I killed him.'

'Good for you.'

She held onto him until it hurt. 'You came for me.'

'I did.'

'But… but…'

He kissed her on the lips. 'I'll always come for you, Sophia. I love you, Sophia Blake. More than I thought I could love anything, I love you.'

'I love you, James.' There were a million things she needed to say but no time for any of it. 'I think I've loved you since I was a little girl.'

'So what now?' she whispered.

'I hadn't quite thought that far ahead,' Faulkner admitted. He looked up and down the companionway. It was empty, although he could hear men talking nearby. Although he was tempted to try to escape the *Dead Reckoning* immediately, Fiora's warnings of the Tallowman's power and tenacity stopped him. He couldn't leave an enemy like that behind. Not when it would pursue Sophia to the end of the world.

'Where's our ship?' she asked.

'No ship. I came on my own.'

'Your own?'

'Long story.' He took her warm hand. 'We'll go this way. For Isaladar's sake don't shoot anyone unless you have to.' When they reached an empty locker he had spotted on the way in he pushed Sophia gently inside 'Wait here for a minute.' He gave her his sword. 'Mind this for me.'

He shut the door before she could argue and then jogged back to the captain's cabin and rolled the corpse over. As the light hit the corpse's face Faulkner started in surprise. The man looked like he must have been at least eighty. 'Evil old bastard,' he muttered to the dead man. He quickly stripped off the man's shirt and pulled it on. The material was bloodstained, but hopefully that wouldn't be noticed in the gloom below decks.

He shut the cabin door behind him and then sauntered along the middle of the deck, doing his best to look like an old hand. As he went he took a storm lantern off its bracket. A sailor called out to him, but he muttered something unintelligible and the man thankfully didn't follow him when he went down the hatch to the lower decks.

Naval architects were nothing if not predictable and it didn't take him long to find the heavy door he needed. As he reached for the latch, he shivered at the feeling of cold eyes on his back. He swept the lamp around behind him, but all he caught were flickering shadows. He put the lantern down, heaved the sturdy doors open and got to work. Once he was happy with his handiwork, he picked the lantern back up and carefully put it down on the single little table in the room. He then shut the heavy doors again and backtracked through the darkness to where he had left Sophia.

'Are you all right, James?' she asked when he let her out.

'No more battered than I was before.'

'Where did you go?'

He took his sword back. 'I left them a surprise. Now let's get you off this cursed ship. Quickly.'

'Let's get *us* off this cursed ship.'

He smiled. 'Preferably.'

They reached the main hatch unmolested. Faulkner quietly climbed the ladder and surveyed the weather deck. Thankfully, the four men at the bow were still making a sloppy go of repairing the sloop's damage. Satisfied the crew were oblivious to his presence, he turned his attention to the open boats. The yawl would have done nicely, but it was far too big and too heavy to ever swing out with just the two of them. He turned his attention to the two longboats. They were lighter, but still far too heavy for him and Sophia to manhandle overboard. He gritted his teeth. He hadn't come this far to trust Sophia's life to strapping her to a barrel and praying some ship chanced across her on the open sea. Fore, one of sailors carrying out the repair suddenly swore loudly.

Faulkner grinned and held his sword, hilt first, down to Sophia. 'Swap. Give me that pistol.'

She took the sword and handed him the gun. 'What now?'

'We need to get a boat over the side but we'll never manage it on our own. As a political radical, how do you feel about our running a press gang?'

'Right now, the idea positively delights me.'

He saluted her and then walked across the deck towards the four sailors. Sophia followed along behind him, sword in hand.

'Evening, gentlemen,' he said conversationally.

The four of them turned slowly to look at him. 'What the—'

'Now, don't go doing anything stupid,' he said. 'I've had an extraordinarily long and wearing day and the first of you to do something dim-witted is going to get himself shot. Do you understand?'

The men looked around in confusion.

Faulkner sighed. 'It's simple. I am a boarder. I snuck aboard and now I'm going to give you orders. If you ignore those orders or make any kind of fuss I will shoot one of you. In the head. Is that clear?'

The *Dead Reckonings* met his gaze and nodded as one.

He turned the pistol on the sailor who had been working with a hatchet. 'Put down that nasty thing slowly and kick it to me.' The sailor did as he was told. Pistol still covering them, Faulkner stooped and picked up the little axe. He stood back up and pointed his gun at the sailor who looked least likely to cause trouble. 'Fetch two lines of about twenty yards length. Tie one line to the bow of each longboat and then fix the other end of each to the gunwales just near the mainmast. That clear?'

The man gulped. 'Very.'

'Are you fine to look after this one, Sophia?'

'Oh yes,' she replied, the sword steady in her hands.

Under her watchful gaze, the sailor quickly fetched the two lines then, one after the other, tied them to the bow of each boat and then to the side of the *Dead Reckoning*.

'Good.' Faulkner motioned for the other three *Dead Reckonings* to join their mate at the boats. 'Now I want you to pick up the boats one at a time and throw them over the side. I suggest you don't capsize or swamp them or you'll be in for a very long swim.'

With a groan of effort the sailors picked up the first boat and heaved it over the side. The longboat hit the water with a terrific splash and for a moment Faulkner was sure it would sink. But it righted itself and quickly fell away to stern, until it was caught by the line and was towed along, bumping and clattering against the *Dead Reckoning's* hull.

'Good. Now the next one. Quickly.'

They repeated the process. Again the boat splashed down hard but didn't sink. Held by their lines the two boats bounced and writhed along in the sloop's wake, grinding against each other and bumping against the *Dead Reckoning.* They needed to hurry. The little boat's timbers wouldn't take much of that treatment.

'All right, gentlemen, into that first boat,' he said.

The sailors clambered over the side and down into the longboat.

'If any of you shout out, I will shoot you.'

Sophia peered out over the side. 'We're cutting them adrift?'

He nodded.

'Can I do the honours?'

'Of course.'

With a slash of his sword she cut the line. The boat with the *Dead Reckonings* in it immediately fell away to stern. None of the men aboard were brave enough to raise the alarm and soon the boat was only an indistinct patch of darkness behind them. Faulkner glanced about them but the deck still appeared deserted. 'You first, Sophia.' He untied his scabbard and handed it to her. 'But sheath that sword first or you'll chop a thumb off.'

She stuck out her tongue but took the scabbard and slid the sword home. Then she climbed over the rail and shinned down the *Dead Reckoning's* side until her feet were being splashed by the sea. The longboat was bouncing and thrashing against the line like an unbroken horse, but she timed her jump perfectly and leapt aboard.

He laughed in relief and swung a leg up over the rail.

An iron grip closed on his shoulder. 'And where might you be taking my next meal?' the Tallowman hissed.

It whirled him back aboard like he was a child. He tumbled through the air and crashed heavily against the main mast. Pain flashed through him and his pistol and hatchet skittered away across the tilting deck.

The Tallowman laughed as Faulkner picked himself up.

'Come on, Captain Faulkner, show me what a Realmsman is made of,' it screamed. The Tallowman knew it was playing a dangerous game. If it was Sophia it would have already cut the line and escaped.

'Show me your nation's famous guts,' it shrieked as it skipped down the deck and kicked Faulkner hard in the stomach. It had to tempt the stupid girl back aboard. Let her believe she could help this fool. The ship rolled in the swell and Faulkner crawled towards the bow. Laughing, it sauntered after him.

'Cut the rope, Sophia!' Faulkner shouted. 'Cut the rope!'

It couldn't have that. It leapt forward and smashed a fist down on Faulkner's kidneys. He crumpled to the deck with an agonised whimper.

'Fight on, Captain! Fight on!'

Rolling away from it, Faulkner lurched to his feet. Spying a piece of heavy chain left by the repair work, the Realmsman snatched it up. He slowly advanced on the Tallowman, whirling the chain around his head like a knight's flail.

'Much more what I expected,' the Tallowman hissed.

Faulkner whipped the chain towards it. The Tallowman held up its left arm and took the full force of the blow. The heavy links broke a bone in its arm, but the Tallowman easily reefed the chain out of Faulkner's hand and threw it overboard with a laugh.

'Better.' It smirked. It punched Faulkner hard in the stomach before he could react and then threw him towards the stern. 'But hardly good enough.'

Out of the corner of its eye, the Tallowman saw it had got what it wanted. Like the idiotic girl she was, Sophia Blake had climbed back aboard. It only needed her a little closer. Just a fraction more and it would have her.

'Face me!' she shouted.

The Tallowman giggled. The girl was carrying a sword. A sword! Against a creature like it! She hadn't even taken the blade out of its scabbard yet. 'My face will be the last thing you'll see,' it said.

She was scared now. It could smell it on her. But, like a fool, she still stepped forward to protect her beloved captain. Now it had her. Even if she tried to dive overboard she would be far, far too slow to escape.

She began to draw the sword.

It leapt towards her.

As the sword left its scabbard, the blade of the sabre flamed incandescent gold, bright enough that a glorious summer day seemed to live trapped within the steel. The Tallowman hissed in fear and slid to a stop, inches from the girl. The light from the sword lit the deck like it was midday. Pain lanced through the Tallowman and the evil flesh within it roiled and rolled in terror.

She raised the sword.

The daemon within it squirmed and thrashed, desperate to escape. The air around them hummed like lightning had struck the ship.

Sophia slashed the Tallowman across its chest.

Agony raged through its body, expanding and threatening to unravel the daemon within it. It screeched as smoke poured from the wound. It knew with cold certainty that another hit from that blade and it would cease to be. Fear overwhelmed it and the Tallowman turned and threw itself down the hatchway like a snake fleeing back into its lair.

Faulkner's mouth was full of blood and his face was so swollen he could only just see. Still holding his sword, Sophia dragged him back to his feet with her free hand. Picking up the pistol, he tottered over to the hatchway. He stopped at the top of the ladder and peered down into the dark. To follow the Tallowman down there was to die. It might have feared the sword, but in the twistings and turnings below decks it would still find him and it would kill him.

'What now?' she asked. The sword's steel was fading and reddening in her hands. Now it looked as if the glow of a beautiful sunset had fallen across the blade.

'Back in the boat.' He slammed the heavy hatch cover shut. 'Hurry.'

She nodded and scrambled back over the side.

He staggered across the deck after her, clambered painfully over the rail and then threw himself awkwardly into the bottom of his second boat for the day.

Sophia cut the line with his sword and they drifted free.

They were a hundred yards astern when the Tallowman appeared at the rail.

'You fools,' it screamed after them. 'Your little bauble won't save you. And when I recapture you I will not kill either of you, oh no. I will do nothing so kind. Faulkner, I will let you watch me consume her! I will tear off your eyelids so you can see me rip the life out of her chest!' It turned away, shaking with laughter.

'It's going to catch us, isn't it?' Sophia whispered. 'We'll never outrun it in this boat.'

'Not if I know my business it won't.'

The Tallowman shrieked orders at the few surviving crew below decks and, knowing their lives depended on it, they raced to carry out its commands.

The ropes Faulkner had braced the wheel with were quickly cut away and the terrified helmsman swung the wheel hard over. In the rigging above, the surviving topmen let go the sails as they turned into the wind. Despite the damage the sloop had suffered, the canvas came down smartly and the cold easterly filled them. The bow of the *Dead Reckoning* swung about, turning after Faulkner and Sophia's little boat and, as the wind hit her abeam, the *Dead Reckoning* heeled over.

Below decks on the table where Faulkner had left it, the lantern rocked back and forth.

Despite the searing pain radiating out from the wound across its chest, the Tallowman smiled. It could still see the fool's boat as a distant speck on the horizon. Did they really hope the night would hide them? It was a creature of the dark.

The *Dead Reckoning*'s deck tilted as she heeled further and further over as she gathered pace. Down in the heart of the ship, the little lantern tipped over. As it rolled across the table, it cast its rippling light on the heavy, almost flameproof timber walls of the powder magazine. The ship rocked again and the lantern bumped over the edge of the table and hung there on the lip for a long moment. Then it crashed down into the pile of loose gunpowder Faulkner had spread on the floor. The lantern smashed and its flame burst free.

The powder flashed into life and set off the rest of the magazine.

The *Dead Reckoning* blew apart with a flash like the birth of a new sun. Timbers and wreckage rained down hundreds of yards from the ship.

42.

FAULKNER'S EARS RANG from the roar and lights from the flash danced before his eyes.

By the time he could see again the *Dead Reckoning* was almost gone. The explosion had devastated the ship and the majority of the wreck had sunk almost instantly beneath the waves. By the time the echo of the explosion had faded, the odd glow from a smouldering plank or spar against the black of the ocean was all that marked where the ship had been.

'Do you think it's dead?' Sophia asked.

Faulkner nodded. 'That explosion would have killed a dragon.'

Reversing his sword, she handed it to him hilt first. 'James, I think it really does have a piece of the Holy Lance in it,' she said.

He took the sword. 'And I've always been swearing at the silly thing and throwing it in corners.'

'It's a link to Prince Isaladar.'

'I've no cleverer explanation for what it did to the Tallowman.' He laid the sabre carefully in the bottom of the boat. 'To think I've been carrying around a piece of the Holy Lance for the last year.'

They sat in stunned silence for a moment.

'So what now?' she asked at last.

Faulkner wiped some of the blood off his face. 'We sail back to Dogwood Island and then on to Stormhaven.'

'No, you idiot, I meant what about *us*. Now this is over?'

Doing his best to hide his pain, he leant forward and kissed her.

'Don't.' She pushed him away. 'We can't be.'

'We can.'

'James,' she said, 'I saw how you looked at me after I healed de Lacey. You were horrified. Disgusted.'

'I was shocked and scared. Not horrified. Not disgusted. I love you.' He tried to smile, but it was hard when his face was so battered. 'It's probably lucky you're tainted. Otherwise a woman like you would be completely beyond the reach of a poor cove like me.'

'Don't joke. People will judge you.'

'Let them.'

'Nothing will be the same. We tainted are pariahs.'

'I don't care.'

'Really?'

'De Lacey got disowned by his own bloody family and gets by.'

'I should have told you.'

'You should have.' He took her hand. His fingers were already black with bruises. 'But we all have our secrets. I don't tell people that when I went aboard the *Agricola* after the Asare Roads I had spilled so much of those poor Caladians' blood that it ran from her scuppers like a waterfall. All I could hear was the screaming of their wounded. I still dream about that sometimes. I think we all have things we hold close and silent.'

'Aren't you worried I'll go mad?' He could tell she wanted it all out now.

'Of course I am.' He forced a grin. 'And aren't you worried that I'll end up a conservative old drunk who can only talk about his glory days? Any love is a risk.'

She leant forward and kissed him deeply until she accidently touched his ribs and he grunted in agony. 'Did that hurt?'

He grimaced. 'Everything hurts. It was worth it though.' He reluctantly turned away from her. 'Now let's see about getting us back to Dogwood Island.'

Sophia shook him gently. 'James, James. I think we're here. But there's a boat in the bay.'

Faulkner forced his sunburnt eyes open and looked around groggily. It was mid afternoon and sure enough, there dead ahead was Dogwood Island. Lying at rest in the cove where they had left the *Game Birds* was a little topsail schooner. Although everything hurt he clambered aft, took the tiller from Sophia and turned their bow towards the island. The long hours in the boat had not treated Faulkner well. Although they had found some freshwater in a canteen, he was still famished, sore and thoroughly baked by the sun. Despite some sunburn, Sophia somehow seemed unwearied by their journey.

'Do you think that ship is friendly?' Sophia asked.

He took her hand. 'Let's hope so.'

Thankfully, the winds and tides treated them kindly and they were able to coast straight into the bay. Faulkner studied the schooner as they slid past her. She was a pretty little ship, spotless, clean and in better condition than many warships. Although a number of her crew watched them pass, no one called out to stop them. A large blue ensign fluttered at her stern.

Sophia pointed to the flag. 'Is that what I think it is?'

'Yes. The King's Ensign.' He didn't need to tell her who flew that flag.

Ahead a crowd had gathered on the edge of the sand to meet them and a great cheer went up when they got close. Faulkner ran the boat up on the beach and the waiting people raced down into the water to help them. De Lacey, Tom and Jenkins reached him first.

'We thought we'd sail back here to wait, just in case you somehow managed to pull it off,' de Lacey laughed, clapping him on the back.

Faulkner grinned at his friend. 'Easy there. I'm three quarters broken.'

'I told them you'd manage it,' Jenkins rumbled.

He shook Tom's offered hand. 'You made it back to dry land I see?'

'It was close.' Tom did his best to look nonchalant. 'But Billy is the best. Though Isaladar knows what trouble I'll be in when I fly back to school.'

'For what it's worth, I'll never forget what you did. Now get me out of this bloody boat. Don't think I can manage it on my own.'

They manhandled him out of the longboat and helped him up onto the dry sand near where he had been shot. A group of grinning *Game Birds* crowded about him. He looked around for Sophia. She was already ashore and was locked in an embrace with her father. Tears streamed down Uriah's face.

Donald forced his way through the press of men. 'Here is a coat, sir.'

Faulkner laughed. 'I don't want a bloody coat, Donald. Go find something for Sophia to eat and drink.'

'But you look—'

'Donald!'

His servant stormed off, swearing under his breath.

Faulkner turned back to de Lacey. 'So who owns that pretty schooner?'

'We do.'

Faulkner turned to his left. Standing alongside Fiora were two middle-aged women and a middle-aged man. Unremarkable and dressed in simple country attire, they were the type of people you would pass on the street every day of the year and not notice.

The taller of the two women stepped forward and shook his hand. 'I am Mrs Chandler.' She nodded to the other woman. 'That is Mrs Smith and this is Mr Bower.'

Faulkner took a deep breath. 'You are Camar Shiem, I take it?'

'We are and we should apologise for arriving too late. We were having some trouble finding the Tallowman until Miss Blake used the largest dash of taint any of us had ever heard.'

The other woman, Mrs Smith, stepped forward. 'Is the Tallowman dead?'

Faulkner quickly recounted their fight aboard the *Dead Reckoning*.

'Finding a holy blade and blowing up a Tallowman – you and Miss Blake have been busy,' Mrs Chandler said with a smile after he had finished.

'I could do with a rest.'

'You've earned one. But first call over Miss Blake, we would talk to you both in private.'

Faulkner, the three Camar Shiem and Fiora walked a few yards down the beach before he turned and called to Sophia. She left Uriah and came over to hold his hand.

'These people are Camar Shiem.'

A flicker of fear showed in Sophia's eyes but she nodded to them in greeting.

'When we get back to the mainland, you will need to come with us, Sophia,' Mrs Chandler said simply.

'Am I your prisoner?'

The Camar Shiem shook her head. 'No. But you have seen our enemy now. You know how powerful they are. We can protect you.'

'And educate you,' Mr Bower added.

'What about my father?'

'Uriah?' Mrs Chandler turned to look at the lawyer. 'We will legally clear his name, but he will not be able to return home.'

Sophia gasped. 'You are exiling him?'

'Of course not, but we are not magic. We cannot undo the fact that two dozen people witnessed him murder a woman in cold blood.'

Fiora put a hand on Sophia's shoulder. 'I will look after your father, Sophia. I swear it on my family's honour.'

Sophia nodded and then looked up and down the sand as if searching for an answer, or an escape. 'Can I talk to James for a moment?' she asked at last.

Mrs Chandler nodded and she, the two other Camar Shiem and Fiora walked back to join the crowd of *Game Birds*.

'I think she's right,' Sophia's said, once they were out of earshot. 'I have to go with them when we get back to Stormhaven.'

Faulkner sighed. 'I know. But just until you are safe. Not to disappear into some asylum forever.'

'Really?' She smiled at him, but her voice wavered.

'Really.'

'From anyone else I'd think that mere bravado.'

'Bravado? I'm rich enough to hire half the country to look for you if they do try to steal you away.'

She laughed and stroked his bloody and bruised face. 'Kiss me, darling.'

He did.

References

- The song the sailors sing while readying *Game Bird* for sea is '*All for Me Grog*', an Irish folk song. The original artist is unknown.

- The poem Sophia quotes at the Royal War Flying College is '*Pine-Trees and the Sky: Evening*' by Rupert Brooke.

- The poem quoted in part by Faulkner to Sophia after the mutiny is '*Beauty*' by John Masefield.

Acknowledgements

I owe a huge debt of thanks to countless people who have helped with *The Game Bird*.

To my friends and family who have put up with me droning on endlessly about my book for years. A special mention to my in-laws and my sister in- law, Courtney, who read and loved the book when it was still awful.

To all the members of my writing groups past and present. But particularly: Sally Egan, Jessie Ansons, Margret Jackson, Diana Threlfo, Maree Gallop, Anna Lundmark, Karen Whitelaw and Elena Terol – your support has been unfailingly incredible.

I've been lucky enough to be spoilt with many brilliant beta readers. I would have never got here without them all, but I especially need to recognise Dorian Walsh, Michelle Goldsmith and Candice Wellfare. These three not only made *Game Bird* a far better book, but made me a much, much stronger writer.

To my brilliant editors Abigail Nathan and Simone Ford. Both of whose touch vastly improved this novel. Any mistakes that remain are, of course, my own.

To my brothers Dorian, Magnus, Fergus and Stirling – not all of whom have been much help with the book, but who are the best mates a man could hope for, are ever willing to road test my worlds and always keen to grab a beer.

To my mum and dad, for being generally fantastic parents and also instilling in me a love for reading and stories (Even if they said I read far too much fantasy on the school bus. Sorry, I still don't love Steinbeck's *The Pearl*).

To my children Freya, Felix and Odette – who make writing a lot harder – but everything else in life fantastic.

Lastly and mostly, to my wife, Libby. For everything really. From putting up with me listening to far too much Springsteen, to being the best thing to ever happen to me.

About the Author

Aidan has loved fantasy and science fiction for as long as he can remember. His tastes have broadened with age, but they have remained deep in his blood. If a religion could convince Aidan that Middle Earth was heaven, he'd sign up immediately.

He lives in Newcastle, Australia with his wife, three children, two dogs and a cat.

Aidan has a personal blog at https://aidanrwalsh.com/ and a slowly expanding encyclopaedia on *The Game Bird's* world at https://unpathedwaters.com/

You can reach Aidan on his Facebook page @AidanRWalshauthor or on Twitter at https://twitter.com/AidanRWalsh He'd love to hear from you.

The Game Bird is his first novel.

www.ingramcontent.com/pod-product-compliance
Lightning Source LLC
Chambersburg PA
CBHW021427240626
47153CB00001B/51